"HAVE YOU ANY IDEA HOW LONG I'VE DREAMED OF THIS?"

Geoffrey's breath fanned the soft curve of her ear.

In answer, Laura turned her face up to his. Their lips met. Quickly the kiss abandoned its languor, became more passionate. Sensations violent and sweet were sweeping them away toward an endless ecstasy. Then she remembered Lisa and abruptly pulled away.

The silence was deafening until Geoffrey spoke. "Something is still there, isn't it?" It was an accusation, not a question.

When she finally answered her voice was intense. "I love you, Geoffrey. Isn't that enough for now?"

"For now? What's coming up in the future?"

Laura sat up and hugged her knees to her naked breasts. A tear trickled down her shin. How could she answer when she didn't know? She just didn't know.

Books by Megan Alexander

SUPERROMANCES

17—CONTRACT FOR MARRIAGE
95—BLOSSOMS IN THE SNOW

These books may be available at your local bookseller.

For a free catalog listing all titles currently available,
send your name and address to:

Harlequin Reader Service
P.O. Box 52040, Phoenix, AZ 85072-9988
Canadian address: Stratford, Ontario N5A 6W2

Megan Alexander

BLOSSOMS IN THE SNOW

A SUPERROMANCE FROM

W RLDWIDE

TORONTO · NEW YORK · LONDON · PARIS
AMSTERDAM · STOCKHOLM · HAMBURG
ATHENS · MILAN · TOKYO · SYDNEY

To Fuzen with love,
and to Tuesday's children
who are full not only of grace,
but of continual help and encouragement.

Published January 1984

First printing November 1983

ISBN 0-373-70095-4

Printed in Canada

Snow laced boughs,
Brittle etchings of winter's pain.
Even so, the plum tree blossoms.

CHAPTER ONE

LAURA CLUTCHED the Kyoto city map in her hand and anxiously walked along the busy boulevard. Monday-morning crowds swirled around her, moving as if they had only five minutes to reach their destinations. Although traffic appeared heavy, taxis zoomed in and out in hysterical competition. Laura's anxiety matched the compulsive tempo.

She was two days late to her new job at the Sato School of Languages. The administration could already have hired a replacement. She tried not to think of the frightening prospect. How on earth would she cope in this foreign city, jobless and solely responsible for a nine-year-old nephew?

She ducked under the awning of a tearoom, studied the map for a moment, then turned off onto an alleyway that appeared to be a shortcut to the school. A frail late-August breeze nudged a row of colored lanterns that hung from the eaves of a tempura restaurant, then succumbed to the warmth and dampness of rising humidity.

Laura hoped she wouldn't look wilted by the time she arrived. How would the administration regard the overdue appearance of the school's new faculty member? Not favorably, she suspected, having already noted the Japanese appeared to be a nation of superconscientious achievers.

She'd called the school and explained Kelly's illness, how she'd just arrived and knew no one who would care for a sick child. The secretary's English had seemed about par with Laura's Japanese, but she'd indicated the message would be recorded and someone would return the call. When Laura received no reply, she'd telephoned twice again with the same vague results. Hadn't the secretary understood?

Maybe the illness of a child was not considered sufficient excuse to miss the two days of orientation and training sessions for new teachers last Thursday and Friday. On the other hand, perhaps the office was just too busy preparing for the opening of the fall semester to get back to her. Had she made a harebrained decision to come here, after all? One scrambled for quick solutions when left in such circumstances.

Two months ago a stroke had snuffed out the life of the grandmother who had raised Laura and Kelly. The will had left the house to an aunt, Grandmother Canfield's daughter, and a small annuity to Laura and Kelly. The two of them were suddenly on their own.

When one of her professors told her about prospective jobs teaching English in Japan, it had seemed a gift from heaven.

"Language schools are springing up as thick as our pizza parlors," he'd said. "The Japanese are heavy into world trade, and tourism is skyrocketing. Businesses are eager for their employees to know the language."

Her degree in English qualified her for the job, although a six-week crash course in conversational Japanese had done nothing to add to her self-confidence.

"Don't worry," her professor friend had assured her. "Many of the directors are American." He'd advised her to apply first to the Sato School of Languages, one of the largest and most prestigious in Kyoto.

Nevertheless, Laura had studied her textbook at every spare moment. Well, she would know soon enough if she had chosen wisely. Making the right choices was what life was all about, wasn't it?

But life had not been all bleak since their arrival in Kyoto. The new apartment, although tiny, was attractive with its quaint mixture of Western and Japanese rooms. Moreover it overlooked a little park, a bonus for Kelly. Their new neighbors, the Matsuis, proved friendly and helpful. Best of all, Kelly's illness turned out to be merely a bad case of jet lag and he showed his same sunny self when she enrolled him in school an hour ago.

Crowds thronged this narrow street, too. Laura soon realized that it proved no shortcut, but she was pleased nonetheless. Kyoto's past wrote its signature here. It held a distinctive ethnic quality still alive and vigorous despite the many signs of Westernization. Color splashed everywhere: the round caps on the heads of bounding schoolboys; a flowered *furoshiki*, cloth carryall, dangling from the arm of a kimono-clad elderly woman; signs and banners lettered in *kanji*, Japanese script, hanging from every available space. Each shop displayed its specialty: fine tea bowls, dolls, bolts of shining silk, pottery, lacquerware, cloisonné and a sushi bar with its popular canapés of raw seafood on pats of vinegared rice.

Laura caught a whiff of incense from a tiny Shinto shrine. *Tiny*. There was that word again. Somehow Japan conjured up adjectives dealing with diminutives: *little* people, *minuscule* gardens, *haiku*, the poem of only seventeen syllables. Even the artwork was frequently expressed by means of *spare* brush strokes.

Now back on a main boulevard, Laura found herself again preoccupied with concerns over her job. It wasn't that she lacked confidence in her ability. After all, she had earned her way through college successfully coaching foreign students in English, and she owned a new teacher's credential from one of Oregon's finest universities. Still, she agonized endlessly over missing out on last week's meetings. Her classes, offering instruction to a clientele of mainly business and professional people, started tonight. Suppose her superiors didn't approve the lesson plans she'd so painstakingly prepared? And how would they view her somewhat unorthodox approach? She'd heard that Mr. Sato, the head of the school, was a charming articulate gentleman, but Laura would work primarily with the evening-school director. What sort of person was he, she wondered: conservative, progressive? Or perhaps the director was a woman. The name was Dr. MacDivitt, if Laura had understood the secretary's heavily accented English.

But adjusting to a new job was not the only matter on her mind. One dark cloud always hung in the sky. Kelly had talked about it incessantly from the minute she'd told him about the move.

"Hey, Laura, wasn't my dad stationed in Japan?"

"Yes, darling, but that was a long time ago." She wished he had forgotten that detail. As far as she was concerned, the very mention of his father defiled the conversation.

"Maybe we'll run into someone who knew him," he said hopefully. Kelly steadfastly clung to the fantasy that his father might appear someday, a be-medaled military-intelligence hero, somehow full of reasonable excuses for his ten-year absence.

Thus far in his young life, Kelly had been spared the truth. Laura knew it was natural for a boy who grew up with an elderly great-grandmother and an aunt a dozen years his senior to long for a father. How could they dash his dreams? But he should have been told long ago. She must find words to explain the ugly facts very soon. A nine-year-old boy was not too young to face reality.

Kelly's father, Major Geoffrey McDermott, had been a debonair young army major on a two-week leave when he swept Laura's sister off her feet at a spring college dance. Three days later they were secretly married, and after a rapturous week-long honeymoon, he returned to his base in Japan.

Soon after, Lisa's one attendant, a sorority sister, happened to run into the serviceman who'd conducted the ceremony and discovered he was not a bona-fide chaplain. The marriage had been a hoax, the entire affair regarded as a lark as far as the young men were concerned. Too late Lisa realized the extent of her naiveté. She didn't even have a piece of paper to give evidence to the fraudulent ceremony. Ashamed and humiliated, she begged the sorority sister to keep the entire matter secret. She never again heard from the young officer who'd conned her into the "marriage."

No sooner had she dealt with this trauma than she found she was pregnant. Frantic, she told no one but wrote to the army, only to learn that Major Geoffrey McDermott had recently received an honorable discharge and lived with his Japanese wife in Tokyo.

Brokenhearted and desperate, she procrastinated telling her parents about her predicament and made one excuse after another to remain at college for weeks after the term ended in June. Then, when Laura's and Lisa's parents were drowned in a midsummer sailing accident, Lisa arrived at Grandmother Canfield's to compound the family tragedies.

Kelly was born four months later, and Lisa had died from complications that could have been avoided had she sought medical attention earlier. Laura often wondered if her sister abetted her death because life had lost significance for her. Even though Laura was only twelve at the time, she would never forget the agony of her sister's heartbreak. Major Geoffrey McDermott. She had never seen him, but how she despised him!

Laura was grateful the man had never known that he'd fathered a son, and if by some unlikely chance this Geoffrey McDermott ever surfaced, she would move heaven and earth to keep him from finding out. It would be impossible for her to relinquish Kelly to such a person. Her nephew was as dear to her as if he were her own little brother.

The events that had happened a decade ago acted as a stone cast into a pool. Ripples reached out to affect others in ways Lisa could never have imagined. Widowed Grandmother Canfield had resigned her job as women's editor of a large daily newspaper to take up the responsibility of raising infant Kelly and twelve-year-old Laura. Her modest investments and the money from Laura's parents' estate supported them adequately, but there were far fewer luxuries. There was to be no exclusive private college in Laura's future. Instead she earned her own way through Oregon State University and now found herself faced with the challenge of parenting a nine-year-old boy.

A test of maturity is accepting responsibility for one's actions, Laura frequently reminded herself. Lisa had lost her head when she was away at college. Her impulsive action still rained fallout. Well, Laura intended to keep control of her own life, especially where men were concerned. Any mistake she made would ultimately touch Kelly.

Laura hauled herself back to the present with an effort. Any thought of her sister's adversity always depressed her.

Now she recognized the Sato school from the description given to her by her neighbor, Mrs. Matsui. It was an architecturally brazen ten-story office building of natural wood and a wide expanse of glass

The school itself occupied only the first two floors. She breathed a prayer that all would go well and walked into the Sato office. Nervously, she wadded the map in her hand into a tight ball and introduced herself to the administrative assistant, Marcia Cole. The tall auburn-haired woman gave Laura a steely-eyed appraisal and explained that the night-school office didn't open until five o'clock.

"I understand," Laura said. "But would it be all right to look over the facilities? Also, because of some mix-up I never received my contract."

"Ah, Miss Adams," the woman said, ignoring Laura's question. "We were wondering if we would have to replace you. A British teacher applied last week—highly qualified, I might add. When you didn't show up, we were sorely tempted."

Alarm chilled Laura. "But I called and explained."

"Strange. We've been snowed under these past few days. Lucky you came in this morning or we'd have called the other applicant. He's standing by. You say you haven't yet signed your contract?"

Was that a threat? "I was told I could sign when I arrived," she said firmly. She couldn't help comparing herself to the tall imperious woman; one tough, cool lady, she decided.

Because of Laura's slim figure, five-foot-two height and thick blond hair that waved naturally to her shoulders, people often assessed her as a kind of fragile girl-next-door, a description that incensed her. She was vulnerable all right, which was why she so often slipped on a protective veneer of self-assurance, as effective as any hard hat, with no one the wiser.

Miss Cole smiled. It was charming but without sincerity. "I hope your tardiness isn't any indication of what we can expect in the future. Maybe you should think twice about accepting this position. Except for you, we have an all-male faculty—more reliable, we've found. Not likely to be absent because of sick children."

A rather eloquent Anglo-Saxon term occurred to Laura, but she bit her lip and headed for the elevator up to the night-school office. It looked as if she had almost lost her job. She must tread carefully.

On the second floor she walked down the hallway, giving wide berth to a painter on a scaffold. She peered through several open doors. Each classroom could accommodate about two dozen students. Sparse furnishings, only blackboards and desks, gave an austere appearance. At the end of the hall she found the office. The door was lettered in both English and Japanese: "Hours: 5:30 P.M.- 9:30 P.M., Monday - Friday." The door stood slightly ajar but offered resistance as if stiff on its hinges. A shove sent something on the other side crashing loudly to the floor, then she heard the sound of running footsteps.

"My God, what a mess!" a male voice cried. The door flew open, and Laura saw at a glance that she had bumped a stool and tipped over a bucket of paint. Why would anyone leave paint in such an unguarded spot? Thick gray liquid oozed across a canvas and onto the highly polished wood floor. Horrified, she looked up to meet the exasperated stare of a tall dark-haired man. If looks had the power to shrink, she could have sat on a pinhead.

He tapped the lettering on the door. "Do you read English?" His tone scorched her.

She nodded dumbly, still looking at the disaster before her. Finally finding her voice, she cried, "Hurry, find something to wipe this up before it spreads any farther!"

He disappeared and returned in a few moments with a bundle of cheesecloth and a roll of paper towels. The atmosphere fairly crackled with his silent denunciation as they mopped up the spill.

Covertly she noted that his profile was sharp and a little forbidding, like a silhouette defined by clean quick strokes, not conventionally handsome but with plenty of character. Actually, if she rated each of his features separately the score would be negligible, but the authoritative jaw, the strong straight nose and the etched vertical line in each cheek all blended into a distinctive whole that thoroughly excited her. In spite of the awkward preliminary, here was a man she would like to know.

Now the dull grayed areas where the fresh paint had removed the waxy sheen from the floor made her feel ill. She gave a helpless shrug. "I don't know what to say, except I'm sorry," she said when they completed the task.

"I guess it wasn't very smart to leave that stool by the door even if it wasn't during office hours." The admission came in a pleasant baritone, and the quality unexpectedly warmed her. Gauging his unrelenting expression, she had expected a more strident tone.

"I'm Laura Adams, one of the new faculty members," she said tardily. "And I sincerely hope you aren't the new director."

He gave a token nod. "In person." He didn't offer his hand. Nevertheless, his eyes granted her an appreciative evaluation.

She took a deep breath. "Would you mind if we started over? Or maybe you'd rather I just faded into the woodwork?"

His mouth twitched slightly. "Generally I prefer a more creative approach. Miss Adams, you say? Ah, yes. You're the one who didn't show last week."

"I'm afraid so. I could blame the international date line for sabotaging my schedule, but as you know, it was a little more serious than that." She searched his face for a glimmer of compassion. He merely raised an eyebrow. From this man it was more intimidating than a ten-minute lecture.

"The Sato school isn't in the habit of rolling out the red carpet for personnel who come waltzing in at the last minute," he said.

She looked up sharply. "But, Dr. MacDivitt, didn't you get my message?"

"No, I didn't. To whom did you give it?"

"I don't know. I'm not sure," she stammered. "I assumed it was one of the secretaries. My young nephew became ill. We had just arrived, and I knew no one who could take care of him."

He seemed to weigh her explanation. No doubt he figured she'd really spent the time wandering around some temple grounds or off gazing at the deer in Nara.

"I'm sorry about your nephew," he said finally. "But unfortunately I have no time to give you a special briefing before tonight. I'm due at a meeting in a few minutes, and since my secretary is already overburdened, I must get some manuals ready for one of the classes. I expect you'll just have to play things by ear."

Her hackles rose at his assumption that she'd come unprepared. "I have made ten weeks of lesson plans and brought along a lot of material."

"I see," he said so uninterestedly that she decided weeping secretaries or hurt children would never carry their problems to him.

She made her tone brisk. "If you'll just point out the book room, I'll not trouble you further."

"First room to the left," he said, and started thumbing through the stack of loose-leaf manuals on his desk. Maybe she'd read him wrong. His whole demeanor suddenly appeared more harried than formidable.

Laura hesitated as she toyed with an idea. Perhaps here was an opportunity to improve her image. At this stage she ought to snatch at anything to earn a few Brownie points, although she suspected it would be a rare experience to achieve full approval from this man.

"Actually I'm free today. Is there anything I can do to help with the manuals?"

He glanced up, apparently surprised that she still remained. "Can you type?"

"Seventy-five words a minute."

A relieved smile spread across his face. Laura

almost gasped. She'd never realized what such a change could do for a person. The hedge of aloofness vanished. Now he seemed to own the kind of aura that reached out and enveloped her. She felt amazed at herself, the way that charismatic expression of his intrigued her, the faint quickening of her pulses. He was obviously younger than she'd first thought, probably in his middle thirties. Unfortunately, the smile disappeared so quickly she almost wondered if she had imagined it. No one could accuse him of scattering wit and charm all over the place.

"Maybe you're an angel in disguise, after all, Miss Adams," he said, and explained the problem.

Apparently a half dozen pages had been omitted from the end of the manuals. If Laura would type and run them off on the copier, students could insert them before class tonight. An easy two hours' work, she judged.

He pointed to a box of master copies, showed her the room where the office machines were located and muttered something about having to dash to a meeting.

After a hassle straightening out several cords at an almost inaccessible outlet, she plugged in the electric typewriter and got to work. By noon she not only had completed all the typing but had inserted the pages, as well.

She hummed a little tune as she stacked the manuals neatly on the counter. "How's that for efficiency, Your Royal Highness?" she sang out, and wondered if he would be able to ante up a few words of appreciation.

At that moment Dr. MacDivitt walked through the open door and glanced at her in a way that surely meant approval. It turned her a little breathless. Strange that she should react that way. She was used to approval. She tried for a smile and wasn't certain it came off. "All finished."

"Finished? You're unbelievable! Do you mind if his royal highness takes a look?"

She felt a flush rise to her cheeks and handed him one of the notebooks. He thumbed through the pages and nodded. Silently she challenged him to find a single error. He bent closer for a few seconds, then tossed the manual aside. "Superior work, but I'm afraid this just isn't our day."

"What do you mean?"

"You typed the wrong master copies. I should have checked them out first," he said with more than a little irritation. At himself? Or her? Well, it wasn't her fault, so let him sputter. Instead he gazed at the computer on an adjacent desk as if mesmerized, then strode over to check the electrical outlet.

"Good Lord, woman! All I wanted was a little typing. Did you have to change our entire electrical setup?"

"I believe it's customary to plug in an electric typewriter," she said stiffly.

"Of course, but, my dear Miss Adams, a little care would have prevented you from loosening the plug of our computer. You have just wiped out the pre-enrollment report my secretary started this morning."

Laura stared at the outlet. "Ordinarily there are

guards on computer plugs, especially where there's a common outlet.''

"And so there is. I fixed it myself earlier today." He clapped a hand to his head. "I fixed it, all right, but I didn't put it back. It's probably still on my desk. My fault, I suppose." He shook his head. "I'll swear the two of us set off malevolent vibrations. If this is a sample of our future working relationship, I'd better run for cover.''

"Likewise," Laura said. "We'll have the place in shambles before the first class begins. However, if you're willing to trust me with the typing, I'll be glad to do it over.''

"No, indeed. Run along. I'll manage.''

The man infuriated her. "Are you saying you don't think we can work together?''

He ran his hand through his hair, ruffling it in a way that added to his harassed expression. "What do you think? If you're asking me to trust my instincts, I'd say the prognosis is definitely negative.''

"Well, I wouldn't want you to doubt your instincts," she said with all the sarcasm she could muster. "This job has been star-crossed from the start. I haven't seen a contract, much less been able to sign one. Your assistant, Miss Cole, tells me a British teacher is anxious for the job. So why don't I bow out right now and save us both a lot of hassle?''

"Impetuous, aren't you? Not an admirable trait in a teacher, you know. Let's see how things go tonight, and we'll talk afterward.''

"I don't like to be kept dangling. It's apparent that several people around here will be relieved if I don't take this job. Oh, I'll teach my class tonight, so you'll have plenty of time to notify my replacement. That is, if you'll trust me with your students for one session.''

His sour expression suddenly vanished, and his dark eyes twinkled. ''I admit it's a risk, but I'll take it. How about you? Do you think the two of us can carry on tonight without burning the place down?''

She would have given a fortune for a good exit line, but she felt too upset. She'd just resigned her job. Was she out of her mind? She fixed her gaze on the scroll painting behind him and knew her eyes glistened suspiciously.

''I'll do my best, Dr. MacDivitt.'' She turned to leave.

He lifted a hand to detain her. ''And by the way, Miss Adams. My name is McDermott. Not MacDivitt. Geoffrey McDermott. And you can forget the 'Dr.' ''

CHAPTER TWO

GEOFFREY MCDERMOTT! Surely not the same man who'd ruined her sister's life! *Please, God, don't let it be true!* Somehow Laura got out of there, walked to the elevator and stumbled out to the street.

The afternoon sun was warm against her back, but a chill crawled up her spine and she felt light-headed. It was after one o'clock, or 1300, as the Japanese reckoned time. She looked for a sushi bar. She needed to sit down for a while and think what to do. Could there be two men in Japan with that same hated name? Fear surged around her like a dark aura. She must find out soon. If the man she'd just left actually turned out to be Kelly's father, he had a legal right to take Kelly away from her! Oh, God, why had she ever come to Japan?

Now she had no job, but that problem paled in light of the larger one. The important action now was to get away from Dr. Geoffrey McDermott until she proved his identity one way or another.

The sidewalks still teemed with people, businessmen in conservative suits, young mothers wheeling babies in strollers, teenagers, both boys and girls, in jeans and bright T-shirts. Only an occasional gray-haired woman in somber kimono stamped the scene with ethnic reminder.

She found a sushi bar in the next block. Usually she would have been fascinated by this Japanese version of a fast-food restaurant, but she barely tasted the dish of vinegared rice and shrimp the chef put before her. She wrestled with the impact of meeting the man called Geoffrey McDermott.

Had he wondered about the way she'd caught her breath, the shock in her eyes, the foolish way she'd gaped at him? The general physical likeness was there, all right. Tall, dark, wavy hair. She could understand why her sister might have been swept off her feet. When he'd smiled, she'd felt the pull of his attraction.

But she'd had the impression Lisa's husband had been a fun-loving individual. Well, a person could change in ten years, couldn't he? Also, the time lapse might have colored her own recollections. She must take into consideration that she was only twelve at the time and had a twelve-year-old's perspective.

She tried to recall Dr. McDermott's reaction when they'd met that morning. His face had shown no sudden surprise at the name Adams, although she had to admit he looked her over with the same interest any male might show. But then, there were Adamses all over the place, one full page alone in her hometown telephone book. Anyway, a man who'd treated her sister so callously was no doubt too thick-skinned to react to any such association.

Nevertheless, the last person in the world she wanted to work for was a man named Geoffrey McDermott. She would not chance his discovering his relationship to Kelly. She was glad she'd resigned first. No doubt he'd planned to ease her out anyway. Otherwise wouldn't he have had her sign the elusive contract today? The omission was no oversight; the man was precise and methodical. She had a mental picture of the British teacher hovering like a vulture, awaiting her demise.

With careful budgeting, she and Kelly could get along for at least a month while she looked for another job. She wouldn't allow herself to think what would happen if she couldn't find one.

Last summer the job prospect in Japan had loomed as a lifesaver. Not only hadn't a position for an English teacher turned up in Oregon, but the trauma of her grandmother's death was followed two weeks later by her breakup with Bill, the young engineer she'd planned to marry after graduation. Instead of a wedding, however, Bill had decided he wanted her to move in with him, without commitment, without Kelly. It had hurt a lot. More than ever the experience reinforced her determination to remain wary concerning any relationship with a man.

So during the shattering days that followed, she'd leaped at the opportunity to go to the language school in Kyoto. She felt desperately in need of a new scene, a new challenge. Kelly was a flexible child. He would take the uprooting in stride.

Laura paid the bill for her sushi and looked at her watch. She had over an hour before Kelly got home from school. If only she could consult her friend Sachiko Kimura, who lived in this city. But Sachiko, the young music teacher whom she'd met at the university last year, was in Tokyo attending a seminar.

Laura walked disconsolately down the street, feeling lonely and strange in the big city. Even the inability to read all the *kanji* on shops and buildings added to her alienation.

The streets were jammed with small cars, all spotlessly clean and moving with such speed she wondered that frequent crashes weren't part of the city cacophony. Motorcyclists and bicyclists zipped in and out, oblivious to peril. She watched with mixed suspense and admiration as delivery boys managed stacks of trays piled with takeout food with one hand and guided their cycles with the other, as precise and agile as any juggler.

Her eye caught a sign, *Burton-Kubo School of English.* The recognizable words appeared like a port in a storm. Saying a little prayer, she followed an arrow and took an elevator to the second floor.

AN HOUR LATER Laura stood in a taxi line, incredulous and a little breathless. After the unhappy morning at the Sato school she could hardly believe her reception at Burton-Kubo. She still felt dazed.

Scott Burton, director-partner in the Burton-Kubo school, had stood up and offered his hand as she entered the reception room. Probably in his late thirties, he had the square muscular frame of a football player. Thick wheat-colored hair framed a face so homely, so ingenuous that Laura immediately felt at ease with him. A wide grin disclosed even white teeth, and his ears, although flat against his head, were definitely oversized, but on this man with the friendly blue eyes, the ears were endearing.

Without false modesty she outlined her credentials and experience, mentioning there had been a misunderstanding about an expected job at Sato, so she'd decided not to stay there. Did he have any openings?

"This is our lucky day, Miss Adams," Scott Burton said, and beckoned her into a chair. "We are a small school and specialize in English only, but an unprecedented evening enrollment finds us bursting at the seams. I've been on the telephone all day trying to line up more teachers."

They plunged into a discussion of language-teaching techniques. Laura saw at once that this school was far more experimental and progressive than the Sato institution. After a spirited conversation he took her on a tour of the classrooms, which were mere cubicles compared to the ones at Sato. But in contrast to Sato's stringent surroundings, here the rooms were full of interesting displays with additional equipment such as phonographs and tape recorders. What a different world! Here, too, the job involved teaching night school. However, the salary was not as high as that offered by the prestigious Sato. No matter. The environment made up the difference.

"I can't imagine the erudite Dr. McDermott allowing a prize like you to slip through his fingers," Scott Burton said back in his office as she signed the contract. "He's one sharp fellow, you know."

"Oh?" Laura murmured noncommittally.

"He certainly is," he said with admirable enthusiasm for his rival. "Did you know that he's a regular columnist for the *Japan Times*? In addition, he's the author of a dozen or more books on Japan, and Lord knows how many magazine articles he's published.''

''He sounds like an impossible yardstick for us ordinary mortals. How does he have time to act as a director of a school?'' Laura asked.

''I believe he's filling in temporarily until the regular man returns from the States. I wouldn't be surprised if he works for free just to get out and mingle with people. Writing is a lonely business, you know. Besides, he and Mr. Sato are longtime friends.''

Lisa's husband a writer? That was entirely possible. Laura didn't recall hearing her sister say much about Major McDermott's job in the army except that he had something to do with intelligence.

''McDermott muffed this one, all right,'' Scott reiterated to himself as he added his signature to her contract.

Laura thought about the paint-spattered floor, the bungled manuals and the disconnected computer. ''I'm afraid I don't fit in over there,'' she said.

Scott leaned back in his chair and ran a square hand through his unruly hair. ''Well, I can understand that. Sato runs a rather conservative plant. I'm surely happy you decided to sign with us, Miss Adams. I know McDermott, and I wouldn't want to proselytize. But as long as you didn't sign a contract, I'm sure there's no problem.''

Problem, Laura thought. More likely McDermott, Cole and company would declare a day of rejoicing at her leave-taking.

She explained that she wouldn't be able to start until tomorrow since she'd already obligated herself for this one evening. He chuckled.

"Aha, practical as well as pretty," he said as he ushered her out. He walked with her to a taxi line in front of a nearby department store. She glanced at her reflection in the window. Girl with Contract. It sounded like the name of a success story. It was, she thought exuberantly. Hers!

When her turn came up for a taxi, he gave explicit directions to the driver on how to reach her address.

"Good luck!" he said, closing the door. Immediately she prayed for it fervently. A sudden start threw her violently against the seat, then with the zeal of a kamikaze pilot, the driver planted his hand on the horn and shot in and out of traffic on both the right and wrong sides of the street as if he were engaged in a game of chicken. She tapped the back of his seat and made frantic gestures for him to slow down. He grinned, waved a white-gloved hand and bore down on the gas pedal even harder. After experiencing several heart-stopping near misses, she closed her eyes and braced herself, vowing that if she ever reached home alive she'd use only buses and streetcars in the future.

Out on the street at last, she stood for a few moments on shaky legs to regain her composure. She had been warned earlier about the wild taxi drivers...but this!

She bought some peaches from the corner fruit peddler and ordered food from a nearby *soba* shop for dinner to be delivered in a few minutes. *Soba*,

buckwheat noodles, was a dish Kelly took to with
relish. The noodles were cooked in soup and were
nourishing and tasty when mixed with bits of meat
and vegetables.

There was no elevator to her third-floor apartment, so she climbed the outside stairway with still-
unsteady steps, opened the door and froze.

Kelly, bare to the waist, sat cross-legged on the
tatami mat, his expression grim and melancholy. He
clutched an open pocketknife in one hand and in a
sudden movement seemed to plunge it into the left
side of his belly, drawing it swiftly to the right and
viciously upward. Then he fell forward on his face.
The entire process took less than two seconds.

Laura screamed and rushed to the prone child. She
rolled his limp form over, expecting to see blood
gushing from his stomach. Not a scratch was visible.
She shook him hard.

"Kelly!" she cried. Silence. Then he opened
sparkling brown eyes and grinned.

"Neat, huh?"

She slumped on the floor beside him. "What on
earth are you doing?"

"Hara-kiri. Gee, it used to be an honorable Japanese custom."

"But not anymore. You gave me a terrible scare,
and you know our rule about knives."

"All I'm doing is practicing."

"Practicing! Don't tell me you learned that in
school?"

"Not *in* school, *at* school. Chizu taught us during
recess."

"Good heavens, who is Chizu?"

"She's a kid in the fifth grade. Her mom is Japanese and her dad is American. She knows all about customs over here."

Laura nodded. "And she's going to enlighten you, I suppose?"

"You bet. She has a club. Only the kids who don't know anything can get in."

"Well, it's certainly nice to know how you rate."

"Come on, Laura. You know what I mean. Only the kids who don't know anything about Japan. It's an honor to get in."

"Who says?"

"Chizu says."

"Naturally. And what is this great organization called?"

"The Chizu Kokasai Bunka Shinkokai. It means the Chizu International Cultural Association."

"Very impressive, I'm sure. And does your teacher know what this kid is up to?"

"Yeah, she thinks it's neat. Tomorrow we're going to have a sit-in and learn all about Buddha."

What kind of shenanigans went on there? Her friend Sachiko, who'd grown up in Kyoto, had recommended this American school without reservation. Well, she would call first thing in the morning. In spite of Kelly's assurances, she could wager that the teacher didn't know what had been going on. Hara-kiri yet!

She looked at her young nephew, who toyed pensively with his pocketknife. He had thick lashes and his chestnut hair curled engagingly around his ears and across his forehead. Now that the mischievous eyes were concealed, his expression took on a cherubic sweetness that never failed to melt her completely. She sighed.

"This is probably one of your dull, run-of-the-mill, Laura-type questions, but were you able to sandwich in any arithmetic or spelling among all that Kokasai Bunka?"

He looked at her in disgust. "Gosh, you know we never get out of that stuff. But it was easy. The teacher said I was ahead of my class. She might even put me up in the fifth grade with Chizu."

"With Chizu?" *Over my dead body,* Laura determined.

"Yeah. I learned how to speak some Japanese, too. Listen. *Uri-no-tsuru ni, nasubi wa naranu,*" he ponderously intoned.

"Wonderful. It sounds very profound," Laura said.

"Oh, it is. It means, 'Eggplants never grow on cucumber vines.' "

Laura sighed. "Who taught that to you, as if I didn't know?"

"Yeah, Chizu. Hey, maybe we ought to invite her over." The idea obviously appealed to him, but Laura interrupted before he augmented it further.

"You'd better open the door. I hear the delivery boy with our dinner," she said.

After they'd finished their meal, Seiji Matsui, the high-school boy who lived next door, arrived to stay with Kelly. Longing for a quick shower, Laura eyed her Japanese bathroom with dismay. It had a tiled drain space where one scrubbed and rinsed and a deep sit-down tub to be filled with very hot water in which to soak afterward.

She settled for a quick sponge bath and would go through the lengthier routine later. She applied her makeup with care and slipped into a blue linen suit, the sharpest-looking outfit in her rather meager wardrobe. Then, lugging two heavy briefcases of material, she headed out for her one-night stand feeling ready to take on the Sato School of Languages, Geoffrey McDermott, director, and even Marcia Cole, the intimidating administrative assistant.

She had no intention of introducing eager students to the English language with the dull assortment of texts she'd found in the book room, even though she would be acting as their teacher for only one session.

By six o'clock, six men and two women were gathered around the table in her room: a department-store manager, a hotel clerk, an engineer, two business executives, a travel-bureau employee, a telephone operator and a secretary. There was nothing traditional about Laura's approach. Her philosophy was to encourage immediate communication without the usual weeks of grammar drill. Grammar would be integrated when necessary.

"How do you do? I am Miss Adams," she said, and wrote her name on the blackboard, then demonstrated a hearty North American handshake. Physical contact at an introduction was alien to Japanese culture so she was not surprised to encounter the hesitant, limp-fingered clasp of her students. Amid much hilarity and chatter, they practiced introducing themselves to each member of the class along with working on firmer handshakes.

The room was a bedlam of laughter and zealous greetings when she glanced up to see Geoffrey McDermott leaning casually against the doorway observing. She gave him an inquiring look, and he waved a hand indicating for her to continue. She had no idea how long he'd been there, nor could she tell what he was thinking. She supposed he considered her noisy class out of control. Well, let him think what he pleased. It didn't matter one whit. Why was she under surveillance, she wondered. Maybe she ought to make his visit worthwhile.

She pulled out all the stops, using every trick in her repertoire, making use of the pictures, objects and charts she'd brought along to motivate participation. By the end of the evening the rapid-fire exchange left her breathless and her students, as well, but all members learned to introduce themselves and carry on a short conversation using a few basic phrases. She had become so involved she was surprised to see that Geoffrey still remained after she dismissed her class. His eyes glowed. He looked anything but disapproving, but his businesslike tone of voice dashed that notion.

"Don't forget to stop by the office on your way out," he said.

"I haven't forgotten," she said crisply. No, she certainly hadn't. She supposed after tonight's rowdy exhibition he couldn't wait to get rid of her. Well, the feeling was mutual, but if the response and enthusiasm of her students were any indication, he had no reason to complain.

A few minutes later she sat down in his outer office. *Darn!* His door was closed. Was someone else with him, or was he exerting executive privilege by allowing her to cool her heels for a few minutes?

A man wearing a dark business suit and heavy dark-rimmed glasses sat across the room reading an English newspaper. Couldn't they even wait until she got out of the building before they summoned the British teacher? She glanced at the office clock impatiently. She'd promised the Matsui boy she would arrive home by ten. Now she'd have to call a taxi in order to make it. Two taxi rides in one day seemed more than she could handle at this point. She looked impatiently at the clock and tried to ignore the frank appraisal of the man who waited with her.

"Are you a teacher here?" he asked finally. His accent was decidedly American.

"I teach English," she said, dodging the question.

"Lucky school!" His eyes emphasized the compliment as they swept up from her trim walking shoes, took in the feminine cut of her suit and lingered on her face.

"Do you teach, also?" she asked.

"No. Just waiting until Geoff is finished. I'm over from the States on a little visit. We're going to do the town tonight."

What was Geoffrey McDermott's idea of "doing the town," she wondered. "Are you two old friends?"

"Former army buddies. We were stationed in Japan together. Haven't seen Geoff since our discharge almost ten years ago."

"Really?" Her voice sounded strangled. Ten years! The hideous truth sent her heart to thudding. Ten years ago her sister had married Major Geoffrey McDermott. An impressionable young girl at the time, Laura could still recall her grandmother's stunned reaction to Lisa's elopement with a soldier her family hadn't even met, then the shock of his betrayal and the heartbreak of Lisa's death when Kelly was born. Even after all these years, tears stung her eyes whenever her thoughts turned to the tragedies.

"So you were both in the army together," she muttered inanely. Oh, God, did she dare ask his rank?

"Right. I was in communications and Geoff was in intelligence."

"Officers, then?"

"Yes. We both made major before our discharge."

So he had been Major Geoffrey McDermott! Two Major Geoffrey McDermotts in Japan at the same time, both in the army? Not likely, but it could be possible. She knew it was wrong to leap to conclusions with so little proof, but the coincidence, if it were such, sent chills through her. She locked her hands in a tight agonized grip. This meeting wasn't going to be easy. Maybe she would just leave, telling the secretary she had to be home to release Kelly's sitter. Better to end any contact with this McDermott now. Further exposure held too many dangerous potentials.

Not a suspicion must cross his mind that she could be Lisa's sister. He might ask questions, and questions would inevitably lead to Kelly. She wiped her sweaty palms with a handkerchief.

"Say, are you all right? You look a little pale," the man said.

"Only a headache," she said, relying on the hackneyed excuse. Just then a couple of students came out of the office followed by Geoffrey.

"Miss Adams." He beckoned her in and waved to his army friend. "Be with you in five minutes," he said, then closed the door. She noted his eyes: dark brown. Brown could become a very cool color. Hair almost black with a coppery sheen. Lisa's description to a T.

"I hope you aren't still thinking of leaving us," he said at last.

"I thought I made my position clear today."

He looked pained. "I didn't think you really meant it."

"You must admit that my contract seemed in doubt."

He scowled, moved his chair closer to the desk and toyed with a note pad. Laura studied his face and realized that if she were honest, she must admit he had a sensitive mouth, and the way that curly lock fell across his forehead just now made him look decidedly boyish. So far his face had shown as fascinating an array of expressions as any actor's; she felt annoyed with herself for the thoughts that accompanied her observation.

Realizing she was gazing at him a little too directly, she switched her focus to an oil painting in the room, waiting for him to arrange the appropriate countenance that made him appear wise and tolerant with the hint of authority that administrators reserved for touchy moments. This was a touchy moment, she decided, and awaited his next words with interest.

"I blame myself for not following through on that blasted elusive contract of yours. Other than that, do you mind telling me if you have other reasons for your decision?"

"Not at all." She'd have liked to see the change on his face if she told him her real reason: *you may be a dangerous man in my life, Major McDermott. I want nothing to do with you.* "Except for the students, this is a very uncomfortable place. From the moment I stepped inside this institution I felt like excess baggage. I don't like it here, Dr. McDermott."

"I see. You're very open, aren't you?"

"Yes, I am."

"Perhaps that's commendable."

"Thank you. I think so."

"On the other hand, it's not very professional of you to take off on such short notice."

"Nor of you to keep me on edge about my contract."

"Oh, come now. Any doubts were all in *your* mind. Not ours."

She widened her eyes. "My goodness, I thought they were all in your instincts."

"Levity. Pure levity. Didn't you recognize that?"

"I recognize when I'm out on a limb with three strikes against me."

He looked pained. "That's a mixed metaphor, Miss Adams."

"I know. It suited my purpose."

He shifted uneasily as if the small office had sud-

denly become smaller. She caught her reflection in
the glass-covered watercolor behind him, her face
blending with the yellow chrysanthemums to create a
montage. She studied her image with a critical gaze
and had a sudden thought. If she were sitting in his
chair, she could read that young woman like a book.
She'd know the kind of college she attended, the section of the country where she lived, her economic
status and that she was probably the type who led
cub-scout troops on weekends.

But what would he think if he knew that this
slender girl in the periwinkle-blue suit, her hair styled
in a casual fashion appropriate for schoolteachers
and visiting foreigners—what would he think if he
knew she were the sole guardian of the son he didn't
even know he had fathered?

"Jobs are not so plentiful now," he continued.
"Most contracts are signed by this time. Perhaps you
should think twice."

"Oh, I agree," she said. "I've thought about it a
lot. My position looked so insecure here that I signed
a contract with the Burton-Kubo school this afternoon." She summoned up the smug little smile she'd
hoarded for this particular moment.

He banged a fist on the table. *"Shikataganai!"*

Her eyes widened. "Is that a Japanese epithet?"

"Yes." He glared as if daring her to ask for a
translation. "And it suited *my* purpose." He reached
for the telephone. "Never mind. I know Scott Burton. I'll call and explain."

She held up a hand. "Please don't. I have every intention of fulfilling my contract with him—as I

would have yours, had I been allowed to sign it this morning.''

He turned on his rare smile. It was full of charm, and she fought against the weakness she felt in the pit of her stomach.

"I admit there were a few unfortunate incidents today," he said. "But that doesn't change the fact that I find you a superior teacher."

He leaned forward, forcing her to meet his eyes. "I saw excitement in your class tonight and real learning, Miss Adams. You're the first teacher I've encountered here who realizes what this kind of school is all about. Quick communication! Not the ability to conjugate verbs in every tense. As a matter of fact, I'd like you to set up some workshops for our other teachers. It could be arranged to suit your schedule. If you'll take on the project, it will mean a substantial increase in your salary."

For an instant she wondered if she might have acted too hastily. Money was a problem. It would not be easy to manage on the Burton-Kubo salary. Cost of living was high in Japan. But she didn't care. Any sacrifice was worthwhile in order to get away from this man. Even if he had not been her sister's husband, he exerted a compelling attraction. Every time she met those dark brown eyes of his she inwardly acknowledged the allure, and she didn't want to deal with the way it confused and disconcerted her. This man had self-assurance to spare and had already demonstrated his aggressiveness. If he were the man she suspected he was, who knew what action he might take if he learned he had a bright attractive son like

Kelly? The farther away from him she could get, the better.

"Well, Miss Adams, what do you say?"

"I'd say that's quite an offer to a person with whom you strike malevolent vibrations."

"You do like to rub things in, don't you?"

"Just human, I guess, but I also have a strong sense of self-preservation."

"In that case, you must realize the Burton-Kubo pay scale doesn't match ours. You mentioned earlier that you have a child to support. Hadn't you better reconsider?"

She rose. Fear slashed through her like a knife. There would be no conversation concerning Kelly. "You have a friend waiting outside, so I'll not take any more of your time," she said. "You needn't pay me for tonight. Perhaps that will help to make up for any trouble I've caused. Good night, Dr. McDermott." She smiled sweetly. He wasn't the only one who could produce charm on demand.

Good manners failed to mask the outrage on his face as he showed her out of the office. She would cherish that look for a long time to come, she thought. Then irrationally she felt a queer kind of regret.

CHAPTER THREE

LAURA SETTLED INTO HER NEW JOB at Burton-Kubo with enthusiasm. She loved the freedom to be inventive, and she hoped the eager response of her students reflected the success of her methods. Scott, like Geoffrey, showed excitement about her approach to teaching, and at his request she had already written a small manual for new instructors incorporating creative and innovative suggestions.

Scott mentioned he'd shown a copy to Geoffrey McDermott at a recent seminar. "He was impressed, let me tell you! I'm afraid I rather enjoyed rubbing in our good fortune at having you on our staff."

Kelly, too, liked his school, if excitement over his science project, something to do with solar energy, was any measure. He'd cluttered the entire apartment with it for days, so it was with relief Laura watched him gather it together one morning, ready to take to class. She offered to help him carry it the three blocks to school.

She could smell autumn in the air that day. The humid heat of late summer was over, and now, mid-September, the sweet-corn sellers who plied their trade along this route had all but disappeared. It felt windy and cool, and the blue-tiled roofs glittered with early-morning drizzle. As they passed a temple, a cloud of starlings rose from a cypress and headed for the hills. She took a deep breath of the clean damp air and wondered if she should have worn a raincoat.

Laura planned to use this jaunt to visit Kelly's principal and inquire about the hara-kiri episode. She would be discreet. Overprotective parents or guardians were not popular with teachers and administrators. Nevertheless, she intended to get to the bottom of Chizu's unique enterprises. She'd dressed with care in her new fall suit, a soft ginger color, and hoped she would not only look smart but communicate smartly. She would not back down if Kelly's well-being was threatened.

As they reached the edge of the schoolyard, a sleek black Mitsubishi Debonaire pulled up to the curb just ahead. Laura stopped in her tracks. The man in the driver's seat was Geoffrey McDermott. Her grip on Kelly's hand tightened and so did her throat as she nodded toward the small dark girl who got out of the car.

"Do you know her name?"

"Sure. That's Chizu, the girl I told you about," he said.

The child waved to Geoffrey and scampered up the walk toward the building.

"That's Chizu?" Laura cried. The announcement had set off a stab of pain. She put the box containing Kelly's project on the sidewalk and rubbed her aching arms. "What's her last name?" she asked huskily.

"Gee, I don't know. Everyone just calls her Chizu. Hey, what's the matter? You look kind of funny."

Laura willed her charging pulses to settle down. "Give me a minute to catch my breath. This is heavier than I expected," she said evasively, and turned her back until she heard the driver rev the engine and shift into gear. A moment later the car sped out of sight.

Could Chizu be Geoffrey's daughter? If so, Kelly and Chizu were half brother and sister! She tried to take in the possibility. Perhaps that was why they'd found instant affinity. Kelly had said Chizu's mother was Japanese and her father American. It certainly added up. Lisa's husband already had a Japanese wife when he went through the false ceremony with her. He must have had a baby daughter at the time, as well. One ominous coincidence after another now appeared, like the leaves that surface as one stirs a bitter cup of tea.

Somehow she helped Kelly get his project to the schoolroom and even managed to coerce her face into an appropriate expression when she met his teacher. Then she fled. The hara-kiri incident paled in importance. She wouldn't complain now. Such a course would inevitably lead to a confrontation with Chizu's father.

Over the past couple of weeks, worries concerning Geoffrey McDermott had faded when it looked as if she would never see him again. But now she wondered. Would episodes such as this one keep cropping up to throw her off balance?

Laura had planned to use the morning to look for another part-time job, but she felt so shaken she decided to go on to school and bury herself in lesson plans. However, she would have to find extra work soon. She and Kelly could manage on her present salary, but nothing remained to build a savings for inevitable, unexpected needs. Scott gladly would have hired her for more hours, but the only openings were in the evening.

At school she became involved in planning a series of situations for students to act out, improvising in English. She forgot about lunch as the hours sped by, and she worked without a break until Scott interrupted her, a strange look on his face.

"McDermott is on the phone, Laura. I hope you won't let him talk you into going back to Sato."

"No way," she said, and went to the office to answer. What did he want, she wondered with apprehension, as she always did whenever his presence disrupted her life.

"Miss Adams?" His pleasant baritone voice came clearly over the wires, and she felt a disturbing weakness in her knees. "I've had a devil of a time tracking you down. Do you spend every waking hour at school?"

"Not really," she said coolly.

"Well, I hope you don't mind my calling you there, but I've been eager to mend any hard feelings you might have for me. If you're free next Saturday, I'd like to take you to see one of Kyoto's prime attractions, Sanjusangendo, sometimes called the Hall of a Thousand and One Buddhas. All of the same god, yet each golden face different. Marvelous portraiture. I know you'd enjoy it.''

She couldn't believe the invitation. Wasn't he married? Was his Japanese wife understanding of even so casual an excursion with another woman?

"Thank you. It sounds fascinating, but I'm afraid next Saturday would be impossible for me,'' she said in a way that she hoped might discourage any further invitations.

"Another time then,'' he said, disappointment obvious.

Back in the teachers' room Laura told Scott that Geoffrey hadn't mentioned Sato. "He just invited me to see Sanjusangendo.''

"You'd never find a better guide,'' Scott said ruefully. They both went back to work, and an hour or so later he poked his head in the teachers' room again. His smile illuminated his craggy features and lent sparkle to his eyes. He showed an engaging shyness combined with an old-fashioned courtly manner. Behind his homely facade lay a keen creative mind and Laura found it a joy to work for him.

"How about joining me for *osanji*?'' Scott asked. "You know the perils of all work and no play.''

"*Osanji?* Sounds luscious. What is it, some exotic drink?''

"Roughly translated it means 'honorable three o'clock.' Snacks, actually. Something like English afternoon tea. And if you can't make it by three, there's always *oyattso*, 'honorable four o'clock.' ''

Laura rose. "Very adaptable, these Japanese. I'd love to join you. Where does one take an honorable three o'clock?''

"Would you believe my favorite coffeehouse is just around the corner?" Scott said.

The place, with its paneled walls, black lacquer tables and creamy bubbles of light from paper lanterns, had the subdued decor of an exclusive club. No traditional music of koto, samisen or flute here. Instead, Laura recognized her favorite Beethoven string quartet, volume judiciously controlled, coming over an excellent sound system. Several young people who looked as if they might be students sat in isolated study, each nursing a cup of coffee.

Scott ordered coffee and a fresh-fruit compote for each of them and they discussed the burgeoning enrollment. "I appreciate your staying with us," he said. "I doubt if Geoffrey will ever get over losing you." He chuckled. "I told him he was going to have to accept misfortune like that famous character of his, Tohaku."

Laura glanced up sharply. "You don't mean Tohaku from the book of the same name?"

Scott formed a circle with thumb and forefinger to acknowledge her acuity. "Precisely."

"But isn't that a novel by K.D. Kano?"

Scott nodded. "Yes. A number of us happen to know that the erudite columnist from the *Japan Times* is also K.D. Kano, the novelist."

Laura felt as if someone had snapped a wet towel in her face. She supposed she looked completely nonplussed as she tried to absorb the incongruity. How could Geoffrey McDermott, the seducer, the philanderer, the cad, be one and the same as K.D. Kano, the author of a half dozen best-selling, insightful novels?

She had barely had time to consider the possible scope of Kelly's and Chizu's relationship. Now this! If this was the same man she'd loathed for so many years, he had to be a Dr. Jekyll and Mr. Hyde. She'd read of such persons. Psychologists documented them as multiple personalities. Geoffrey's world accepted him as a brilliant writer, but she knew his dark side. She stared at her coffee as if she could find an answer in its depths.

At last she understood why her sister could have been overwhelmed by this man. The serious brown eyes that could swiftly change to look at one with such warmth, the handsome muscular body, the sharp mind and self-assurance—all were potent charms that could dazzle any young woman. A few minutes ago even she was astounded to find herself wondering what it might have been like to remain at Sato, to work with this eminent exciting man. No wonder Lisa had regarded him as a stranger from paradise!

What a different man Laura had envisioned all these years, a shallow, slick lightweight. The actuality was far more dangerous.

As she and Scott walked back to school, she barely heard his conversation. Already, she acknowledged, she thought of Geoffrey as the man who "married" her sister. So much evidence was hard to ignore. Anyway, all her actions had to be guarded until she found out for certain.

Scott caught her arm to detain her as they entered the foyer of the school. "Miss Adams? Laura?"

She looked up at him, concerned at his anxious

tone. He looked as if he had just been turned loose in a ring of lions. It still seemed amazing that such a big man could be so shy. She smiled warmly. "Yes?"

He shrugged. "Oh, skip it."

"What were you about to say?"

His frown deepened but he didn't speak.

"Osanji," she said. "A civilized habit I plan to acquire. I loved it. Thank you."

"Likewise. Happy you could come."

"The weather is dampish, but I think it's rather pleasant."

"Yes, very pleasant."

"There must be other topics you would like to discuss?"

"Damn it, Laura, would you believe I was all set to invite you to see Sanjusangendo when McDermott called and asked you?"

"Well, why not ask me then, Scott?"

"The second viewing is never the same thrill as the first," he said wistfully.

She threw him an expression of mock disgust. "Didn't you hear what I said? Ask me. I have no intention of going with Dr. McDermott."

He bowed low in Japanese fashion. "Well, then, Miss Adams, may I have the pleasure of your company in visiting the Hall of the Thousand and One Buddhas next Saturday?"

She solemnly returned the bow. "Delighted. There. Was that so difficult?"

"You're something else, you know that?" he said, but he needn't have uttered a word. His grin spoke a thousand and one thank-yous.

She hurried home to fix sandwiches and a salad for Kelly, who was going to a baseball game and picnic with his team that evening. She ate her own dinner and had barely arrived at school for her classes when she answered the ring of her in-house telephone.

"Please come to the office and take a call. Someone named Kelly wishes to speak with you," the secretary said.

Laura raced down the hall. Kelly would never call unless there were a real emergency. What could have happened? Her throat tightened as she picked up the phone.

"Kelly?"

"Laura?" His voice sounded strained.

"Is something wrong?"

"Well, yes. . .no. I mean, Miss Kimura is here."

"Sachiko? Wonderful! She promised to come and see us the minute she completed her Tokyo music seminar. She knows I get home late. Show her where to find things, the tea and all, and go on to your picnic."

"Well, okay, but. . . ."

"But what? Tell Sachiko to come to the telephone, Kelly."

"Gee, Laura, I don't like to bother her."

"Bother her! Isn't she right there in the room with you?"

"No. I'm calling next door from the Matsuis. I got sort of worried. Miss Kimura is sitting on the tatami like one of those Buddhas. She's crying up a storm but she doesn't make a single sound. It's weird, Laura. What shall I do?"

CHAPTER FOUR

IT WASN'T EASY for Laura to keep her mind on her teaching that evening. She'd met Sachiko last year when the young woman had lived in the United States giving demonstrations at colleges and conservatories of the famous Suzuki method for teaching music to young children.

After Kelly had enrolled in one of her violin classes, the three had become good friends and continued to correspond after Sachiko returned to her home in Kyoto. What disaster sent the attractive Japanese musician running to her American friend instead of to her own family?

Laura dismissed her class promptly and skipped the usual coffee and discussion with Scott and the other teachers in order to catch an earlier bus. Tonight the two-mile ride seemed to take forever. By the time she scurried up the two flights to her apartment, she was breathless and apprehensive. But Sachiko, now looking serene and untroubled, sat reading on the small sofa in the Western-style living room. Laura hid her surprise.

"Sachiko, how wonderful to see you! Sorry you had to spend the evening alone."

Sachiko rose to greet her. Laura, small by

American standards, felt gawky alongside the diminutive Japanese girl whose economical movements flowed with a dancer's grace.

Sachiko hunched her shoulders in a minimizing motion. "Don't worry. I used the time to try to 'get my head together,' as you Americans say. Anyway, Kelly-kun arrived home from his baseball game not long ago and we had a nice visit before he hopped into his futon."

Laura made a fresh pot of tea, and over the steaming brew they caught up on each other's activities, tiptoeing around any mention of the emotional storm Kelly had reported. Sachiko had changed into a blue *yukata*, a lighweight, informal kimono, which enhanced her perfect ivory complexion. Tonight she looked pale.

"You've lost weight, Sachiko. You must be working too hard."

The young woman's posture stiffened. "Never. My work is my food and drink. I would starve without it." Her soft musical voice showed an unaccustomed edge.

"But I feel something is worrying you. Do you want to talk about it?"

"You are perceptive as always, Laura. But I must not aggravate your patience with my own inconsequential problems," she said, lapsing into her native habit of self-deprecation.

"Nonsense. I'm your friend," Laura said warmly.

For a moment Sachiko put her shining dark head in her hands as if struggling for control. Then she straightened abruptly. To Laura's amazement, bitterness, not grief, marked her expression.

"You faced many difficulties when your grandmother died, leaving you responsible for Kelly," she said. "But I saw you make decisions quickly, objectively. I was impressed. Tell me, what would you do if your parents insisted you give up your career?"

"They want you to give up your music! Are your parents ill? Must you care for them?"

"I would gladly do so if such were the case. But it is a far different predicament. Oh, Laura, they insist on *omiai*!"

"An arranged marriage? I thought that rarely happened anymore."

"On the contrary. It is on the upswing. I wouldn't be surprised if almost half our marriages were conducted through *omiai*. The difference today is that it has become more of an introduction system. Couples are rarely forced to marry against their will. I have a friend who went through the custom fifteen times before he found a compatible girl."

"Then why are you so upset? Is there something offensive about the man your parents wish you to meet?"

Sachiko's mouth took an unfamiliar cynical twist. "Kenzo Okita appears to be every parent's dream of an ideal match."

"Kenzo Okita?" The name sounded familiar.

Sachiko looked startled. "Do you know him?"

The name instantly conjured up a young man in Laura's class the only night she taught at Sato. His pronunciation had been hopelessly garbled and she had tuned in to his frustration, offering extra help, but he hadn't called. Laura explained her recollection. "I can assure you he's one handsome young man."

"Oh, yes. His uncle, the go-between, insists he is both handsome and intelligent. Not only that, he has a fine position in a prestigious corporation. As soon as his English is good enough, he will be sent abroad to represent his company."

"Heavens! You'd better run, not walk, to meet that man!"

Sachiko's eyes snapped angrily. "Never. *Kekkon wa josei no haka de aru.* 'Marriage is a woman's grave.' I choose to marry no one. My vows are all dedicated to my music."

"But why?"

"Why? I have only to observe my parents. If we have guests, mother serves them but remains in the kitchen. Father never takes her out socially but spends his evenings more often with his cronies than with us. The only time he talks to my mother is when he issues orders regarding his food and clothing. Why would I trade my music for a life like that?"

Laura felt amazed. She knew that compared to North American males, Japanese men could be considered somewhat dictatorial, but she'd never had it spelled out like this.

Sachiko seemed wound up now as she spilled her grievances. "When my mother was ill in the hospital for a couple of weeks, did my father visit her even once? No! He spent the entire time with his Miss Number Two."

"A mistress?" Laura asked.

"What else?" Sachiko's tone was scathing. "I happen to know that he had his Miss Number Two from the time he was in his early forties, and so do many affluent men. It's a status symbol like owning a yacht.''

"But surely your parents aren't typical.''

"You must understand that here a woman's role is rigidly defined by tradition and most women accept the situation as did my mother.'' Sachiko snapped her fingers. ''*Fusho fuzui*. 'When the husband beckons, the wife jumps!' ''

Laura was not convinced. "But I have seen many Japanese couples traveling happily together in the United States. Aren't times changing?''

"Oh, yes, but far too slowly and for far too few. And never in my conventional family,'' she said bitterly. "When and if I marry, I want to be able to talk to my husband. When I reach out, I want someone to be there, someone who cares.''

"Don't all women?'' Laura murmured. She felt at a loss as to how to help her friend. How could she, an orphan, identify with Sachiko's dilemma? No strong family traditions dominated Laura's actions. Her decisions were her own and she took full responsibility for them. "Have you explained your feelings to your parents? Surely they want your happiness.''

"Happiness,'' Sachiko jeered. '' 'You are twenty-three years old,' they say. 'Your duty is to marry and raise children.' They view music as a mere stopgap between school and marriage. I must toss it out of my life like used clothing.''

"But, Sachiko, you admit times are changing. Maybe this man thinks as you do. Can't you have both a career and a marriage?''

"That's hardly likely. His mother and sister have

waited on him all his life. Why would he want to change? I would be expected to give up my music and follow the pattern. Never!''

"Have you seen him?''

"No, and I don't want to,'' she said vehemently. "But he has seen me. As a result of attending several of my concerts, he apparently convinced his parents to find a go-between.'' Sachiko wilted. "Our first meeting is scheduled next week at a coffeehouse near my home, but I tell you truly all I think about is how to avoid it.''

"Sachiko, for your own peace of mind, you must meet him.''

She shook her head. "Dabble a toe in quicksand and you are lost.''

Laura looked at her friend thoughtfully. "He must love music, Why else did he go to the concerts? Might that not mean he is sympathetic to your career?''

Silence stretched as Sachiko considered the idea. "We often accuse Americans of being flippant and lacking finesse, but they do face up to situations,'' Sachiko said at last. "We Japanese take a more roundabout route and are more likely to rely on intuition. All right, I'll meet him, but I won't give up my music for any man, not even for the handsome Kenzo Okita.'' Her gaze moved wistfully to her violin case by the door.

"Play something for me,'' Laura said.

"Oh, no. I would disturb Kelly-kun.''

"Never. Once he's asleep, an earthquake wouldn't wake him up.''

"Music heals,'' Sachiko said more to herself than

to Laura. She opened her case, adjusted and rosined the bow, then with head bent in a musician's listening pose quietly tuned her violin. Each caring movement spoke of her passion for the instrument.

At last she played. Laura recognized the poignant Bach "Air in G" and knew she heard not a mere performance but true communion between composer and artist. Technique was not sufficient for such a profoundly simple work. One heard humility as well as fierce human strength.

As the music ended, Laura felt too moved to speak. She thought of the poem written recently by one of her students.

> From the yearning of her heart
> Music lifted,
> The incense of her soul.

Sachiko smiled and put her violin away. Music indeed had restored her. Laura felt relieved and hoped she'd given her friend sound advice. She didn't want to interfere, yet she wanted to be the friend Sachiko needed.

They chatted for a few minutes more, then, clear-eyed and composed, Sachiko thanked Laura for her sympathetic ear and bid her *sayonara*.

Perceptive, decisive, objective were the fine words Sachiko had used to describe her American friend, but not one of those traits was evident in the irresolute, doubting individual Laura became when dealing with her own recent problems.

What would she do if the little Japanese-American

pixie, Chizu, were actually Kelly's half sister? Revealing the stunning information to him would involve telling him about Geoffrey. She refused to worry now, not until the real truth surfaced. Even then she wasn't sure she could tell Kelly. No, later, much later, when her young nephew could handle it— or more precisely, when she could.

But she must find out, and soon. The uncertainty tore her apart. She didn't want to keep remembering every inflection of Geoffrey McDermott's voice, to recall each change of his expressive face. She wanted no part of the new emotions that seemed to surface ever more frequently.

THE NEXT MORNING was Saturday. Kelly slept late and dashed in just as Laura finished the dishes, to remind her it was almost time to leave for the outing with his scout troop.

"Is my lunch ready?" he asked.

"Heavens, no. I'll fix it now. I forgot all about it." Laura hastened to put something together for him. Meanwhile Kelly opened the refrigerator and poured himself a glass of milk, liberally spattering the shining counter.

"Hey, I almost forgot something, too. The teacher said we have to pick up the rest of our stuff from the Science Fair by noon today. They need the auditorium for something else. I brought part of it home last night, but there's still more."

"*We*, you say? You should select your pronouns more carefully, my boy. It looks as if first-person singular gets stuck with the chore." She wiped the counter, mentally sighing at her nephew's high-handed rearrangement of her Saturday morning. Now she would be rushed for time. Scott was to pick her up at eleven for their luncheon date and visit to the hall of golden Buddhas.

She handed Kelly his sack lunch.

"Thanks," he said with a smile, his upper lip now sporting a milk mustache. He made a beguiling picture.

"Young man, you catch on fast to these Japanese customs. I see it's *fusho fuzui* already."

"Fusho fuzui?"

" 'When a man snaps his fingers, the lady jumps,' " she explained.

His eyes gleamed. *"Fusho fuzui."* He rolled the words on his tongue as if savoring a piece of candy. "Wow, what a neat idea." He flashed her a disarming grin. "I'm going to organize the guys into a *Fusho Fuzui* Club first thing Monday morning."

"You'll do no such thing."

"Why not? Chizu and her Samurai Sisters Lib group made the boys walk three paces behind them all week."

"I'd like to have seen that," Laura said.

"And something else," Kelly continued. "Put a circle around September twenty-fifth, next Friday night. That's open house at school. Our class earns special points if our folks come."

Laura's face fell. "You know I teach evenings, Kelly."

"Golly, couldn't you get off just this once? I'll feel funny if no one comes for me."

"I know you will, darling, but I can't afford to take any time off. Things are going to be pretty tight around here until I find another part-time job. I'm sorry, but that's the way it is." She cursed the fate that ganged up on orphans.

He ducked his head and stared at his shoes but not before she saw him blink away the film of moisture in his eyes.

"Look," she said with forced brightness. "Why don't I write a note and explain? Since I'm unable to be there, maybe your teacher will excuse you for the evening."

He shook his head, which he kept averted. "She won't. I have a part in a skit. But if my mother and dad were alive, they'd come, all right. Man, dad would really wow 'em with all those medals."

"Of course he would," Laura hedged, distressed as always when Kelly mentioned his father. How much longer ought she to go along with this myth?

Laura often worried that she couldn't be more supportive of Kelly's school activities. She had volunteered to write and edit the Parents' Club monthly bulletin, and the officers had overwhelmed her with praise at the first edition. Such work came easily and she enjoyed it. However, to a child, being present at his performance held much more meaning than writing some dry bulletin.

Mercifully a horn sounded announcing his ride. Looking somber, he clutched his lunch and manfully trudged off to join his scout troop.

Laura picked up her new *furoshiki*, the flowered square of silk traditionally used as a carryall, found a plastic shopping bag and started to leave when the telephone rang.

"I can't believe my rotten luck," Scott said, and poured out his predicament. It seemed his partner, Mr. Kubo, had suddenly taken ill and Scott had to fill in for him at an important conference. "A heck of a spot at the last minute like this." His distress was only too evident.

Laura insisted she understood, not to worry, and yes, she'd love a rain check. But she had to admit she was disappointed. She had been so busy settling into her schoolwork this past month she still hadn't had time to explore the city, and she had really looked forward to spending a carefree day with the big gentle man. He had a way of putting people at ease, and his old-fashioned gallantry came so naturally that she frankly basked in it.

Outside heavy clouds darkened the sky, and wind whipped her skirt around her legs. By the time she reached Kelly's school, rain had begun to fall in gusty streaks. Inside the auditorium she found the remaining parts of Kelly's project, his name tacked conspicuously on it along with a blue ribbon that he'd failed to mention. The school was only three blocks from the apartment, but it would be some feat to manage the bulky parts. Next time she would suggest that he tackle miniatures.

Laura lumbered outside into the downpour with her unwieldy burden. She hauled a large cardboard backdrop done in poster paint, two broomstick-size poles and a number of indiscriminate items jammed into a hefty box. The shopping bag and *furoshiki* were no help at all. She struggled out to the sidewalk, then set everything down and tried for a more efficient arrangement. A taxi came in sight and she signaled frantically as the driver zoomed by staring heartlessly straight ahead. She threw an envious glance at several children and parents loading projects into warm dry cars, then determinedly tied the *furoshiki* around her head—a futile effort, she realized as the downpour soaked it immediately.

She bent into the wind juggling her cumbersome load. People turned to stare from under their umbrellas as if she were some weird apparition. For two cents she'd dump the whole thing into the nearest ash can. There was little storage space in the tiny apartment anyway. The backdrop flapped back and forth, wilting fast, threatening to disintegrate. Purple, green and yellow paint dribbled into a dismal mixture as it ran off onto her skirt.

A car skidded against the curb, a door flew open and a tall man got out. It was Geoffrey McDermott, raincoat flapping. He reached her in three long strides. Without a word, he grabbed her load and stacked it in the back seat of his car on top of what must have been Chizu's project. Oh, Lord, why was it that every time she ran into this man she looked like a blithering idiot? Just once she'd like to look cool and collected, even sexy and glamorous. Good heavens! What difference did it make?

"No weather instincts at all, I see," he said as he propelled her into the car and took his place at the wheel. "Are you freezing?" His face showed real concern but his tone indicated casual interest. She'd noticed the curious disparity before. It was as if he always needed to temper emotion with words, or words with emotion. "Where do you live?"

"Straight ahead two blocks, then just around the corner," she said meekly. "My nephew left earlier on a scout trip. I forgot there was so much to carry or I would have made other arrangements."

"Kids!" he said, and his inflection suited her sentiments precisely. He peered through the streaming windshield, giving full attention to the street.

Awkwardly she strove to make conversation. Trifling words piled on words could build a hedgerow between them. That was what she wanted, wasn't it? No, she admitted while sneaking a sidelong glance at him. She wished he didn't look so inscrutable, that his profile wasn't so ruggedly handsome, that she didn't have to fight this crazy emotional confusion that welled up inside her every time she got near him. She wished. . . .

She nodded toward the back seat. "So you got stuck with picking up a project, too?"

"Right. Chizu's effort was no great shakes, but she's too much of a ham not to participate. A bright child, all right, but science isn't her forte."

But arrange a little hara-kiri demo and the tempo would pick up, Laura thought, and modestly refrained from bragging about Kelly's blue ribbon.

"This the place?" he asked, coasting to a stop in front of her apartment.

"Yes, it is. And thanks for the rescue. I can manage if you just leave everything here on the sidewalk."

He scowled as if she were demented and gathered the sodden props. "Lead on," he commanded. It was ridiculous to stand in the rain and argue, so she hurried up the stairs and he followed. He set the load on the landing as she fitted the key into the lock.

"Thanks again," she said with a polite smile, a dismissing action that he ignored.

"Oh, no, you don't. I need a hot cup of coffee and so do you. Instant will do." He peered over her head into her apartment. "Anyway, I've been curious about where you hang your hat. Don't worry. I won't stay long. As a matter of fact, after you change, we can head for the Kokedera Moss Gardens. Rain or mist provides perfect viewing."

What a despot! Under the circumstances, she supposed she at least owed him coffee. But the Moss Gardens were out as far as she was concerned.

She led the way into the apartment and pointed to the section of the L-shaped area that served as the kitchen, feeling relieved she'd left it tidy.

"Help yourself, but none for me." No, sir. Not on a bet. The ill-humored gremlin who hovered over the two of them would no doubt manipulate her into tipping over the pot, scalding anyone within reach. "As for the gardens," she said, "thanks, but I won't be able to join you."

"Why not? Your nephew is off on an outing. You just said so."

"Count me out, but help yourself to the coffee while I change."

He stared at her. No doubt she looked like someone's bad dream, her hair flattened and separated into limp strands, her skirt and sweater bunched and clinging revealingly to her figure.

"Too bad about your skirt. Fresh paint, right?" Something about the way he lifted an eyebrow told her he recalled only too well the paint episode in his office.

Angry and embarrassed, she went to the bathroom, slipped out of her sopping clothes and hung them over the tub. Standing nude she unconsciously crossed her arms over her breasts as she thought of Geoffrey sitting in the next room. It was as if a fire had been suddenly kindled in this cold place. *Damn!* What was this man doing to her?

She hurried back to the bedroom, where she put on a soft, rose wool dress, last year's, but she knew it was becoming. She toweled her hair and took another five minutes to shape and blow it dry, meanwhile chiding herself for even bothering.

Ready at last, she joined him and found that he'd turned on the radio and was listening to music that sounded like a Spanish dance. Its exuberance filled the room with whirling melodies and pulsing rhythms.

He looked up as she entered, but the way his eyes shone behind the dark curl of his eyelashes, she could see his mind was no longer on the music.

He turned down the volume and made a comprehensive gesture. "Great little place you have here."

"The bath and bedrooms are Japanese-style, and as you see, this room and the kitchen, what there is of it, are Western."

What a well-shaped head he has, she thought. The

rain that had ravaged her own appearance had perversely turned Geoffrey's hair into an appealing curly cap. Thank goodness he couldn't guess the amazing vagaries that plagued her during their mundane chatter.

"So you're already finding out that the Japanese have two styles of everything," he said. "Architecture, clothing, music, anything that touches their lives. They can arrange a traditional art alcove, the *tokonoma*, with one hand and a silicon chip with the other."

"The Far East and the Far West at the same time?"

"Precisely. I've had a love affair with the place my entire life. Japan is one provocative lady, mysterious and beautiful, but you'd better forget logic if you want to understand her."

"You've lived here a long time, then?"

"Yes. During my teens my father was in the diplomatic corps. Because of my facility in the language, I spent my army years here. Afterward I went back to the States to complete my Ph.D., then returned to make it my home ever since."

Had his graduate-student days coincided with the time he met Lisa, she wondered.

He glanced at her one good print and the bowl of bronze chrysanthemums she'd arranged that morning. "These places are pretty much alike, but you've made it yours." He walked over and ran his fingers across a shelf of the few favorite books she'd brought along. Then he shot her a quizzical look as if to add up her personality from the sum of the titles.

Good luck, old boy, she thought as he took in the array of authors, everything from Dickens, Ibsen, Steinbeck and a couple of poetry collections to a lot of recent science fiction, along with K.D. Kano's latest novel. She hoped he wouldn't ask about the plain leather folder that contained her recent attempts at haiku. She didn't want a man of his literary reputation poking his nose into her amateurish writing. But he didn't notice it, nor did he mention his own book. Instead, he tapped the nineteenth-century-poetry anthology.

"Let me guess. Your favorite is Swinburne. Right?"

"That sensualist," she scoffed.

He chuckled, and she knew she hadn't fooled him for a minute. She'd rarely seen him laugh, and his attractive smile always came as a surprise in his thoughtful face. Very compelling. If a smile like that could make Laura's head swim, what had it done to her sister?

In spite of her directions, Geoffrey had made a full pot of coffee, found the cups and served her now as if she were the guest. She tasted it. The man knew how to make a good cup of coffee, but nevertheless she felt wary in his presence. In contrast, he settled back on the sofa as relaxed as if he'd just come home. Only pipe and slippers would have completed the picture.

Was it Geoffrey's self-assurance her sister had found so appealing? It was disturbing, no doubt about it, she thought wryly, startled to find herself wondering how it must have felt to be kissed and held by him.

"Hey, is my brew all that potent? I've made the same comment at least three times. 'Yea, though we sang as angels in her ear, she would not hear,' compliments of Swinburne, as you no doubt know."

Why didn't he go on to the next line? It was far more appropriate. "Let us rise up and part," it said. She felt sorely tempted to quote the words but hated to confirm Swinburne was indeed her favorite poet. Sorry, I was thinking about a problem."

"Problem? What do you say we avoid problems? I love everyone today. I'm a bundle of sunshine, a model companion for your first visit to the Moss Gardens."

His words were flip but the look in his eye unnerved her. It seemed to suggest something far more serious and she felt her own senses sharpen in response.

She tried to meet his glance with impersonal ease, then took a too large sip of coffee and felt it burn all the way down her throat. She coughed and wiped her eyes.

He leaned forward and turned her chin so that she faced him. His hand felt surprisingly gentle. "Now what's all this about a problem?"

"Actually, it has to do with Chizu," she said when she caught her breath.

He looked incredulous. "Chizu! What has Chizu to do with us? I can't imagine that child doing anything other than making this world a happier and more fascinating place to live."

"You're prejudiced, naturally. Still, I admit she is precocious."

He nodded. "She is indeed."

"With a flair for leadership."

"Ab-so-lutely."

"But," Laura said, finally allowing all her pent-up anger to escape, "demonstrating hara-kiri with pocketknives goes too far."

He threw back his head and laughed with a heartiness she hadn't known he possessed. "Well, I'm sure you agree she does have a flair for the dramatic."

"I don't find violence amusing," she said stiffly.

"Nor do I, and I expect this is all my fault. Chizu asked me to explain the old custom in some detail recently. She was so interested I should have guessed what she was up to. In case you haven't discovered, her present mission in life is to educate her ignorant American classmates in all aspects of Japanese culture."

"I would have preferred flower arranging or even the tea ceremony," Laura said dryly.

He waved a hand. "Don't worry. She'll get around to those."

"Somehow I don't think they are very high on her priority list. At the moment I gather she is promoting some kind of girls'-lib group, and last week it was Belly Band Day, whatever that is." She made a face.

His lips twitched. "She does choose colorful topics. Belly Band Day," he repeated. "Ah, yes. In some circles there still remains a superstition that a male must keep his navel warm. Relax. I'm sure your nephew takes Chizu's ventures in stride."

"Are you making light of this situation?"

He parroted her tone. "And aren't you making

mountains out of molehills? I'm certain that Chizu's pedantic exploits are harmless. In fact, the kids might learn something. But I can see you're upset. I'll mention the hara-kiri bit to her mother.''

"Her mother! Don't you assume any responsibility for your daughter's discipline?'' Laura cried.

Geoffrey stared at her, his face a mixture of emotions. "Chizu is not my daughter, Laura,'' he said quietly. "I'm not married, but if I ever have a child—and I can't tell you how much I want one— I only hope he or she will be a lot like Chizu.'' The wistful quality of his voice more than underlined his sincerity.

Color flooded Laura's face. "But I thought...I mean...'' she stammered. "I saw you drop her off at school. You picked up her project. You spoke of her as if she were your daughter. I assumed ....'' Her voice trailed away.

"Yes, I can see how you might believe that,'' he said. "Chizu and her parents are my neighbors and longtime friends. Bill Thompson and his wife are in Hong Kong for a few weeks and left Chizu with another neighbor. I've been helping out with transportation occasionally and filling in on fatherly duties.'' He shrugged. "That's it.''

Laura's mind reeled. Chizu Thompson. Not Chizu McDermott! *Thank God!* Life suddenly became enormously less complicated without having to deal with a half sister in Kelly's life. Still, that fact didn't diminish the threatening specter that remained. Everything she had learned about this man pointed toward him as Kelly's father. Army records existed to verify his background. He'd stated only too plainly just moments ago how much he wanted a child of his own. She felt an inward shudder as she recalled the longing in his voice as he said it. His desire now took on a far more frightening aspect. If he learned about Kelly. . . .

He rose and she did, too. She felt shaken and hoped he'd leave without any further disturbing conversation. He hesitated as if trying to make up his mind about something. She felt uneasy at the sudden intimacy of his gaze, the way he studied the dust of pink that now rose in her cheeks. His appraisal drifted to the pearl buttons at her neckline, then moved slowly down to rest on her slim waist.

"Laura," he said at last. If she hadn't known better, she would have thought he was searching for words.

"Yes, Dr. McDermott."

He shook his head in hopeless reaction to her continued use of the formal address. "Let's face it," he said. "I got off on the wrong foot with you, and I can't seem to right myself. Can't we start over? I feel as if I'm up against a brick wall, a barbed-wire fence and a firing squad. Is it because you thought I was married?"

This was an unexpected turn. "Yes, I did believe that."

He walked over and put his hands on her shoulders. Their firmness and warmth penetrated her dress, and her shoulders burned as if no cloth existed. Her vision blurred as if the outside mist now permeated the room.

"I can understand your resentment, then," he continued. "But you needn't be concerned on that score. I'm a bachelor."

The information both relieved and worried her. What had he done with his Japanese wife? Deserted her as he had Lisa? "A bachelor of the confirmed variety, no doubt."

"Yes, I'm afraid I do have that reputation. I guess I figured I couldn't write unless I was free from emotional involvement."

"An odd assumption for a writer."

"True, and I've spent the last ten years trying to prove it." He paused. "There was a girl...you're not at all like her except for certain inner qualities." His solemn expression gave way to a softer mien as he studied her face. "There's a unique sweetness about the mouth, and I don't mean naiveté," he said as if describing someone else. "And of course there's the quick intelligence." He touched her cheek briefly. She caught her breath as she felt some inner tension building.

Laura swayed slightly and Geoffrey steadied his hands on her shoulders. "What was her name?" she whispered, and closed her eyes, not wanting to hear yet passionately needing to know the answer.

He shook his head. "I'll fill you in someday. But enough of the past. I'm eager again for a future and I want you in it, Laura. More than anything in my life right now I would like us to mean something special to each other." He earnestly searched her face for reaction, his dark brown eyes warm with gold highlights. Then he leaned down and kissed her on the lips. The kiss was not overlong but it was definitely persistent, like the man who initiated it. His arms encircled her, pulling her close, and it seemed as natural as breathing to lean her head against his shoulder.

He held her firmly but with a touch that somehow imparted gentleness and laid his cheek against her temple. She was instantly aware of his hard determined jawline and felt her breathing quicken. Was it irrational to allow herself a moment or two to savor his nearness, the feeling of protectiveness and comfort he offered? It was a feeling she yearned for, needed.

They clung to each other, swaying gently, and wherever their bodies touched, the sensation was acute, delicious. It was as if she'd never known that such a feeling existed, and experiencing it filled her with exhilaration.

For a little while everything seemed to grow more vivid. Below on the street, a priest's seashell horn blared plaintively for alms, and a faraway temple gong sounded, its echo fading into the distance. Her pulse raced in dismay. She felt completely bewildered by her reaction. Hadn't she resolved to be wary about admitting men into her life, this one in particular?

What made her respond so quickly? She'd never thought of herself as a singularly passionate woman. Affectionate and tender, yes, at least in her relationship with Bill, her only serious love affair. But not like this. The way her entire body kindled just now frightened her. Oh, God, were these the same emotions Geoffrey had awakened in Lisa? What lunacy had come over her?

She tried to pull away but Geoffrey's embrace tightened at once. The moment demanded she stay in his arms. She felt torn. It was as if her renegade inner voice were pitting her against all her instincts. She had been Kelly's pillar of strength for a long time. Now it was her turn to lean on someone, to feel desirable, attractive to a man like K.D. Kano.

A sweetness like blossoms seemed to surround them as she listened to Geoffrey's quiet deep voice tell her how lovely she was, how intriguing, how much he wanted to know her and how deeply he regretted his petulance that day at the language school.

She tried not to think about her own arms around his neck, how his hands smoothed back her hair, how they gently cupped her face, then drifted down to span her waist as if to prove to himself how small it was.

She tried not to visualize how he must have made love to Lisa with the same gentle beginnings, and did her best to dismiss her own emotions until later, later when she would feel composed enough to sort out her reactions and motives and put them into proper perspective.

Geoffrey kissed her again, then released her.

"That's for a fresh start," he said, and looking so much like Kelly she could have wept, he gave her a little salute, said goodbye and left.

She leaned against the door listening to his steps grow faint and disappear. Her knees were weak and her head pounded. She felt drained, exhausted. She could use a fresh start, too, beginning about ten years ago. Ironically, these were almost the same words she'd used the day she met Geoffrey, *before* she knew he had been Major Geoffrey McDermott.

But there could be no fresh starts for them; only endings. Growing up with Lisa's bitter misfortune clouding her life left Laura skeptical of the integrity of any man who came on strong so early in a relationship. Now the mocking specter of the Geoffrey McDermott she had always pictured grinned cynically from her memories. She'd heard all about that silver tongue from Lisa and she dared not put any faith in it.

CHAPTER FIVE

FOR THE REST OF THE WEEK, Laura tried to make sense out of the incident. By stretching credulity, one might rationalize away a quick kiss as merely her appreciation for being rescued in the rainstorm. But that was no quick kiss she and Geoffrey had enjoyed. She could argue that he swept her off her feet as he had Lisa. But Laura was no ingenue. There had been ten years of forewarning concerning this man. She visualized dozens of ways she could have prevented the intimate interlude but the exercise proved futile. What was done, was done.

Well, she wasn't going to let it worry her. Fortunately, he hadn't followed up on his invitation to show her the Moss Gardens, nor had she seen him, so she felt convinced that he had phased himself out of her life as quickly as he had Lisa's. So it would be inappropriate to feel let down or abandoned, right? Right.

Nevertheless, she kept hearing his resonant voice telling her how earnest he was about wanting to know her, which was doubly distressing because he sounded so sincere, so convincing. She kept remembering his face when she first caught him listening so intently to her radio, how the music had seemed to send him journeying to some unreachable place. Perhaps it triggered some poignant recollection. Even the controlled Dr. McDermott could appear vulnerable, it seemed.

It was difficult to see how a man could wear so many hats: the stern administrator of the Sato language school, the man who wistfully professed his longing for a family, the grave intellectual who cherished privacy and the charming companion who made himself at home in her apartment.

Oh, forget it. She hated the way he invaded her thoughts, and she feared the threat he posed to Kelly. Still, it appeared that her worries might be over. At least, the next few days went so smoothly that Laura decided her fates must have held a committee meeting and voted her a stint on Olympus. The sun shone, her students responded with unusual enthusiasm, she didn't miss the bus home from work even once and she had a perfect day with Scott exploring the golden Buddhas of Sanjusangendo. Her spirits soared during such interludes. She was an incurable romantic, happiest when everyone smiled, said pleasant things and looked forward to cheerful endings. Ah, delusion.

It hadn't taken long for the week to return to normal. Kelly had worn out his shoes in just over a month, and her tooth required a root canal instead of a filling. Their electric bill was astronomical even though the apartment was unheated except for the *kotatsu*, the table with the warming unit on its underside. The final blow occurred when, instead of the long-expected annuity check from her grandmother's estate, a letter arrived from the lawyer stating that probate would not be concluded for another four or five months. Panicky, she called an employment agency and got an appointment for Saturday afternoon. She should have done it weeks ago.

On her calendar she noticed that parents' night was scheduled for that evening. Apparently, Kelly was no longer upset that Laura was unable to attend. At least, she saw no signs of depression or other unusual behavior and was thankful her nephew was a secure enough child to take such a disappointment in stride.

"Don't worry," he said when she again voiced her regrets that morning. "It doesn't matter that you can't come." He did a handstand ending in a neatly executed back flip and landed on his feet. She appraised his apparent nonchalance. *So don't ever get the idea you're indispensable,* she warned herself wryly.

"I'm proud of you for acting so mature," she complimented him.

"Oh, it's okay. Chizu and I worked it out."

"Chizu! What on earth has Chizu to do with it?"

"Her folks can't come, either."

"Oh?" she said uneasily, then dismissed the apprehension in the probability the two children supported each other in their common problem.

But that evening when she arrived home from teaching, Kelly was not there. The school program should have been over an hour ago. Seiji Matsui, the high-school neighbor, was to have spent the evening with Kelly. She went downstairs to the Matsuis' apartment. All was dark. What had happened? Seiji had always been completely dependable. Back in her little kitchen she put a kettle on for tea. Nothing like tea to sustain one.

Moments later she heard a clatter on the stairs, and Kelly burst into the room followed by Geoffrey and an elfin child whom she recognized immediately as Chizu.

"Hey, Laura, guess what? We won! Our class won!" he cried. "And you want to know why? Dr. McDermott was our pretend father, that's why."

"Your what?" Laura cried aghast.

Geoffrey gave a snappy military salute. "Surrogate father reporting. Just another of my hidden talents."

Good Lord! What insidious fate had thrown Geoffrey and Kelly together?

"I was worried," she said coolly.

Geoffrey frowned. "But I told Seiji to leave a note."

"Well, he didn't," Laura said, simultaneously spotting a folded paper propped in plain sight on a lamp table. How had she overlooked it?

She apologized, squirming inwardly at Geoffrey's amused expression. At least Kelly remembered *his* manners.

"Laura, this is Chizu. Chizu, this is my Aunt Laura." So here was the incomparable Chizu at last. Where was the hoyden who demonstrated hara-kiri and conducted all those cultural sessions single-handedly? There was an aura of poetry about this child. Delicate features combined the best of both Oriental and Caucasian. Though her hair was cut in a no-nonsense style, it couldn't detract from her delicate beauty. Neither did her stubby shoes nor the plain navy coat. One still sensed the presence of a Titania who spent her days scalloping from thistle to thistle. Actually, it was her eyes, a startling green, that denoted the provocative nature of this child.

"I'm so glad to meet you, Chizu-chan," Laura said tardily. "Sit down, all of you, and tell me about the program." She forced a smile and tried to keep the electrifying sensation of Geoffrey's presence from engulfing her. Why did this man insist on intruding into her life?

Geoffrey settled into what he already apparently considered his favorite chair. "The kids gave a great performance, and since there's no school tomorrow, I took them out for ice cream."

"I had two double-deckers," Kelly said, his eyes sparkling at the recollection. Laura said nothing.

Geoffrey looked at her with concern. "Hey, I didn't intend to butt in. A guy doesn't go out of his way to offend someone he likes a lot. Rule number one, two and three, as well. As far as I was concerned, it all boiled down to how the kids would feel if they had no one to represent them."

The children stared wide-eyed and Laura sighed.

"Very commendable of you." Yes, indeed. He was always at least a dozen steps ahead of her.

"Thanks. So am I forgiven?"

She nodded warily. "Yes, you are, and you're also a con artist if I've ever seen one."

He grinned and Laura fixed her attention on the children so that she didn't have to meet his laughing brown eyes. Their knowing gleam had a way of enfolding her and turning her witless and incoherent.

"It did occur to me that the ice-cream gambit might enable me to see you again," he said. "But I was mainly concerned with fair play for the children."

"Thanks. I'm sure it meant a lot to them," she said stiffly, and knew that it did.

"You're welcome. Now, it would mean a lot to me if you would accept an invitation."

"Yeah, Laura, we can all go back to that ice-cream place," Kelly said.

"Not so fast, young man. I prefer to issue my own invitations. May I take you to lunch tomorrow, Laura? Then we'll make another try for those elusive Moss Gardens. You kids can stay home and play Monopoly or something."

"Thanks very much, but I have an appointment," Laura said.

"You could break it."

"I'm afraid not. It's very important."

"It sure is," Kelly piped up. "Laura has to get another job. We're practically down to tea and beans," he said cheerfully, quoting one of her earlier remarks.

Laura felt herself blush and glared at Kelly, hoping he wouldn't find it necessary to repeat any more of her comments.

"Too bad you moved over to that poor-paying Burton-Kubo outfit. Our offer still holds, you know," Geoffrey affirmed.

"I'm looking for something part-time," she said

with as much dignity as she could muster. "Typing, tutoring or secretarial work, preferably mornings so I can be home afternoons when Kelly returns from school."

Geoffrey leaned forward "Mornings, you say? I seem to recall a note posted on our school bulletin board offering part-time work of that nature. Let me call right now. Someone is bound to still be around."

"I'd appreciate that," Laura said, trying not to sound too eager. She indicated the telephone in the hallway, handed him a pen and pad, then went to join the children, who were spread out like octopuses on the floor playing one of Kelly's electronic games. Already they were in a world of their own.

In minutes, Geoffrey returned and handed her the pad. "How does this strike you?"

She skimmed his large clear handwriting, then read it again. It sounded too good to be true.

Wanted immediately: Expert typist. Minimum: 75 words per minute. Speed and accuracy essential. Hours: 9:00-12:00 mornings, Monday-Friday. Apply A.M. only.

The address followed.

"It's exactly what I want," Laura cried, no longer able to curb her enthusiasm. "Oh, I hope it's not filled."

He shrugged. "Probably not or the notice wouldn't still be there. I'm familiar with the area. Why not let me drive you there in the morning?"

"Oh, no. I wouldn't think of troubling you," she

said firmly, but jotted down the directions he gave her along with which bus to take.

He rose. "Come along, Chizu-chan. I won't earn any Brownie points if I don't get you home."

They left then as Laura and Kelly thanked him again, Laura so elated about the job prospect she could hardly speak coherently.

As soon as she got Kelly off to his Saturday scout meeting the next morning, she called the employment agency and canceled her appointment, praying she wouldn't have to make another one after her interview for the typist's job. She dressed with special care. She was sure of her skills but could she make a good impression? Ruefully she considered her first day at Sato. She seemed to have a penchant for blowing critical moments. Well, she would be extra careful this time.

She worried that she might not look the part of a supercompetent typist whose prime concern was speed and accuracy. Her blond hair when worn casually waved around her shoulders, giving her a decidedly youthful appearance.

Frowning into a mirror, she pulled her hair severely away from her face and wound it into a French knot. Better. Last year's classic brown suit was no doubt more professional-looking than the feminine cut of her new ginger one. Yes, much improved, she decided after changing. For a final touch she added a pair of reading glasses. The results satisfied her in a blurred sort of way. It was as if she viewed everything through a fishbowl. She tucked the glasses into her purse and would put them on at the last minute.

Everything seemed to bode well when the designated bus showed up almost immediately. *Please, God, let me get this job,* she prayed repeatedly. The bus lumbered along slowly through heavier and heavier traffic. She couldn't get used to the human density. Still, in a country that held a population of half that of the United States in an area smaller than the state of California, she needn't have felt surprised.

She looked at her watch for the hundredth time. This ride was taking forever. Geoffrey had said the place was located in a suburb about forty-five minutes away. Already she had traveled a half hour and she was still in the city. Then she remembered. "Take the west bus," Geoffrey had said. This bus indisputably headed east. Her spirits plunged. Was it better to stay on the bus until it completed its circuit, or should she jump off and hail a taxi?

She showed the address to the bus driver, who gave a broad grin, nodded vigorously and pointed vaguely off into the distance, chattering incomprehensibly all the while. She sat down in despair, watching the minutes tick away on her watch. "Apply mornings only," the notice had said.

At precisely quarter to twelve she ran up the steps of a handsome condominium. On the porch she paused to catch her breath. She put on her glasses and rapped smartly. The door swung open so quickly that someone must have been waiting for her. She stared up at the fuzzy face that oscillated dizzily in front of her.

"What took you so long?" Geoffrey McDermott said.

CHAPTER SIX

ASTONISHMENT, THEN ANGER rendered Laura speechless as she took in Geoffrey's amused expression. Her first impulse was to turn and run, but the thought of such lack of poise restrained her.

Geoffrey held the door open. "Come in. I've been expecting you," he said pleasantly. She found herself following him through an entry hall and into a spacious area, a kind of combination library and living room furnished mainly in traditional Western style. Bookshelves lined two of the paneled walls. Leather chairs, brass and cloisonné lamps and a massive teakwood desk provided a masculine environment warmed and softened by an Oriental rug in shades of burgundy.

She took the chair he indicated and folded her hands in her lap, trying to appear composed.

"I take it this is some kind of game," she said.

He leaned back in his chair and tapped his fingers together as if to give her comment thoughtful consideration. "Game? I'd say it's a business proposition. You need a job and I need someone with your abilities."

"So why all the playacting? Why didn't you say so last night?"

"Yes, I would have preferred that myself. But would you have accepted? I doubt it."

"Doubt," she said. "That's the operative word here, all right."

"Now, don't go in for dissembling. I believed you might be more interested in the job if you saw what it entailed."

"A job that starts out with subterfuge doesn't rate very high in my book." She made a conscious effort to relax her rigid shoulders, unwind her tightly clenched fingers.

He shot her a quizzical glance. "How about a little port?" Without awaiting her reply, he reached over to a decanter and poured them both a glass. She willed her hand steady as she accepted hers. They sipped the ruby liquid in silence for a few moments. She felt his eyes on her, unwavering, as if he could read her thoughts, and he probably could.

"What on earth have you done to your hair?" he asked, his expression clearly showing his opinion.

She fingered the French knot, which had begun to loosen. "I can't see that it concerns you."

"Now, don't get defensive. It's a guise, isn't it? Your idea of the perfect secretary." He grinned. "So you don't object to a little playacting, after all?"

She glared at him. This was all too humiliating. "You're treating me like a child!"

His voice suddenly deepened and his eyes moved over her appreciatively. "Believe me, Laura," he said earnestly, "I regard you as anything but a child."

"But I fell for the whole scheme!" How could she have been so gullible?

"And everything I told you was true."

"Oh, sure. What was all that business about a note on the bulletin board and the telephone call?"

"But there *was* a note on the bulletin board. I put it there myself. Fortunately, thus far there was no response. I admit the telephone call could be classed as artifice. But in your case, I considered any ruse justifiable."

Why, she wondered. As far as she knew, all he had to judge her work by was the day she'd spent at Sato. And that had been a disaster. "What about Marcia Cole at the language school? I understand she's very competent."

He finished his port and poured another glass. "Marcia fills in for me occasionally when work piles up, but she already has a full-time job. She's okay but not in your class. It's not easy to find a person with your qualifications, one who wants only part-time work. You're speedy and your degree in English will come in handy for copy editing. Let's face it, fate keeps throwing us together. You can't deny it, so why fight it?"

His voice seemed filled with genuine appeal and she wanted to hate him for the way it turned her light-headed, lessening the fury over the way she had been duped.

She lifted her chin. "I believe a person has some say over her fate."

"Amen," he said, and walked over to his desk and lifted the cover from a typewriter. "It's a brand-new electric. Does everything but make up the beds. Have a look." He started demonstrating the various functions. Unable to restrain her curiosity, she walked over to watch. Typing on this machine would be like performing on a Steinway after owning a tinny player piano.

"It's a dream," she said, but without inflection. *I won't argue anymore with this man. I won't,* she resolved. *It leads only to disaster.* For a few seconds their eyes met and held. Then he picked up a thick manuscript and handed it to her.

"My new novel ready for you to type."

She skimmed the first page. As always she savored Kano's lyrical style and original turn of phrase. The story intrigued her immediately. With an effort she refrained from turning the page to finish the paragraph.

He flipped through the pages indicating margin notations, sections numbered out of sequence and arrows pointing in all directions. "I'm a hopeless typist. See what you're in for?"

"I think you'd be better off with someone who's experienced in cracking codes," she said dryly. "This sort of copy is not conducive to speed typing."

"You've analyzed my needs exactly." He named an hourly figure and she almost gasped. It was considerably more than she earned for teaching.

"Deadline for this manuscript is the end of the month but I could probably wangle an extension."

"I see. The job is temporary, then?"

"Not at all. I always have work in progress, a weekly column, lectures, a big backlog of research notes, not to mention a wide correspondence. I've been without a secretary for a couple of weeks. Mine got married and moved to Tokyo. Marcia has been helping out until I find someone.''

Laura took in the quiet elegance of the room, the fine typewriter and the K.D. Kano manuscript. If anyone had told her a year ago that she would have an opportunity to work with this eminent novelist, she would have been ecstatic. But now?

"I'm sorry, but I can't accept your offer," she said quickly for fear she might weaken.

"Why not?" he demanded. "We each have something the other needs. Can't we accept that and go on from there? What's your reason?"

"Well, for one thing, all your instincts advised against me the very first day we met."

He threw up his hands. "So I made a lamebrained remark. Are you going to hold it against me forever?"

"Yes, I am."

Her answer seemed to amuse rather than provoke him.

"I can guarantee we could work well together."

"No, you can't."

"Oh, yes, I can. After all, we're both fans of Swinburne."

"You don't make sense."

"And that's the whole thing in a nutshell, isn't it?"

"Yes. I don't care to work for you, Geoffrey," she said in a low voice, wishing she could sound more decisive.

He reached over and gently removed her glasses, then pulled the pins from her hair, allowing it to fall to her shoulders and curl again around her face. She felt uneasy. What if he might take a notion to pull off more layers of her facade? He held her at arm's length, forcing her to meet his eyes.

"So says the job applicant. What says the real Laura Adams?"

He smelled subtly of soap and his hands on her arms touched off a mysterious response that unnerved her.

"You are lovely, little Laura," he said softly, and let his fingers drift through her hair. She was startled by his expression, which was as caring as his words had been. Her pulse began to hammer and she hoped he wouldn't notice the rhythmic rise and fall of the brown wool above her breast.

On that day at Sato he'd sworn that the two of them set off malevolent vibrations. Was this what he meant? She held herself as still as possible. If she pretended she was invulnerable, perhaps he would back off. He felt her lack of response at once.

"I can't figure you."

"And I can't figure you. Why are you so set on hiring someone who hasn't produced a single reference? Why me?"

He pulled her into his arms again, gathering her close against him. "My darling little Laura. How blind can you get? Do you know that I stay awake nights plotting excuses to see you? Have you any idea what an outrageous combination you are? Brains, beauty, ability plus, all wrapped up in a package that's so desirable it's all I can do to keep from whisking you off to some remote hideaway." He looked at her hungrily, searching her face for answers.

Danger! She recognized it in the intensity of his gaze, in his words, smooth and persuasive, in the hot feel of his cheek against hers and in the fragrance of his clean hair. Oh, yes. She knew where it could lead.

He was very practiced, this Geoffrey McDermott, the man of the gifted pen and the silver tongue. His words flowed easily and carried about as much substance as the air it took to speak them.

He lifted her hand, uncurled her fingers and kissed her palm. Slowly then, his lips brushed a feathery trail across her cheek to her mouth, ending in a firm determined kiss that took her breath away. The kiss claimed, demanded. Her limbs grew weak and she found herself grappling with an incredible yearning to return kiss for kiss, embrace for embrace, to revel in the sensations. But every nerve ending shrieked a warning. *Remember! Remember!* She struggled out of his embrace.

"The real Laura Adams doesn't care for this part of the game plan."

His expression was enigmatic. She could only guess at his reaction.

"I see," he said quietly. "So it's the employer who's the fly in the ointment. I'm sorry you got the wrong impression. Well, believe it or not, I have so many deadlines that I wouldn't have time to bother you. How does this strike you? During working hours you'll have the place entirely to yourself. I'll leave work assignments on your desk and come around only when it's absolutely necessary. As a matter of fact I'm taking off the first of the week to spend a few days in Tokyo. My housekeeper, Mrs. Fujii, comes twice a week but usually only afternoons, so you can settle into the job with complete freedom.''

"You're taking a leave from the language school?"

"I've been filling in as a favor to my old friend, Ken Sato, until the new man arrived.'' He observed her hesitancy. ''Okay, how about on a trial basis, say a month or so, or until you finish typing my novel? Then we can reevaluate the situation.''

A month, she thought. She knew she could complete the book by that date and in the meantime, she hoped, find another job. She needed money now. The work fitted in perfectly with her own schedule and the salary turned out to be much more than she'd expected. If only she could work for K.D. Kano and not have to deal with Geoffrey McDermott.

"A month, you say?"

"Any time limit you prefer, and I promise to keep everything very businesslike.'' His smile was sardonic. ''We can even resort to formal address if that would make you any happier,'' he added as if to offer one more inducement.

"All right, and I insist on the trial period. One month, or until I complete the manuscript. Either of us may terminate the position then.''

He smiled. ''I'll go for that.'' Obviously, he'd rather play by her rules than turn her off completely.

She picked up her reading glasses and put them in her handbag. "I'll report Monday morning at nine."

"Good," he said, taking a key from the desk drawer and handing it to her. "For the house." He smiled, turning on charm as vibrant as the noontime sun now streaming through the windows. "Would our business agreement during working hours preclude an after-business-hours invitation to lunch? I make a superb omelet."

"I'm surprised you'd even mention it." She started for the door.

He followed. "Or better yet, why not a short sightseeing jaunt? I'm an expert on Kyoto."

She knew what he was up to. "To the Moss Gardens, naturally. Thanks, but no thanks."

He sighed. "I see. Well, then, a very good good-afternoon to you, Miss Adams."

She was out on the porch before she remembered her manners, but he'd followed her. She turned with a slight nod of her head. "And a good-afternoon to you, too, Dr. McDermott."

On the way home Laura mulled over the past hour with Geoffrey. It had been a battle of wits and she wasn't at all certain she'd won.

She tried to think how she would feel about him as a man and as her employer had his name not been McDermott, but she found it impossible. All she knew for certain was that she responded to his every word, his every facial expression and even his touch far more than she had to any other man. Well, that was natural, wasn't it, if the man was who she suspected he was?

He handed out a lot of smooth talk, all right, but even though he was much older than she and obviously a man of considerable experience, she was on to him and she hoped that he was getting the picture.

She was glad that she had a date that afternoon to meet Sachiko for *osanji*. She wanted to take her mind off the entire experience.

She was always pleased at an opportunity to visit with her friend. Their schedules didn't mesh well, so they'd started the habit of snatching an hour together whenever possible. The Japanese, even Sachiko with her American exposure, preferred to meet in a coffeehouse or restaurant rather than entertain in their homes. Occasionally, Laura was able to coax Sachiko over to the apartment, but not often. Now Laura was anxious to hear how the arranged marriage was progressing.

Sachiko had already found a table. She looked as feminine in her navy suit as she had in her *yukata*, the lightweight kimono she'd worn on the night she'd been so upset about *omiai*. Her eyes were discreetly lowered as befitted a young Japanese woman alone in a restaurant. For all her vows of independence, Sachiko still found satisfaction in some traditional habits.

They ordered coffee, and after a few amenities Laura couldn't confine her curiosity any longer.

"So how did it go? Did you have a problem finding each other?" She caught herself immediately. "Forgive me. I know I shouldn't ask."

Sachiko's laugh was melodious as always. "That's what I like about you, Laura. Straight to the point. Another Japanese girl and I might sit here all afternoon dying to know answers and never once broach the subject.'' She wrinkled her tiny nose. ''Actually it's a very dull story. Just as the go-between said, Kenzo Okita is handsome, moneyed and has a brilliant future.''

Laura noticed the edge to her voice. ''Well, then?''

''And he's a robot!''

''So off with his head?''

''Precisely.''

''Maybe he's shy. That elegant cool of yours may intimidate him. Surely you can give him at least one plus.''

Sachiko gave an exaggerated frown as if to search every corner of her memory, then shrugged her shoulders daintily. ''I doubt it. At the rate he communicates it would take him ten years just to give me his vital statistics.'' She repeated some of the remembered conversation.

'' 'The nights are suddenly cold,' he said.

'' 'Yes, winter comes early,' I agreed.

'' 'Already chestnuts are roasted on street corners,' he continued.

'' 'Indeed. And the small leafed maples are turning scarlet.' ''

Laura laughed heartily. ''I love it. You're almost speaking haiku.''

Sachiko's frown deepened. ''It's far from amusing. That kind of talk predicts the future. I can hear it now.'' She lowered her voice and spoke sternly. '' 'Where is the paper? What time will dinner be ready?' Sum total of day's communication.''

"Are you telling me this is the end of the arrangements?"

"How I wish it were so! But I promised my parents I'd see him one more time. However, this can't go on long. One is expected to make a decision soon. Too many meetings cast bad vibrations. It is especially embarrassing for the parents. Perhaps the two of us can issue a joint refusal so no one will lose face."

"I don't understand how you can tell whether or not you want to marry him after so few dates."

"Because you must realize that in the arranged marriage, all the so-called basic requirements have been scrupulously checked: the ages and health of the couple, how many certificates the bride holds, the groom's ability to support a family, social status, ancestry. . . ." She pursed her lips. "Some men even specify whether they prefer round-faced or long-faced girls. Others won't accept a bride born in the Year of the Horse. Now do you understand?"

"I can see some advantages in that procedure, and I'll bet *you* have a few requirements to add to the list."

"Indeed I do, and I intend to air them."

"Aha, I think I hear a message from the S.D.O.I.," Laura said.

"S.D.O.I.?"

"Sachiko's Declaration of Independence!"

Sachiko looked thoughtful "Marriage is a big word. It should have at least twenty-five syllables. I want a man I can talk with, someone with whom I can share feelings and ideas, and I want him to share his with me. I want us to like and respect each other. I admit this man is attractive, but who knows what's going on in Tongue-tied-san's head? Believe me, if I can't find out the next time we meet, I'm calling the whole thing off!''

CHAPTER SEVEN

TWO WEEKS LATER as the mellow chimes of the wall clock struck 11:30, Laura typed the final page of the new K.D. Kano novel. She had pushed hard to finish it. She stretched her arms high, then rubbed the back of her neck to ease the stiffness.

Geoffrey had followed his promise to the letter, communicating mainly through memos left on her desk each morning. He nodded pleasantly in passing, addressing her always as Miss Adams. After a few days she caught herself regretting their agreement to keep their relationship strictly business. A little cordiality would have relieved her lonely work.

Nevertheless, she felt justifiably smug as she locked the completed work in the fireproof safe where Geoffrey kept work in progress. He had suggested it would take at least a month to do the job and later hinted about an extension if necessary. He'd gone to Tokyo again yesterday, saying he might not return until tomorrow. She would like to see his face when he found the finished manuscript waiting for him.

The book, like all of K.D. Kano's novels, had touched her deeply. It was the story of an interracial marriage destroyed by prejudice. The characters had come alive for Laura and she had wiped away tears when the relationship of the American soldier and the Japanese girl had ended in heartbreak.

Laura felt disenchanted by a sudden insight. No wonder he wrote with such conviction. If army records were accurate, he, too, had been married to a Japanese girl.

As she worked in the solitude of Geoffrey's spacious library, Laura came to think of K.D. Kano and Geoffrey McDermott as two separate individuals: Kano, compassionate and profound; McDermott, Machiavellian, the man who had ruined Lisa's life, someone whom Laura could not trust.

At times as her fingers sped over the keys, she almost believed her own fantasy. Indeed, she decided, a sensitive individual like Kano could have a passion for anonymity. Geoffrey could very well have offered to impersonate him even to the point of hiring a typist who had only read but never met K.D. Kano. Everything she knew about Geoffrey added up to prove him capable of such a conspiracy, but in the end she had to admit it was really fantasy, after all. As much as she wanted to believe it, she knew it couldn't be true.

She glanced around the room. It exuded tranquillity from the muted varicolored rows of books to the fluid lines of a jade vase and the framed floral print in shades of apricot, gold and turquoise. The place provided a frankly nourishing ambience. If she found another job, she knew she would miss working here. However, although she had tried, she had been unable to find work that fitted into her schedule.

Suppose Geoffrey continued his unblemished behavior. Would it be safe to stay? Well, she still had two more weeks to consider it.

She looked at her watch and debated whether to start something else. She hated to profane the mood of the novel. Fifteen minutes remained of her normal 9:00-to-12:00 work hours, not that she owed Geoffrey anything. She'd worked past noon every day this week in order to complete the manuscript. But 9:00 to 12:00 were the hours she'd promised, so she found a small batch of research notes and estimated she could finish them in the remaining time.

Today was *Jidai Matsuri*, the October Festival of Eras. Kelly had been invited by a school friend to see the parade and spend the night, and Laura planned to catch up on some long-neglected chores. When she first learned of the *matsuri*, she had hoped Scott might take her to see it, but he'd mentioned a house full of visiting relatives.

Well, she could use a free afternoon. A stack of ironing awaited her, and new material to sew into kitchen curtains had been lying in a drawer for several weeks now. Mainly, she needed to shop for groceries again. As Kelly had so publicly announced, they were virtually down to bare cupboards.

Geoffrey had thoughtfully given her a check before he left yesterday. After paying her bills, she had about 15,000 yen, or sixty dollars left. Although she was not a spendthrift, her modest bank account had melted away in two months instead of the six which she'd counted. Cost of living was much higher here than at home. But working part-time would solve her problems moneywise, she amended.

She typed the research notes with dispatch and had just settled the cover on her typewriter and put on her coat when she heard an insistent knock.

At the door stood a handsome bearded young man, attaché case in hand. Heavily built, he nevertheless moved with a kind of rhythm as if he were listening to music. His dark eyes surveyed her figure and left no doubt that she passed inspection. There seemed something vaguely familiar about him, but then men in dark suits carrying attaché cases were legion in Kyoto.

"Hello, there, I see something new has been added," he said with excessive inflection.

"Dr. McDermott isn't in," Laura said, somehow unable to take offense at his uninhibited scrutiny.

"I'm Neil Anderson. Just passing through. I usually stop by to see old Geoff whenever I'm in Kyoto. He's at the parade, I suppose?"

"No, he's in Tokyo and won't be home until tomorrow."

Disappointment briefly clouded his expression. "What a shame. I have a magnificent old wood carving I know he'd want to see. I deal in antiques, by the way."

"Perhaps you can see him tomorrow, then. I'm Laura Adams, his secretary."

He raised an eyebrow. "Secretary, eh? Marvelous taste in secretaries."

She smiled in spite of herself. The man was a bit brash, but there was something about his easy attitude that was kind of contagious, and he was definitely attractive. One could almost say he was dipped in pizzazz. She started down the steps and he followed.

"Hold on. Are you off to the festival?"

"Not this time. I have some chores that won't wait."

"You're skipping *Jidai Matsuri*! Have you ever seen it?"

"No, but—"

"Well, I can't allow you to do that. It just happens to be one of Kyoto's top attractions. Let me take you. I know a perfect viewing spot."

"Thanks, no. I really have my afternoon scheduled." She looked at his eager face and almost wished she hadn't refused.

He shook a finger playfully. "Schedules ought to be ignored occasionally, else they tend to manipulate you. I'm a seer in my spare time, you know. Old Geoff will be very upset with me if I don't take you. He's a nut on Japanese culture." He gave her a provocative wink. "Has he invited you upstairs yet to view his collection?"

What collection? "No, and thank you for the invitation but—"

"Ah," he interrupted. "You're worried about my credentials. I assure you I'm perfectly reliable." He handed her a card printed in both English and *kanji*. N.J. Anderson, Fine Oriental Antiques, it said, and gave a Kobe address.

"Have you lived in Japan a long time?" she asked.

"Ever since I got out of the army."

"You and Dr. McDermott were army buddies, then?"

"Old buddies, okay, but not in the army, I'm afraid. Old Geoff was a major and I was a private. So what do you say? Shall we go? Run away from chores and see a *matsuri*? You can trust me. My rules for clean living are absolutely infallible," he said pontifically.

She laughed and reconsidered the invitation. Technically, Geoffrey's friend might not be classed as a complete stranger, she rationalized. Perhaps the occasion was even made to order. An old friend might enlighten her on Geoffrey's background. A discreet question thrown in the conversation now and then could clear up volumes. So she agreed. Neil was so clearly delighted and flattered by her acceptance she felt reassured.

They climbed into his sporty little Nissan and in minutes reached his special viewing site, a friend's second-story fabric-store window.

Apparently the parade had gone on for some time. A cacophony of flutes and drums filled the air. The sight was breathtaking: highborn ladies, faces whitened; armor-clad samurai; geishas and their apprentices, the lovely young *maikos*; sandaled farmers wearing awkward straw garments and mushroomlike hats—all passed in extravagant procession. The variety seemed endless, a panorama of history dating back to the eighth century. Laura had never seen anything like it.

The minute the last contingent passed in review, Neil hustled her back to the car. "Come on, let's hurry so we can beat the crowds up to the fire festival. It always follows *Jidai Matsuri*. The drive's less than forty minutes to a mountain village. It's the kind of bash that's right up my alley. Lusty! Noisy! God, you have to see it.'' Neil was almost shouting in his enthusiasm, and Laura got caught up in the spirit.

''What's keeping us?'' she said.

He flashed a wide grin as he helped her back into the Nissan. He chatted in continuous monologue about Kyoto's charms and weaknesses and primarily about his antique business. ''It's a compulsion. Some men hunt animals. I search for beauty. I have an eye for it, you know.'' His glance assured her that his pursuit was not confined to antediluvian objects. ''How long have you known old Geoff?''

''I met him at the language school when I arrived late last August, but I've worked for him only a couple of weeks. And you keep saying 'old Geoff.' You two must surely be around the same age.''

He grinned amiably. ''Geoffrey was born old, my dear. A smart guy, though.'' Did his voice hold a grudging edge?

''Yes, a real talent,'' Laura said.

''But reserved as hell.''

''Even with you?''

Neil's mouth twisted as if at some unpleasant recollection. ''I'll wager not many people get close to him.''

''Probably not. He's a very private person,'' Laura said, and thoughtfully phrased her next question. ''You imply that he's lonely. Has he ever been married?''

Neil glanced at her sharply. "Hasn't he ever told you?"

"No. Why should he? Just wondered," she said.

Neil lit a cigarette and inhaled. "He was married during his years in the service, and you can take it from me that marriage almost destroyed him."

"Destroyed him?"

"The girl left him soon after his discharge."

"She left him?" Laura repeated numbly. Had his wife discovered Geoffrey's affair with Lisa? "A girl he met over here?"

"Yes. I only saw her once, but let me tell you she was one classy lady and from an affluent family, too. No wonder he virtually became a recluse."

"So he has changed?"

Neil hesitated for a moment. "You could say so. Anyway, that's when he started to write. Spilled all his feelings on paper, I guess. I didn't see him for several years."

"What about you? Do you have a family?"

He smiled at her with tolerance. "No, my dear, I'm not married. Haven't found the right girl yet, or maybe I just don't like to be fenced in."

There was more she wanted to ask, a lot more, but Neil had already noted her inquisitiveness. They had climbed the mountain road for several minutes now, and he suddenly pulled over to park the car. "Nice, huh?" he said, pointing to the blue-tiled roofs of Kyoto. They seemed to spill from a fold in the mountain to cover the entire city, the color muted in the late-afternoon haze. A flock of birds, all tinted the same hue, whirled and headed south. Patchwork fields fanned out from the city's edge, cultivated in a way that indicated strip-cropping. Not an inch of ground remained untended. The intensely nurtured Japanese countryside made a distinct contrast to America's vacant lots and vast unpeopled lands.

Neil drove back onto the road and twenty minutes later nosed his Nissan into an impossible parking space in a cul-de-sac just off the main street at the far end of the little village.

Laura pointed to a sign that seemed to indicate no parking, but Neil dismissed her concern, saying that during festivals one could ignore the sign.

They strolled down the main street. It was almost dark now. A full pumpkin moon hung above and a bonfire somewhere ahead crackled and lit up the sky. She inhaled the fragrance of green tea and burning wood and of sweet potatoes roasting on vendors' carts.

"Yaki imo, yaki imo," one vendor cried in a deep, drawn-out, melancholy voice. A noodle seller played a thousand-year-old tune on his toy tin trumpet. Wind chimes and the rustle of paper streamers decorating shops and houses provided a continuous chorus.

"No wonder the Japanese love festivals," Laura cried. "But what has fire to do with this one?"

"Who knows?" Neil said. "And what's more, who cares—except maybe old Geoff. There's at least one *matsuri* a month just around Kyoto. And why not? The Japanese are a nation of workaholics. They deserve any excuse they can find for a celebration."

They stopped to watch two men slapping cooked rice on a wooden mortar with heavy mallets. "*Mochi* pounders," Neil explained. "The paste is made into a kind of biscuit. It's no French pastry, hard as nails, but one can acquire a taste for it."

He bought a few and they munched them as they watched the men swing their mallets with fiendish disregard for each other's safety, barely missing heads, bodies and fingers. The crowd that gathered raucously cheered the pounders on to greater daring, and Laura felt certain they might kill each other any minute.

"All part of the fun. Don't worry, they know what they're doing," Neil said, dismissing her concern.

They walked from house to house admiring the objects the villagers displayed in front of their houses on this occasion: handmade dolls, an eight-fold screen, a handsome cloisonné vase, an inlaid koto, watercolors on silk, a wealth of heirlooms. Neil kept up a running commentary on the treasures as easily as if he were a scanner on a computer.

"You're unbelievable," Laura said.

He squeezed her hand. "And so are you. Remember me? I'm an expert on quality."

She laughed. It was easy to laugh with Neil. He seemed upbeat and uncomplicated. Obviously no hang-ups clouded his outlook. He tucked her arm through his and kept her close to his side as crowds rapidly thickened. Fireworks went off with earsplitting noise. All around them bonfires roared fiercely, the glow turning people, trees and shrubs into black silhouettes against the soaring flames.

Excitement permeated the crowd and shouts of approval reached a frenzied pitch as rockets blasted the sky. Torches were lit along the parade route and the procession began at last: banners, floats, masked dancers and palanquin after palanquin. Strong-armed youths in head kerchiefs and brief corded skirts carried the gilded litters that bore images of Shinto gods.

"Wasshoi, wasshoi," the young men chanted continually.

As the final palanquin lumbered in front of them, it suddenly lurched and pitched sideways and for a moment the carriers almost lost control, swerving with the heavy litter into the crowd. People screamed in panic. Shoving and pushing, they surged en masse back and forth across the street in a human riptide. Laura found herself boosted upward, then toppled to the ground amid a swarm of flailing arms and legs. *My God!* She was going to be trampled! She clawed at someone's coat and struggled for a foothold, feeling her own sleeve tear from the shoulder. Terrified voices ricocheted around her and she knew the crush of bodies would suffocate her. An awful roaring sounded inside her head. Then her mind whirled sickeningly and settled into darkness.

WHEN LAURA REGAINED CONSCIOUSNESS, she found that she was stretched out in the doorway of a little shop. A small circle of silent people stood around her, their faces frozen into masks, barely visible in the dimness. Where was Neil? Someone helped her to her feet. She took a few steps and the group dispersed, apparently satisfied she had recovered.

She examined her torn stockings and rubbed an aching arm. Had Neil also been hurt in the mishap? Where could he be? She looked around. Everything seemed different. The former crowds had thinned to stragglers and the only light came from dying embers of the bonfires. How long had she lain in the doorway? It was getting dark and cold. The moon, now remote and unfriendly, was seeking refuge behind a cloud.

She tried to arrange the torn sleeve of her coat but it still gaped, hanging by a few threads at the seam. Suddenly she felt for the shoulder strap of her purse. It was gone. Every cent she had to her name and all her identification. What would she do if she couldn't find Neil? Surely he must be looking for her, too. Or was he lying injured in some hospital?

There was always the train back to Kyoto. But she had no money! Her hands grew clammy in spite of the chill, and her mouth felt so dry she wondered if she could speak. What did it matter? With her poor Japanese, she wouldn't be able to articulate her predicament with any clarity.

Neil must be waiting for her at the car, the logical place, of course. Why hadn't she thought of that immediately? She walked up the block, but nothing looked familiar on the dark deserted street except now and then a wilted banner or a few tattered streamers, flotsam from the procession. In alarm she ran several hundred yards farther, then crossed and hurried back on the other side. Cars passed now and then while she fearfully hugged the shadows.

Streaks of light and piercing sounds like gunshots brought her to a sudden halt. Her heart pounded frantically until she identified the source as the final gasps from a dying bonfire. But in the flash of light she'd recognized the mortar where she and Neil had watched the *mochi* pounders. Thank God. At last. Relieved, her adrenaline pumping, she hurried around the corner into the cul-de-sac. But the place was empty. The car was gone.

CHAPTER EIGHT

TERROR SEIZED HER NOW. Why would Neil leave without her? It seemed the final devastation. Her knees felt weak. She leaned against a tree. A cricket gave a melancholy chirp and the breeze rustled the leaves in a dry whisper. Never had she felt so helpless.

Suddenly, brakes screeched and a car swung around the corner, blinding her with its headlights. She ducked her head and flattened herself against the tree. Someone jumped out of the car and ran toward her. Neil! He grabbed her shoulders.

"Laura! Are you all right? My God, I've been out of my mind trying to find you!"

She clung to him as an avalanche of relief washed over her. He walked her to the car and helped her into it, where she sat with her head in her hands. "I thought you went off and left me."

"Left you! I've searched every nook and cranny in this entire village. What happened?" He started the car, picking up speed as he left the village, driving the mountain road with skill and assurance. From time to time he cast a worried glance at her. He seemed considerably subdued, his earlier mood routed by the unexpected turn of events.

"I waited in the cul-de-sac as long as I could, but the damn police gave me a bad time for parking there," he said with a trace of irritation.

"Rotten luck all around. I lost my purse."

He turned to her with concern. "No! Anything of value?"

"All the money I have left in the world to last until my next paycheck," she said bleakly.

He reached over and patted her hand. "A damn shame. How much?"

"In yen I guess it amounted to about sixty dollars."

"Well, don't worry, I'll take care of that. Anything else of value?"

"Some identification, that sort of thing," There were also a couple of family snapshots in her wallet. One was the only picture she had of Lisa and the man she had married. His features were shadowed and indistinguishable under his officer's hat, but the elation on Lisa's face was unmistakable.

She directed Neil to her apartment and they arrived a short while later. He walked her up the two flights and they paused on the landing while she found her key. Meanwhile he took out his wallet and counted out the amount of yen she'd lost.

"You're a dear, Neil, and I'll pay you back as soon as I get my check."

He dismissed her offer with a wave of his hand. "Oh, no, you won't. It's my fault for not taking better care of you."

She felt relieved. For a little while she'd had the vague feeling that he might have been annoyed with her. "Blame the fiasco on me," she said. "I should have warned you. I tend to provoke disasters, but both the *matsuris* were marvelous."

"And so are you." His eyes sparkled merrily in the porch light, and his carefree manner seemed completely restored. "Next time I'll handcuff you to me. That ought to invite some interesting possibilities. You're a sweetheart. I leave early tomorrow for Sendai, so I won't see you again until I come to Kyoto." He gave her a quick hug and kiss. The kiss was light, impersonal, more like a pat on the head, not at all like Geoffrey's, which demolished her poise and filled her with obscure alarms.

Except for the frightening aspects of the evening, Laura had enjoyed her time with Neil. The excitement of the *matsuris* had added dimension and color to her routine existence. She looked forward to tasting more of this exciting city.

She could imagine the well-chosen words Geoffrey would deliver her for taking off with a perfect stranger, not that she cared nor that he even need know. It was none of his business.

Neil seemed fun and upbeat and she'd enjoy having him for a friend. Moreover, she was anxious to get well enough acquainted so she could frankly pry deeper into Geoffrey's background. She'd have to be subtle about it; she didn't want Neil mentioning her inquiries to Geoffrey.

If she really wanted to face up to her dilemma and put an end to her worries about losing Kelly, all she needed to do was to leave Kyoto and go back to Oregon. If Geoffrey was really Kelly's father, the more contact she had with him, the more danger she courted. It would take only a chance remark or some vague memory to alert him to the relationship. If Geoffrey learned Kelly was his son, there was not a doubt in the world that he'd initiate legal proceedings to claim him. No court would deny a prominent man like Geoffrey McDermott the right to his child. The thought devastated her. Lose Kelly? She couldn't bear even to think about it.

But she was trapped, at least for the present. She had a contract to honor at Burton-Kubo's and she couldn't contemplate moving anywhere until she'd saved some money.

Reviewing her efforts to find another job, she admitted she hadn't really tried very hard. She had answered a number of ads, but not one of the positions had fitted into her schedule. To be truthful, she knew that she didn't want another job. She loved working for K.D. Kano.

MONDAY MORNING SHE RAN up the steps of Geoffrey's condominium. Midway into the library she halted when she saw him looking through a desk drawer. "Good morning," she said.

"Ah, Miss Adams, Right on time as usual. I'll be out of your way in a minute." His tone was brusque. As he sorted through some papers she couldn't help but notice that he moved with the well-knit precision that spoke not only of a man in excellent physical shape but of someone eminently in charge of himself. His irregular masculine features appealed to her far more than Neil's markedly handsome ones. Laura suddenly realized as she watched him that every nerve in her body had come alive. He looked up at her.

Their eyes met, and she could see the reflection of her own in his. Was this symbolic? Some magnetic force seemed to draw her close, leaving her with neither the will nor the desire to remain indifferent. No wonder Lisa had been overwhelmed. Geoffrey had the power to intensify a woman's emotions, to make her think loving thoughts one moment and hateful ones the next.

"Something wrong?" Though his lips wore no smile, she noticed the tiny creases near his eyes that were the beginning of laugh lines.

So he'd caught her watching him. "I don't know what you mean," she said stiffly, and looked at her watch.

"Okay, I'm leaving. Just let me get my things together."

"Any priorities concerning my work this morning?"

"One only. Finish typing my manuscript."

She made her tone elaborately casual. "Oh, I finished it last Friday."

He looked startled. "Finished! Surely you're not serious?"

She pointed to the adjacent room where he kept his files. "Look for yourself."

"My editor will be positively delirious!" He strode to the small room and returned with the manuscript. Still showing disbelief, he thumbed through it. "Beautiful work, Miss Adams, and I've never known anyone so speedy. You're a treasure!"

"Thank you," she said, and suddenly wondered about the agreement concerning the length of her employment. Now was the time to quit, wasn't it? Actually, she had two more weeks to locate another job before she gave notice. The thought of leaving upset her, left her feeling oddly bereft. "Do you have something else for me to do this morning?"

"Take the day off. You deserve it. And, Miss Adams?"

His voice had a resonant baritone quality. Did he sing? She must ask him sometime. "Yes?" she said belatedly.

His face broke into a smile that suggested they shared the most cordial of relationships. It wasn't his even white teeth that caught her attention, but something that glinted in his clear direct eyes. Amusement? Eagerness? She couldn't tell.

"Chizu's birthday came earlier this week," he said. "I promised her a treat on Saturday. I'm taking her and a guest of her choice to lunch. Not surprisingly she wants Kelly. I hope you'll give your approval."

Laura frowned. She didn't like this at all. Any togetherness between Kelly and Geoffrey was precisely what she had hoped to avoid. Of course, as far as Kelly knew, his name was Canfield. The family had never mentioned the name McDermott even once in his presence. But there was always a chance that Kelly might discuss his background, bring up his mother's name or relate some incident that would trigger a connection for this intuitive man.

"I'm afraid Kelly has a scout meeting," she hedged, hoping the excuse would end the discussion.

"What time is it over?"

She hesitated. "One o'clock. But they often play baseball afterward."

"Well, if they don't and he wants to join us, tell him I'll pick him up as soon as he gets home."

What could she say? "Well, all right." She didn't even try to hide her reluctance.

"Don't worry. I'll have him home by five. Chizu will be delighted. And thank you, Miss Adams," he said, and left somewhat more abruptly than good manners would dictate. Did he think she would change her mind?

The continued use of the formal address, which Geoffrey made a point to exaggerate, had become a bit silly, she decided, although she'd agreed to it at the time. Still, any device that would keep Geoffrey at a distance could be considered an asset as well as a necessity.

GEOFFREY AND CHIZU appeared promptly at her apartment the next day. Contrary to Laura's hopes, Kelly had been eager to accept the invitation. Hands and face scrubbed and still wearing his scout uniform, his scarf tied in a lopsided knot, he carried a beribboned package and looked like the perfect model for a Norman Rockwell painting. *How dear he is,* Laura thought fondly, and at the same time told herself to stop worrying about a harmless little birthday celebration.

Rationalize. That's all she ever did anymore. Nevertheless, the fear that Geoffrey might discover Kelly was his natural son always clouded her life. She didn't have positive proof, of course, but everything she'd learned thus far underscored the possibility. If only there were someone she could ask without having to divulge Kelly's true identity. Well, she would bide her time. When she saw Neil again she'd question him for the answers she wanted no matter what he thought of her nosiness.

As the three rose to leave, Chizu walked over to Laura.

"Please come to my party, too. I've already asked permission." She glanced at Geoffrey for confirmation.

"She has indeed. It was entirely her idea and I heartily concur."

Laura hesitated. "Thank you, but I believe this is a special treat for just you and Kelly."

Chizu eyed her solemnly. "I think I know why you don't want to come, but you needn't worry. Uncle Geoffrey and I aren't superstitious."

"Oh?" What did superstition have to do with it, Laura wondered apprehensively.

Chizu held up four fingers. "It's because there are four of us, isn't it?"

"Four?" Laura asked, even more puzzled.

"Four is an unlucky number in Japan, the way thirteen is in America," the child said. "But we don't believe that, do we?"

"We certainly do not," Geoffrey promptly

agreed. "So put on your hat and coat and don't keep us waiting."

It seemed that *shi*, the word for "four," was also the word for "death." Many hospitals, hotels, airplanes and even schools shunned four as a room or seat number, Geoffrey explained.

Laura eyed the three expectant faces. She was no match for their hopeful expressions. At least she would be present to divert the conversation in the event that any dangerous topics surfaced. Yet, as Geoffrey helped her into her coat, she couldn't help thinking how could she go on like this, always worrying, always afraid.

For the luncheon Chizu had chosen one of the popular *shokudos*, the eating emporiums in department stores, for two reasons, she informed Laura in her precise English.

"Number one, there is a fun amusement park on the roof garden. Number two, Kelly and I can choose what we want to eat from the samples in the window."

Geoffrey rolled his eyes. "Organized and knows her own mind, this kid," he said in an aside to Laura. But when they arrived, Laura understood. The windows displayed astonishingly accurate plastic replicas of each dish on the menu. The children chose without indecision while Geoffrey muttered something to Laura about not expecting *shokudos* to cater to gourmets. But the food was attractive and tasty, although the place was so noisy that conversation proved almost impossible. The noise didn't faze the children, and Laura found she welcomed the distraction.

Lunch ended with ice cream. Chizu opened her presents, then they took the elevator to the roof garden, which featured a small zoo, several rides and strolling entertainers. The day was cool but sunny, and Laura watched the children with pleasure as they scrambled over a dragonlike jungle gym, which they soon abandoned to give a mime artist their undivided attention.

So far Geoffrey had said little except now and then to respond to the children's excited chatter when they ran over to join them from time to time. With Laura he remained studiously courteous. They might have been two people who had met casually once before. He stood beside her now.

"You look unusually attractive today, Miss Adams. I hope that your heart is filled with cherry blossoms?"

"You're being obscure again."

"I thought just the opposite."

"Cherry blossoms?"

"Yes, a symbol for restoring good fellowship, Miss Adams."

"Miss Adams, Miss Adams," she repeated with exasperation. "You're doing that on purpose, aren't you?"

"I expect I am, now that you mention it. I'm glad that you find it as ridiculous as I do."

"I didn't say that."

"But you implied it."

"I can't believe the way you manipulate people. I bet you're a demon at fencing or chess."

"Oh, I am."

"And that ability of yours to turn people into putty."

"Oh, come now. Can't we just have a nice friendly conversation?"

"As long as you don't get personal. Weather, current events, inflation, K.D. Kano's new novel, whatever you like, but leave me out."

His amused expression disappeared. "That's something I can't do, my dear, leave you out."

A chill went through her. She'd typed the same sentence from his manuscript quite recently. "Sounds familiar. In fact, it's downright plagiarism, excerpting that line right out of your novel."

He looked genuinely taken aback. "Did I? Well, I meant it sincerely, whatever the source." Something in his eyes reached out and touched her, but she turned away, pretending interest in the gold and bronze chrysanthemums spilling from a row of wooden planters. Now the children headed toward a merry-go-round. She strolled over to watch them and found a stone bench shaded by a tubbed maple tree, its brilliant leaves brocading the autumn sky.

Geoffrey followed and sat down beside her. They watched Kelly and Chizu each choose a mount, and as the carousel wheezed into action they could hear Kelly's shout.

"Hi ho, Silver," he cried, slapping his horse's flank. But Chizu, chin up and reins gracefully held, was a grand lady on a white charger. Laura smiled despite her mood.

"Chizu is a charming child, so different than I imagined."

"And how was that?" he asked.

"From Kelly's descriptions, I imagined a combination rip-roaring whiz kid and Betty Friedan."

"Chizu could have invented feminine mystique. Did you notice how she wraps Kelly and me around that little finger of hers? I'm fortunate that my friends the Thompsons share her with me, and now that I have your Kelly occasionally, my frustrated fatherly instincts are satisfied now and then."

Laura studied his face as he watched the children and was surprised to observe what appeared to be an expression of genuine longing.

Up until now, she'd thought the only place this seemingly invulnerable man would exhibit his emotions was in his novels, where he could control them.

He lifted a hand to salute the riders, and the joyous, unaffected communication between the man and two children fused with the background of sky, sunlight, dappled shade and maple leaves into a moment of intolerable perfection.

Later Geoffrey drove them home, the children happy and tired and she and Geoffrey not talking at all. Laura felt shaken by the day's events and tried to find an explanation for her distress. Was it that she couldn't escape the shadow of the past? That she no longer seemed to have the freedom to act independently or to love when she chose? And that she resented the restriction? She needed to think more clearly.

Nevertheless, she admitted to an ache in her heart, poignant and consuming, wishing that things could be different, that Geoffrey had never met a girl called Lisa and that his name were Smith or Jones or anything except McDermott.

CHAPTER NINE

LAURA WORKED HARD NOW preparing her students for mid-term examinations, volunteering extra hours for those who needed help. Some of the young businessmen seemed under special pressure. Apparently they needed a passing grade in order to win a promotion in their company.

For others, a chance to be sent abroad depended on their success. The students who held jobs dealing with the public were also diligent workers, but a few in the class were indifferent to their progress. Laura wondered if they attended primarily for the school's monthly social functions such as dances, picnics and excursions.

There were also girls whose prime motivation appeared to be to collect one more certificate. Sachiko had mentioned that all young women collected certificates in such skills as flower arranging, the tea ceremony, sewing, cooking and piano to make them more attractive on the marriage market.

During Laura's morning job, Geoffrey had turned more and more of his research over to her, saying that she had a knack for zeroing in on essentials. She loved this part of her work for him and was glad for the variety and challenge it offered. Somewhere in the back of her mind she wondered if she was also glad that adding this dimension meant that she now saw Geoffrey on a daily basis.

Nothing more had been said about terminating her position when the month was over. Geoffrey seemed pleased with her work, if his continual compliments meant anything. It was up to her, wasn't it, and she knew quite well she had no intention of leaving. She loved her job. It brought not only satisfaction but a meaning to her life that no other kind of employment ever had.

She began to worry less when Geoffrey showed no interest in her background other than what she'd told him, and not a thing suggested he thought either she or Kelly could have held a part in his past. *His past.* She wished she could lock it out of her mind.

Since the day when he promised to keep their relationship totally businesslike, he'd conducted himself accordingly. It seemed no effort for him to slip back into the role of impersonal employer and casual friend, detached, courteous and at times full of fun. She envied him the ability and at the same time resented it, wishing she could blow from hot to cold with as much ease. But then, a man with his past would have no problem, would he?

Today she found herself listening, hoping for his footstep in the hallway. Mrs. Fujii, Geoffrey's housekeeper arrived, poked her head into the library, smiled and nodded and left to work upstairs. Laura wondered about the room somewhere up there. Did he really have a private art collection or had Neil been kidding? He did, she decided. She sensed that

Geoffrey was a man who liked to possess, to be in charge, but in spite of his self-assurance, indeed perhaps because of it, he was reluctant to share his private self. They were two of a kind as far as that was concerned.

It was Thursday, and she'd worked again without seeing him. For some reason he seemed present anyway. She kept remembering how he looked at her from those steady brown eyes in a way that seemed to take her in and keep her out at the same time. In spite of all her arguments to the contrary, it was beginning to appear that passing superficial judgments on this man was not enough.

At noon she covered her typewriter and slipped out of the house, wishing the knot in her chest would disappear. Music could heal, her dear friend Sachiko had maintained. Well, today she'd see if it could bring serenity. Sachiko had invited her to a student recital that afternoon to be held at the conservatory where she taught.

The young woman showed extraordinary skill with young children, and Laura listened with pleasure, impressed with the musicianship of the students. Today, considering the lengthy and enthusiastic applause and frequent camera flashes, the audience must have held a generous proportion of approving relatives.

"What a fine teacher you are," Laura said afterward, as the two had a cup of tea together at a nearby *kissaten*.

"Oh, they could have performed much better, but I'm glad you liked my poor efforts."

"Poor efforts! I'll bet you worked like a fiend to prepare your students for today's concert!"

Sachiko smiled. "Yes, I worked hard, but only to you may I admit it. My heritage clings with a heavy hand."

"Then perhaps you should be more understanding of your parents and the young man who wishes to marry you."

"Perhaps so, but this is the twentieth century. His parents wanted to know how many certificates I possessed. Certificates do not guarantee a good wife. I do not wish to produce them."

"Is Kenzo interested in certificates?"

"He says not, but who knows? He says very little, that one. But last week he sent me an Isaac Stern record, my favorite artist. How did he know?"

"You probably dropped a remark some time. He may not talk much, but he's obviously a good listener."

"He no doubt wanted to make, as you say, a few cub-scout marks."

"Brownie points, Sachiko."

"But I am not fooled."

"Poor Kenzo."

"Not poor. He is number-one son in family. Do you know what that means? He is spoiled beyond belief."

"Can you blame him then if he wants to be number one in your life?"

"If a man is number one in my life, then I must be number one in his."

"Good luck. Have you thought of a grand challenge yet?"

Sachiko's eyes crinkled mischievously. "Oh, yes. I have a splendid idea."

"Go on. The suspense is killing me."

"I have always heard that men let down their reserve with geishas."

Laura rolled her eyes. "Don't tell me you would encourage your young man to visit a geisha? Anyway, how would you know whether he talked to her or not?"

"Oh, I would know," Sachiko said with a provocative little smile. "I shall be the geisha!"

"You!" Laura cried.

"Why not? With the white coating on my face and dressed in authentic costume, I don't believe there's a chance he would recognize me." She tilted her head at a coquettish angle, pitched her voice high, made it breathy and rattled off something in Japanese sounding completely unlike herself.

Laura looked at her in amazement. "What an actress you are! But, Sachiko, this kind of caper only works in the movies. I wonder if you can get away with it?"

"I'm convinced I can," she said with assurance. "And if not, what does it matter? How he reacts or *if* he reacts will give me the answer."

They turned into Laura's street and Sachiko parked in front of the apartment. "Don't count on instant action," she said. "I haven't even figured out how Miss Clever Lotus Blossom is going to arrange meeting with Tongue-tied One."

Was the plan only a passing whimsy or would Sachiko go through with the scheme, Laura won-

dered. She was surprised to feel her sympathy go out
to the unsuspecting young man.

THE LAST WEDNESDAY in October was Laura's birthday, and she'd almost forgotten it until she spotted
the package of cake mix Kelly had hidden in his
futon. He probably planned to bake it that evening
while she was at school. Darling boy! How many
nine-year-olds would be so thoughtful?

On her way to work she recalled last year's celebration, her twenty-first birthday. Bill had given her a
ring, and her grandmother had hosted a small
birthday-engagement party. How her life had changed
since then! Dear Grandmother Canfield was gone,
and Bill had suddenly opted against the conventions
of marriage. Now he was living with another girl. The
Adams sisters had not been lucky in the men they had
loved.

As she entered Geoffrey's library, her eye caught
the bonsai maple that stood on her desk. A card with
her name was propped against it.

"Lovely, lovely!" she cried aloud, and bent to examine the tiny tree, painstakingly cultivated to retain
its perfection in miniature.

She opened the card. There was a poem written in
kanji. The translation followed:

> How my spirit lifts
> To recall that moment
> Under the flaming maple,
> Because its shade
> Fell upon the two of us.

Beneath, Geoffrey had written, "All my good wishes for a happy birthday," followed by his signature.

The moment on the roof garden when they'd sat under the maple tree and watched the children on the carousel would stay with her forever. So he had felt it, too. The poem was distinctly K.D. Kano, she thought, and felt curiously light-headed.

She reached out to touch the bonsai's tiny leaves as if to make certain they were real.

"Good morning," Geoffrey said from the doorway. She whirled around, unaware that he had been standing there.

"It's beautiful! I've never owned such a treasure," she said, feeling unexpectedly shy. He walked over to join her.

"I'm glad you like it. Our time together with the children last week was very special to me."

"To me, too, and what a lovely reminder. I hardly know what to say!" She felt breathless with pleasure at the significance of the little maple, almost overwhelmed. Impulsively she threw her arms around Geoffrey's neck and kissed him. "Thank you, Geoffrey. I love it!"

He caught her to him, nuzzled her hair, then returned her kiss with much more passion than her own had deserved. For a moment she found herself responding, then pulled away gasping.

"Oh, Geoffrey, I'm sorry, I didn't mean...." After all, she'd been the one to insist on the "businesslike" arrangement.

His eyes twinkled. "Didn't mean what?"

"Well, you know, I was thrilled with your gift, it was so thoughtful."

"Perfectly natural, my dear girl, and I appreciate no end *your* appreciation."

She wished she didn't feel such a fool. "I just don't want you to misunderstand anything."

He couldn't have looked more serious. "Oh, I wouldn't do that for the world."

"Really, I mean it. I guess I'm overly sentimental."

"Good. I'm beginning to realize how much I've missed out on sentiment. You've made my day." He smiled as if totaling his private satisfaction.

Realizing her cheeks were burning, she again gave her wholehearted attention to the bonsai, taking in its beauty, its leaves a shower of crimson and gold. Tucked among the branches she saw a small pamphlet with a set of directions regarding its care. Plucking it out, she studied it with diligence as if not to miss a single word.

A moment later she glanced up and caught Geoffrey's amused expression, then suddenly realized the directions were written in *kanji*. Oh, Lord, she hadn't even noticed until now.

"Don't worry, I'll translate it for you," he said with a chuckle.

She held up the birthday card. "How did you know?"

"I keep a stable of spies. School files aren't too shabby, either."

Of course. One's birthdate usually appeared on a job application. She moved the little tree to an adjacent table. "Thank you again, Geoffrey. I'll treasure your present, but don't you think it's time I got to work?"

He pulled a long face. "Is that a hint?"

"It's your time I'm wasting."

"So waste a little more."

She couldn't help feeling distressed and no doubt she showed her discomfort. It would have been easier if he'd acted a little more like the Geoffrey she was used to. All this sweetness and light proved disconcerting.

"Okay," he said with an exaggerated sigh. "You don't have to hit me over the head." He ambled toward the door, then turned. "And, oh, yes, Laura, there's not a damn thing wrong with enjoying a kiss, and although I wholeheartedly wish it, you needn't consider it a commitment."

CHAPTER TEN

AT WORK THE NEXT DAY Geoffrey asked her to condense the pertinent facts from a lengthy article. It had to do with the activities of a group of unscrupulous artists in Thailand who had perfected a technique that enabled them to create, in a few days, works that resembled antique originals so closely that even experts could be fooled. The aging process involved soaking the pieces in seawater and burying them in earth for a relatively short time. Each one cost around five dollars to make and was sold for thousands by corrupt dealers.

As she finished, Geoffrey came in and sat next to her reading her copy. His shoulder brushed hers, and she caught the fresh scent of his immaculate white shirt. How on earth could she concentrate when he was so near, his cheek only inches from hers? If only there were some way to hide her sudden breathlessness.

"Have you run into any such fakes?" she asked, hoping the subject would allow her time to recover her composure.

"Yes. Unfortunately a friend of mine got taken. His Ming vase turned out to be one of those Thailand replicas. I want to pass on these notes to him so that ne can be more cautious in the future. Incidentally, have I told you how gorgeous you look today? Also lovely, charming and appealing, a breath of spring in autumn." He scanned her reddening cheeks with a gleam in his eye, and she could almost feel the strength in his hands even though he made no move to touch her.

She tried to discourage him so she could continue with her work. "I never trust more than one adjective at a time."

He chuckled. "Don't tell me my sunny secretary is turning cynical?"

"You're impossible. I can't earn my salary when you hover over me like this."

"Take five. You've earned it. Anyway, I don't like to be rushed when I'm in the presence of real beauty. Allow me to stay a little longer and feel thankful."

"You're embarrassing me."

"I'm admiring you. Every day I look at the woman sitting at this desk and think I can't be luckier by a single iota. Comes another day and another iota. What do you propose I do about it?"

"Lock yourself in your office and hang up a sign: No Admittance. Man Inside Bursting With Iotas."

"You're heartless."

"Only between nine and twelve."

He gave an exaggerated sigh. "Okay. I'll get out of your way, but only until twelve. After that I make no promises, and you could at least spare me a kind look. I need something to sustain me."

She took in his woeful expression and laughed in spite of herself. She didn't mind this kind of sparring, and Geoffrey's gentle teasing even amused her. But she hated scenes. Anger demolished her. She could never seem to hold her own in an argument. If only she could maintain this easy rapport between them, keep things frothy and light, perhaps she could keep her head together, after all.

As it turned out, she didn't have to worry about either the repartee or Geoffrey's presence for at least a week or two. He announced the next day that he was leaving on a tour of speaking engagements, radio and TV appearances sponsored by his publisher.

"I despise this sort of thing. I'd much rather stay home and write," he said. "You wouldn't care to come with me?"

"Don't tell me that even K.D. Kano doesn't adore all those fawning females turning him into an intellectual pinup?"

She knew his invitation was not meant seriously but she also knew that if he'd looked at her closely he would have seen the instant acceptance in her eyes. *Control yourself,* her sensible inner voice warned her, while at the same time she wondered if there were something in the genes that caused sisters to be attracted to the same man.

NEIL DROPPED BY her apartment a few evenings later just as she was preparing dinner. His beard was trimmed as neatly as before, but by Japanese standards, his plaid sport coat was almost flamboyant.

"Just as beautiful as I remembered," he said as she beckoned him inside. His voice carried a lilt not unlike that of his Scottish ancestors, Laura thought, amused by his enthusiastic appraisal.

"Hope I'm not intruding, but I didn't know until the last minute I would be free. How about joining me for dinner?"

"I'm sorry, Neil. I teach evenings. Would you care to take a quick potluck here instead? Just leftovers."

He sniffed appreciatively. "Home-cooked leftovers add up to a gourmet trip for me, lady. I accept! Next time I'll call ahead, I promise, and we'll do the town."

"And I accept," she said. "That is, if you guarantee no surprise endings."

He grinned. "It's a deal."

She made a green salad and took the pasta casserole out of the oven. "You're on your way to Tokyo again?"

His face clouded for a second. "Got to keep hopping in this business. Just got wind of some old Chinese fans and screens that are for sale."

"I typed a report for Geoffrey today on some Thailand fake antiques. Do you know anything about them?"

"Count on old Geoff to be on top of that skulduggery. Sure, I've seen a few, but a dealer ought to be able to spot one a mile away. By the way, who was that little tornado who shot down the steps just as I arrived?"

"Probably Kelly. I'm his guardian."

"You!"

"Yes, he's an orphan." She wouldn't say more and risk it getting back to Geoffrey.

"Must be tough raising someone else's kid."

"Not this child. He's like my little brother."

"Sure. I just meant it takes patience, not to mention money, to bring up kids these days."

"You don't think about things like that when you love someone," she said, suddenly defensive. "Kelly is just about the most delightful little boy in the world, intelligent, sensitive, charming—"

Neil laughed and held up a hand. "Hey, I'm only kidding. What a tiger you are!"

"You'd better believe it where Kelly's concerned. What about you? Do you like children?"

His smile faded. "Can't say I've ever been around 'em much. Never won many popularity contests with kids—women, either. Now, you take old Geoff. You might not believe it, but he has a fan club that stretches from Ohio to Tokyo."

She caught her breath. "Ohio!"

He looked at her oddly. "Yeah, our home state."

Kelly came in then, and Laura made introductions. Kelly immediately regaled Neil with a detailed account of his soccer game. Ordinarily Laura would have admonished Kelly, but now she was grateful for the distraction that gave her time to assimilate this new piece of evidence. Ohio, the state where Lisa went to Inglewood College. When Geoffrey went home on leave, he would travel to Ohio.

She had to hurry to make her classes on time, and Neil left when she did, promising to call her very soon. His information rode roughshod over her evening, and it took all her effort to keep her mind on her teaching. She almost wished Neil hadn't divulged it. Still, she'd have no rest until all the pieces fitted together. When Neil came around next time for the promised "night on the town," she'd try for the final answers.

She was glad Geoffrey would be away for a while. It would give her time to deal with this latest revelation. Her loyalty to Lisa now warred continually with emotions for Geoffrey she still dared not admit.

HOW THE WEEKS HAD FLOWN since they had arrived in Japan, Laura thought the next evening as she prepared dinner. Kelly sat nearby, explaining the festival that would come up in a week or two, *Shichi-go-san*.

"It's special for kids seven, five and three years old," he said. Laura had noticed that shops recently had been featuring lavish displays of children's clothing, both traditional and modern.

"Kids go to shrines with their parents and get candy and presents."

"Sounds like a fun time. I imagine Chizu told you all about it."

"Yes, and so did the teacher." He flashed an endearing grin. "So can we celebrate *Ku-shichi-go-san*?"

"Hey, wait a minute. How did that "nine" get in there, as if I didn't know?"

"Well, since I haven't been here before, don't you think it would be nifty to include age nine? You want to learn about all this culture stuff, don't you?"

"So we widen the age range."

"Everyone gets dressed up. Sometimes the boys get spaceman or cowboy outfits."

"Oh, yes. Presents are involved."

"Sure. Why else would we want to celebrate?"

"Why else indeed? Well, Chizu just recently turned ten. We might as well make it a ten-nine-seven-five-three day, and we'll take a picnic and go to a shrine."

"Good idea," Kelly cried with sudden enthusiasm, as if the suggestion had arrived unsolicited out of the blue. But he found that Chizu's parents planned to visit relatives in another town on that day, and when he called a friend in his scout troop, the boy said he was going on a fishing trip with his father.

Kelly slumped in a chair looking desolate. "That's what I'd like to do, go fishing with *my* father."

"I know," Laura said gently. "But at times when something goes wrong or we're terribly disappointed, we have to rely on our special ability."

His usually sunny face wore a pout. "Special ability, what's that got to do with it?"

"Everything. You and I know that we have always been able to manage when we run into difficulties. We miss a great deal by not having our fathers, but we also know that we have the ability to handle it. *Ganbaro,* they say over here."

"Not me," he said stubbornly. "All the time I see kids with their moms and dads, and I wish like everything that I had mine."

"Of course you do, and so do I."

"Well, I know what happened to my mother, but we don't know anything about my dad. How come? You could go to the army or the F.B.I.; I'll bet they'd help. But you don't do anything, Laura." He rose and his eyes were bright with unshed tears.

Laura walked over and reached out to touch his shoulder, but he jerked away.

"You don't care, do you?" he cried. "You won't even try to find him." He backed farther away as if he couldn't bear to be near her.

"Darling, listen. Your mother checked with army headquarters before you were even born. I wasn't a lot older than you at the time, but I remember perfectly."

Kelly turned on her furiously. "Somebody has to know what happened to him. How could he just disappear? He was famous. He had a lot of medals, didn't he?"

"Who told you?"

"No one. I just know. He was Major Canfield, U.S Air Force Intelligence, wasn't he!"

Laura took in the belligerent pose that scarcely masked the vulnerable little boy underneath. Should she allow him to deceive himself forever? Delay the truth until he had greater maturity?

"Kelly," she said at last. "Remember what I said about *ganbaro*, our special ability to face up to things?"

"Yeah," he said, but his eyes remained narrowed and watchful."

"Well, I'm going to tell you something about your parents now, because I believe you're ready to handle it."

Laura cringed when she saw the sudden fear that gripped him, but she continued. "The army assured us that your father was not missing in any kind of action. It's true he served in Japan as a major in intelligence; he was honorably discharged, and we know when and where. It has been ten years. If your father had wanted to come home, don't you think he would have done so by now?"

His chin began to quiver. "But why wouldn't he want to come home by now, Laura?"

"Sometimes people rush into marriage too fast, then realize they've made a mistake. I believe that was the trouble. You see, your father was home on a two-week leave when he met your mother. She was only eighteen at the time, far away from her family at college. It happened very fast. They never saw each other again after those two short weeks."

He stood quietly, trying to absorb the terrible inference. Suddenly he rushed over and flung himself into her arms.

"But he didn't know about me, did he?" Sobs racked his body. "Did he?" he begged and clung to her in desperation, obviously hoping for one last crumb of solace.

Laura felt a fierce surge of anger. "No, Kelly, he didn't know about you." She held him close. His breath came in shuddering gasps as the dream died within him.

At last he grew quiet. He pulled out of her embrace but still clung to her hand and turned his tear-stained face up to her. "If he knew about me, do you think he'd want me?" he said barely above a whisper.

Laura gripped his hand as much for her own sustenance as for his. Would Geoffrey McDermott want Kelly? Oh, God, she didn't even have to ask! At least she hadn't revealed to Kelly that he was born a McDermott. She looked down at the expression of longing in the little face that had become so precious to her and hugged him again.

"Yes, darling, he'd want you. How could he help but want you!"

CHAPTER ELEVEN

KELLY'S OUTBURST HAUNTED LAURA continuously as she probed her conscience. Did she have the right to keep father and son apart? Without a doubt, Geoffrey would be the most ecstatic man alive if he knew Kelly really belonged to him. Geoffrey adored children. One could not ignore that part of his nature. But would a man with so many question marks in his past make the kind of father Kelly deserved?

At least this afternoon would provide a distraction from this constant battle in her mind. Kenzo Okita, the young man involved with Sachiko in *omiai*, had asked Laura to meet him for *osanji* to discuss "very important matter." Laura was frankly curious. Sachiko had mentioned that Kenzo was making great strides in his English with a private teacher. Did this industrious fellow want still more help? She recalled her offer to give him special assistance the evening at Sato when he had struggled so pathetically. She arrived promptly at the coffeehouse and found him waiting.

He had a different air about him, far removed from the troubled, insecure student she recalled from her classroom. As he rose to bow, he looked taller than she remembered, but his understated composure was still distinctly, traditionally Japanese.

"Thank you for honoring humble invitation," he said as they seated themselves.

"I'm happy to come," Laura replied, and wondered how long it would take to get to the point of the meeting, if ever. *Be patient,* she charged herself, trying to keep in mind the Japanese dislike for directness. Not unexpectedly, she found herself joining in superficial conversation on several unrelated topics.

After more than an hour, Laura grew nervous. If Kenzo didn't get to his "very important matter" soon, she would have to leave in order to fix Kelly's supper and get ready for her evening class.

"I recall my promise to help you study English," Laura said, hoping to bring the conversation on course.

"Not to worry about English. I have fine private tutor. You hear improvement?"

"I do, indeed, Kenzo. You won't need me after all."

"Oh, yes. Have need for other kind of lesson. I wish very much to marry Miss Sachiko Kimura."

Laura inwardly sighed. What did that have to do with lessons, she thought in despair, wondering if they were launched on still another subject. "I'm not sure I understand."

"Sachiko is modern lady. I think you call it 'liberated.' Words won't come when we are together. I don't know how to talk to lady of liberation."

Laura stared in disbelief. "And you want me to teach you?"

"Yes. I think you know much about this subject. You also are liberated lady, yes? Tell me what to do, what to say. I pay well for such lessons."

Laura was astounded. "I don't think it would work, Kenzo."

"I study hard. Have good I.Q. I can learn."

"But are you sure you want to? It isn't possible to change your beliefs, overturn traditions so quickly."

"I want Sachiko for my wife," he said resolutely.

Laura observed the determined set of his chin. He meant it. In spite of all she'd heard about the Japanese male's disdain for romantic love in marriage, it seemed as if Kenzo might truly be smitten.

"Well, Kenzo, you don't need lessons. I can sum up the whole matter for you in a few words."

"You can?" he asked, amazed.

"Yes. All you have to remember is that every woman, liberated or not, yearns to be treated as a complete human being the same as you."

"Beg your pardon and very sorry, but not true. Man has one place in life, woman another. Different," Kenzo said firmly.

"Of course, we must acknowledge some differences, but our human needs are the same."

"Very sorry again, Miss Adams, but you have it wrong. Human feelings not important in *omiai*."

"This time I think *you* have it wrong, Kenzo. You are a highly eligible bachelor. You could marry practically any woman you want. If human feelings don't enter into marriage, why are you so determined to marry Sachiko?"

For the first time he ducked his head as if he were

embarrassed. "Sachiko is from excellent family. Intelligent woman. She will make fine mother for my children and run my household with distinction," he said stiffly as if he resented the need to qualify his answers.

"I see," Laura said. "And why do you think she ought to marry you?"

He looked taken aback. "I make good salary. I take family responsibilities seriously."

Laura smiled. "Ah, but I haven't heard you say that you love her. I assure you that liberated ladies want to hear that."

He sat tall and quite still, but Laura knew she had hit her target. "She knows I regard her highly."

"Oh, you've told her?"

"Not necessary. We are more subtle about such things in Japan."

Laura sighed. This was a losing proposition. "I hear that you want Sachiko to give up her music."

"You know Sachiko?" The implications seemed to alarm him.

"She was my good friend in the States, so I know how much her music means to her."

"Sorry, but you hear only half-truth. I am proud she is excellent musician and plan to buy her fine Yamaha grand piano. She can play all she wants, teach our children both violin and piano. But career not necessary for Japanese wife."

Laura felt certain she could never get through to this nice young man. He longed for a talented, intelligent, beautiful wife, but he wanted her to fit into the traditional role. "I see," she said thoughtfully.

"Sachiko tells me that you are a fine tennis player. Do you intend to drop your team when you marry? Teach tennis only to your children?"

"Why do that? Tennis a healthy sport. Have fine friends on team. Tennis necessary to my well-being."

"Oh, so you do think feelings are important? Listen, Kenzo. Creativity is a human need. Everyone reaches out to fulfill it in his or her own way. Sachiko's career does this for her. It would kill her spirit to give it up."

He pondered her remarks. "In Japan woman finds creative outlet in home. Paint, sew, cook, arrange flowers. I think you not understand."

"I understand very well. That's why I say I can't give you lessons. We don't think alike."

"Please," he said, now clearly distressed. "I must succeed. I try to understand. I promise. Give one assignment. I will practice. We meet in two or three weeks, and I give progress report. Progress report," he repeated as if he liked the sound of the words.

"All right, Kenzo, but I can tell you for certain that you can build her the biggest home in Kyoto and furnish it with the finest concert grand, but you won't get anywhere with Sachiko unless you accept her as a person with feelings and needs the same as yours." Had she made any impression? She didn't think so.

"Assignment, please?" His eyes shone with eagerness.

"Okay. You asked for it. Communication is your goal for the week. Talk to Sachiko, and I don't mean just to discuss the weather. Ask her what she wants out of life and tell her your dreams, too. Listen to her. Confide.''

He sucked in his breath and shook his head. ''Okay. But I don't believe Sachiko cares to talk about such subjects.''

''Try her, Kenzo. Try her.''

Laura gave her promise not to tell Sachiko of the ''lessons,'' and they rose to leave, bowing. She'd heard that women should always bow lower than men to indicate male superiority, but she deliberately kept her gesture at precisely the same level as his. She might as well condition him right off to liberated ladies. Kenzo didn't blink an eye at her audacity.

SCOTT HAD BEEN more than attentive lately, Laura realized several days later as she went directly from Geoffrey's to school in order to use the copy machine. What a good friend Scott was, both to her and to Kelly. Apparently he adored Kyoto as much as Geoffrey did, and he took delight in introducing it to her.

They had gone to see the lengths of newly dyed textiles washed in the Katsura River and spread out like banners on its banks, visited the silk weavers in the grilled, narrow houses in the Nishijin district. He showed her a garden so stark in its simplicity that it consisted of only fifteen rocks rising like islands out of a swirling sea of carefully raked sand. And last Sunday they took Kelly with them to nearby Lake Biwa for an afternoon of boating.

An awareness of beauty in nature as well as in man's creations seemed ingrained in the Japanese.

Laura, too, began to appreciate this philosophy and pondered how much one missed in life when one ignored it. Geoffrey, perhaps even more than Scott, seemed steeped in this cultural characteristic. It emanated from the pages of his books. "One must never rush through life at so fast a pace that one doesn't have time to marvel at the beauty of blossoms, the symmetry of a vase or the fullness of an autumn moon," one of his characters had said.

At school she hurried to the room that held the copy machines. Scott stood at a counter thumbing through a folder. His face lit up as she entered. She loved his off-center smile, the strong homely face that was wonderfully redeemed by warmth and openness. He looked such a bear of a man, yet one sensed at once his underlying gentleness. "Suave" was a word that could never be applied to Scott. A universal father figure, Laura thought, in spite of the fact that he wasn't a father.

"Just in time to join me for lunch," he said. "There's a new seafood place around the corner. Let's try it."

Laura offered no resistance. The apple she'd munched on the way over hadn't had much staying power and Scott's comfortable company was just the tonic she needed.

Although the little restaurant they entered might have been classed as a fast-food place, its uncluttered decor gave the illusion of space. Their order, promptly filled, arrived on red lacquer trays, the food placed on gray stoneware dishes. There was a clear soup containing vegetables cut like flowers, and fish arranged on a sea green leaf with a helping of snow peas alongside.

"This type of soup is clear so that the diner can see what floats within," Scott said. The colors, proportions, shapes and textures became a subtle artistic composition. It was as important for the food to please the eye as the palate, Laura had discovered.

"I've missed seeing you this past week," Scott said. "I've been unusually busy."

"Too much nightlife or too much work?"

"A combination of both, what with first one brother and his family arriving for a visit and then another."

"You have two brothers?"

"Three, all younger, all married."

"All but you?"

"To my sorrow, yes. Dad passed away about the time I graduated from college. I was needed at home."

The classic case of the sacrificing eldest son, Laura thought. "So you put your brothers through college?"

"It was worth it, and believe me, they paid me back handsomely. Besides, they presented me with a mint assortment of nieces and nephews."

Could anyone ever really repay that kind of sacrifice? "So no regrets?" Laura asked.

"I wouldn't be normal if I said I had none. I've always fancied myself fair material for a family man."

And he was, she thought. The woman would be

lucky who married him. "You talk as if your life is over, Scott. You're still young."

"Already turned forty."

"Life begins at forty."

"I admit I still cherish the dream," he said wistfully. He told her then how he had supported his mother and brothers with a job in a prestigious export business in San Francisco. There he found he had a facility for Japanese and was sent often on business trips to Japan, where he eventually met his present partner, Kazuo Kubo.

"I was a business major in college and in many ways not the most likely guy to set up a language school, but Kubo-san wanted an American who was fluent in Japanese and could manage the business end. I did a lot of research on teaching language, and we've been very successful. Over the past ten years we've developed a chain of ten schools reaching from Hiroshima in the south to Sendai in the north."

The waiter brought the usual fragrant green tea and they sipped it for a while without talking.

"So what kept you so busy all week besides visiting relatives?" Laura asked finally.

He toyed with the handleless cup for a moment. "Actually, I've been wanting to talk to you about that, although I hadn't thought to bring it up today. My partner and I are planning to open another language school in Nara, and we hope to get it rolling by spring. I've been spending a lot of time getting it organized and will probably move there next year."

"Leave Kyoto? Oh, Scott, we'll miss you!"

He studied her a bit shyly, she thought. "That's what I'd like to discuss with you. Would you consider moving there?"

"Nara? Why, Scott, I'm flattered that you'd ask me. I'd have to think about it, you know, what with Kelly established in school here, the lease on my apartment and all. Would the teaching position be the same?"

He reached over and took her hands in his big ones, and his lips moved soundlessly as he seemed to struggle with apparently difficult words. Finally he spoke.

"Not to teach, necessarily, unless you want to. Damn it, I hadn't meant to bring it up like this. What I'm trying to say is. . . I'd give the world if you. . . I want to take you to Nara as my wife, Laura."

Her amazement must have shown clearly. He let go of her hands and lifted his own in a helpless gesture.

"There, you see, I've blown it, jumped in too fast, haven't I?"

Laura swallowed hard. "I'm surprised, that's all. We haven't known each other very long, and, well, I've never actually thought of us in that way."

"I know," he said. "And I apologize. You see, I'm in love with you, Laura. I've been living with the idea all along, so it seems perfectly natural to me. But don't worry, I promise I won't press you."

They were silent for a moment while she tried to form a reply that wouldn't hurt him. His eyes turned anxious.

"Maybe you think there's too great an age difference? Eighteen years, you know."

"Oh, no, Scott. Age doesn't matter."

"And I didn't even ask if there was anyone else. At one time I wondered if McDermott might have his eye on you."

Laura flushed. "There's no one else, Scott," she said firmly.

The relief in his face was palpable. He reached for her hand and hid it completely between his two large ones. "As usual I blundered in like a bull in a china shop. Would you believe I had it all worked out in my mind a lot differently? There's a charming inn just outside the city. It has a magnificent view and beautiful gardens. I had wanted to take you there in a week or two and talk about us then." He shook his head at his impetuousness. "But you looked so lovely today I just couldn't wait. I had to spill the beans at high noon in this fish restaurant!"

Laura laughed, relieving the tension. She played for time while she drank her tea. "I need to think about this, Scott. There are some priorities in my life that need looking after, and of course there's Kelly. You know he's my sister's child, but there's a lot I haven't told you."

"You know I don't care what happened years ago. Surely you realize I'd want to adopt him. He's a great kid and having a son like Kelly is all part of the dream."

Her eyes filled with tears. Such a dear man. She'd rather die than hurt him.

He flashed her the comforting grin that was as good as a bear hug. "Don't fret. I promise not to bring it up again until you're ready to talk about it."

She nodded. "Okay." The lump in her throat prevented any more comment. They went back to the language school then, and Laura sat most of the afternoon staring at her lesson plans without writing a word.

"Don't fret," he'd said. How on earth could she not? Marry Scott? She loved him as she loved anyone dear to her. How could one help but love Scott? But she was not *in love* with him.

There was no question that he would be an adoring husband and father, the kind of father Kelly longed for and deserved. And if she moved to Nara as Scott's wife, her worries about Geoffrey would be over. But was it fair to marry this sensitive man without giving him the kind of love he had a right to expect? She would be using marriage to Scott as a panacea for what truly ailed her. Geoffrey.

During the following days, Scott's proposal dominated her thoughts. Perhaps she ought to consider the Japanese approach to *omiai*: marry, and if all the factors for a good marriage were present, hope that true love would develop. She felt certain that getting to know Scott could be a lifelong and richly rewarding experience.

Her feelings waxed wildly ambivalent. One minute she was set to rush into Scott's office and cry, "I'll marry you this minute!" Then up came the stumbling blocks again. In spite of *omiai*'s philosophy, how likely was it that a satisfying marriage could be fashioned from a one-sided affair? Did the ingredient called passion really count in the long run, or could she be content with comfort and companionship?

She recalled the time Geoffrey had held her in his arms, and she wondered if that quality of intimacy, so intense, so urgent, that feeling of wanting to be close forever...was it all just a reaction to their physical attraction, which might rate little importance in a lasting marriage? Not once had she ever felt that depth of emotion for Scott. He was a vulnerable man. She must proceed with caution.

Kelly and his "Uncle Scott," as he called him, had an excellent rapport. They had already gone to a sumo match together and several ball games, but now Scott wisely refrained from pressing his advantage, a discretion Laura appreciated.

As the days passed, she worried that their relationship might become awkward. But Scott appeared as natural and understanding as ever. Just occasionally she caught the silent appeal in his eyes when he looked at her, and she would want to rush over and put her arms around him. To offer comfort? Reassurance? Oh, why, she thought in despair, why couldn't she feel for Scott that same rush of physical excitement she felt for Geoffrey?

CHAPTER TWELVE

LAURA SURVEYED THE BASKET of mending. She'd worked ever since lunch and had barely made a dent. Mending was the one chore she tended to procrastinate with, and she sometimes wondered if Kelly might grow up and go away to college before she ever got to the bottom of the basket.

She let down the hem of a pair of his jeans and abruptly quit the task to spend the next hour writing *haiku*. She had composed several dozen of the short poems since her arrival in Kyoto. She'd written poetry since she was a child, and this form particularly enchanted her. What a challenge to express an emotion or fleeting impression in a mere seventeen syllables! Still, if one can't say something succinctly, it probably isn't worth saying, she thought.

Kelly's footsteps bounding up the stairway on his way home from school broke her concentration, and she put the *haiku* away in the folder where she kept the others. Conscience stricken, she eyed her mending. Why hadn't she kept at it? Now she had little to show for her afternoon. Then she reasoned virtuously that everyone needed a little time to be creative.

Kelly headed for the refrigerator to find a snack.

Between consuming cookies and milk, he gave her an account of his day that proved about as concise as haiku and considerably less enlightening. When he finished, he picked up a deck of cards Scott had brought home from Tokyo and shuffled them with impressive flair.

"Gee, it was super of Uncle Scott to give me this card-trick set. We sure have a lot of nice friends."

"Yes, and aren't we lucky!"

"Uncle Scott is always doing nice things for us, sort of as if he wants to take care of us, just like Grandma Canfield. And I like Miss Kimura a lot. She's pretty, but you still get the feeling you ought to be extra good when she's here."

Laura smiled. "It's the schoolteacher in her."

"Mr. Anderson is okay, but I don't think he's very interested in kids."

"Well, you haven't had much time to get acquainted. And Dr. McDermott?" she felt compelled to ask.

Kelly brightened. "Oh, he likes kids a lot."

"Oh, how can you tell?"

"Well, he looks at you when you talk to him and he listens as if what you say is important."

"I see. Well, you certainly have everyone pegged." And not too shabbily, either, she thought, and wondered if now was the time to mention Scott's proposal. She wanted to believe that his offer made sense, so every time she pictured Scott and Kelly trudging off somewhere hand in hand, why did the man always turn out to be Geoffrey?

And whenever she thought of herself at the altar

with the blue-eyed Scott, why did she look up and see
a tall man with dark shining eyes?

GEOFFREY HAD RETURNED several days early from
his promotional trip in order to prepare for an international conference of journalists in nearby Arashiyama, a suburb located up in the hills. "I need
someone who will go along and make tapes and accurate notes of the various sessions. How about it?
Time-and-a-half pay, if that's any incentive?"

Laura hesitated. She wasn't certain she could
handle an all-day trip with Geoffrey. Besides, the
conference was on Saturday, and she didn't know if
she could find someone to take care of Kelly. "Can't
you get anyone else?"

He frowned. "I would prefer your help in this
case. As I've mentioned before, you have an incisive
mind and the ability to zero in on essentials. This
conference is important to me, Laura, vital as re-
source material for upcoming columns."

"I'll let you know," she said, and was later relieved to learn that the Matsuis planned to be out of
town on the weekend and were unable to take care of
Kelly.

"Never mind," Geoffrey said when she told him.
"I'll call Chizu's folks, the Thompsons. I know
they'd be happy to take him if they have no other
plans. Probably they'd want him overnight."

"Overnight! How long does this conference last?"

"Late afternoon, but Arashiyama is such a spec-
tacular place I would like you to stay and have dinner
with me."

"Well, I'm not sure," she hedged, but Geoffrey was off to the telephone before she could say any more.

"All arranged," he said a few minutes later, and grinned provocatively when he saw her chagrin. "Just wanted to save you the inconvenience of coming up with any more excuses," he explained. "And in case you planned on producing a few sneezes or a limp or something, forget it. You won't be sorry. Arashiyama is glorious this time of year, one of the most famous viewing spots for fall color in all Japan. November is the perfect time to see it." So it was decided.

She hated to acknowledge the way her spirits leaped at the prospect of the excursion. The fall color sounded glorious, but so did the idea of spending an entire day at Geoffrey's side. Yes, she wanted to be with him, she admitted, not just sit home with make-believe, remembering the sound of his voice, the sheen of his dark hair, the way he'd smiled at her when he issued the invitation.

The trip was tempting, all right, and dangerous. She was all too aware of the hazards such a day could bring. There was something irrevocable about sitting beside him in his car, feeling the sharp existence of that something special between them, knowing the day could be enough to break her heart. At times like this, she felt as if she were tiptoeing through the dark, ready to plunge into disaster at the first misstep.

Nevertheless, Geoffrey had firmly tossed the ball into her court. "I won't lay a hand on you unless you

permit it," he'd said in so many words, and he'd surely keep his promise. So it was up to her. Very well.
There would be no scenes. They would not quarrel.
She wouldn't allow herself to become trapped in any
questionable situations. Absolutely not. She would
stay in charge.

GEOFFREY PICKED UP Laura and Kelly early Saturday morning, dropped the excited boy off at the
Thompsons, then headed out of the city and up into
the outlying hills. Geoffrey looked exceptionally distinguished today. He had a head of thick wavy hair
that would no doubt someday be classed as leonine.
His white shirt had a crisp freshness, and his
charcoal-gray suit, in keeping with the Japanese
male's preference for dark colors, was perfectly
tailored to his broad shoulders. Occasionally she
caught a subtle whiff of soap, clean and masculine.
She didn't dare define the sensations that were filling her right now.

He flashed the sudden smile that always changed
his face so dramatically and made her breath catch a
little. Someone ought to tell him he wouldn't startle
people so much if he would go at that smile more
gradually.

"You're mighty quiet this morning," he said.
"Office hours now open for confidences, confessions
or just spouting off."

Well, they could talk about how he would feel if he
knew his son had been in the car with them this
morning. "Just enjoying the scenery," she said.

"I have a hunch it's more than that. I've been

watching you lately. Something's eating you, isn't it?''

"My, my, I didn't realize my companion was going to be Dear Abby, or are you just feeling plain old nosy?" She hoped her flippancy would discourage him. Every time he tried to enter into her personal life, she had trouble keeping her mind on the proper track.

He gave an exaggerated sigh. "It's your loss. You'll miss out on some fantastic solutions."

"I'll try to live without them," she said.

"One of those 'I'd rather do it myselfers,' eh? Well, remember this, Laura," he said, dropping his bantering tone, "it never hurts to try a little communication."

He was right, of course. Communication would certainly clear up matters, but not in the way he expected. Laura darted a swift look at his profile. There was that unruly curl that fell across his forehead exactly like Kelly's, the straight authoritative nose and the mouth with the faintly cynical curve. Acknowledging the emotional confusion she felt, she looked out the window trying to sort through it as she watched the passing scene.

Skeins of morning mist still threaded stands of green pine, spruce and cherry, then thinned to bright sunshine as they arrived in Arashiyama. The town was situated on a densely wooded ridge. Shades of vermilion, scarlet, orange, yellow and crimson fired the hills in a breathtaking exhibition.

"I've never seen fall color like this!" Laura cried. "Autumn must be Japan's loveliest season."

"People are very season-conscious here, particularly when it comes to autumn. I guess it has something to do with the transience of our existence."

"Are you going philosophical on me?"

"It's a fact. Think about it. In autumn, the shorter days, the chill in the air, the turning leaves all remind us of life's impermanence."

"I hear K.D. Kano speaking," Laura said. This time his smile was easy and slow, and it was as if she had found something she had lost. The sensation proved heady, and it was all she could do to return the smile without appearing as confused as she felt.

Now they left Arashiyama and climbed more steeply. The conference site was a new hotel dramatically set on a bluff overlooking the Oi River. Terraced gardens swept green-tiered skirts down the hillsides all around the structure. Its architecture, serenely defying the twentieth century, was reminiscent of a Japanese inn, but it contained the latest in modern amenities, Laura found after they'd parked and gone inside.

Geoffrey handed her an identification pass and a program of events with notations to indicate the sessions he wanted her to cover.

"I have a hell of a schedule today," he said. "Mainly interviews. I probably won't see you until it's all over. There's a lunch for you up in the Garden Room, but I'm having mine with a panel of journalists with whom I'll appear later." His eyes were already on someone on the far side of the room, and his thoughts, as well, it seemed. He gave her an absentminded nod, and with a hurried "See you later," he was gone.

Good. She had been afraid this trip might include too much togetherness. Then why did she feel abandoned? It didn't make sense. She pondered her seemingly irrational feelings. Gathering up her natural dignity, she checked the schedule and headed for her first assignment.

Since it was an international conference, the lectures were given in many languages. She monitored the simultaneous translations, which were frequently given in heavily accented English. She had to strain to catch every word and felt doubly pressured because of the confidence Geoffrey had expressed in her. For reasons she preferred not to investigate, it became important to her to do an outstanding job. By noon she was so tense she decided to forgo the luncheon and stroll through the edge of the town.

Streets were filled with small specialty shops carrying goods to attract the eye of tourists: umbrellas, dolls, lanterns, bamboo ware, fans...an endless choice.

A cook broiled eel over a charcoal stove in front of a restaurant, men fished from a bridge and children skipped a coarse rope, probably removed from the straw sacks of charcoal that were beginning to be delivered to residences of late. After stopping at a sushi bar for a rice roll filled with egg and vegetables, she went back to the hotel.

The afternoon went far easier. The last event was the panel of English-speaking journalists on which Geoffrey appeared. Each member spoke briefly, then all answered questions put to them by the audience. Laura saw a different Geoffrey on the podium and wondered if she knew this man at all. He even looked different to her. He acted as moderator and there was no doubt that he was in charge, not aggressively but giving the audience the pleasant feeling that matters would be kept well in hand.

Nevertheless, his own answers were swift and shrewd, demonstrating a confidence that left no room for ambiguity. The lock of hair fell against his forehead now, and he leaned forward eagerly, taking in every word. When he spoke, his voice seemed much deeper. "Charisma" was the most likely word to describe the image he projected.

Once during the session his eyes searched her out, and finding her, they gleamed with recognition and something else. For a moment it was as if only the two of them were in the lecture hall. In the middle of this important session he still thought to look for her! She felt as if a fire had been kindled in a room that had been austere and cold.

The conference ended in late afternoon, and there was a general exodus. Laura waited in the lobby for almost an hour, but Geoffrey didn't arrive. He was probably still talking with reporters and the other journalists, she thought wearily, and decided to take a walk. Let him wait for her for a change.

She strolled out onto the terrace. Dusk gave way to darkness turning the hills into amorphous contours. Persimmon lanterns glowed, lighting a pathway that meandered among bamboo, a rock garden raked in swirling patterns and trees pruned both to reveal and to conceal the secrets of gnarled trunks.

She paused by a pond of indolent carp, then walked under an archway of maples, their colors grayed and lifeless at night, not even faintly reminiscent of their daytime splendor. The dramatic change affected her profoundly, and she took a note pad from her purse and put down her feeling in haiku.

The crunch of footsteps broke her mood, and Geoffrey strode around a stone lantern to join her. She hastily stuffed the haiku back into her purse.

"I thought I'd find you here," he said. "How was your day?"

"Not easy but stimulating."

"Mine, too, but I got some good interviews. Sorry I had to neglect you." He took her arm and they continued to walk. Her traitorous senses soared at his touch, and she couldn't help but imagine how life would be with a Geoffrey who was innocent of all wrongdoing. Why couldn't he even look the part? It would be so much easier to deal with a scoundrel who looked like a scoundrel instead of this attractive, magnetic man.

With an effort she continued the conversation. "I liked your speech. Well organized, meaty and to the point."

"Come now, it couldn't have been that perfect."

"Oh, I didn't say it was perfect," Laura added quickly.

He threw back his head and laughed. "Okay, let's have it."

"I thought your opening was too blunt. I realize you had to be brief, but you didn't have to jump in feetfirst. An opening is not the place for shock tactics. It took your audience a while to catch up.''

He thought a moment. ''You're right, you know. I'll watch that in the future. I'd better take you along more often.'' He laid an arm lightly across her shoulders and pointed to the moon just rising above the treetops. She looked up through a silhouette of pine branches clustered against the silver light.

''Like shadows on a *shoji*,'' she said a little breathlessly.

He squeezed her shoulders, and his touch sent the pulse in her throat throbbing so that she could barely swallow. She gazed at the moon as if it had bewitched her.

''You're becoming a real native,'' he said. ''Are you aware that Kyotans consider the moon their special province? During certain full moons they cook up a storm, write music and haiku and traipse by the hundreds to designated spots solely for moon viewing.''

''A custom I could learn to love,'' Laura said.

A fragrance like jasmine floated around them. Moonlight strained by mist clothed the garden, and the music of silence wove the scene into completeness. Geoffrey stood quietly beside her. With a knowing and loving eye, he seemed to absorb the beauty around them, becoming a part of it. She adored this quality in him and knew it denoted a man of rare sensitivity. She gazed at his strong profile touched by light and shadow and felt a poignant longing. If he should turn and look at her now, her eyes, her face, even her body would reveal the rising desire that clamored for his touch.

Be careful, she cautioned herself. Good sense dictated she ought to leave. Now. Flee from this man whose dark eyes embraced her far stronger than his arms ever could; leave behind the deep compelling voice that relentlessly questioned the restraint she strove so hard to maintain.

"Come along," he said, taking her hand. "Let's see the rest of the gardens. Our dinner reservation isn't for another hour yet." Now the terraces were a study in moonlight and shade. The architect must have placed every plant, rock and tree keeping in mind the effect of its shadow. They strolled down to a small open-air teahouse that overlooked the river. Somnolent branches of wisteria wrapped themselves around the structure that was now deserted and illusory in the thin mist rising from the water below.

They slipped off their shoes and walked on the tatami. Inside, the effect was not unlike a gazebo. A chorus of croaking frogs rose from the river below, and the skittering of a night creature rustled the reeds on the bank. Farther away came the faint tinkle of wind chimes.

"A little night music," Geoffrey said.

He stood so close she could almost feel the warmth from his body. His breath touched her cheek, and she felt an electrifying awareness of intimacy draw them closer together. A sudden splash below broke the spell. They peered over the railing and looked down at the river. Perhaps a diving bird, a loosened stone or the night fisherman who now rowed his boat across the moon path. Reflections from the lanterns danced and twinkled on the surface of the water.

He turned her around so that her face was bathed in moonlight. His touch, though brief, had whetted her appetite for more. Much more. "Tell me, what are you thinking, Moon Girl?"

"Moon Girl?" she whispered, trying to steal a little time to recover her reason.

He smiled, his face full of tenderness. "Yes. Cool, remote, infinitely intriguing. What's inside that lovely head of yours?"

"Autumn leaves, the inconstant moon. I think I've caught that Japanese feeling of impermanence."

He drew a deep breath. "Yes, I feel it, too, but there's something else, something I don't understand. A reticence, some secret cloak you draw around you that prevents you from being totally yourself."

She remained silent. He appeared intuitive beyond all belief. "There are times when I catch a glimpse of the real you," he continued. "A brief warmth in your eyes when you look up at me, a wistful thoughtfulness in your expression when you sit at my desk and sometimes even a secretive smile if I happen to come into the room unexpectedly. Then quick as a flash you shut me out. I can't live with glimpses. I want all of you."

Their eyes met, and she felt the attraction between them, at once both fragile and intense. Even in the shadows she saw that his eyes were warm and appealing. She willed her response not to happen, but the sudden emotional tide that swept her senses was too strong to resist. Her hand reached out to him, and suddenly she was in his arms.

"Oh, Laura, do you know how I've longed for this moment?" he asked, and brushed his lips across her temple as if to savor the sweetness of her skin. She felt a melting sensation almost impossible to tolerate and slipped her hands beneath his jacket, spreading her fingers to take delight in the feel of his broad shoulders and hard lean back. Geoffrey sighed with pleasure, and his hands slid downward from her shoulders tracing the curve of her breasts and her hips, then encircled her slim waist crushing her against him. The subtle sexuality that had existed between them all along now exploded into passion.

In the dim light of moonglow she felt his eyes like flames touch her everywhere. They clung together, teasing each other's lips, then kissing deeply, allowing hunger and longing to obliterate past and future.

She didn't care that his kisses left her breathless, that he was aware of her wildly beating heart, that he saw her enchantment.

After a few minutes he held her away from him and cupped her face in his hands to look into the depths of her eyes, reading all that he could see there. She returned his gaze, her eyes silently beseeching him to kiss her again with all the fire and hunger they were both feeling.

With mindless disregard, she'd turned from the path she'd charted for herself. Now she headed into unknown territory. There remained one certainty: she was in love with Geoffrey. In a way, it was a relief to admit to the feeling that had smoldered so long inside her. She realized she was opting for a divided loyalty. Was that possible? But he was a different Geoffrey. Not the one who had played such a ruthless role in her sister's life. Laura had a right to love, didn't she? Anyway, she wouldn't tell him she loved him yet, but as long as she secretly acknowledged it, she could stop doing battle with herself.

When the enigma of the past was finally solved she'd try to deal with it, and if the answer to Lisa's torment never came, she'd endeavor to handle that, too. *Ganbarone!*

Oh, God! Lisa! Her sister's grieving face seemed to hover in the mist, adding yet another element to destroy the ambience. Laura dug her fists into her eyes to blot out the illusion.

"What's wrong?" Geoffrey cried.

"Something, someone," she mumbled inanely.

He peered out of the teahouse and listened. "There's no one," he said, and laid an arm around her shoulders. She drew away and they faced each other in silence for a few seconds, two figures cast in stone. Suddenly she heard his sharp intake of breath and became frightened at the way his eyes narrowed to angry slits, the compressed line of his mouth exhibiting both hurt and bitterness.

"Don't tell me you're into playing games," he said, his voice dangerously controlled.

"No, Geoffrey, never!"

He took her by the shoulders again, and this time his grip was not gentle. "What's with this on-again, off-again technique, then?

"I'd never do that!"

"Why else do you play loving and warm one minute, then give me the brush-off the next?"

She turned away from him and leaned against the railing. "You've misunderstood completely." She began to tremble and had to force herself not to cry.

His hands were in his pockets now, and he stood over her, menacing, huge, like a dark cloud. "Okay, then, fill me in. Make it concise. Try for three short sentences."

Here was the perfect moment. *Answer him. Tell him the whole truth. Get it over with.* But she knew if she did he'd be furious. Ultimately, he would have to reject her. She couldn't think of facing a future without Geoffrey any more than she could think of facing one without Kelly. Oh, God, what to do? She forced the coldness of steel into her voice. "Working hours are over, Mr. Employer."

He stared down at her, his face a mixture of anger and bewilderment. "Can't we talk? I'll listen. I want to listen. Your mixed signals are killing me!" Suddenly he seemed to wilt. "It's Scott, isn't it? I suppose he's asked you to marry him?"

"Well, yes, but . . . ."

"Damn it, you don't love him. Tell him. What's so difficult about that?"

"There are other considerations."

"You mean you'd marry him after the way you responded to me? What kind of woman are you?"

Suddenly, he drew her back into his arms again and claimed her lips in a long, caring kiss.

Her throat convulsed. She longed to love him freely in a world where she felt no guilt, where she could forget all the yesterdays and respond with an abandon that would silence her warring conscience.

She felt the tension in his arms increase. "Talk to me, Laura. Say something," he implored. It was obvious he needed more than just her physical response. She couldn't answer. A desperate scenario running through her mind all but silenced his plea.

This was the way he'd kissed Lisa, lovingly, tenderly. That young woman had felt the strength of his encircling arms as Laura did right now. She'd listened to the same endearments and had become caught up in the same magnetism.

She felt a stab of pain. This constant comparison was something she was going to have to live with in their relationship. Could she deal with these ghosts from the past? She suppressed a sob, but tears ran down her cheeks. Geoffrey's posture stiffened immediately. *Not that old ruse,* his expression clearly said.

He glared at her a moment and then apparently decided she was truly hurting, after all. He laid a gentle hand against her wet cheek, and when he spoke, his voice was just above a whisper. "I'm sorry, Laura. I didn't mean to hurt you. It's just the way you kissed me. I thought it meant something to you."

"I know, Geoffrey, and I meant every kiss I gave you. You were perceptive from the beginning. I *am* dealing with something in my life right now that is tearing me apart, something that has to do with my past." She searched his face for some glimmer of recollection, some sudden comprehension, but she saw none, only a puzzled frown.

"Surely you can give me credit for being even a little understanding, a little compassionate. Why can't you allow me to help you?"

She shook her head. "This is a problem I must solve myself. No one else can do it for me. Can you accept that for the time being?"

He gazed at her for a long time as he thought over her request. Was he doubting her sincerity? His expression told her nothing. "For the time being then, but if this is as impossible for you as it is for me, you'll do something about it." His voice was as cool as the evening mist.

He probably doesn't trust me, she thought. Well, they were even. She wasn't sure she trusted him, either. They walked from the teahouse and started up the hilly terrace. Silence hung between them like a curtain, both of them lost in their own private thoughts.

Now the garden appeared stark and forlorn, and a sharp breeze tugged at their clothing. Once, when they passed under a lantern, she darted a glance at Geoffrey's face. Was it remote, bleak or full of anger? For a brief instant she wanted to reach out and touch him, but he was far away from her now.

Desperation closed in on her. If only she'd kept her head instead of acting like some star-struck schoolgirl who'd succumbed to the magic of Arashiyama moonlight.

CHAPTER THIRTEEN

SOMEHOW SHE GOT THROUGH the rest of the evening even though she had been painfully conscious of the barrier she'd built between them. Dinner in the beautiful dining room of the hotel looked and probably tasted superb, but she would never know; the events of the evening had rendered the meal flavorless. Their secluded table, no doubt reserved for a price, overlooked the illuminated garden, but she rarely looked at it, not wanting to recall what had just taken place there.

Later Geoffrey drove her home, not in silence. No, they determinedly discussed the fine points of the lectures like two intellectual strangers who just happened to spend an evening together. A fiasco.

Well, Geoffrey had promised to back off for a while, so now it was up to her. To begin with she would give Scott her answer. Dear, wonderful Scott. She would not marry him without bringing him the kind of love he deserved. True, she'd considered his proposal seriously when she watched him with Kelly. There was no doubt that he would make a firm and loving father. There already existed mutual respect as well as real friendship between the two.

She'd had lunch with him again last week, and as he'd promised, marriage was not mentioned. No, she would not "use" Scott. She would tell him at the very first opportunity.

LAURA RECEIVED A CALL from Kenzo Okita that evening. He reminded her that they had an appointment the next day for the "progress report." She had relegated Kenzo's plan for courting Sachiko to the back of her mind. The events of the past few weeks convinced her that she was the last person on earth who should counsel Kenzo or anyone else on affairs of the heart. She was a stranger to his culture, and Kenzo to hers. Cultural change was a gradual process, not something one accomplished over a few cups of coffee at a *kissaten*.

However, Kenzo's eagerness and beguiling courtesy over the telephone was more than a match for her planned refusal, so she met him again on the following afternoon at the same coffeehouse.

What a startlingly handsome Japanese man he was, with his lean athletic figure and fine-boned intelligent face. He and Laura sat down at the small table, and his serious dark eyes regarded her now.

"Tried hard on lesson. Not sure if it worked," he said.

Laura took a few seconds to recall all that she'd told him. "Ah, yes. Communication. How did it go?"

He frowned. "Maybe better. I talk about virtue of classics. She listen. She talk about French impressionism. I listen. We do not agree, but we listen."

"Excellent, Kenzo."

"Not so sure."

"What else did you discuss?"

He shifted uncomfortably. "Conversation very brief. She helped me short time with English pronunciation. End of meeting."

"Is that all?"

He nodded. "But some improvement, you think so?" He seemed to need her approval.

"Yes, indeed, but try to be natural, Kenzo. Let the conversation flow where it will."

"Difficult. When I look at beautiful girl, tongue stops working. Nothing comes naturally. Not one thing."

"You can always ask questions, about her teaching, her goals, if she has any fears. Then share your feelings."

"I believe she thinks I am not too smart."

"Well, I can assure you that's not true. Speak up, surprise her. All you need is a little practice. Isn't there any woman friend with whom you can talk, your sister, a secretary?"

He looked askance. "Not possible. Never!"

"What about a geisha? I hear they are very skilled in conversational art. I'm told that many wives wish their husbands would talk to them with the same freedom they do with geishas."

"I think you are mistaken," he said, but fingered his coffee cup uneasily.

"No, Kenzo. Liberated lady or not, a woman wants her husband's respect for her opinions as she shows respect for his."

"Wife who expresses opinions in public causes husband to lose face. Man speaks; woman listens."

"Well, then, I think you must give up the idea of marrying Sachiko. You know she is intelligent. Why would you want to ignore her?"

He straightened his posture so that he looked down on her in the way a teacher determines to enlighten a not quite bright pupil. "I think it is time to give you a lesson, Miss Adams. You do not understand Japanese way. Woman is free one. Man has great obligations. He is controlled by *giri ninjo*, the code of human obligations. It is more important than anything else in life here. I must guard family honor, make all important decisions, take care of money matters. *Giri ninjo* is stronger than human affection. It is number one for all men, especially if he is the eldest or only son, as I am. Obligation lasts all my life."

Laura considered the young man's words thoughtfully. She had not realized the influence of *giri ninjo*. "Still, despite your heavy responsibilities, you are able to carry on with great freedom. Sachiko tells me that her father spared himself no luxury while Sachiko and her mother had to be very frugal. Sachiko saw little of her father, and her mother was desperately lonely. Moreover, he has an expense account that includes gourmet meals, geisha parties, country-club memberships and extended business trips, not to mention the patronage of bar girls and, in his later years, a mistress, all of which he enjoys while her mother remains at home. Her mother never even calls him by his first name, always the formal term, *anata*.

Do you consider that freedom for a woman? Sachiko doesn't.''

"But I shall provide her with fine home, one of best in Kyoto."

"A cage is a cage, Kenzo. No matter how golden."

"The West has tainted her," he said bitterly.

"Perhaps so, but I think the concept is spreading in your country. Maybe you should visit the States for a while. Then you could appreciate Sachiko's point of view."

"She will be satisfied once she settles into marriage."

"Don't count on it, Kenzo. You expect your wife to make some changes, so you'd better be prepared to make some compromises, also. And, Kenzo, do you realize that you have been carrying on a perfectly good conversation with a liberated lady?"

He looked at her with his nice shy smile. "True. Prospects not so bad, after all. I tell you, Miss Adams, I want Sachiko for my wife. I am determined. So, ready for next lesson."

Laura sighed. She couldn't be sure he'd really been listening. "Try a little empathy this time. Put yourself in the role you wish Sachiko to fill. Ask yourself how you would react to it."

He stared at his empty coffee cup and muttered something in Japanese as if reminding himself of something. "Okay. Try again. I talk; she listens. She talks; I listen. Then do empathy. That's it in a clamshell. Yes?"

Nutshell, Kenzo, she corrected silently, and knew she ought to tell him that such a concept could scarcely be reduced to fit into such a small space. They bowed and went their separate ways.

Laura thoughtfully considered the conversation and wondered if Kenzo would be doomed to discontent. Obviously, he loved Sachiko, but he knew he would be the object of derision among other men if his wife acted too independently.

Now she wished she hadn't become involved in the whole affair. If there were a prize for a bungling go-between, she would be the number-one candidate.

THE NEXT NOON as she left work at Geoffrey's, she planned to head straight to school to prepare some exercises for her evening classes. Instead, on impulse she stopped by the little park across the street from Geoffrey's house and sat down on a stone bench. Actually, the park amounted to hardly more than a landscaped strip of green, no doubt designed to give the illusion of space to this area so densely populated with condominiums. At any rate, it provided a far more pleasant setting to eat her lunch than in the crowded teachers' room.

A raw wind came up, sending dry leaves scurrying to huddle finally against a stone lantern like a family of quail. Two old women sat on a bench across from her, their faces turned toward the sun. Laura nibbled a sandwich and looked up at the second and third floors of Geoffrey's condo, wondering if the little balcony that faced the park fronted the room in which he worked. She had never been in any part of his house other than the library and his file room.

Did Geoffrey actually have a room upstairs where he displayed his fine art collection?

Clouds scudded across the sun, and she turned up her jacket collar against the increasing, coolness. Autumn slipped quickly into winter in Japan, it seemed. She wrapped up the rest of her sandwich and put it back into her bag, then rubbed her cold hands together. She'd better take the bus to school, after all.

As she turned out of the park, a hand touched her shoulder.

"Are you out of your mind picnicking in this weather?" Geoffrey asked.

She hadn't seen him since last Saturday at Arashiyama, and she'd wondered if he might have gone out of town. For a moment their eyes caught and held in a wary communication; questioning, remembering, passing silent signals, finally agreeing to carry on without recriminations, at least for the time being.

"I'm going to buy you a thermometer, a barometer, a rain gauge and maybe even a windchill indicator," he said.

Alongside Geoffrey, sensibly dressed in overcoat and muffler, she probably did look foolish in her lightweight suit, but the sun had shone with such crystal-clear promise that morning.

This time his eyes were full of laughter, but they were tender, too. She felt herself grow warm in spite of the chill. It would be convenient if she had a kind of automatic pilot to take over in this kind of situation until she could get hold of herself.

"Actually, I didn't notice the cold until a few minutes ago. I guess I'm unusually warm-blooded," she said.

"Oh, I agree," he said heartily.

She bit her lip at the unfortunate reference, and he looked amused at her confusion. As always, his nearness made her resolve all but vanish.

"Lucky I saw you from my window," he said. "I was certain it was you, although I couldn't quite make out your face."

"Don't tell me you're into spying?"

"Only at small blondes who don't know enough to come in out of the cold." He took her arm. "I've got a pot of soup on the stove. Just what the doctor ordered."

She hesitated. "Well, I do have a busy afternoon ahead, but hot soup does sound infinitely better than a cold sandwich." *You're rationalizing again,* she decided as they walked back across the street to his condo.

He led her into a large cheerful kitchen. Shining copper-bottom pans hung in convenient reach from a central chimney above the stove. *Mikans*, walnuts and dark Aomori apples filled a hanging tiered wire basket, and as far as she could tell, not a single modern appliance was missing.

What would it be like to live here as Geoffrey's wife, to share his bed, to work side by side with him in this warm attractive room? She tried not to think about it.

"So you're a gourmet cook along with all your other accomplishments?" she said, gesturing around the well-appointed kitchen.

"You bet. Wait until you taste my soup. Sensational!" He removed his coat and muffler and hung them on hooks near the door, washed his hands and ladled two steaming bowls of soup. "It's mulligatawny," he said, setting them on the table in the dining nook.

She inhaled the appetizing aroma, tasted the soup, then formed a circle with thumb and forefinger. "Superb!"

He nodded, sitting down to join her with the lofty assurance of a master chef. She found his pride endearing. What a complex man he was. The years stretched ahead with unbelievable loneliness at the thought she might never get to know him completely.

He ate with appetite. "A soup for all seasons and particularly winter," he declared.

"I agree. What's in it?"

"Lots of chicken, vegetables, apples, real cream and a heavy hand with the curry. I'm glad to see that you have an appetite. You've lost weight, haven't you? I'd begun to wonder."

"'Wonder,' now there's an intriguing word. Full of potential," she said, hoping to forestall any more personal observations.

"This lunch is not aimed at any wrinkle-browed reflection," he said.

"Oh, no? Almost anything you say needs defining, Geoffrey,"

He leaned across the table and gave her the sincere look that always alerted her defenses. "I'm not that profound, Laura, and you very well know it. Actually, I did have something in mind other than lunch. I thought it might be a good idea if we took some time to get to know each other a little better.''

She felt startled. They must be on the same wave length. She'd had the same thought only moments ago. ''We've been acquainted for some time now.''

''Vital statistics aren't what I'm after, and I already know you're the world's best secretary, that you're unconscious when it comes to matters of climate and if there's a disaster pending, you'll turn up in the thick of it.''

Then you know about as much as I'm prepared to tell you, she added silently.

''But,'' he continued, ''I want to learn your candid opinion of Bruckner, if you sleep on the right or left side of the bed and what you were like when you were a little girl. You seem to have simply appeared, like that mythical woman who rose from the sea on a half-shell. You never mention your family.''

''Good heavens,'' she said uneasily. ''Do you have the rest of the afternoon? I don't care for one-sided conversations. Perhaps there ought to be a little reciprocation.''

''Good. I can see progress ahead. I sometimes get the feeling you consider me part of the furniture.''

She couldn't help smiling. ''But classy furniture, Geoffrey.''

''Thanks a lot. So what do you want to know about me? Today I'm an open book.''

She caught her breath. *The only thing I need to know is why a man like you once behaved in a manner that appears completely illogical.* She needed to acquire several coats of armor before she could handle

Geoffrey's answer to that question. "Well, Geoffrey, let's see. This could get pretty personal, you know—such as how has a well-known writer and eminently eligible bachelor like you escaped marriage?"

"I've been waiting until you came along, naturally. What else? There are many sides to my fascinating personality."

"How about naming a few of your secret vices? You must have a few. Also, someone told me that you were King Midas with a roomful of treasure. Is that true?"

"Yes, it is, and I'd like nothing better than to show it to you the minute we finish lunch, if you'd care to have a look."

"And the vices?" she asked.

"Equal-opportunity time here. Your turn now. No manipulating the conversation. That's quite a technique you have to keep nosy people like me from invading your privacy. I suppose you aren't ready to tell me why you build that wall around you?"

She went over to examine a hanging plant that had become a bit droopy. "Poor thing, you could use some bone meal," she said to it. "It's not cross-examination time yet," she said coolly. She hoped he wouldn't persist in raking her over the coals in order to find something in the ashes.

He followed and stood close behind. He didn't touch her but she had the feeling he'd wrapped both his arms around her.

"You're trembling. Why? Surely you're not afraid of me."

"I'd say I was more afraid of myself," she said.

"Do you mind if I speculate? I think you must have been terribly hurt by some devastating experience, something that keeps you from trusting men, something that makes you afraid to love. But that's the puzzle. You have perseverance and courage to spare."

He reached for her hand and she allowed him to twine their fingers together for a little while so that she could savor the small intimacy. It was the caring way that he accomplished the brief touching, as now, or when he helped her on with her coat or helped her into the car, that often gave her a strong feeling of his sexuality. Perhaps it was the thoughtfulness he showed or his protective manner that seemed so distinctly male.

"I would hate it if you continued to think you couldn't be open with me," he said. "I want trust between us, my love."

She felt tears sting her eyes. "So do I, but people do follow patterns and I wonder if they ever change. You're a strong person, Geoffrey, and you have a way with words, both spoken and written. Sometimes I'm not certain whether you're speaking truth or fiction."

"Good Lord, what reason have I ever given you to be suspicious?" he demanded.

"Since we're into revealing our pasts today, what about that poor girl you sweet-talked into marriage when you were in the service, then abandoned? Someone filled me in, Geoffrey."

He laid a hand against his cheek as if she'd slapped him. She was shocked by his pained expression. He walked across the room and stood looking out of the window for a moment. His silence terrified her.

"Scott told you, I suppose," he said dully at last. "You're mistaken, though. I didn't abandon her. She left me. The wounds went deep, as far as I was concerned. In fact it's pretty arrogant of me to accuse you of being afraid to love again. I might as well have been talking about myself."

Laura knew she looked astonished. "You! Afraid?"

"Yes," he said. "For ten years I avoided serious relationships; then you came along."

"Are you telling me that the girl you married when you were in the service left *you*?"

"That's right. It was a bad time for me. We were very young and deeply in love, but neither of us was mature enough to handle the prejudice we encountered."

"Prejudice?" What did prejudice have to do with Lisa?

He gave her a steady look. "My Midori was a beautiful Japanese girl, Laura." His expression turned bleak and she could feel him go far away from her.

Laura wondered if she looked as shocked as she felt. For a moment she clung to the back of a chair to steady herself. Japanese! Major Geoffrey McDermott was already married to a Japanese woman at the time he married Lisa. The army records were specific about that. The implications tore through her like a gunshot. Here at last came the clue that irrevocably identified him. "Japanese wife!" she cried as the full impact of what this meant overwhelmed her. "Oh, no, please tell me you weren't married to a Japanese!" She caught the disbelief on his face.

"My God, Laura, surely not you, too!" he said, and reached for her as if a touch might erase her words.

Laura struggled against clarifying his misunderstanding. Let him think she was prejudiced against interracial marriage. Had his dalliance with Lisa been so fleeting that he'd completely forgotten her? Or had it in reality added fuel to the breakup of his marriage to Midori? Laura couldn't say another word, not now when her world had shattered around her. She picked up her purse and walked from the room. Geoffrey watched in silence, disappointment, hurt, rejection all clearly etched in his desolate expression.

Blindly she made her way to the bus stop. Halfway to school she didn't even remember boarding the bus, much less paying her fare. Moreover, she'd left her briefcase with the material she needed to work on that afternoon.

The information that Geoffrey had been married to a Japanese girl was not unexpected. She'd heard the army report discussed over and over by Lisa and her grandmother. It was just that she'd hoped desperately never to find this damning evidence in Geoffrey's background. There could have been errors, coincidences, she'd kept telling herself. If he'd been married to a woman of any other nationality, she would have been ecstatic.

For weeks she'd prayed for a clue that would prove Geoffrey innocent, anything that would establish that he couldn't have been involved in the deception. Instead, one negative sign after another continued to surface. Now came this one from Geoffrey's own lips, the most conclusive yet.

She realized she hadn't tried very hard to verify this latest fact. Weeks ago she could have found some diplomatic way to frame her question. But she hadn't wanted to. If one didn't look for trouble, one wouldn't find it. Is that what she believed? A fine philosophy for a woman who lectured a nine-year-old boy on the virtues of facing up to life.

Still dazed when she arrived at school, she went straight to Scott's office, but the secretary said he was in Nara again. She walked slowly back to the bus stop. As she waited, Shigeru, one of the nisei teachers, curbed his shining new motorcycle near her.

"Hi, Laura-san, may I give you a lift?"

She thought a moment and knew she could make the trip back to Geoffrey's to pick up her briefcase a lot faster on a motorcycle than on the bus. She looked dubiously at the demon machine. She'd never ridden one before.

"You're sure you have the time?" she asked.

"The rest of the day if you need it," he said, obviously anxious to show off his fancy new Yamaha. She gave him the directions to Geoffrey's condo and climbed on behind Shigeru, clasping him around the waist in the customary hold.

Shigeru weaved in and out of the traffic with skill and daring, and they reached their destination in a few minutes. A bit shakily Laura slipped inside and retrieved her briefcase without running into Geoffrey. Meanwhile Shigeru revved the motor of his bike as if each raucous surge was music to his ears.

As they skidded away from the curb, Geoffrey stepped out on the porch, his face a perfect picture of bewilderment. How ought she to carry on during this awkward situation?

Wave, she decided wearily. Add a little mystery to his day. Let him reconcile her apparent prejudice and her busy afternoon to a cozy motorcycle ride with a handsome Japanese male.

CHAPTER FOURTEEN

ALREADY LAURA NOTED small signs of approaching winter. Her neighbor, Mrs. Matsui, had taken down her wind bells, and the little pottery shop down the street now featured stacks of stoneware braziers. Although today's clear November sunshine seemed not to warrant it, almost everyone wore scarves, coats or jackets.

At Geoffrey's she typed furiously, making an unaccustomed number of errors. She hoped the repetitive clack of the keys would take her mind off the fact that Geoffrey was probably holed up in his room working on his new novel. He'd said it dealt with postwar occupation in Japan, and every morning she hoped she'd find the first few chapters on her desk. They would be full of typos and the usual hopelessly marked-up out-of-sequence sentences and paragraphs. She loved getting them into shape. It was like digging a diamond out of rough sandstone.

Every time she paused she found herself listening for his step. Perhaps he was on one of his frequent jaunts to Tokyo, after all. Good. She needed the time to decide what to do about her appalling behavior that day in his kitchen. On the surface they appeared inexcusable. All she could do was to apologize, say there was a misunderstanding and hope he wouldn't pursue it.

Everything in her told her to forget the past. But no matter how she reasoned, not one thing had changed except her own willful emotions. She must act soon. No more shilly-shallying. It wasn't fair to keep Scott out on a limb, and she must either tell Geoffrey what she knew of his past and accept the consequences or else lock it in her mind forever and throw away the key.

Life had grown so complicated she sometimes felt as if her head had turned into a battleground. As a child, when she felt pressured she would climb a rugged old sycamore in her grandmother's yard. There in the leafy green haven she would allow the solitude to revive and nourish her until she regained perspective. She could use a sycamore tree now.

That afternoon she received a call from Scott. "How do you feel about last-minute invitations? My partner, Mr. Kubo, and I are invited to a geisha party this evening, but he called just now to say he's not feeling well. How would you like to go in his place?"

Laura was amazed at the invitation. "But, Scott, I understood that women weren't welcome at such parties, and anyway, what about my classes?"

"Not to worry. I can get one of the afternoon teachers to sub for you. I checked out the guest list and found that a couple of other women are included. And so is Geoffrey McDermott, who's an old friend of our host, Mr. Fukukita. So I'm certain you'll feel comfortable."

She almost gasped. Comfortable! With Geoffrey

there? "I'd love the opportunity, if you're certain it's okay."

"Mr. Fukukita welcomes you. I've already checked it out with him. It isn't easy for foreigners to gain entrée to a bona-fide geisha affair, particularly for a woman. However, Mr. Fukukita is in the publishing business, and educational material happens to be one of his interests, so several heads of local language schools are among the guests tonight."

He told her when he would call for her. She thanked him and thoughtfully considered the evening. If only it wouldn't prove awkward. She hadn't talked with Geoffrey since last week when she fled his kitchen leaving him with an erroneous impression. The deep hurt and disappointment that clearly showed on his face had haunted her ever since.

She decided to wear her long robin's-egg-blue chiffon dinner gown. It was cut princess-style and she knew it flattered her slender figure, flowing gracefully when she moved. She smiled to herself as she pressed it. She could as well wear jeans. Tonight all eyes would focus on no one but the lovely geishas.

As she washed her hair, she caught herself wishing it were Geoffrey who would escort her to the party. She imagined her arm tucked in his, the feel of his body close to hers that never failed to quicken her heartbeat. She simply must put an end to Scott's hopes that she still considered marriage. Every time she accepted an invitation, Scott would surely take it as proof positive she was leaning favorably toward such a decision. It was grossly unfair to him. Maybe tonight would provide the opportunity that seemed to evade her. Perhaps she would talk to him coming home in the taxi, or better still, she would invite him in for coffee or a drink.

She decided to try on the dress to see if it looked appropriate for tonight's occasion, after all. As she pulled the zipper, it caught. It wouldn't budge and she was afraid to force it. Kelly was at the park next door playing soccer. He would never hear her voice over the noise. Perhaps Mrs. Matsui was home from work. Laura ran quickly down one flight to knock on the door. The woman promptly answered, and Laura explained her predicament.

"Would you believe I'm going to a geisha party?"

Mrs. Matsui was an attractive woman, probably in her mid-forties, now a part-time legal secretary. Except for Seiji, her children were grown and married. Since her firm dealt with many American companies, she spoke excellent English. Now she wore her usual *yukata*, but when she went to work she dressed in the smart tailored suits favored by most businesswomen.

"So you are going to a geisha party. I have never gone, but of course my husband has many times," she said, carefully working at the zipper. Her expression was tranquil, tinged with a quality that could only be described as bittersweet.

"Do you mind that you can't accompany him?"

She brushed her hand across her stylish coiffure. "Oh, no. Geisha houses are primarily for the diversion of tired businessmen. Men are under much pressure in this country. Geishas provide relaxation, pleasant conversation and a little entertainment. A busy man does not expect this level of feminine companionship in his own home.''

"Amazing," Laura said.

"I do not begrudge visits now and then to the geisha houses. Geishas are skilled and accomplished in their arts. They are not sexual playthings. It's the bar girls who call themselves geishas who make wives unhappy.''

"Don't wives say anything?"

Mrs. Matsui pursed her lips. "A good wife takes charge of her home and family and makes no complaint.''

"Not American wives! They'd never stand for it. Are all Japanese wives so compliant?''

"This zipper has caught some of the material," Mrs. Matsui said. "I shall have to work carefully so as not to rip it. Do wives complain about bar girls?" she continued. "Yes, many speak out, especially women who have reached high places in government positions. But I can assure you these same ladies assume the age-old passive role when in their own homes with their husbands." She frowned and shook a finger. "Tradition," she said sternly as if the word held earthshaking power.

"But aren't times changing?" Laura insisted.

"Yes, gradually, especially among the young. General MacArthur gave women legal rights, to vote and to share in their husbands' property, but we still have a long way to go in becoming equal human beings." Mrs. Matsui untangled a bit more material from the zipper. "It's coming," she said. "Would that personal problems could be solved as easily. My own sorrow is that my husband and I never truly communicate. I am not his confidante nor even his good friend. But men need to communicate with women. That's why they seek their pleasure with geishas and bar girls.''

''In our country we have an expression that says, 'What's good for the goose is good for the gander.' What would happen if a woman sought out another man?''

Mrs. Matsui drew back, appalled. ''Oh, no. A husband would lose face.''

''Some equality,'' Laura said dryly.

''Ah, Laura-san, you must realize equality is relative. A Japanese man takes the support of his family seriously, so his job comes first. He must produce well and socialize frequently with members of his company.'' She wrinkled her nose slightly. ''It fosters company spirit, and if he stops off every night on his way home for a drink and a little 'diversion,' well, a man has human needs.''

''And doesn't a woman?'' Laura asked sharply.

''But it's not proper for a woman to admit them.''

''Count me out as ever becoming a good Japanese wife!''

''I know. You Americans have many times our divorce rate.''

''But how do women feel about their husbands seeking pleasure with these women?''

Mrs. Matsui stared off into the distance, her posture a study in resignation. ''When a woman is in love with her husband, she is heavyhearted.'' she said softly.

Laura ran the freed zipper its full length and back again. "Fine, and no damage, either," she said "*Arigato!* Thank you."

Arrangements were made for Seiji to stay with Kelly until Laura returned that evening, and after expressing appreciation for Mrs. Matsui's skillful help, she hurried home to bathe and get ready for the party. She ached for the pain her neighbor obviously suffered. Regardless of tradition, one truth emerged: a woman's heart reacted the same in Japan as anywhere else in the world.

In a subdued mood, she met Scott at the door a couple of hours later.

"You look lovely," he murmured as he helped her into her velvet evening jacket. He bent to kiss her lightly and she responded, feeling like Judas. Scott no doubt would consider the kiss encouraging. But she couldn't marry him now, could she? Yes, she could, and two dear people would be happy, Scott and Kelly. Living in Japan, it might be easier to adhere to the Japanese philosophy of marriage.

At the thought, something tightened around her lungs like a steel band restricting her breathing. Tonight after the party, no matter how late, she would talk to Scott. She would be honest.

"I'm surprised women are included," she said as they got into the waiting taxi.

"I'll have to say that it is rare, although it is arranged from time to time for foreigners. Understandably, geishas feel restricted by wives and tone down their acts."

"I admit I'm curious and a little confused about them."

"Most people are. Actually there is no other profession like it in the entire world. First you must realize that a geisha house is not a brothel, nor is a geisha a prostitute. Literally translated, geisha means 'talented person.' She is a highly skilled and trained entertainer and intellectual companion for men and is apprenticed as early as seven years old. Her house provides for her education, food and clothing until she is able to earn her own way. By that time she owes them thousands of dollars."

"I hear that bar girls sometimes call themselves geishas."

"Unfortunately that's been true since the Second World War. But real geishas occupy a respected position in Japanese life. The difference is clearly apparent."

The Gion district, where the party was to be held, was located in a dimly lit area of rows and rows of houses. Lanterns shone on decorative signs showing the name of each house. Scott translated as their taxi cruised slowly through the area. "Flaming Glory, Heavenly Blossom, Pleasure Garden, Sweet Pine Shadow...." The names sounded like labels on exotic perfumes.

"The parties are held here in one of these teahouses. The girls don't live here. Moreover, one doesn't just walk in off the street; it takes considerable arranging and is very expensive," Scott explained. "No doubt our host has excellent connections. We are being entertained by one of Kyoto's top geishas and in one of the finest houses."

The taxi stopped at the entrance of The Silver

Willow. The two-story structure had a distinctive air of its own, like an elderly dowager, well preserved, old-fashioned yet confident of her role in life.

Laura and Scott got out of the taxi and walked through the small garden to the entrance. They left their shoes at the door and followed a maid up a stairway to a spacious tatami room. A low table about eighteen inches high occupied the center. At one end of the room the inevitable alcove displayed a landscape scroll and a simple arrangement of dried grasses. Creamy lanterns bathed the guests in a tranquil setting. Occasionally, an elusive fragrance begged identification.

Scott introduced her to the host, Mr. Fukukita, who bowed and welcomed Scott warmly, but she considered his greeting to her quite remote, and she wondered if she should have invaded this distinctly male province, after all. Thank goodness for the two British couples, or she would have felt highly conspicuous. Guests were introduced to one another, then seated on the cushions the maids distributed around the table. Mr. Fukukita sat at the head. Laura saw no Mrs. Fukukita. Naturally. Good Japanese wives remained at home.

A chuckle from across the table lodged a sudden stone in her throat. Geoffrey? Why couldn't he have sat at the far end of the table? Fortunately, at the moment he was deep in conversation with Mr. Fukukita. Perhaps she would have time to gather her poise before he noticed or spoke to her. On the other hand, after their recent strained parting, perhaps he might choose to ignore her.

She began to engage Scott with breathless little freshets of conversation, anything that popped into her head, keeping her tone scintillating, her face glowing as she gave him her undivided attention. Scott responded as if he found every observation profound and exciting. Darling Scott, her guardian angel. Well, later tonight she must disillusion him. One didn't string along guardian angels.

As she considered the men in her life, she realized she had molded them into the family she didn't have. Scott, her dependable big brother; Neil, a carefree, unpredictable cousin; Kelly, her nephew but more like a little brother; and Geoffrey—the one man in the world with whom she shouldn't have fallen in love.

She stole a quick look at him. He still conversed cordially in Japanese with his host. It seemed obvious they were good friends. Geoffrey, a longtime resident of Kyoto and a man of importance, would be bound to have a wide acquaintance.

Laura moved uncomfortably on the cushion. She sat properly on her heels, as did the other guests, but in less than a minute she felt positive she would sprawl ignominiously, limbs askew, in front of all the guests. She saw that Geoffrey had observed her struggle to maintain her posture.

"*Komban-wa.* Good evening." His somber greeting included both her and Scott. "Sit with your legs crossed in front of you, Laura. Your host understands very well the inadequacy of Western muscles."

"*Komban-wa,*" Laura murmured, and with embarrassment rearranged her aching stiff legs to fit under the table and scooted close so her position was not so noticeable. She glanced at the English ladies, who stoically maintained a proper Japanese posture. Bully for them, Laura thought with both awe and envy.

"This *is* a surprise," Geoffrey said, addressing himself to her again. "I'm beginning to see what you meant by your busy schedule." His voice was as deep and composed as ever, but his hands were set before him in a bone-whitening clasp. Was he still angry and hurt over her apparent display of prejudice toward his marriage to a Japanese girl? If only he knew that her pain surpassed his in this case.

Laura tried to become engrossed in the food the maids now served and listened attentively as Scott explained each dish. Once she glanced briefly at Geoffrey, and he met her eyes coolly. The intimacy, the tenderness or whatever it was that once flared between them had vanished as if it had never existed.

Sliding doors parted, and two young girls, not a day over fourteen, entered with mincing steps. It was as if two exquisite dolls had suddenly become lifelike. Long wide sashes on salmon-colored kimonos, plus willow sprigs and silver pins in their hair, denoted them as *maikos*, or apprentices. They were followed by two geishas, probably in their early twenties, wearing the richest silk kimonos Laura had ever seen, sky blue at the shoulders deepening to a midnight blue at the hem, the entire garment embroidered exquisitely in cherry blossoms. The wide sashes, obis, were of rich brocade.

Their movements flowed from one position to another as in ballet, and although their whitened faces were masklike, their scarlet lips curved alluringly and their eyes held a provocative gleam. Laura realized she was as mesmerized as the men.

At once the *maikos* and geishas served sake and sweetmeats first to the men, of course, then to the three women. It was amusing to see how differently the girls behaved to each sex. Laura, the object of circumspect gestures and bows, felt both amused and irritated at being treated as if she were a venerable grandmother. But the geisha who served Geoffrey sat very close to him and from time to time allowed her hand to flutter tenderly against his as they chatted with animation in Japanese. Geoffrey clearly lapped up the devotion and laughed so frequently that Laura envied the girl's seeming wit and expertise. These girls were professionals in dealing with men in social situations. If only she could pick up a few clues on how to handle tonight's delicate session with Scott.

Once when Scott and Geoffrey laughed uproariously at something one of the girls said, Laura asked what was so amusing.

"The girls are very good at making puns and jokes. It's all part of the package," Scott explained.

"What did she say?"

"It wouldn't make much sense in translation. Anyway, it's pretty risqué. Remember it's all a game. Don't let the way these pretty dolls pamper us men bother you. They are never grossly sensuous. Eroticism never goes beyond a pat or a squeeze. Part of their skill is merely to suggest the romantic possibilities between men and women.''

There was magic here, all right, Laura admitted. The walls of the cozy room receded as she consumed the warm sake. Languor seeped through her limbs while she watched the geishas' dedicated ministrations and listened to their lilting conversations. Their laughter came frequently as they devoured every male pronouncement, and their expressions ranged from solemn adoration to coquetry. Only occasionally did their lips form a rosebud pout. Meanwhile their fans wafted a heavenly scent. No wonder a man yearned to experience such perfect femininity.

Laura watched the geisha who attended Geoffrey lean to gaze into his eyes with a pose that was positively worshipful. Then the girl's hand slid down his arm to linger on his hand in a gesture of sweet regret as she left him to devote her charms to one of the other guests. Geoffrey grinned at Laura for the first time that evening when he saw her watching the little tableau.

"So what do you think?" he asked.

She spread her arms to take in the room. "A dream world."

"But a carefully structured one," he said. "Everybody movement, every spoken word has been studied with the prime object to give pleasure. Each significant gaze has required hours of practice. Years of study prepares these girls to converse intelligently on almost any subject. The more artful the girl, the higher the price tag. The sole function here

is to give the illusion of devotion, perfect companionship and delight. Nothing more. As for me, I prefer
the genuine article,'' he said sotto voce, even though
the girls could not understand English.

Oh, sure, tell me all about it, Laura thought,
recalling the little scene she'd just witnessed. Nevertheless, she admitted a man would have to be made
of stone not to bask in such an atmosphere.

Later the geishas began a dignified slow-motion
dance accompanied by the *maikos* on flute and
samisen. There was nothing voluptuous or erotic.
The movements were deliberate and classical.

"Such gorgeous komonos!" Laura murmured to
Scott between dances.

"They cost several thousand dollars, and the girls
must pay for them out of their earnings. Still, these
girls can make more money in one evening than an
office girl makes in a month.''

What this party must be costing! "Where do the
girls live?''

"Some live in quarters like a sorority house with a
kind of housemother. A few live at home or in an
apartment like any working girl. They can be hired
singly or in groups as hostesses, entertainers or com-
panions for an evening such as at a play or concert,''
Scott whispered as the girls started to perform again.
This time they did the *Beisuboru Dansu*, a series of
comic gestures based on the baseball game, a sport as
popular in Japan as in the States. After more dancing
and some singing, the *maikos* and geishas bowed out
through the folding doors. Clearly the evening was
over.

Everyone expressed appreciation to Mr. Fukukita, and he departed first, as was the custom for hosts. Laura felt a strong sense of rejection when Geoffrey followed without a backward look in her direction. Scott took her arm and they walked out of the building while Laura tried not to feel let down.

"It's early," she said. "Could we go somewhere and talk for a while? I think we could use some coffee after all that sake." If she had only a portion of the geishas' expertise, perhaps she could cushion the difficult hour to come.

Scott squeezed her hand. "Would you believe you took that suggestion right out of my mouth? We do have things to say to each other, don't we?"

Outside Scott hailed a taxi and gave the directions to a coffeehouse. They left the curb and eased past a sleek shining car parked just ahead. It looked as if one of the blue-clad geishas sat with a man in the back seat. So the girl's evening wasn't over, after all. Perhaps a little more work as a scintillating, intellectual companion? Laura's eyes strained hard to penetrate the darkness. Mr. Fukukita? Or Geoffrey? The shadows held the secret.

At the coffeehouse Scott ordered and they drank leisurely, inhaling the fragrant aroma while they listened to a recorded pianist playing a Chopin nocturne. The plaintive, emotional music seemed to set the stage for her role in a poignant drama, except she couldn't remember her lines. She gripped her cup, searching for the words that would soften the impact of what she was about to say.

"Scott, darling?"

He reached over and took her hand between his two large ones, and his familiar crooked grin almost unnerved her. "Yes?" he said.

"About our getting married . . . ."

He patted her hand. "Everything is okay. You're upset about telling me, aren't you?" he said kindly. "Listen, my dear, I released you almost the same day I asked you. I realized at once what was happening between you and Geoffrey."

"I'm afraid that won't work out, either," she said.

The answer didn't startle him. "No? I predict otherwise. I've never seen two people more suited to each other."

Laura swallowed but couldn't speak.

"A marriage for us was never right for you and possibly not for me, either," he continued. "We should have talked earlier. It wasn't very gallant of me to put you through all this turmoil."

"Scott, dear, you're the most gallant man I've ever known. I do love you in a very special way. I guess the trouble is that I always considered you the big brother I always wanted."

"I like that," he said gently. "I never had a little sister, you know."

Laura's eyes filled. One of the reasons she adored Scott was his quality of absolute integrity. She hoped she hadn't added too much new hurt to the old disappointments he'd suffered. They talked quietly for a while until they both seemed to feel a climate of relief. Truth granted the serenity that now flowed between them. If only she could remember that.

Later he took her home, and she thanked him again for taking her to the exotic evening with the geishas. He squeezed her hand and kissed her lightly, his touch and his homely smile enveloping her in a sense of comfort and reassurance.

CHAPTER FIFTEEN

GEOFFREY CALLED MONDAY MORNING just as Kelly left for school to inform her she could have the week off. "There's nothing pressing. I see you're all caught up. When my novel is ready, I'll give you a ring. With your hectic schedule, I imagine you can use the time." Did she detect a note of sarcasm?

"Thank you," she said coolly, and hoped the mindless quivering that went on inside her couldn't be heard over the phone. "Don't call me; I'll call you," his message implied. Did that mean he was easing her out of her job? The thought plunged her into despair.

The impact of the geisha party had lingered during the days that followed. On the surface it appeared to have been a lighthearted evening attended by four beautiful and carefully schooled girls. But extensive dynamics surged beneath such occasions. The whole focal point was man's relationship to woman, his attitude toward her as a human being. Clearly a Japanese man desired a woman's companionship. How sad that he couldn't find it with his wife. But tradition stated that man must separate home life from human needs. But if Mrs. Matsui was right, Japanese wives secretly longed to replace the hours a husband spent with these special women outside the home.

In Japan, man's promiscuity was considered natural, not immoral or sinful. This fact was made abundantly clear to Laura when she learned that a bride traditionally wears a wide headband to hide her horns of jealousy, a potent reminder that she must not expect fidelity from her husband or grow jealous when he eventually becomes unfaithful to her. No wonder Sachiko found it difficult to follow the tradition after several years abroad, where she absorbed a totally opposite philosophy.

Unused to free mornings now that she didn't go to Geoffrey's, Laura caught up on housekeeping chores and tried not to think about him. Did he punish her because he was still angry or hurt? She walked around watering the plants. "At least sentimentality isn't your problem," she said to the club-like cereus.

The morning seemed endless. She made a batch of fruit bars and set aside half of them for the Matsuis, then got out her writing materials and tossed off half a dozen haiku, all dealing with the arrogance of men. When she finished, she wadded them up and threw them into the wastebasket. Concentration didn't come easily today. A recurring thought that she'd kept pushing to the back of her mind finally demanded her attention.

Didn't she have a right to love the person of her choice? Her sister had been young and headstrong during that long-ago interlude. Perhaps Lisa should have shared some of the blame in the affair. But

Laura had no more than salved her conscience than came back again to haunt her.

When the telephone rang, she leaped to answer. It was Neil. She hadn't heard from him in ages.

"Lucky me to catch you home! I stayed all night at Geoff's, and when I saw you weren't working today, I thought I'd give you a ring. How do you feel about Kabuki?"

"I haven't seen it yet, Neil."

"Believe me, you'll love it. It's playing at the Mikamiza Theater this morning. What do you say?"

"This morning? I'd love it." Yes, she would. Maybe an hour or two in Neil's upbeat company would be a tonic for her doldrums.

"It starts at eleven and goes on for several hours. See you soon." His pleasure crackled over the wires.

Neil couldn't have provided a more timely diversion. She quickly changed to her ginger suit and added a flowered scarf. Neil arrived a half hour later lugging a large crate.

"Mind if I leave this here?"

"Antiques? Are they valuable?" She didn't feel comfortable about storing such expensive goods.

"You'd better believe it. A buyer is coming from Nagoya to meet me in Kyoto in a few days. My car is filled to capacity." He looked around the small apartment. "Maybe we ought to put it in a closet. I mean, the boy, well, you know kids, a little roughhouse now and then."

"Our closets are brimming, but you needn't be concerned about Kelly."

He shoved it in a corner. "Keep it quiet. I'd just as

soon word didn't get around. Some valuable ceramics in there.'' He took in her concerned look. ''Don't worry, I'm not planning on turning you into a storage outfit. I'd have left it at Geoff's, but I just picked it up a few minutes ago.'' The large crate diminished the apartment by its size. Well, it would only be for a few days.

When she got into his Nissan a few minutes later, she saw what he meant. The back was piled with cartons and boxes. But the exterior was clean and shining, and she noticed that Neil followed the Japanese habit of keeping a feather duster in his car. No wonder all the automobiles here were so spotless.

''You look very businesslike this morning,'' she said, eyeing his neat dark suit, white shirt and dark tie.

He smirked. ''We adults have to jump out of the same mold over here. The nail that sticks up its head gets pounded.'' His tone held an unaccustomed sarcastic edge. Had he and Geoffrey got into an argument that morning?

''Tell me about Kabuki. I've heard the actors are all men, some dressed as women.''

He brightened. ''True, and some are world famous for their female impersonations. It's superlative theater. They invented the turntable stage long before anyone else ever thought of it, and they can provide anything from a typhoon to an earthquake and fire right before your eyes.''

They found a place to park and after taking care of the admission hurried inside barely in time to find their places in a first-floor box. Lanterns glowed softly all around. Suddenly the sharp beat of the *hyoshigi* sticks cut the air like pistol shots.

The audience grew quiet, lights dimmed and a black-green-and-vermilion curtain parted. Laura was projected into the most dynamic sights and sounds she had ever experienced in drama. Onstage, chalk-faced actors pranced larger than life with masterfully controlled body movements, trailing ten-foot silken trains in ravishing colors.

Fairly visible black-clad prop men manipulated everything from dancing fireflies to prowling animals. The musicians, also onstage, performed quavery, tuneless music on flute, samisen, koto and drum while the voices of the chorus alternated between bansheelike wails and swallowed syllables. Excitement intensified whenever an actor whipped himself into a frenzy to ever faster beats of the *hyoshigi*. His eyes seemed to widen and cross, his teeth gnashed furiously and his head gyrated as if it was almost independent of his body. Then abruptly all sound ceased, and the actor froze in a stunning tableau.

To Laura's surprise, Kabuki proved to be a variety show including a one-act play, several dances and an extract from a classical drama. Lengthy intermissions became a time for socializing and partaking of refreshments from one of the restaurants or bars in the theater.

"I adored it!" Laura cried a full four hours later, when they left.

"Ripsnorting theater," Neil agreed.

At her apartment she asked him up for coffee, and again he thanked her for storing his antiques. "Anything I can do for you in return? Fix a leaky faucet? Oil a squeaky door? I'm not a bad handyman."

"Not a thing." Except he might fill in another piece of Geoffrey's background. She decided to inquire before she lost courage. "By the way, Neil, I've been intending to ask since you remarked that you and Geoffrey grew up in Ohio, did you ever hear Geoffrey mention a girl he met at Inglewood College? I used to know someone who went there who said she dated a Major McDermott a number of years ago."

Neil leaned back in his chair and frowned as if trying to recollect. "God, I don't remember. Geoff really went for all those sorority chicks."

"Sorority chicks?" She almost choked on the words. "Do you recall any particular one?"

"Hell, no. Why don't you ask him?" He looked at her with sudden interest. "Hey, don't tell me some girl is still holding a torch for old Geoff after all these years?"

"I doubt it. Just wondered. It would be quite a coincidence, wouldn't it?"

"You better believe it!"

Kelly arrived home from school then, and Neil said he had to get on with his deliveries. She was grateful for Kelly's chatter, something about baseball scores, to cover her agitation over this last bit of information.

Sorority chicks. Lisa had met Geoffrey at a college sorority dance. If Neil's memory was correct, he'd just handed out one more piece of evidence that pointed to Geoffrey. One would have thought she would be used to these bits and pieces by now, that they wouldn't even faze her. Instead, she felt as if she were headed down a mountain precipice like a snowball gathering layers of hurtful debris. Would it all end in one final, shattering collision?

AGAIN, ANOTHER DAY OF LEISURE intimidated Laura, since she felt compelled to fill it with worthwhile activity. Clear skies had taken a leave of absence, too, turning gray and misty, reflecting her mood to perfection.

She took out her overstuffed mending basket and patched the knee on a pair of Kelly's jeans. Listlessly she sewed a button on a blouse and listened to the negative sounds that accompanied her task. Someone across the way practiced the koto, always the same piece, always the same mistake. A passing taxi driver leaned on his horn endlessly, and a neighbor banged open a sliding door, dragged out a futon to hang over the balcony to air, then pounded it as if it had given serious offense.

Ordinarily she didn't even notice such commonplace noises, but today she felt edgy and vulnerable. *Get out of the house; go for a walk; do something to settle your jittery nerves.* Perhaps, finally, it was time to vist the Moss Gardens. Rain or mist was the time to view them, Geoffrey had said. Now they loomed as an anodyne to her dark mood.

She put on raincoat and boots, wound her hair into a knot and tucked it under a floppy rain hat that drooped to curtain her face.

On the way downstairs she stopped at the Matsuis with a plate of the fruit bars she'd baked yesterday.

"*Arigato*. Such a treat!" The discerning Mrs. Matsui no doubt noticed the lateness of the hour as well as Laura's wan expression.

"I'm not working today. I'm having a little vacation," Laura explained in answer to the question Mrs. Matsui was too polite to ask. Would she soon have to admit she'd lost her job for good? "I thought I'd go to see the Moss Gardens."

"A perfect time to view them, and a fine place to get to know oneself," Mrs. Matsui said. One could never fool Mrs. Matsui for a moment.

Laura hailed a taxi and soon reached her destination. The gardens were deserted today except for a priest in his bell-shaped garment and parasollike hat. He was standing in an attitude of meditation, so motionless he might have been a stone lantern.

Laura walked along a path that meandered among dripping trees, glossy rocks and around a pool. Shades of velvet green moss, sparkling with droplets, covered the grounds. A flat rock slab overlooking the pond offered a spot for contemplation. She sat down, drew up her knees and clasped her arms around them. Just below a crane stood still in shallow water.

Gardens in Japan were resolutely structured to look unstructured, Geoffrey had told her. The Japanese viewed them as "happenings" where one could reflect on life as it interwove the changing seasons.

She watched a red leaf fall into the pond, curl and glide away into the mist, celebrating the completion of its cycle, true to itself to the end. Could she remain true to herself? Was it possible for her to parent Kelly with wisdom? To be loyal to Lisa and at the same time be hopelessly in love with Geoffrey? What if his call never came asking her to return to work? The thought turned her despairing. In a garden one looked to nature for answers, but here she found none.

A rustle startled her, and she realized someone had sat down beside her.

"Ah, a little wood nymph," a male voice said. "I hoped I might run into one."

Laura kept her chin on her knees. Her hat brim drooped effectively to screen out intruders, but she didn't have to move her head to recognize this one.

"I can't believe this. Don't tell me you just *happened* to come here today?"

"I'm afraid I can't own to any ESP. Mrs. Matsui was a veritable wealth of information when I stopped by. I'm glad you finally got around to a visit."

She shrugged. "I decided I'd better see it before someone turns it into a conglomerate of apartment houses."

"Never. The country would rise up in arms to prevent it. This is one of the oldest gardens in Kyoto, designed in the fourteenth century. So how have you been?" he asked as if it had been months instead of a few days since he'd seen her.

"Okay."

"Good. I hoped you wouldn't be all mean and moody. Did you enjoy the geisha party?"

"Yes. Charming and enlightening. And you?"

He lifted one shoulder as if to indicate the trivial nature of the occasion. "A mirage. Pure fantasy."

She peered out from under her hat to take in his eminently satisfied expression. "Baloney!" she said.

"That's a rather harsh evaluation."

"It's true, though. You lapped up every minute of it."

He grinned. "Yes, I did, but there were some mitigating factors. Think about it. Consider the beleaguered writer, worn to a frazzle, at cross-purposes with a certain lovely lady, bereft of female companionship. Surely you wouldn't begrudge him a therapeutic evening?"

"You're eating my heart out!"

He nodded sadly. "The standard hardhearted female reaction—and would you mind coming out from under that atrocious hat? I feel as if I'm trying to carry on a conversation with a broken umbrella."

She folded back the brim from her face, and he smiled his appreciation. She adored him when he acted like this. It made her feel safe and natural, and his lighthearted banter dissolved the restraint that was becoming second nature to them. Would this be the right time to say something that needed saying? The wrong word now could turn into another gate banging closed between them.

"I believe it was Lady Menderall who said the best time for an apology is as soon after the fact as possible," she said carefully.

He looked up sharply. "Lady Menderall? Who's she?"

"Actually, I made her up. What I'm trying to do is to apologize for what I allowed you to believe concerning your wife, Midori. Our conversation that day happened to touch off bitter memories that upset me. My reaction had nothing to do with prejudice, please believe me,'' she said all in one breath, wanting him to understand at once so there'd be no need for long explanations.

Geoffrey nodded. "I said to myself after you left, 'Everything I know about this woman doesn't add up to her reaction. Therefore, I'll trust what I know.'"

She closed her eyes to hide her sudden tears. If only she could do the same. "I want to be truthful, Geoffrey, but the truth takes time."

Geoffrey answered with a smile that somehow still managed to look somber. "You're forgiven," he said.

There was an undercurrent going on here that she didn't want to dissect or analyze now. They were skating on thin ice. Much better to keep matters light.

"Good," she said, relieved. "So you won't have to rave and rant a lot or give me one of your hundred-dollar lectures."

"I charge a lot more than that. Besides, you know I'm unfailingly cool and collected."

"Oh, sure, like a roaring lion. I can even see your muscles ripple when you go into one of your diatribes."

He pulled a long face. "You really know how to hurt a guy, don't you?"

She tapped her watch. "Hadn't you better get back to your typewriter? I happen to know that you have some important deadlines."

"Impossible. I can't work when I'm full of green monsters."

"You? Never!"

"I mean it. Watching you batting those long lashes of yours at Scott all evening just about drove me up the wall."

"Ha! You were so busy holding hands with the geishas, how could you notice?"

"I noticed. Have you told Scott yet that you aren't going to marry him?"

"We'd both come to the conclusion it wouldn't work, Geoffrey."

He held her chin so that she had to meet his eyes. "Say it. Say you're not going to marry Scott!" He wasn't teasing now.

"I'm not going to marry Scott Burton," she repeated firmly.

He dropped his hand and gave her a searching look. "And while we're at it, what's all this business with my cousin? You've kept that mighty secret."

"Your cousin? What on earth are you talking about?"

"Neil, Neil Anderson. I heard him call you from my place with the invitation to Kabuki."

His cousin! No wonder she'd felt something vaguely familiar about Neil. "I had no idea you were related. I wonder why he didn't mention it?"

Geoffrey frowned. "He's not the most stable character."

"I've only seen him a few times, but he's always been perfectly charming."

"That's what they all say, and he is most of the

time. Unfortunately, he's an on-again, off-again alcoholic, and I have the feeling he's been hitting the bottle again recently.''

"I've never seen him anything but sober."

"I suppose you met him at my place one time when he stopped by?"

"Yes, you were out of town."

"Well, I'm not happy about it. My advice is to keep away from him."

What was it with Geoffrey? Was he jealous of his cousin?

"Would you care to know anything else about my social life? Shall I send my calendar to you for approval?"

"Good idea. And one more thing, who was that good-looking Japanese fellow you were carousing around with on a motorcycle when you were supposed to be so all-fired busy?"

She stared, disbelieving. "Do you realize you could have hired yourself out during the Spanish Inquisition? I think I'll let you sweat that one out. Since you're doing your darnedest to turn me into a femme fatale, I'd better maintain a little evidence."

"I'm serious. There's someone in your life who's done a magnificent job of confusing you. A man, no doubt. Were you ever married? Engaged?"

"Engaged, but I don't care to discuss it. I don't pry into your private life. I'm not asking about Marcia, Midori and most likely Alice, Linda, Rachel, Lois and Mehitabel."

"Mehitabel!"

"She was probably one of the girls you forgot.

After all, when a man has a fan club that stretches from Ohio to Tokyo, he's bound to forget a few.''

"Good Lord! Where did you get that information?"

She lifted her chin. "I have my sources."

"Well, they're completely inaccurate."

"I wonder."

He sat for a long time, silent as the crane that still remained motionless in the water. "Trust," he said at last. "It's a way of loving, isn't it?"

"You and I don't qualify. Right?" She lapsed into a bleak silence.

"I have a plan," he said after a few moments. "It's called 'Retroactive Cancellation.' You accept me, I accept you. We forget the past and ignore all misunderstandings. How's that for plan A?"

"And plan B?"

"Just this," he said, and swooped her up into his arms. She stiffened but made no actual movement to resist. The garden seemed caught in a breathless hush with only the sound of dripping trees faint in the background.

Her heart began to pound, and it suddenly seemed that her entire body had turned into one aching pulse. She wound her arms around his neck and lifted her lips to meet his.

His cheek was wet and cool with mist, but his kiss was warm, possessive, sweet and totally satisfying. He filled her ears with endearments and turned her light-headed. She wanted to lean back on the mossy rock, open her arms, her lips, all of her to him. She returned his kisses, responding instinctively. She couldn't hold back if she had wanted to. Call it intoxication, mindlessness, whatever, she couldn't hide her love from him when he touched her. At last they drew apart, breathless, his eyes still devouring her.

"Really," she said, straightening her coat, then pointing to the crane, which had now ducked its head. "Is that any way to behave in front of that poor innocent bird?"

"Come on," he said. "I'll take you to lunch. If we stay any longer that bird might become over-educated. Besides, this moss has a tendency to cover everything. I'm not partial to green-faced girls."

"I'm already blue with cold. Let's hurry. I'm starved."

So he took her to lunch where they had a private room, and they chatted as if they'd just met and wanted to learn every exciting thing about each other. She felt dreamily anesthetized and hoped the magic would never end.

He took her home in time for Kelly's arrival from school, and she spent the rest of the day wondering if the meeting in the gardens held any significance or if it had been one of a kind, filled with dreams, mist and illusion. The latter, she suspected. After all, Geoffrey hadn't once mentioned a date to return to work for him.

That evening as she took the bus to meet her classes at Burton-Kubo, she considered the past two days, the exotic Kabuki, the sour note introduced by Neil, the idyllic afternoon with Geoffrey in the misty gardens, at times whimsical, yet something much deeper, too. What a complex man he was. Continual-

ly she felt the urge to understand him more fully. But
that was part of what love was all about, wasn't it? A
commitment to one's best understanding.

Abruptly she turned her mind to the evening
ahead. A week ago Scott had asked her to give a demonstration, using her own classes, for a delegation
of visiting English-language teachers. The demonstration had to be moved into a larger room to make
room for the visitors, but by the time she'd arrived,
several of her students had the room set up and
ready. Her classes seemed inordinately proud at being selected, and she knew they'd respond well.

She'd perfected her lesson plans several days ago,
but she hadn't mentioned any part of her procedure;
she wanted the lessons to be completely spontaneous.
Part of the activities would involve the observers in
an impromptu skit where they would act as imaginary applicants for various business firms while
certain students would interview them for prospective jobs. She would also show special techniques for
teaching the parts of speech and ways to learn vo-
cabulary. She'd learned long ago that involving the
onlooker was a surefire way to engage his or her enthusiasm.

Scott praised her work continuously, almost to the
point of embarrassment. He offered her the director-
ship of the Kyoto School when he moved to Nara,
but she refused. Having observed Scott, she realized
the job entailed long hours as well as a lot of
meetings and travel. She had precious little time with
Kelly now. A director's job would eliminate a lot of
that. Maybe sometime in the future. At the moment

she adored teaching, and she felt certain she wouldn't find the same satisfactions in an executive position as she did in the classroom. However, she had not a doubt in the world that she could handle it. Then she wondered how much of the decision was influenced by the fact she'd have to give up her job with Geoffrey.

Scott had been in Nara for several days but promised to return in time for that evening's demonstration, to brief the visitors and make introductions. However, he had not yet arrived. It wasn't like him not to keep his word. Something unusual must have happened to detain him.

At the appointed time when he still had not come, Laura gave the greetings and spoke briefly of her philosophy of teaching languages, then plunged into her presentation. As always, she became so caught up in the learning process in action, she forgot everything else. At the evening's close, she accepted the enthusiastic accolades of the delegation and headed for the office to check out. She wanted to get home quickly. It had been a long day.

She stopped cold at the secretary's ashen face. The woman spoke something on the telephone and with a shaking hand replaced the receiver in its cradle. She met Laura's questioning glance, then bowed her head in her hands. "Scott is missing," she said, her voice breaking. "He was last seen rescuing some children from a burning building in Nara."

CHAPTER SIXTEEN

"MISSING!" LAURA MARSHALED all her defenses against shock and disbelief. "Didn't anyone see what happened to him?"

"No one has seen him since the building collapsed in flames."

"Oh, no," Laura moaned. "The children, were they found?"

"Yes, but they were toddlers, too young to communicate."

How like Scott, selfless as always. "There must be someone we can call, something we can do!"

The secretary began to cry. Laura walked over to the counter phone and dialed Geoffrey's number. She drew a relieved breath when he answered. In terse sentences she broke the news.

"My God! How awful! Are you all right?" he cried.

"Just tell me what to do, Geoffrey. You know how inadequate my Japanese is. Does Kyoto have a bureau of missing persons?"

"Does anyone know whether he escaped the burning building? What a ghastly thing to happen! Listen, sit tight. I'll check with the chief of police in Nara—I know him. Then I'll start calling all the hospitals. We may locate him yet. There's always a lot of confusion around a fire. Chin up. I haven't acted very decently about you two, but it was only because I was so damn jealous. Go on home. I'll call you the minute I find out something.''

Geoffrey, her rock in a crisis. The minute she arrived at the apartment, she camped by the telephone as if Geoffrey could miraculously track down Scott in less than twenty minutes. But it was near midnight before he got in touch. The solemnity of his tone sent her spirits plunging.

''Tell me.''

''City Hospital. Intensive care. He was identified only a short while ago. An ambulance brought him, but he didn't have his wallet or other identification.''

''Thank God you found him. How is he?''

''Badly burned.''

She felt drained and weak, barely able to hold on to the phone.

''Laura, are you there?'' His concern leaped over the distance.

''Yes, I'm just trying to absorb the implications.''

''I understand. Remember, Scott's a strong, healthy guy. He has that going for him.''

''What about the language school?''

''I promised Mr. Kubo I'd fill in until the new Kyoto appointee arrives next week. I'll keep in touch. Get some rest now.''

The more she tried to turn Geoffrey into a Svengali, the more he proved himself peerless. The tug-of-war between her emotions and her loyalty to Lisa had been like a knotted fist inside her. Why did she allow doubts to diminish every positive action? In any emergency he proved strong and helpful. Only a small, mean mind would accuse Geoffrey of being so concerned about his own adventures and misadventures that he could not be concerned or caring about the lives of others. Particularly friends. ''Trust me,'' Geoffrey had begged. Couldn't she do any better than this?

KELLY HAD REMAINED HOME from school for a couple of days with a mild case of the flu, but he returned that morning, his usual sunny self. Mornings proved long in the cold little apartment. Laura had wakened with a headache and she didn't look forward to another lonely day.

Now she knew how happy she'd been working in Geoffrey's beautiful library while he pounded away upstairs on his beat-up old portable. They were a good team. Their minds seemed to compliment each other. Even Geoffrey had said so.

She wanted to get back into his life. She needed the satisfaction she received from working with him. She hungered for the emotions he aroused when he touched her, to see the light leap in his eyes when he kissed her.

He'd called every day to give her the latest bulletins on Scott's progress. After a little small talk, the conversation ended too quickly. How unreachable he seemed. But even everyone at school seemed to be emotionally inaccessible as long as Scott hovered between life and death.

Then that morning as she drank her third cup of

coffee, Geoffrey telephoned with the news that Scott was out of intensive care and had made significant improvement. Relief washed over her.

"Thank God!" she said fervently.

"Amen," he replied. It sounded as if he were going to hang up, and she grew panicky.

"Geoffrey, listen. Scott's tragedy has been devastating, but there isn't anything wrong with me, and I feel as if I have a bad case of cabin fever. Work would be therapeutic. Say it out straight, do you or don't you want me to come back to work? I can't stand being in limbo."

"Oh, you can't?"

He paused, the silence full of possible meanings. *Now you know what you've been putting me through*—was that what he meant? But perhaps it was only her guilty conscience.

"Are you certain?" There was no mistaking his eagerness. "Believe me, I need you. I hated to ask, what with all the worry about Scott, and I knew that Kelly had been sick."

"Oh, thank you, thank you!" she cried in a rush of exuberance, and didn't care if she overwhelmed him with it.

"Hey, maybe we both need a change of pace. I finished my stint at Burton-Kubo. The new director has arrived. How about a little break before we get back to our desks? I'm free until noon, then I have to be back at my place for an important call from my newspaper editor. All calls from newspaper editors are earthshaking," he said dryly. "Most likely he wants a column or two on that dissident scientist who's making such a ruckus at some of the universities. I used to know him. The editor will want the columns yesterday, naturally. I'll pick you up as soon as I can get there." He sounded as elated as she felt.

Quickly she changed into the blue suit Geoffrey admired, even though it was more appropriate to spring than to autumn. She checked her appearance in the mirror and noted she looked a bit pale. Drat the headache. Of all times when she wanted to feel her best! She dabbed a little color on her cheeks and swallowed a couple of aspirins. By the time Geoffrey arrived, she felt more than equal to the occasion.

He looked as if he might have just stepped out of the shower, skin glowing and hair curling damply. She felt a stirring in her body at his presence, so engaging yet so enigmatic.

In minutes they joined the traffic headed for the heart of the city. The day matched Geoffrey's mood; dazzling sunlight spread its brilliance over bustling crowds, enveloping them with its warmth, drawing out lethargy and sending them racing. The excitement of the impromptu decision deepened Laura's appreciation of the man beside her, and she was afraid to speak, thinking her voice might give her away or she might somehow disturb the marvel of the day.

"Have you chosen our destination?" she asked finally.

"Why not let the car decide? Might prove interesting."

"Unusually easy today, aren't you?"

He gave her a sly glance that seemed to acknowledge their mutual anticipation. "And you're unusually beautiful." He reached over and gave her a quick kiss on the cheek. "I've wanted to do that for the last fifteen minutes. Have you any idea what you do to me?"

She found it difficult to swallow. "Let's not pursue it, at least not right now in front of the Daimaru Department Store."

He grinned. "Bad timing. Okay, then, let me hold your hand and fantasize."

A while later they passed the railway station and Geoffrey pointed out the immense wooden pagoda of the Toji, East Temple, and coasted into a parking spot.

"This is the Kyoto Flea Market. You've probably never seen one quite like it. Let's have a look."

They got out of the car and walked toward the vast complex, which Geoffrey said was held only on the twenty-first of each month. The place stretched for acres, most of the booths protected by a framework of bamboo or canvas awnings.

It was a beehive of activity with sights and sounds vigorously vying for attention. Stalls were jammed one beside the other displaying everything from singing crickets in tiny cages, baby chicks, live crabs, clothing old and new, to hardware, pottery and food of every description. Was there anything under the sun one couldn't find here? At times the noise was deafening as vendors competed, crying out their wares. Laura and Geoffrey joined a crowd that gathered around a frantic auctioneer.

"The process is different here," Geoffrey said. "It starts with one item. If that doesn't sell, the auctioneer doesn't lower the price. Watch."

"What a charming little teapot!" Laura cried as the man offered a tiny blue-and-white pot for only a thousand yen. No one bought it, so he quickly placed two on the table, offering both for the price of one. To Laura's surprise, no one snapped up this bargain, and the man went through a paroxysm of suffering as he now set out three pots for the same price. His anguish proved excruciating.

"I can't bear it," Laura whispered.

"Just part of the act," Geoffrey said, and when the auctioneer placed five teapots on the table, all for only one thousand yen, Geoffrey stepped forward and bought them. The man wrapped them in newspaper, and Geoffrey presented them to her with a flourish.

Laura laughed gleefully. "What on earth will I do with five teapots?"

"Hang on to them. We may have five children someday."

For a moment she closed her eyes to visualize an infant with dark curly hair and a deep dimple in its cheek exactly like Geoffrey's. Then the face faded into Kelly's. A spasm of dizziness suddenly overtook her, and she swayed, almost losing her balance.

He caught her arm. "Anything the matter? You look pale."

"No, nothing. Just a headache." She forced a nonchalant smile.

Concerned, he led her to a bench. "Rest here. I'll

get you a cup of hot tea, and how about a snack? Have you tried a *bento* yet? It's a staple feature of daily life here.''

A few yards away a vendor hawked a stack of the snacks, which could be compared to box lunches. Geoffrey purchased a couple and handed her one. "Too early for lunch so I got small ones." They were flat boxes made of thin wood and attractively wrapped in flowered paper.

"Oh, no!" Geoffrey cried as he opened his. "I should have checked. I got *hinomaru bentos* by mistake. Well, you might as well become initiated." He indicated a little carton of rice with a red plum in the center. "That represents the Japanese flag, but treat the plum with respect. It will eat the enamel right off your teeth."

Laura tasted it and almost strangled. It was the bitterest fruit she had ever sampled. How could anyone eat it?

"Some people believe if you hold the plum against your temple, it will cure headaches."

Probably bores a hole right through to the brain, Laura thought. The rest of the food was tasty, a tidbit of sausage and a sweet seaweed dessert called *mitsu mame*, but she was unable to finish it. Something had happened to her appetite.

Geoffrey looked for a bin to deposit the empty boxes. By the clutter in the area, it appeared the *bentos* caused a major litter problem.

"How's the headache?"

"Okay," she said brightly, determined to continue their morning together if it killed her.

Once she picked up a *kokeshi* doll and examined the workmanship, her head pounding like a bass drum. He bought it for her, and she thanked him solemnly.

"Why so serious, my girl? It's only a very small present." He bent down and kissed the tip of her nose hoping for a smile in exchange. Involuntarily, she drew away. If she were coming down with Kelly's flu bug, she didn't want to pass it on to Geoffrey. But he misinterpreted her action and stiffened. "Why do you run away from me every time I get close to you?" he'd asked her often. She cursed all viruses, plus headaches in particular, while observing his obdurate expression.

"I didn't mean that the way it seemed, Geoffrey. I have a feeling I'm contagious with something, and I don't want you to get it." Did he believe her?

He glanced at her sharply. "We'd better get you home, then. Anyway, it's almost time for me to get back for that phone call." The morning that had started with such promise now wilted completely. She'd try to make sense of it later. Now she ached all over. All she could think about was crawling into bed.

As he walked her up the steps, she stumbled. He swung her easily into his arms and carried her up into her apartment. She rested her head against his shoulder. She could absorb the comfort it brought her without his knowing, couldn't she? Before he set her down on the sofa, he laid his cheek against hers, then quickly withdrew it. Was he trying to give her a taste of her own actions? Well, even in so small a way he succeeded.

"Good Lord, girl, you have a fever, all right. I should have brought you home earlier. Do you have to wait until you fall on your face before you complain?"

"I guess it's the flu. I didn't think it could hit so quickly."

He settled her on the couch, went to the bathroom to rummage in a cabinet and returned immediately with a glass of water and a couple of aspirins. He found a blanket and covered her, then looked down at her anxiously. "Don't get up. I'll come back as soon as I go home and take that call." She felt Geoffrey slip a pillow under her head and rest his hand gently for a moment on her forehead, then heard him leave.

The time passed unevenly and sometimes she sank into oblivion. She woke once shaking uncontrollably, so chilled she wondered if she would freeze, but before she could summon the effort to find another blanket, she was seized with such intense heat she cried out for water. What had happened to her inner thermostat? Vaguely she was aware of Kelly and Geoffrey, but it was more as if she were in another world observing them from afar.

Eventually she drifted into a troubled sleep, dreaming she'd been swept into an icy sea, clinging with desperation to a lifeboat. Geoffrey kept swimming nearby, but in the dark night he couldn't find her. "Geoffrey!" she screamed over and over, her throat so parched she knew he'd never hear her. Still she forced his name in a rasping whisper, but it was too late. The dark sea had claimed him.

A firm shake on her shoulder roused her. "Laura, wake up! What's the matter?" With effort she opened her eyes. Geoffrey's concerned face loomed above as his hands steadied her until she stopped trembling. She tried to reconcile the angry black waves with her rumpled blankets and sheet. How had she gotten into her nightgown and into her futon?

She drew a hand across her eyes. "Sorry, dreadful dream. I thought you were drowning, Geoffrey." He reached for her hand.

"I'm right here, darling."

Kelly stook looking down at her, too, his face drawn in alarm. "Golly, Laura, you really scared us."

"Just a nightmare. I'm okay."

" 'Okay,' she says. Burning up with fever, head banging her out of her senses, and she's 'okay.' "

She gave them a weak smile. "I do feel better, honest. Would someone bring me a drink of water? About a gallon would do. And what time is it?"

"Saturday morning, eightish." Geoffrey said.

"Saturday! What happened to Friday?"

Geoffrey felt her forehead. "Fever's gone, I'm certain. What happened, indeed?"

"But my classes?" She sat up in alarm.

"The world won't come to an end because you missed one class. Don't worry. Kelly and I took care of things. Do you feel like breakfast?"

"Yes, I do. I'm starved."

"Good. My partner and I will tend to it immediately—that is, if we can fight our way through all those houseplants. What goes? Are you running a nursery on the side?''

"Oh, we're tending them for a neighbor who's out of town," Kelly said. "Laura gave them all names and talks to them. Boy, are they growing!''

"Well, I guess. It's like trying to navigate a rain forest.''

Laura laughed. "I suppose I should have warned you about my green thumb.''

"I'll make the coffee and fry the bacon," Kelly said, and took off to do so.

"And I'm running you a bath, my girl. I've no intention of dining with such a sorry sight.''

Laura passed an arm across her damp forehead and tangled hair. "You're not exactly an example of sartorial splendor yourself," she said, noting his clothes were rumpled and he needed a shave. On the other hand, as a knight in shining armor he'd do very nicely.

He ran the bathwater and came back to help her out of the futon. She gasped at the chill. "Who got me into my nightgown and into my futon, I'd like to know?''

"Unfortunately, I missed that opportunity. Mrs. Matsui was very accommodating. But I'll be delighted to help you out of it.''

"I'm competent. Just hand me my kimono.''

He leaned over and kissed her bare shoulder and held her close for a delicious instant before he gave her the garment. She managed to walk fairly steadily into the bathroom. He watched to see that she made it, then went to join Kelly in the kitchen.

After soaping and rinsing, she settled into the hot tub of water, relishing the cleansing sensation. She washed and dried her hair and put on her heavy winter kimono, a *dotera*, meanwhile inhaling the fragrance of percolating coffee and frying bacon. She listened lovingly to the sound of Geoffrey's and Kelly's chatter over the clatter of pans and dishes. Fresh and ready at last, she looked forward to joining her two men for breakfast. She felt a catch in her throat at the homey, family situation. She would cherish this experience.

Although she felt weak, she recuperated rapidly, reveling all day in the tenderness and concern Geoffrey and Kelly showed her. Contrary to her fragile appearance, she had always been unusually healthy. Without a father for the past ten years, she'd never been exposed to this kind of caring from any man, much less her self-centered fiancé, Bill. Kelly's and Geoffrey's devotion touched her deeply. She felt a richness that was hard to explain.

The entire day brought comfort as well as ultimate soul-searching. After breakfast she lay on the couch and watched Geoffrey and Kelly clean up the kitchen. Then Kelly got out a backgammon board and the two bent earnestly over it, heads almost touching, the contours of their profiles heartbreakingly similar, and always that unruly lock across their foreheads.

Their faces, highlighted by a lamp against a darker background, could have been a portrait by Rembrandt. *Father and Son,* she thought, and her vision blurred. Was there some malicious spirit in her life that kept the precious things just beyond reach? The

backgammon game over, Kelly went to play soccer
with some of his friends, and Geoffrey sat down at
his portable typewriter.

*A man stood by the woman he loved both in sick-
ness and in health,* the traditional wedding vow or-
dained. Well, she could not have asked for greater
commitment. She tenderly watched Geoffrey now engrossed in his work. He hadn't asked her to marry
him, at least not in plain words. "We may have five
children someday," he'd said playfully when he
bought the teapots at the auction. Still, didn't his actions during her illness say he cared for her enough to
marry?

*Oh, Lisa, I want to marry him. Can you forgive me
for falling in love with the man who hurt you so
deeply? Can't you see how he's changed? Nothing
you told me about that unfaithful young man mat-
ches what I know about this one. He adores his son,
Lisa. Surely it's wrong to keep them apart.*

Was maturity alone responsible for the transfor-
mation? Had some traumatic event turned the
charming charlatan into a man of integrity?

Or did he play the same old game, after all? Perhaps he had a dark side that came out only in his relationships with women. Challenged by the age-old
chase, he led them on until they gave in, then took
off for greener pastures. No. She didn't believe that.
Neither had Lisa, who'd loved and trusted him. The
negative conclusion revolted Laura.

Geoffrey stayed all day, fixing meals, checking her
temperature, teasing her one minute and being dead-
ly serious the next, insisting she rest and allow him to
wait on her.

That night after Kelly went to bed, Geoffrey knelt by her futon. "Good night, darling. I have to go home and tend to some deadlines. I'll see you tomorrow. Mrs. Matsui has promised to check on you in the morning."

"I've kept you from your work. I'm sorry."

"You're my priority, always."

She reached for his hand. "You're quite a doctor, doctor."

He smoothed back her hair with his other hand, then let it linger on her cheek. She laced her fingers in his.

"You make me feel safe, wanted," she said softly.

"Well, at last, my darling, you're getting the picture. For a bright woman, you can be remarkably slow. Sometimes I have the feeling that I ought to write 'I love you' in fifty-two languages and have it notarized."

"Do you mean that, Geoffrey?"

"Laura, when are you going to believe me, trust me?"

Suddenly he slipped into the futon and clasped her to him. It was a tender embrace and she absorbed the warmth of his body as she had the words he'd just spoken. He held her firmly as if to sustain and reassure her.

A sudden intimate touch, a sensual kiss could have sent their passions spiraling. But she didn't want that now, and she sensed that neither did he. Instead they savored the touching, the closeness, the feeling of belonging.

This, too, was a way of fulfilling one's need for intimacy, and it was also a way of manifesting one's sexuality. Love's pendulum swung in a wide arc, nurtured at both extremities. She sighed with satisfaction.

The time had come to put the past aside, to disregard its bitter indictments, never to allow them to come between her and Geoffrey again. The present was her true reality. Disaster lay ahead if she continued to allow the past to entrap her. Tranquillity stole over her at last, and her eyes grew heavy.

Laura wakened slowly the next morning. Beneath her window, birds chirped brief bits of conversation, brittle as tinkling glass. She glimpsed frosty roofs sparkling in the sunshine and sat up suddenly, recalling last night. The bed beside her was empty. She hadn't heard him leave. She felt an instant of panic. Were those moments when he held her so tenderly all part of another dream? Relief washed over her when she saw the indentation of his head still in the other pillow. She picked it up and hugged it to her, verifying the reality of the man she loved.

CHAPTER SEVENTEEN

By Tuesday, Laura felt strong enough to return to work, eager to become active and busy again. Her illness had produced some revealing insights into her relationship with Geoffrey. She thought about him often, hoping the time would soon come when they could discuss their future.

Geoffrey had left a note on her desk saying he had to go to Nagoya, something about interviewing the dissident scientist, but practically ordering her to take it easy, and he'd see her in a few days. She made a face at the assignment he'd left, some correspondence that wouldn't fill half the morning. His new novel had to be around somewhere. He'd completed it, and she couldn't wait to start working on it. Sure enough, a short search found it in the fireproof safe in the file room.

She looked fondly at his usual scratched-out passages, notations in the margins and meandering arrows. What a challenge, and she loved every minute of it. She worked without a break until noon, engrossed as always in the story, then went straight home. As she walked in the door, the telephone rang.

"*Moshi, moshi?*" she said.

"*Konichiwa.*"

"Sachiko! Aren't you teaching today?"

"Two of my students are ill with that flu that's been going around, so I thought I'd call for a little chat. I have something to tell you." Her voice bubbled with excitement.

"Don't tell me you pulled off that geisha caper?"

"Oh, yes, I did."

"It worked?"

"Perfectly! Such fun! Kenzo believed I was a genuine geisha. What did I tell you? Men are easily fooled."

"But how did you arrange it?"

"Oh, we were very proper. I have a cousin whom I took into my confidence. He was so enthusiastic I could hardly restrain him. He arranged a little dinner party at a teahouse for Kenzo. It's not uncommon for relatives to look over prospective brides and grooms. One of my friends from the studio acted as the other geisha. It was marvelous. Even my cousin couldn't tell us apart at first. We rented wigs and wore our prettiest kimonos. A friend who applied the makeup changed the shape of my mouth and eyes. She's very skillful. I wish you could have seen me!"

"But what about all that traditional entertainment?"

"Why, Laura-chan, you ask that of a musician? I played the koto and my friend is skilled in classic dance. We were superb. Our singing was a little shaky, but we kept their sake cups filled, and they thought we were nightingales."

"But, Sachiko, a lot goes on at geisha parties besides music and dancing."

Sachiko giggled. "Oh, yes. I had excellent information from my cousin. I tilted my head most demurely and made soulful expressions like a wounded fawn when I looked into Kenzo's eyes."

Laura burst into laughter. "So did you loosen Kenzo's tongue?"

"A few cups of sake and a few soulful looks, and he opened up like a dictionary. Whatever the topic, he discussed it brilliantly. And," she added portentously, "not once did he tread on my feminist toes."

"I'm impressed," Laura said. "So your Kenzo is talkative, after all."

"At least he's not tongue-tied with a geisha, but whether he can communicate with a prospective wife is another matter. He invited me out to dinner next week. I shall use a few geisha tactics without the trappings, and we shall see what happens."

"You're certain Kenzo didn't recognize you?"

"Never! I hardly recognized myself. Not a word to anyone, you promise?"

"I promise, but remember this, Sachiko, no one is perfect."

Sachiko's voice turned serious. "Life is a puzzle, no?"

"True," Laura said. "Life is a puzzle, yes."

Laura had no more than hung up the telephone when it rang again. This time it was Kenzo. He had to go out of town on business for a few days, so he couldn't meet her at the coffeehouse to give his "progress report." Could they get together next week instead?

"Of course, Kenzo, and how are your lessons going?"

"Very well. You would be proud of your most difficult pupil."

"I'm glad, but then you are an excellent student."

"*Arigato,* and you are fine teacher."

Here we go again, Laura thought, and did her part in continuing the polite little game, repeating that only a good student would make such progress. Meanwhile she was consumed with curiosity concerning his reaction to Sachiko's geisha triumph. Patience, she reminded herself. She might not learn the answer for months.

"So you are learning to communicate with Sachiko?" she asked hopefully.

"*Hai, so desu.* Oh, yes. A-plus grade."

"Wonderful, and how about empathy?"

"*Kekko desu.* Okay. Such fine thing happen I think I must tell you, but must give promise not to tell Sachiko. You give?"

"Of course, Kenzo."

"Sachiko's cousin invite me to excellent dinner with two beautiful geishas."

"Lucky you."

"Oh, yes. Very fortunate man," he said emphatically. "One geisha called Gentle Moon Flower, most beautiful lady in entire world. Talented, too. She played music for me on koto. We do lesson number one, and we do it right, talk and listen, talk and listen. Wonderful. Don't you think so?"

"Yes, indeed, Kenzo, I do think so."

"And I tried lesson number two, also."

"Empathy? Was it difficult for you? I'd be interested in knowing how you accomplished it."

"This geisha a very intelligent lady, begged my opinion, said it was very important to her. She wanted to know if ladies should give up koto when they marry."

"Yes, the question does demand empathy."

"*Kekko desu,* so I remember what you said about my tennis, and I say, 'Miss Gentle Moon Flower, if such lady is as talented as you, she must not deprive family or public of her talent. Give concert at any time she wants.' "

"A plus on lesson number two, also, Kenzo."

"Now I tell you best part. I can't keep eyes from this beautiful geisha, and soon I see something exciting. Miss Gentle Moon Flower is same as Sachiko."

"You mean that the geisha and Sachiko have both beauty and talent in common?"

"*Hai so desu.* Yes, because one and same girl. No one else has ears like Sachiko, like sculptured shells from seashore. No one else holds chin with such special pride." He lowered his voice as if someone might overhear him. "I also notice tiny mole on back of Miss Gentle Moon Flower's neck is same mole in same place as Sachiko's."

A plus for observation also, Laura thought with amusement.

"And how did you feel about Sachiko playing such a game?"

He paused, then laughed. "Who can tell how mind of liberated ladies works? But now I know I can communicate with Sachiko."

"Do you think she realized you recognized her?"

"Oh, no. Positive, and we must not tell her. She learn something at this party; I learn something. Enough. So, honorable teacher, I ask for one more lesson, then I'll be no more bother to you."

"I don't think you need any more lessons, Kenzo."

"Oh, yes. Liberated ladies are complicated females. Need more ammunition."

"Information, Kenzo."

"Almost same thing."

"Well, I can think of one more important lesson, but I realize it is not traditional in Japan to adhere to it."

"Please tell me. Otherwise I worry."

"Fidelity, loyalty. Do you know what I mean?"

He sucked in his breath and laughed heartily. "Easiest lesson of all. No problem. Miss Gentle Moon Flower and Sachiko are two exciting ladies. More than enough female for me. *Arigato. Sayonara.*"

Laura smiled as she hung up the telephone. She had become very fond of the earnest, persistent young man.

ON SUNDAY, LAURA AND KELLY went to the hospital to visit Scott, taking along a card on which she'd written an amusing haiku. A tiny Japanese nurse stood guard at Scott's bedside like a diminutive samurai, timing their visit to an exact five minutes.

Bandaged from heat to foot except for one side of his face, Scott looked like a mummy. He didn't speak but managed a half-smile. Seeing the big man so immobilized, Laura felt desolate but wished him well and promised to return soon. Kelly had watched solemnly and added his goodbye, then suddenly leaned over and whispered, "Remember *ganbaro*, Uncle Scott."

The nurse's eyes were bright as she adjusted Scott's blanket with tender concern. Scott nodded almost imperceptibly and seemed to drift into sleep.

He's in good hands, Laura decided as she and Kelly tiptoed to the door. The nurse held up the card. "I'll read it to him later," she said in soft Japanese.

As they left the hospital, Laura wished she'd written something in a more serious vein. The haiku was meant to amuse, but now she wondered if it might seem flippant or harsh. Kelly had drawn a cartoon to illustrate it, something about not being able to tie a good man down. But Scott was tied down, and for long weeks apparently. The verse somehow lost its humor and seemed almost callous. She hoped the pert little nurse would forget to show it to him.

Back at the apartment she struggled with a more appropriate theme, man versus nature, for a haiku, but today the words wouldn't come. She kept seeing them like butterflies in the mist of her mind, but she could not capture them on paper. Why did she write the verses, anyway? She didn't know if they were any good. She'd tried a few in Japanese recently. Someday she would gather courage and ask Sachiko to critique them.

When she called the hospital a week later to ask about Scott's progress, Nurse Mariko was summoned to answer her questions. Laura recognized the voice of the young woman who had tended Scott the day of the visit. Her Japanese was so clear Laura could understand every word. Between her students, Kelly, Sachiko, Geoffrey and everyone else, she was becoming pretty accomplished at conversational Japanese.

"Much improvement. We are very pleased. He liked your haiku, shared it with all visitors. It made him laugh. Good medicine. Write some more," Mariko said.

Laura thoughtfully considered the folder that now held dozens of her little poems. Perhaps there was a use for them, after all. She would compile the best ones and give them to Scott. One of those attractive flowered binders she'd seen in stationery stores would do as a cover. Short verse matched the brief interest span of invalids. She'd even thought of a title, a Japanese proverb: *Jinsei wa fuzen no tomoshibi*. It was appropriate to the subject matter, which dealt mainly with nature and the fragility of the human condition. Perhaps even better it described her own past year. "Life," said the proverb, "is candlelight in the wind."

CHAPTER EIGHTEEN

LAURA TOOK THE HAIKU COLLECTION to work with her the next day intending to ask Geoffrey if she could use his typewriter to type it. For the first time since she'd started back to work, he was in the library when she arrived. On her desk was an article he'd written for a magazine. He wore a blue sweater that complemented his dark complexion, and his eyes were lively that morning, free from the fatigue she'd noticed there of late. She appraised again, as she had hundreds of times, his firm yet sensitive mouth and blushed when he caught her staring.

"Do I pass inspection?"

"Of course. That's a good-looking sweater," she said. An exquisite tenderness filled her, almost too private for Geoffrey to see. For a moment he waited expectantly as if she hadn't quite said what she intended, then inclined his head to acknowledge the compliment. "I have to get that piece in the mail today. I promised it by December first, tomorrow, but I'd like you to check it over before you type it. I'm not satisfied, but I'll be damned if I know why. It needs your expert editorial eye."

She looked up at him with amusement. "The lowly Adams advising the eminent K.D. Kano?"

He grinned. "Kano feels secure enough in his genre but McDermott doesn't. I value your instincts on these things. Will you do it?"

"Yes, but I'd prefer you okay any changes before I type it."

"When you finish, come on upstairs and we'll go over them. My workroom is on the second floor."

Upstairs in his private domain? Was it as elegant as the library? She felt intensely curious. A man's surroundings gave insight into his personality. Had she seen only one facet? "And, Geoffrey, would you mind if I stayed after hours today to do some work on your typewriter?"

"Help yourself anytime. Schoolwork, I suppose?" He looked at her leather folder with interest, but she ignored him and picked up his article. She didn't want a literary man of his caliber to see her amateurish efforts.

Less than an hour later she took the manuscript and walked up the stairway, following the rapid clack of a typewriter to the end of the hall. He was hunched over a massive desk that almost filled the small room. Reference volumes, maps and papers were piled haphazardly before him. Bookshelves were jammed to capacity. Through a large window she could see the little park across the street. No wonder he'd spotted her so easily that day she sat shivering, eating her lunch.

"You've found me out at last," he said, gesturing across his untidy desk. "I want to have everything within arm's reach."

She handed him the manuscript, feeling suddenly

embarrassed by her temerity. "I found little to change. Actually, it seemed to boil down to a matter of emphasis." She showed him a cut she would make in the introduction, a couple of places that needed more explanation and the rearrangement of several short paragraphs.

He skimmed through her marginal notes. "You've got it," he said with enthusiasm. "We make quite a team, you and I. How did I ever manage without you?"

"Exceedingly well."

He grinned. "I'll rewrite the places you indicated and bring it down in a few minutes."

Geoffrey's art collection must be housed up here somewhere, she thought as she went back downstairs, but doors were closed. As Neil had commented, one probably needed a special invitation to see his "treasures." Whom did he welcome into this special sanctuary? Glamorous women? Art connoisseurs? Good friends? Apparently not his secretary. Or did he hoard treasures like Midas, strictly for his own pleasure?

She was aware of his sexuality continually: when he'd laid a casual hand on her shoulder as she sat at the desk; when his eyes had swept over her in a way that was clearly appreciative; and even now when he was upstairs in his office but still under the same roof.

A little later he brought down the manuscript and she typed and readied it for mailing. After time out to eat a sandwich, she changed the round element in the typewriter to the one that produced the attractive script writing and set to work on her haiku. Perhaps she would ask Sachiko to illustrate some of them with the sparse brush paintings she did so well. She finished typing them in a couple of hours and proofread them, making notations of illustrations that might be appropriate.

Geoffrey walked in, startling her from her concentration. "Good heavens. You're looking at me as if I were Dracula complete with fangs and billowing cape." He walked over and picked up the top page. "Haiku, is it? May I read it?" he asked, already doing so.

If only she'd slipped them into the folder before he arrived. She held out the envelope containing his article, hoping to distract him. "Would you like me to drop this off at the post office?"

He didn't answer but kept reading, eagerly now, as if he couldn't consume them quickly enough. Finally he set them down on his desk.

"Schoolwork, eh? Who wrote these? Not your students."

"I did, Geoffrey, but just for fun." She reached over and put them in the leather folder.

"So my little secretary continues to surprise me—a superior typist, a crackerjack editor and now a poet!"

She shrugged. "Just a hobby."

"Hobby? These are good, really good. They sound as if they were written by a Japanese."

She was beginning to feel flustered by his enthusiasm. He gestured toward them.

"Sending them off to a publisher?"

"Oh, no. I'm just getting them together as a little present. I'm going to ask a friend to illustrate some of them."

His face lost its animation. "For Scott, I suppose. I haven't seen him since last week. How is he?"

She flushed at his accurate guess and wished again she could control such obvious clues to her emotions. They turned her into her own jailer as well as the victim.

"He's coming along much better than expected, but he still has a rough time ahead. He may have lost the use of one of his arms, and vision in one eye is impaired."

"A damned shame. I'll get over and see him again soon." He looked at her appraisingly. "Haiku, a gift from the heart. Right?"

She couldn't answer. Only two things seemed animate in the room, the monotonous hum of the electronic typewriter and Geoffrey's piercing eyes. Finally she managed to say lightly, "I think I hear one of Dr. McDermott's analytical lectures coming on."

"Yes, you do, and I want you to pay attention." He picked up the haiku. "I was practically raised on this stuff, and I've read some of the finest authors. Believe me, yours are every bit as good. It so happens that I have an appointment with my editor tomorrow, and I'd like to show them to her. Her company publishes poetry. She might be interested."

Laura was incredulous. "Surely you're not serious?"

"You bet I am. I can't promise anything. There's not much money in poetry, but whether they accept them or not, these have quality. It takes a while, so you'll have to dream up something else for your stricken hero."

"Geoffrey, I admit that being around you is sometimes like standing in the middle of an artillery zone, but I never thought you were mean."

"You're absolutely right. A very cruel thing to say and I apologize. It's my damned ego. It hurts like hell that you didn't share your writing with me. I feel as if we're in this literary thing together." He actually looked crushed. Laura was amazed at his reaction.

"It never occurred to me to let you see them. They seemed trivial to me, and I wrote them only when I didn't want to do something else. Truly, I thought I'd be wasting your time!"

Her distress must have been evident because his expression softened. He tilted up her chin, and as always, his touch sent a gratifying wave of pleasure through her.

"Ah, Laura, how you underestimate yourself."

She felt an inward quiver. "You can't imagine what you've done for my ego! Everyone yearns to create something genuine during his lifetime. I'm starry-eyed!"

"Yes, you are, and it's mighty becoming." He kissed her, then took her hand. "Speaking of creativity, I'd like to show you my new prize. I was lucky enough to acquire a piece by Hamada."

Hamada? She'd heard about this man who was considered a great creative artist in the field of ceramics. Japan had the unique custom of singling out people as well as objects and buildings as national cultural treasures. Hamada had been chosen for this honor.

They walked up to the third floor. Geoffrey unlocked a door, and they entered a darkened room that appeared even more spacious than the library. There were no rugs, only polished floors and dark paneled walls, almost black. He pressed a switch, and at once, indirect lighting and carefully placed spotlights turned the place into a dramatic exhibition.

Laura caught her breath at the treasures she saw. A pedestal held a handsome cloisonné vase in myriad shades of blue. A set of *kokeshi* dolls captured childish innocence to perfection. There were paintings, carved wooden figures, a three-fold inlaid screen, a stone lantern, ceramics .... It looked as if not a single art form was missing.

A snarling red dragon kite slithered above them across the entire length of the room suspended on invisible wires. She walked over to admire a metal sculpture of a rooster. Every line in its spread wings and arched neck registered self-appreciation.

Laura was no stranger to museums—she had visited them all her life—but this room was unique, arranged with the same care as a Japanese garden, with infinite regard for space, light and shadow.

"It's beautiful," she said, feeling almost moved to tears. He smiled as he recognized her sincerity.

"We all have escape valves. This is mine, like your haiku. Wandering among these timeless treasures has a way of setting one's life in perspective. I'm as compulsive as any addict. A special find gives me a genuine high.'' He led her to a tiered glass shelf and pointed to his most recent acquisition, the Hamada tea bowl. By most standards, it was heavy for such a piece and it had an abstract design in black and gray, almost ascetic in its simplicity.

Geoffrey picked it up and cupped it in his hands. His careful handling showed his regard for its artistry. ''Hamada's pieces sell out in a few minutes whenever they appear in a show. He was so modest he wouldn't sign them, but his style is still distinctive. There's no mistaking his works. You must understand that the Japanese attach a kind of mystic meaning to their ceramics that completely escapes Westerners.''

They walked among the collection, and Geoffrey explained each object. He was about to skip a beautiful kimono that hung inside a glass case, but she stopped him.

''I've never seen such a lovely one!'' she said. It was creamy white, and the obi was patterned in varicolored autumn leaves with the design repeated on the skirt. The motif recalled the time she and Geoffrey sat under the maple tree at Chizu's birthday party.

''I bought it recently at the Nishijin Textile Museum. The maple leaves intrigued me.'' His eyes gleamed. ''Would you like to try it on? I can guarantee it will fit.''

''Oh, no, I wouldn't touch it.'' Geoffrey didn't insist. They moved on, touring the gallery, Geoffrey supplying her with continuous explanations. Finally finished, they left, and he turned a dead-bolt lock on the door.

"Would you like to see the rest of the house?" he asked as they walked along the hallway and down the stairs to the second floor. "There are two bedrooms on this floor in addition to my office." One was done in browns and the other in blues, both totally masculine. "Mine is the blue one. Small but functional. How do you like it?"

"Tidy, understated. I think it suits you more than your office, and blue is your color."

"Why do you say that?"

She couldn't tell him how her heart had leaped this morning when she saw him in his blue sweater. "Oh, you look good in blue but maybe it's something esoteric like sympathetic color vibrations."

He looked amused. "You may be right."

She walked over to view a sepia portrait of a lovely young woman. "Your mother?" she asked, but needn't have. The direct, intelligent brown eyes were exactly like Geoffrey's. He came over and stood behind her, his hands on her shoulders.

"Yes, beautiful, wasn't she? I suppose you've heard the old cliché that men fall in love with women who resemble their mothers. Although you two show little physical resemblance, you're alike in other ways."

"For instance?" she couldn't resist asking.

"To start with, you both slay dragons to protect the ones you love, but you're vulnerable as hell when it comes to yourselves. Also stubborn."

"So our writer is now an analyst," she said, and

started for the door. It was time to change the subject.

"You bet. You're not the only one with multiple talent." They walked downstairs to the library. Laura paused before picking up her briefcase.

"This has been a very special day for me, Geoffrey—your evaluation of my haiku, getting to see all the beautiful things in your gallery. I'm so touched I hardly know what to say."

"No words necessary. I knew what you felt." His eyes sparkled roguishly. "Of course, if you'd care to reward me with a small kiss, I'd be everlastingly grateful. To be perfectly honest, I want one so much you could say I've reached the starvation point."

Without hesitation she walked over, stood on tiptoe, pulled his face down to hers and kissed him quickly, then again with special tenderness. In quick succession amazement, surprise and gladness swept across his face, then his arms encircled her, holding her close. They swayed in silence for a few moments, Laura's head against his chest, listening to the increasing beat of his heart.

"Oh, Lord, I've been wanting to hold you like this. Every minute of the day I've longed for it."

"How well you hide your feelings!"

"I've been playing by your rules. I didn't want to lose you."

She grew very still in his embrace, feeling the urgency in his body. "You won't lose me, Geoffrey. I need you, and I'll probably need you even more in the future. Keep holding me." As she spoke she could see the electrical impact her words had on him. He gripped her almost roughly by her shoulders.

"Say that again."

She was startled by this intensity. "I need you, Geoffrey."

"Again!"

"I need you, and I love you. I've loved you all along, but I couldn't tell you."

"Do you realize this is the first time you've said it? My God, can you imagine the nights I've stayed awake hoping, praying for those very words? You're certain now, aren't you?"

"I'm perfectly sure." Yes, she was. Perhaps their love would become more invulnerable because of the pain it had survived. Her eyes glistened.

"Tears?" he asked.

"Of happiness," she said. "I feel as if I've come home after a long journey." He crushed her against him until she was breathless.

Suddenly he scooped her easily into his arms and carried her back upstairs into his room, set her on the bed and lay down beside her. He half sat up, leaning on his elbow, and looked at her, her hair spread out on the pillow, her eyes steady and holding. With one hand he ran his fingers through her hair, lingered against her cheek, then held her chin and bent to kiss her, teasingly at first, then deeply exploring, tongue against tongue.

A slow fire ignited the desire that had been accumulating within her for months. Now they kissed greedily, and she arched against him, loving the feel of his strong body responding eagerly, loving the way his eyes, his voice, his hands made love to her. Uncertainties faded leaving only wonder.

Everything in the room became more intense. Early-afternoon sun shone sharp, slanted patterns through the blinds to project Roman-candle splendor all around them; a cloisonné vase filled with pink ceramic blossoms sparkled proudly and a symphony on a radio, from somewhere down the hall, built to a thundering climax. She thought of a blaze of maple trees and was filled with a wild, almost painful longing.

Their fingers found buttons, and unhurriedly they helped each other from shirt, sweater and blouse, tossing them to the foot of the bed. Laura's hands burned, anticipating his lean hard flesh, and she sighed softly as she fanned her fingers against his chest.

He held her close, and they savored the tantalizing satisfaction of skin against skin.

"How soft, how fragile you feel," he said.

"You make me feel feminine, precious."

"And so you are, my love." He traced the curve of her ear with a series of feathery kisses, then down her shoulder and to her breasts, teasing them to firm arousal. He cupped them gently as they swelled above their lacy covering, caressing with a special grace, anticipating her desire with lightning sensitivity. His hands moved with surprising delicacy, urging her obvious hunger to overcome her natural reserve.

Her hand drifted to explore him, storing in her memory the crisp thickness of his hair, the firmness of his body; inhaling the clean soapy scent of his cheek; remembering dark eyes behind sooty lashes, his swift smile and the way he said her name as she touched him.

He took one of her hands and pressed it into the base of his throat to feel his throbbing pulse. "See what you do to me!" he whispered. Her own pulses raced, and she basked in their mutual pleasure, feeling a happiness she could scarcely contain.

Suddenly his embrace changed, became urgent, less subtle, and she gasped at his intimate searching.

"Don't be afraid," he said.

"I'm not really."

"You're running away again. Come back to me."

"I'm right here."

"What's wrong? Am I rushing you?"

"You're perfect. I love you. You excite me beyond all reason."

"My self-contained Laura? Never."

"I have a thin protective coating, Geoffrey."

"You're trembling."

She hesitated. "Just my inexperience showing."

He tipped up her chin, and his eyes grew soft. "Are you telling me that you've never made love before?"

"I hoped it wasn't too obvious. Do you mind?" she asked gravely.

His answer was to cradle her close, and they remained locked in each other's arms until their hearts beat in a steady rhythm. She felt uneasy. If only he wouldn't take her reaction as one more rejection. Couldn't he tell that it was anything but that? Had her renegade heart controlled her responses for so long that she couldn't now answer to her most basic desire for love?

She glanced up at his face and saw he wasn't angry, merely watchful. This sensitive man seemed to know that love needn't be hurried. Slowly, they separated and dressed with an outer casualness. A small tender smile flickered between them as he tied the bow on her blouse. He bent down and kissed her sweetly on the lips. *It's okay,* she thought. *He's letting me know. Everything is going to be all right.*

CHAPTER NINETEEN

LAURA SAT IN THE TEA SHOP where she was to meet
Sachiko in a few minutes. Her friend had called
earlier and asked her to come. Laura felt tempted to
beg off; she was tired and a little depressed, but
something in Sachiko's voice had alarmed her.

Geoffrey was out of town again. He'd left a note
saying he had some business with Neil in Yokohama.
The note was not curt, but nor did it include the kind
of message she might have expected after their tender
interlude yesterday. Surely he didn't think she had
backed away from him again. A man would take
only so much of that kind of treatment.

Schoolwork had piled up in unusual proportions
requiring many extra hours. The new director who
took Scott's place seemed determined to make a
name for himself as quickly as possible, confusing
frequent faculty meetings, reports and paperwork
with the real purpose of the school.

Perhaps she could solve problems with more dispatch if she weren't the kind of person who had to
poke at things, to cross-examine and practically do a
research paper on them.

Laura saw Sachiko coming toward her now. On
the surface the lovely Japanese girl never failed to ap-

pear poised and tranquil, but Laura had learned to look for small clues to her moods. Today Sachiko held her shoulders a little too tensely, and her eyes looked large and wistful, as if she hungered for something. A dusty pink touched her honey cheeks. Was she nervous? Angry? In her black suit and tangerine flowered blouse, she looked like a miniature New York model. No wonder Kenzo was smitten. Beauty, brains and talent were incredibly wrapped in that small stunning package.

They chatted over their tea for a while, although Sachiko barely tasted hers.

"You must be a busy lady these days with a certain gentleman filling your calendar."

Sachiko fingered her cup, then set it down. "Yes, these weeks have been exciting."

"Good. Then you've changed your mind about men?"

"I admit I'm always too quick to judge. Kenzo appears more and more a man to respect." Sachiko laced her fingers tightly together. "What Kenzo does no longer concerns me."

Laura was startled. "Why, what do you mean?"

"I had reason to have a complete physical checkup last week, and I learned that I may never be able to have children. No man will want me now." Her eyes glistened with tears.

"Are you certain?" Laura said, trying to absorb the disturbing information. "You must get a second opinion."

"I did, and also a third. The chances are slim."

"But new things are being discovered every day. What about adoption?"

Sachiko's lips trembled. "A man wants his line to continue. He preserves his eternity through his children. I will not deceive anyone. When I tell him, you'll see, he will take off faster than the bullet train."

"Not Kenzo," Laura said resolutely. "I'm sure he loves you. How do you feel about him?"

"Love? Who can say? Love means many things to me. Remember, I'm pure Japanese with only a thin layer of new freedoms. I am determined to continue my career, but I still haven't sorted out my feelings about marriage. Now I won't have to," she said.

Laura offered comfort and urged her to find the names of leading specialists in Tokyo.

"Interesting, is it not, Laura-san, after all the to-do we have made?" She looked at her watch. "I have a rehearsal, so I must go. Thanks for tea and sympathy. Just consider me your own private soap opera. Tune in next week for the next episode. I may even accompany myself with some heartrending music on my violin." She smiled bravely, but Laura saw a tear hover on her lashes.

Laura said goodbye with a feeling of inadequacy. She'd done nothing more for her friend than act the good listener. Everyone had problems. Healing would come only if one faced up to them. Life never promised to be fair. Sachiko had the inner resources if she'd use them.

ON THE FOLLOWING SATURDAY AFTERNOON, Laura finished some household chores, then went to visit Scott. She pulled on her gloves as she hurried to the bus stop. Rooftops were still frosty in the late afternoon, and the surrounding hills were dusted with snow. Her breath trailed vapor clouds in the clear cold air. After Oregon's token nod to seasonal change, Japan's distinctive contrasts were prompt and resolute, even dramatic.

Already in mid-December Christmas trees, angels, mistletoe and red-coated Santas appeared in shop windows, and carols blared endlessly at the crowds. Apparently Japan embraced Christmas with its usual enthusiasm for festivals.

She got on the train, and her mind turned to Scott. He was improving rapidly, alert and talkative now, although Nurse Mariko still timed his visits and scanned his expression for signs of fatigue, shooing out visitors at the first indication he'd had enough.

There were scars on his body, but at least on his face, skillful surgery guaranteed little disfigurement in the future. Laura often wondered if Mariko deserved major credit for his rapid recovery. She seemed to have made Scott her special project. Her bright eyes were watchful, her soft voice encouraged increased effort as he worked at the painful exercises and her smile of approval became a frequent blessing. Perhaps it was the first time in his life that Scott received such caring attention, and he indulged himself with uninhibited pleasure.

At the hospital Laura welcomed the warm temperature and hurried down the hall breathing in the familiar antiseptic atmosphere. Nurses, attendants, doctors, chaste and impersonal all, uniformly rendered her superfluous as they glanced at her in passing.

In Scott's room she walked to his bed, leaned over and kissed his cheek.

"Laura, great to see you." His face lit up.

She pulled up a chair near him. "You're looking lots better."

His face crinkled into a boyish grin. "Never had so much tender loving care in my entire life."

"And you love every minute of it."

"I admit I perked up plenty when they told me I'd have at least partial use of my arm again. Can't raise it above my shoulder anymore, but I'll still be able to give you ladies a bear hug."

Laura sighed with relief. "The best news I've heard in ages. And your eye?"

"Some vision with a good strong lens. But enough about the patient. What's the latest with you and Kelly?"

"Getting ready for the holidays," she said and pointed to the wreath in the window. "It's disconcerting the way Japan is going all out for Christmas."

"Not really. One more *matsuri* is right up their alley, especially one with such an international scope. Besides, it harmonizes with the positive philosophy of Shintoism. Several of their ancestral deities such as Hotei and Ebisu ran around with bags of treasures on their backs like Santa Claus. I'll bet Kelly is delighted. Where is he today?"

"Off on a ski trip with his scout troop." She didn't add that Geoffrey was one of the chaperons. Certain boys had been asked to volunteer fathers for the chore, and to Laura's surprise, Kelly, without consulting her, called Geoffrey and made the arrangements. From Kelly's account, she gathered that Geoffrey was pleased.

The conversation turned to shoptalk for a while, and Scott spoke enthusiastically of the new Nara language school, which he hoped to open himself shortly after the first of the year.

"Then you won't be coming back to Kyoto?"

"No, I have a new apartment near the school, and Mrs. Kubo has already seen to moving my things there."

Mariko came in then and scanned Scott's face with an anxious eye. She walked over to adjust the window shade, then took his temperature. On a previous visit, Scott had mentioned that his nurse was a thirty-six-year-old widow who had lost both husband and child a dozen years ago in a car accident. She had a natural sweetness quite different from Sachiko's fragile, exotic qualities. Laura could read the character in Mariko's face; the pain and discipline, all hard-earned values that she seemed to have honed to a special luster.

Mariko removed the thermometer and took Scott's pulse. Their eyes met and held, and Mariko's expression softened unbelievably. Laura suddenly had the feeling that she was intruding, so she waved goodbye and slipped discreetly out of the room.

Geoffrey and Kelly planned to be home from the ski trip around seven that evening. Before she'd left to visit Scott she had made a batch of the lemon bars Geoffrey liked so much. The table was set with some new tangerine-colored placemats of matchstick bamboo. She had spent almost an hour working to achieve an artful centerpiece of camellias. According to the principles of ikebana, there were usually only three flowers and some foliage allowed in any arrangement. She would make hot chocolate and coffee, and the three of them would sit around the *kotatsu* in a cozy family circle, warming their feet and talking over the day on the ski slopes.

Now she looked forward to the evening with special excitement. After Kelly went to bed, would they plan their future? Make wedding plans? Would tonight also prove the right time to reveal Geoffrey's relationship to Kelly? Somehow fate not only had had a hand in their meeting, but had determined the two belonged together. She still wasn't certain about revealing that news yet. Timing could be crucial, but she felt certain she'd recognize the suitable moment.

New policy, she thought. Laura Adams is determined to be open and resolute when the time comes. She ought to take a cue from Geoffrey and Scott. Neither one ever straddled a fence. "We're part of every person we've ever known," someone once said. She wished she could choose which part.

Before going home, she stopped off to buy the special brand of coffee she knew Geoffrey enjoyed. With two hours to pass, she decided to browse in her favorite book shop, where she found an English translation of one of Geoffrey's earlier novels in paperback. She would read it again. A book revealed its author, didn't it? Perhaps she could get more insight into the complicated man she wanted to marry.

As she started to take the book from the shelf, she

stiffened. Straight ahead at the cash register near the front of the store, Laura thought she saw Geoffrey talking with Mr. Ishimoto, the owner. A tiny Japanese lady wearing a kimono was with them. They were some distance away, but there was no mistaking Geoffrey's dark curly head and the familiar camel's-hair coat he frequently wore. Laura felt as if someone had just jabbed her midsection. What was Geoffrey doing here? He was supposed to be on a ski trip with a carload of boy scouts.

She stared unbelievingly as Mr. Ishimoto wrapped Geoffrey's purchases in two separate packages. Geoffrey put the smaller one in his overcoat pocket and presented the other to his companion. She bowed gracefully, as did Geoffrey, and they went out of the shop laughing and talking spiritedly in Japanese. Laura left Geoffrey's book on the shelf and walked to the entrance, trying not to look as if she hurried, arriving in time to see the couple get into Geoffrey's car.

Her mind raced, trying to avoid the obvious conclusion. Geoffrey hadn't gone on the scout trip, after all. And who was the woman in the lovely kimono?

CHAPTER TWENTY

LAURA WENT BACK into the book shop and stared at the row of titles without reading a single one. There was an answer. There had to be one. Geoffrey was not a man to renege on a commitment, especially to a group of boy scouts. Nevertheless, she felt let down knowing there would be no cozy session around the *kotatsu*. Obviously, someone else would deliver the boys home.

It was a long climb up the frosty steps to her apartment, and inside, the place felt freezing. The pretty table set with such care mocked her now. She put the dishes and mats away so she wouldn't have to look at them and tried not to think how much different the evening might have been.

After turning on the electric *kotatsu* under the table, she sat down and stretched her feet toward its warmth, speculating on the scene in the book shop.

Loving meant trust, Geoffrey had said. If she were to be honest, not once since she'd known him had he ever given her reason to doubt him. It was her own imagination that provided the stumbling blocks. Even now, despite her resolve to ignore the past, the dreaded uncertainties crept in to haunt her. Would it always be this way?

The door bell startled her. Kelly? But it was Geoffrey, alone and immense in his heavy topcoat and fur earmuff cap.

"Geoffrey! Where's Kelly?" she cried, peering around him.

"Some welcome to warm a man's heart. Ask me in, for crying out loud, before I freeze to the floorboards." She stood back to let him pass. "If you'd stayed home for five minutes, you'd have received my call," he said. "The slopes were so crowded we brought the kids home early. One of the boys wanted Kelly to stay overnight, and since you weren't home, I gave my permission."

She sighed with relief and at the same time condemned herself for having doubted him. "Let me take your coat. I'll put on some coffee."

He lifted her off her feet, giving her a hug. "Not tonight. We're having champagne. Grab your coat. Have you had your dinner?" He sounded irrepressible.

"Well, no," she said after he put her down.

"All the better. I know just the place."

"Sounds marvelous," she said, feeling almost overwhelmed by the sudden turn of the evening. In the bedroom she ran a brush through her hair and slipped into her coat, her spirits already soaring.

Geoffrey eyed her approvingly. "Good, I always did admire a girl who didn't dawdle."

"Not too difficult when it comes to choosing champagne and dinner in a nice warm restaurant over coffee and an inadequate *kotatsu*."

"And I thought it was just my company that made

it so appealing," he said as he hustled her out to the car and tucked a lap blanket around her.

"Now what's this about champagne?" she asked as he put the car in gear.

"Celebration time!"

"Is it a secret, or are you sharing?" Even in the car's dimness she caught the sparkle in his eyes.

"Congratulations," he said. "You'll soon be joining me on the bookshelves."

She tried to assimilate this news. "A riddle, I take it."

"Your haiku have been accepted, you goose. You'll soon be a published author."

"Don't pull my leg, Geoffrey."

"I'm not. It's true. After I delivered the scouts home this afternoon, I dropped by to see my editor, Mrs. Matsuda. She said your poetry is pure Japanese in spirit. She loves it. What did I tell you?"

Laura could only shake her head in disbelief. "They're publishing all of them?"

"Right. In one volume. It will be one of a series on Japanese culture. There are others on such subjects as ikebana, the tea ceremony and such. We went to Sam Ishimoto's to pick up one so you can see how yours will look. They all share the same kind of cover."

"I can't believe it!" she gasped. As they drove, she plied him with questions. Would the book be illustrated? When would the galleys arrive? What was the publication date? Would Mrs. Matsuda be her editor?

As obviously pleased as she was, he answered her

questions all the way to the restaurant. The place specialized in Western cuisine and had small private dining alcoves that surrounded a central fireplace. The room felt blessedly warm after the piercing cold outside.

After they were seated, Geoffrey gave his full attention to the menu, and Laura took the opportunity to look around. Lights were turned low and candles burned on the table. A Christmas tree stood near the fireplace, its ornaments on fire with reflected flames. A stereo played a symphonic arrangement of Christmas carols. All else seemed to blend into the background in respectful deference to the quality of the evening. She watched the flickering light play on Geoffrey's dark head as he studied the menu. She'd never be able to keep love from her eyes and voice tonight.

He glanced up suddenly, catching her staring. "Hey, look who has stars in her eyes!" he said, and handed her the small package she'd seen him shove into his pocket at the book shop. It was the book on ikebana from the series. Bound in a soft cover with double-folded rice-paper pages, it had an outer removable hard cover that closed with bone fastenings. Laura had never seen such an original binding and tried to imagine her verses encased in the charming volume.

"Lovely," she murmured. "How can I thank you?"

Geoffrey lifted the champagne from the silver ice bucket and poured two glasses, handing one to her and raising his own. "To the new member of the haiku set!"

Her cheeks felt warm and she trembled a little as she touched her glass to his. "And to you, Geoffrey, who had faith in me."

"Pay-up time," he said, and leaned across to kiss her, one of his firm no-nonsense kisses. *You're mine,* his lips seemed to say. *And don't you forget it.* Her emotions now seemed charged with far more effervescence than the champagne she now sipped.

"How did the skiing go?" she asked when she thought she had her voice under control.

"Nothing like a dozen boy scouts to put a little zip back into your life. We had a great time. Actually, I'm a pretty damn good father figure."

"Yes, Geoffrey, you are," she said with such vehemence that he looked at her sharply. She downed the rest of her drink too quickly. This was not the moment. "How did Kelly get along?" she asked, not wanting to delve any more into the subject of fathers.

"A natural. He'll be a first-class skier in no time."

"Too bad you couldn't have stayed longer. By the way, was that Mrs. Matsuda I saw you with at Ishimoto's earlier?"

Geoffrey set down his glass. "You were there? You saw us!" he cried, astounded. "Why on earth didn't you join us? You could have met her and heard your news on the spot."

Laura hoped the shadows would camouflage her embarrassment. "Well, I didn't know the ski trip had been cut short, so a few other thoughts ran through my mind when I saw you with the lady in the attractive kimono."

He gave a hearty chuckle. "Aha, I see what you

mean. Don't tell me you were jealous? Good! I hope
so. It's one of the best compliments you've paid me.
Hai so desu! Laura is jealous. I think I'll frame it in
gold and hang it in my office. My dear, that lady is
one of the most charming, intelligent people I
know—and old enough to be my mother.'' His eyes
sparkled with amusement.

Geoffrey placed their order, and the waiter promptly brought their salads followed by a marvelous crab
dish. Throughout the meal, Laura felt Geoffrey's eyes
on her. He poured another glass of champagne.
''There must be something else you'd like to toast,''
he said, ''now that we've taken care of the new
author.''

She looked at him to see if he was joking or not.
Often she couldn't tell. ''I thought you'd never ask,''
she said, opting for humor but quickly becoming
serious. ''I was under the impression you and I had
made some kind of commitment at your place a few
afternoons ago. I wondered if we would discuss it.''

He feigned a puzzled expression. ''Commitment?
Ah, yes. Are you for it?''

''Yes, I am.''

''Oh, not me. Never!'' he said with a sly grin. She
knew she looked stunned.

''Unless it's for eighty or ninety years,'' he added.

She laughed a little shakily and held up her glass.
''To eighty or ninety years!''

With a deliberate movement he reached for her
hand and slipped a ring on her finger. Pearls set in
gold. The moment was too fragile and special for
words. He took both her hands in his, and they

smiled the secretive smile they'd begun to exchange of late.

"I'm afraid to say anything because words will sound inadequate," she said.

"You only need three."

"I love you," she whispered.

He bent and kissed her fingers, then let them go. "This needn't be the official engagement ring. We can get to that later, the stone you want, and properly fitted."

"But this one fits perfectly!"

"I guessed well, then. I wanted something for right now, this minute, to make it official. A bird in the hand, you know."

She turned the ring on her finger, admiring the creamy sheen of the pearls in the candlelight. When she looked up she observed that he was watching her anxiously despite his teasing tone.

"I don't want another ring. I love this one. I've always preferred pearls to diamonds. If we weren't in a public place, I'd show you how much I like it."

He grinned. "In that case, I'd better get you home. I recall what happened the other day when you thanked me for something."

"About the other day. . . ." she said earnestly

"Yes, what about it?"

"I was afraid you thought I didn't want you It wasn't that at all. I hardly know how to express it, but, well, does it make any sense to say I wanted you and felt shy all at once?" There was a sudden flare of candlelight illuminating Geoffrey's face, but she couldn't tell what he was thinking. "I do want you to understand. It's like doing anything for the first time. You're excited and scared at the same time. Maybe I was a little more scared than excited.''

''Don't worry, my love, we'll remedy that soon.'' He raised his glass. ''To commitment!''

''Does that mean you want to marry me?''

He gave her an impish smile, and he'd never looked more endearing. ''Well, I was considering it. Do you have any preference, such as morning, noon or night, say within the next week or two?''

''Next week or two!''

''Well, how about tomorrow?''

''Be serious.''

''I couldn't be more so. I can get a judge who just happens to be a friend of mine to perform the ceremony, then all you have to do is pack your suitcase, bring along Kelly and move in. The only thing we'd have to do is register. A marriage isn't legal here until one registers it, and that can be done anytime following the ceremony. Some couples even wait a year to see how things work out. If it doesn't, no hassle, no divorce necessary, goodbye and good luck—unless, of course, there is a child.''

''I see,'' she said thoughtfully.

''Don't get any ideas. I'm registering our marriage five minutes after the ceremony.''

She smiled, not without relief. ''How about the first week in January? My schoolwork will have simmered down by Christmas. That will give me time to get organized.''

''The sooner the better. I hope you don't want a big bash.''

"A little bash suits me perfectly. I have no family except Kelly, you know."

"Neither do I, except for my parents, who live in Ohio. In the meantime we can decide where we want to go on our honeymoon. Right now I just want to look at you."

"Same here," she said. "Would you think I sounded crazy if I told you that you're the kind of person who makes me feel whole?"

"That goes both ways, my darling. Do you have any idea how much I love you?"

"No, Geoffrey, and I do wonder why."

"Listen, goose, that was your cue to say, 'I love you, too, Geoffrey.'"

"I love you, too, Geoffrey," she repeated solemnly. "But considering what we've been through, I'm curious to know *why* you love me."

He rolled his eyes. "Can't we just exchange knowing glances and leave the rest to fate?"

"I have a fondness for specifics and so do you."

"What a time for analysis!" He stroked his chin and cocked a scrutinizing eye on her. "Well, you smell nice, and the way you feel when I touch you just about demolishes me. That brain of yours isn't too shabby, either." He dropped his bantering and leaned forward. "What I mean is that you're the one woman I want to have and to hold, to talk and be silent with, to laugh with and to love. Okay, my darling?"

"High expectations. I hope I can meet them."

"You already have."

"You're my world, too, Geoffrey. I've wanted to

tell you for a long time, but I've been busy with a tug-of-war, not to mention a few hang-ups."

"I know. That's why I gave you some time off. I thought you needed some space to help you make up your mind, in case you didn't notice."

"Oh, I noticed, all right. I thought you were easing me out of your life."

He groaned. "What I'd give for some good old-fashioned communication."

She had to smile. She'd passed that advice around to everyone but herself. Even now fear nagged her. She still hadn't revealed the most vital information of all.

She stared at her plate. Empty! She barely remembered eating a bite. The waiter served a French pastry, then Geoffrey ordered a liqueur as the conversation turned to the practicalities of their future. Give up her teaching? No, they agreed, but she'd ask for a morning session as soon as there was an opening. Kelly would have the brown room. They'd bring in bunk beds so he could have an overnight guest on occasion. They'd retain the housekeeper...there was so much to talk about.

When they discovered the time, it was midnight.

"Good Lord! We're closing up the place," Geoffrey said as he handed money to their patient waiter.

A little later as they stood on her small porch they clung in a long embrace.

"This has been a day to remember. I'll dream of it all night," Laura said.

"In three-dimensional technicolor with me in the leading romantic role?"

"Oh, yes. And a choir of angels and the London Symphony."

He gave her a long, tender kiss. "Good night, my darling. I'll enjoy sweet dreams, too, knowing you've finally exorcised your demons, that no barrier remains between us."

CHAPTER TWENTY-ONE

KYOTO'S DECEMBER had turned harsh and irascible. Icy winds swept down from the snow-covered mountains shoving temperatures down to freezing. Christmas decorations that formerly swung on storefronts and streetlights were stiff and unyielding.

Nevertheless, sidewalks were jammed with people bundled in layers of clothing, waddling from shop to shop in frenzied buying. The month bustled with activity because it was also the time of *shiwasu*, when it became one's duty to clear up all obligations before celebrating the New Year. New Year in Japan was the biggest *matsuri* of them all, a time that was family-oriented, more like a Western Christmas.

Obligations. Laura resolved to join the ranks of the Japanese and clear up one of her own. In her euphoric condition Saturday night, she had found it easy to talk herself out of telling Geoffrey about his son. On Sunday she'd wrestled with the problem all day and finally decided she could not deny her moral obligation. The results could very well prove disastrous for her. *Shiwasu!* She vowed to tell Geoffrey before the New Year. In a way, it was a relief to set a deadline. In the meantime, she would treasure every moment with Geoffrey, suspecting it might be her last.

Arriving at work, she felt glad not to find him in the library and immediately plunged into editing and typing a series of his columns. Perhaps hard work would help banish worry.

An hour before noon everything was completed. There was no sound in the house. Maybe he wasn't home today.

After clearing her desk and filing his manuscripts, she decided to leave and make up the time another day. Perhaps she would stop by Daimaru's and pick up some Christmas gifts.

As she entered the hall she heard footsteps. A few seconds later Geoffrey came down the stairway. He wore a silver gray topcoat with a blue-plaid scarf tucked in at the collar. As always his appearance excited her: the aristocratic profile, the directness of his intelligent eyes, the quiet air of authority. Their eyes met, meaningfully communicating emotions that lingered from their special evening together. Then they said good-morning with a familiarity that established their more intimate relationship.

"I completed the work you set out. Do you have something else?" she asked.

He gave her a look of admiration. "I'll never be able to get over how speedy you are. Take the rest of the morning off. You deserve it."

"Thank you, Geoffrey. I'll use it to get in some Christmas shopping." She started for the door, and he called to her.

"Hey, wait a minute. Why don't you come with

me? I'm headed up to an arts-and-crafts fair in the
Mount Hei area, a great place to shop for gifts. On
the way you can see one of the best panoramic views
of the city you will find anywhere. I'll get you home
in plenty of time to meet your afternoon schedule.''

The prospect of a few hours alone with Geoffrey
sent her pulses racing. ''I'd like to go,'' she said, then
her spirits abruptly plummeted. *Shiwasu* would hang
over her like a dagger, reminding her continually of
her resolve. Well, she had two more weeks yet.
Nevertheless, the imminent self-imposed deadline
cast a shadow on the day.

As they settled in the car, Geoffrey cheerfully
whistled ''Smoke Gets in Your Eyes,'' and she
wondered if he was making some kind of musical
comment on her mood. He glanced at her now and
then as if checking a barometer.

They hadn't gone far up the mountain road when
they reached the snow level. Trees and shrubs became
anonymous white sculptures gleaming in the cold
sunlight. Geoffrey pointed to a pine branch bent low
over the road with its frosty burden.

''A favorite subject for Japanese artists,'' he said,
and fixed his attention on his driving. A half hour
later he pulled into the parking lot of the exhibition
hall adjacent to a large modern hotel.

Inside, crowds clustered around the risers where
individual artists demonstrated. Geoffrey and Laura
wandered among dyers, weavers, sculptors, painters,
doll makers, flower arrangers and origami artists
who deftly folded scraps of paper to create dozens of
delicate objects. In one corner a young woman knelt,

performing pensive music on her thirteen-string koto. Laura had never seen such a kaleidoscope of creativity under one roof.

"It's a feast," she murmured.

Geoffrey nodded. "It should be. All of the artists you see here today are pupils of that select group known as Japan's national treasures. You recall Hamada is one of them? There are about seventy of these masters. Wisely, the government records their techniques on film for posterity. You'll see quality today in the work of their students."

Later they had hot soup and tempura in the hotel restaurant. Geoffrey's acquaintances kept stopping by to speak to him, which prevented their own conversation. It was just as well; something about the day kept her tongue-tied. The moment they stepped back into the hall, Geoffrey was buttonholed by another friend, and Laura wandered around by herself. She watched a potter fashion a bowl on his wheel with such mystic dedication to absolute perfection that she, too, became caught up in the spell. Perhaps such consecration formed the ingredient that separated the great from the near great, she thought.

She bought a set of tea bowls for Sachiko and a dragon kite with a shining silver tail for Kelly. At an adjoining booth she saw Geoffrey pick up and admire a lacquer tray, then almost reluctantly set it down. After he left she slipped over and unobtrusively purchased it, ignoring the fact that it all but demolished her Christmas budget.

Geoffrey finally extricated himself from one of the many persons he seemed to know and came over to take her arm. "We'd better leave now, or I'll never be able to get you home in time for your classes."

Outside the wintry dusk predicted early darkness, and they caught their breath at the impact of the cold. The soft slushy snow had turned to ice, and Geoffrey drove cautiously over the slippery road.

"Careful does it, I don't have chains," he said. Frequently they felt the wheels spin as the car skidded a few feet, but Geoffrey always managed to correct them in time. They were silent as he bent forward, every muscle taut in intense concentration.

"If we can only get down below the snow level, we'll be okay. I think it's only a few more miles."

Laura willed the car to hold firm on the glassy surface. A mile took an age, it seemed. Then, as they rounded a curve, the car suddenly skidded off the road and lurched over on its side in a shallow ditch. Icy water seeped in on Laura's side, and she cried out in shock as she tried to right herself. Geoffrey worked frantically at his door, which had now become the ceiling in their awkward angle.

In minutes he managed to prop open the door, then braced a foot in the ditch and helped her out, holding her tight against him until they regained their footing.

"Are you okay?" he asked.

"I think so," Laura gasped, and even though she felt almost paralyzed with fright she could still feel the broken ice nudging her ankles. They clawed their way up the bank and stood shivering on the road.

"We must hurry," he said, holding her arm firmly. "With these wet clothes, we have to find shelter soon."

"Surely someone will come by and pick us up, what with all those people at the exhibition."

"Don't count on it. They're mostly members of a convention staying at the hotel. I had a special invitation." They plodded along, sliding, sometimes falling, sustaining each other as best they could. She berated herself at every step. She never should have come today. No one knew of her plans. Kelly would be frantic, and what about her classes?

Suddenly Geoffrey pulled her around, reversing direction.

"Why?" she cried. "There haven't been any lights for miles."

"I just remembered there's an old *ryokan*, inn, just off that last lane we passed. We'd better head for it."

Laura's feet and legs throbbed so painfully she bit her lip to keep from moaning, and her wet clothing clung to her body, hindering her progress. *Manage one foot at a time,* she told herself, and calculated each step with caution.

At one point she stopped for a few seconds to glimpse Kyoto far below in the distance. Lights twinkled in the clear atmosphere as if imitating the stars, and the snow-laden branches wrote *kanji* against the moonlit sky. She wasn't certain whether the pain she felt was a reaction to the exquisite scene or that she was freezing to death.

Geoffrey tugged her arm roughly. "Come on. For heaven's sakes, keep moving." Was there really an inn around here, or was Geoffrey hallucinating? They reached a graveled path and gained a sure foothold at last. Laura gave a whimper of relief as they glimpsed the lights of the *ryokan*. It was a large, three-story wooden structure that looked like a palatial home snuggling comfortably into the forested mountainside.

Geoffrey glanced anxiously up at the lighted windows. "I hope they have room for us," he said.

"We're going to stay here all night?"

"What else do you suggest?" he asked dryly.

Just outside the foyer they took off their soggy shoes. In spite of herself, tears filled Laura's eyes at the excruciating ache in her feet. She turned away quickly, but Geoffrey saw and bent down, lifting one foot at a time, giving each a vigorous massage.

"Thank God this inn has central heating. A lot of them don't," he said. The spacious entry hall contained only a flowered screen and a recessed *tokonoma* with its customary scroll and ikebana. Polished wood floors gleamed. As cold and miserable as she was, Laura saw that the very simplicity created an air of elegance.

A maid appeared, bowed low and handed them each a pair of slippers—a bit too small, Laura noted. Geoffrey spoke rapidly in Japanese, and the maid, looking distressed, bowed and disappeared.

"Something wrong?" Laura asked.

"Apparently there's only one room left, and it's reserved, although the people haven't shown up yet."

One room, Laura thought, and felt sudden warmth

return to her icy limbs. The maid soon reappeared, all smiles and bows, and beckoned them to follow her down the polished corridor.

"What happened?" Laura whispered.

"Don't ask. We've been rescued, haven't we?"

The fragrance of green tea wafted past them, and Laura inhaled thirstily. At their room they exchanged slippers for mittenlike socks before walking on the tatami mats. Laura sank down on one of the cushions at the low table and stretched her feet toward the bed of coals underneath. The warmth felt heavenly.

A glance around the room verified the same Spartan simplicity, unpainted wood both textured and polished, *shoji* panels, subdued lighting by means of creamy paper lanterns, a *tokonoma* and, in a far corner, two futons side by side. Through an open door she glimpsed the bath.

"Stay here and get out of those wet clothes," Geoffrey said. "I'm going to telephone your school and see about Kelly."

"What are you going to say?"

He looked at her with tolerance. "The truth. We're stranded. We are going to have to spend the night."

The maids helped her undress and held out a heavy kimono, then gave her a hot damp cloth to wipe her hands and face. They rolled her clothes into a bundle.

"Clean and ready in the morning," one of them said in her quaintly accented English.

Geoffrey came back soon smiling confidently. "No problem. Seiji will stay overnight with Kelly, and the director will take your class.'' He rubbed his hands briskly, then went through the same procedure with the maids, who helped him remove all his clothing.

Apparently inns didn't hold with modesty, she thought as she caught a glimpse of Geoffrey's tall, lean, naked body. She quickly averted her eyes and studiously regarded the painting hung in the *tokonoma*.

He chuckled at her behavior. ''Embarrassment at nudity is a cultural hang-up, not Japanese, I assure you.''

She wrapped grateful fingers around the bowl of hot tea and tasted the bean cakes the maids now brought along with the register for Geoffrey to sign. She tried to see what he wrote without appearing too nosy, but he caught her glance and regarded her with amusement.

''Don't worry. I preserved your reputation. I signed us in as Geoffrey and Snowflake McDermott.''

''Snowflake? You didn't!'' She burst into laughter.

''The inn isn't concerned with our personal arrangements, only our comfort.''

Personal arrangements! The words had an electrifying effect.

''I've ordered dinner, but it won't be served until after our bath. The maids will take care of us soon.''

Laura looked uncertainly through the doorway. ''Are you saying that the maids will attend my bath?''

''*Our* bath,'' he corrected. ''Absolutely. Take it in

stride. Anyway, their presence should make you happy.''

''Happy?''

He couldn't help but tease her. ''Chaperons. Right?''

She lifted an eyebrow. ''It's a unique experience, all right, all this company in the bathroom!''

The maids knocked and entered, bowing and smiling like two windup dolls. Each carried towel, soap and washcloth and motioned their two guests into the bathroom.

''Come along,'' Geoffrey called, ''or you'll cause an international incident.'' She followed.

Just pretend you do this every day and twice on Saturdays, she told herself. A round tiled tub, about six feet in diameter, occupied most of the area. Alongside were two low stools and two wooden buckets.

The maids helped their charges out of their *yukatas*, and Laura sat down on a stool with her back toward Geoffrey. The one dim lantern and clouds of steam cloaked them in temporary privacy. Geoffrey alternately whistled or bellowed out something that sounded like an aria from *Madame Butterfly* while the maids scrubbed their backs and poured buckets of rinse water over them.

''No soap in the big tub—an unwritten law, as you know,'' Geoffrey sang out as he stood up. Laura involuntarily cast a quick look over her shoulder. She had never seen a completely nude man before. Through the evaporating steam she realized his body was firm and muscled, not an ounce of spare flesh.

"Approval?" Geoffrey asked with a grin, and eased into the bath.

"Absolutely. You're what I'd call a beautiful man. I might even go so far as to say you could have modeled for one of those handsome museum statues."

"Careful," he said. "Such compliments could turn me into a madman.'

"I withdraw it, then. Just say I'm suffering from wearing too many pairs of rose-colored glasses."

He flicked water at her with thumb and forefinger, but she ducked and plunged into the bath up to her chin, caught her breath and shot up again.

"I'm scalded!" she cried.

"Don't tell me this is your first honest-to-goodness Japanese bath?"

"No, but I've never had one of a thousand degrees Fahrenhait!" she said, and settled gingerly back into the tub.

"This water is piped in from a hot spring. Relax. You'll love it." Heat began to dissipate the cold and tension from their walk in the snow, and she reveled in the blissful sensation. Suddenly she realized the maids had vanished.

"So what happened to the chaperons?"

Geoffrey gestured carelessly, water dripping from his palm. "Oh, I told them to let us soak for a while. They'll return a little later."

They faced each other across the steaming water, and she could hardly fail to notice that his body gleamed a uniform olive through the moisture, that his dark hair curled engagingly around his ears, that the elusive dimple in one cheek had never been more prominent.

The awareness that filled her now radiated with far more heat than the bath. She undulated slightly in the water, just enough to keep it moving and render it opaque. A delicious languor filled her. What a heavenly experience.

"You've grown mighty quiet," he said. "Office hours now open if you need to get a load off your mind."

"I seem to recall a similar offer not too long ago. Acting the good listener must keep you busy."

"Not at all. I'm particular about my clients. I like only blue-eyed blondes on snowy evenings."

"Whose first names are Snowflake?"

"Absolutely."

Her laugh rippled across the water. He suddenly reached over and took her hand, pulling her toward him. "Come here. You look so appealing I can hardly stand it, your cheeks all rosy and flushed, those blue eyes of yours driving me crazy, not to mention several dozen other attributes." In slow motion she drifted over to him. He cradled her in his arms, and she knew that more than anything else in the world right now, this was the place she wanted to be.

The feel of their bodies gently touching, fluid, buoyant, sent her senses reeling, and she found it difficult to breathe. He kissed her gently as his hands explored, searching, teasing, caressing. She turned to face him, hovering gently for a moment, then closing against him.

Half-floating, legs entwined, they relished each

new intimacy, the newness, the awareness all sweetly sensuous in the incandescence of the hot spring water. She felt his watchful eyes and knew he deliberately proceeded at an unhurried pace, his concern only for her pleasure. She sensed his control in the caring way he first cupped, then held her breasts, not boldly, his fingers like fronds from some sea plant rippling softly against her. She yearned to offer instant and total commitment. Wrapping her arms around him with sudden intensity, she gave the invitation.

The maids knocked. She'd completely forgotten them. He held her close, and his eyes shone with promise.

"Lucky I'm up to my chin in water," she murmured. "Something inside me is catching fire."

He finally released her to answer the maids, who entered holding large fluffy towels. Leisurely, Geoffrey helped her out of the tub with the same nonchalance that he might have had helping her fully clothed from his car. He bent and kissed her shoulder, and they turned to allow the maids to rub them down.

The maids bowed again and offered clean *yukatas* and warm kimonos to wear over them. Such ceremony! Laura felt as if she was taking part in some solemn ritual and hoped she carried it off with as much aplomb as Geoffrey.

"I ordered sukiyaki tonight," Geoffrey said as they walked back into the other room and seated themselves at the low table. "Not strictly Japanese, but they've adopted it for tourists and prepare it well here. Incidentally, you look mighty alluring in that kimono.''

Did he also observe her wildly escalating emotions? "I'll get up and bow if you add that I look bright-eyed and brainy," she said.

"That goes without saying."

"And charming, too?"

"Always—or rather, nearly always." He raised an eyebrow and gave her a meaningful glance. She ignored him and gave her attention to the food that now arrived, hot miso soup with bits of tofu floating in it. One of the maids set a pot on a brazier next to the table, and the other one carried in thinly sliced beef and raw vegetables as artfully arranged on the platter as if they were a study in ikebana. When the fat sizzled in the pot, the maid dropped in the beef and prepared the sukiyaki.

Laura inhaled the rich aroma. "I'm ravenous!" she said, and looked across at Geoffrey, who consumed his soup with dedication. His face held all the enchantment she ever wanted or needed. Again he caught her glance and grinned widely.

"Would you be conjugating sensuous verbs?" he asked slyly.

"You're arrogant."

"Not so, or I'd never have become a writer. What I am is an unreformed mood analyzer."

She laughed. "Sounds like some electronic monstrosity." Good. Keep things frothy, and she'd be able to handle them. Her eyes rested on the two futons side by side, and her breath caught a little.

The sukiyaki was delicious and so were the cold

shrimp, cucumbers and dressing served on a chrysanthemum leaf. Dessert proved to be fresh oranges sliced to form a spray of blossoms across the plate. Meanwhile the maids kept their cups filled with warm sake. They had a way of accomplishing tasks so smoothly that they appeared to be performing a self-effacing ballet. Now they whisked away the dishes, turned back the futons and bowed out of the room.

"I'm not sure I could get used to all this attention. I'd probably grow completely helpless," Laura said.

"Live it up. The Japanese inn is the world's last bastion for such service."

"What next? I suppose they'll tuck us into bed?"

"Oh, they won't come in again tonight. I told them we're on our honeymoon."

"You didn't!"

"You said that before."

"Well, you keep bowling me over."

He rose and pulled her to her feet. "Come over here and have a look." He laid an arm across her shoulders, and as always his touch brought that inner quickening. He slid back the *shoji* to reveal a glass window. Bright moonlight illuminated the garden, covered with an immaculate white blanket except for a gnarled plum tree whose iced branches made lacy patterns against the wall. Wind bells tinkled brittlely from the eaves as if they were frostbitten. The cold reached through the glass, and they moved closer together.

"Not a blemish, not even a footprint," Laura said in a hushed tone.

"The Japanese believe one must not disturb a fall of snow any sooner than necessary in order to show gratitude for nature's gift. Now, there's a theme for your haiku. Get busy and write it."

"Now? This minute?"

"No. This minute is reserved for something else." He removed his arm and she suffered a moment of disappointment, but he only walked over to turn off the lamps. Now the softly lighted garden scene formed a wintry mural. Inside, the darkened room closed around them, full of warmth and silvered shadows.

He pointed outside the window. "See that ancient plum over there?"

"The one whose bare limbs make all those squiggles against the sky?"

"It's an early bloomer," he said. "It will be a shower of blossoms soon after the New Year. Does that give you any ideas?"

"Such as the perfect setting for a wedding?"

"Definitely. Ours. Right here at the inn, and we can stay in this same room for our honeymoon."

"Two honeymoons! The maids will think we're crazy." She pretended hesitation. "Well, if there's a full moon."

He snapped his fingers. "I'll arrange it."

She sighed. "Full moon and plum blossoms. I'd be a fool to refuse."

He tipped up her chin. "You have lovely eyes, but changeable. I've never decided whether they are sky blue or sapphire." He brushed his lips against her eyelids, his touch as light as gossamer. "My love," he murmured. Suddenly he swept her up into his arms and carried her over to the futon, easing her down upon it. He lay down beside her and drew her close, and his kiss was tender, a lover's kiss.

She heard the sound of his quickened breathing and felt the fall and rise of his chest against her breasts, or perhaps it was her own heart beating a rhythm of jubilation. A miracle, she thought, truly a miracle that they were lying in each other's arms, that the long ache was over, that they'd found under-standing at last.

Her hair tumbled around her shoulders, and he buried his face in it. He smelled fresh and warm. Slowly he raised himself above her, his eyes probing hers for restraint or fear. He smiled at her silent answer, unfastened her kimono and slipped it off, then the *yukata*. Now she lay before him clothed only in moonlight and shadows.

"You're lovely, beautiful," he whispered, and kissed her neck, the curve of her shoulder and the soft place between her breasts. Wherever his hands and lips touched she felt herself turn to liquid gold, hot and shimmering.

She reached up to stroke his shoulders, then put her hands on his face, her curved fingers tracing the contours of his cheekbones, then resting on his temples. She inhaled the subtle fragrance of soap, the clean masculine scent of him. He seemed to anti-cipat her every caress with breathless pleasure, remaining almost motionless as if to sustain the sen-sations.

A little shyly she opened his kimono and *yukata*

and helped him out of them. With growing eagerness she trailed her fingers along the length of him, feeling, exploring. The varied textures of his skin excited her. He was elegantly formed, this man of hers, and endearingly gentle. Touching, yes, touching the one you loved provided nourishment beyond all belief.

"Afraid, my darling?"

"Oh, no," she whispered.

Their desire quickened as his hands outlined her hips, then her breasts in tender strokes almost as if he was sculpturing her. He tasted the softness of her breasts, then their tautness, and girdled her waist with kisses. All the while she sensed by his every touch that he wanted her to remember this night forever. *I love you,* she thought. *You're everything I've ever wanted. I love your mind, your body, your tenderness, all of you. It's all precious to me.*

His hands moved more intimately now, searching, gently teasing, trailing fire, and she arched against him, freely acknowledging her own desire for total commitment. The long months of confusion and uncertainty gave way. She felt no recriminations now, no holding back or remotely wanting to, as she basked in their lovemaking.

The futons were soft and deep, and the moonlight reflected from the snowy garden provided a gauzy blanket. The room was hushed; not even the sound of wind chimes outside the window or the swish of footsteps passing by their door could be heard. It was as if the world had retreated in respectful regard for the enchantment that only lovers knew.

"I feel as if I'm moving in some fantasy," she said.

"Fantasy? Thank God this is real." His lips moved across her cheek and traced the soft curve of her ear. "Do you have any idea how long I've dreamed of holding and loving you like this, having you respond without reservation? I've coped with fantasy long enough. I want reality—*you*. I want us to be totally devoted and unafraid to say so."

She turned her face up to his, and they kissed. A moment later her lips parted, and his tongue answered the invitation in mutually deepening ardor. Suddenly the kiss abandoned its languorous exploration, became more passionate. His embrace tightened, and she felt the urgency in his body. Sensations, violent and intense, swept through her. Legs and arms entwined, they became caught up in instinctive age-old rhythms. Propelled on a wake of ecstasy, they melded into one being in a climax that both seared and consumed.

Later, she nestled in his arms and savored the descent back into the shadowed room, the moonlit garden now a scene by Hiroshige. Tears of happiness clung to her cheeks. At last he moved away, but it was as if he still held her. Did he own a special wizardry that allowed him to set her free yet enfold her at the same time?

He wiped away her tears with a corner of the sheet. "Are you okay?"

"Oh, yes. It's all my happiness spilling over. I hardly know how to deal with it."

"You're wonderful. Everything's all right. I love you."

She snuggled against him. "I know."

"So never, never go away again," he said.

"I don't want to go anywhere without you, Geoffrey."

"We're home free, my darling. I thought it would never happen."

Unwittingly she stiffened. No, they were not home free. Not entirely. Not until *shiwasu*.

At once she sensed his withdrawal, although he hadn't actually moved. She kept her head pressed hard against his chest so that she didn't have to meet his eyes. Suddenly he gripped her shoulders and with one hand tipped up her chin so that she faced him.

"Look at me! Don't tell me you're still holding back? Something is still there, isn't it?" he asked wearily.

How could his voice change so quickly? Fear made her almost inarticulate. "I love you, Geoffrey. Isn't that enough for now?" she asked, her voice breaking.

"For now? What's coming up in the future, may I ask?"

"Please, this evening has been heaven for me. Perfect. I don't want to spoil it."

"Spoil it? Not unless you're not leveling with me." He spoke quietly, and the hurt in his eyes brought a lump to her throat. He got up and put on his *yukata* and tossed hers down on the futon. She slipped into it and sat hugging her knees.

"You're the man I love. There's no one else. Can't you believe me?"

"Well, then, what is it? I thought we had this pro-

blem solved. You were wonderful tonight, Laura,''
he added softly. ''So why do you fall back into that
same old pattern?'' He strode over to the far side of
the room.

She got up and walked over and touched his arm.
Oh, God. What was happening to them?

He stepped away. ''Damn it, what kind of relationship will we have if there are always these reser-
vations? I'm not interested in any fine print. I've had
it with evasions!''

The moment for truth had arrived at last. The timing was singularly inappropriate, but then she'd
never expected it would be easy. With a sense of
fatalism she met his eyes without flinching. ''I
wonder if you really want to hear about the demons
I've wrestled ever since I've known you, Geoffrey? I
wonder if there's any way you'll understand?''

He gripped her shoulders so hard she had to hold
back a cry of pain. ''Tell me,'' he demanded.

''It's Lisa, my sister, Lisa,'' she said numbly.
''Doesn't that name mean anything to you?''

Geoffrey dropped his arms to his sides, his expression incredulous. ''My God, what has your sister got
to do with us?''

Laura had a sinking sensation. ''Don't tell me you
can't remember Lisa Adams?'' She closed her eyes.
Don't let him lie to me, she prayed.

Geoffrey paced the floor, then stopped abruptly.
''Believe me, my dear, you're the only Adams I've
every known, and I'm beginning to think I'm lucky I
haven't met any others.'' The words pelted her like
darts and proved as hurtful.

She lifted her chin and retied her sash with vigorous thrusts. "Perhaps you'd better let me refresh your memory then. Apparently it was convenient for you to forget. Think back, Major McDermott. Think back to eleven years ago this coming Easter, a dance at a college sorority house in Ohio where you met, married, then deserted a girl named Lisa Adams."

He stared at her unbelievingly. "Well, I'll be damned. Where did you ever come up with that cockeyed story?"

She turned away to hide her disappointment. She had been certain that he would not lie. She walked over to look out the window. The moon had gone behind a cloud, and the garden looked desolate, dark and menacing. She turned to face him. "Kelly is proof," she said. "You didn't know you'd also deserted a son, did you?"

His face showed an entire range of emotions, bewilderment, anxiety, anger. "Are you saying that all these months you believed I was Kelly's father and you didn't tell me?"

She nodded miserably, not trusting herself to repeat the charge. He walked over and looked down at her, his eyes smoldering. He didn't touch her, and she knew she'd lost him.

"Tell me exactly what happened."

Dazed, she repeated the story as if reciting dry details and events from a history book.

"It's true I was home then on leave," he said slowly, as if gradually remembering. "And, yes, I was in Ohio, but I spent my entire leave in a hospital in traction. I was in a car accident. There are hospital records to prove it.''

"And I have army records to prove my allegations.'' She flung the words at him. "But Lisa found out it wasn't convenient for you. You already had a wife then, didn't you?''

He almost shoved her away from him. "You actually believe that, don't you? You really swallowed the whole thing, hook, line and sinker. You have me confused with someone else. Can't you see that? My God, I wouldn't do that to any woman! What kind of opportunist do you think I am?''

"I thought you'd changed.'' Her voice trembled. She was afraid of his obvious fury. His eyes had narrowed to slits, his fists were clenched tightly, and his voice was filled with so much rage she wondered he didn't shout at her.

"If you really believe that ridiculous story, how could you allow me to make love to you? How could you even give me the time of day? And in heaven's name, if you really thought Kelly was mine, why didn't you tell me?''

She had to get through to him, make him understand. "Please, listen to me, Geoffrey. At first I was afraid I'd lose Kelly. Then I was terrified that I'd lose you, too. I know I was a coward but when you love—''

He held up a hand. "Don't bother. I know exactly what happened,'' he said, and she knew he hadn't heard her. "It happens all the time. The only surprise is that you're so credulous. Your sister got pregnant, and her family would believe almost anything to protect her virtue. True? But the real question here is how she happened to pin her folly on me."

"What about Kelly's striking resemblance to you? You can't deny that! I saw it immediately." She felt her heart break as she flung her trump card at him.

"So we both have curly dark hair. That means absolutely nothing. I'll bet your family never saw the guy in this mythical marriage." He leveled a hard look at her. "Did they? Did you?" he demanded.

Laura shook her head miserably. No, they hadn't. But Lisa would never have manufactured such a complicated story, would she? Besides, Laura had seen the letter from the army. Lisa was naive, trusting, gullible, but she wouldn't lie.

Geoffrey was doing a masterful job of turning the tables, but then, words were his trade. Everyone was flawed. No one was perfect. Had he blocked out his one lapse of character, persuaded himself that it had never happened? She stood tall, facing him squarely.

"If there was one thing I counted on in this whole sordid affair, it was your honesty, Geoffrey." Her voice broke. "I trusted you to tell the truth."

His face was a magnificent study in injured innocence. "Trust!" he cried, his voice edged with bitterness. "Lady, you don't know the meaning of the word!" He strode out of the room, sliding the doors shut with such force the sound ricocheted around her. She was alone, and the room grew silent, chilled and hollow.

CHAPTER TWENTY-TWO

LAURA WOKE UP the next morning feeling exhausted. Her eyes were swollen from weeping, and she felt burdened with an impossible weight that had resulted from the quarrel. She'd waited hours after Geoffrey left the room, hoping for his return. She wanted to explain, wanted to reach out to him, prayed that he wouldn't hate her.

She thought he might have slipped into his futon sometime during the night, but she wasn't sure. The moon had disappeared behind clouds, and only the darkness held the answer. Pain and disappointment had suddenly thrust her into an uncertain world. This morning he was gone.

She dragged herself into the bathroom and bathed her eyes in cold water, then found her clothes in a neat pile where the maid had left them, clean and ironed.

After getting dressed, she walked down the hall to the entrance of the inn. A group of tourists stood waiting for their bus to Kyoto. A providential escape route? She hurried back to the room, found pad and pen in her purse and quickly scribbled a note. "Goodbye, Geoffrey. I've found transportation home. Please believe I never meant to deceive or hurt you. Laura." She would give it to one of the maids and ask her to hand it to Geoffrey if and when he returned.

At once, something inside welled up in protest. What about *shiwasu*? She'd promised herself to face up to problems, not to back off, not to procrastinate or run away. But she'd faced up to Geoffrey last night, and look what happened.

Nevertheless, she knew what she had to do: deal with this crisis now; have done with ambivalence. One way or another it was bound to become a turning point in their relationship. He was so angry and hurt last night that she knew he hadn't heard her. Maybe now he would listen. She crumpled the note and put it into her pocket.

Her love for him was in everything she saw, his rumpled futon next to hers, his kimono folded across a cushion, the lamp he'd turned off so they could more readily view the moonlit garden, in the very air she breathed. Outside, the plum tree's bare limbs were laced with snow. Would blossoms really dare to burst forth on those icy branches?

A maid walked into the room with a breakfast tray. She chattered earnestly in Japanese. The gist of the conversation seemed to be that Geoffrey had gone to see about his car.

"Do you know when he will return?"

The little maid shook her head. She didn't know. Disappointment dulled Laura's appetite, but to please the anxious maid she sat down at the low table and ate a few mouthfuls. If only she could talk with Geoffrey while her resolve was strong, try to explain her illogical behavior.

Somehow she would make him understand how much she loved him, how she wanted to put the past behind her, how she trusted the Geoffrey she knew. Hadn't he pleaded for that very course the day they met in the Moss Gardens?

Minutes later Geoffrey strode into the room, his face as chilly and unyielding as the cold that had whipped color into his cheeks. His remoteness was incredible, surrounding her with a loneliness that almost overpowered her, seeming to sink into her very bones.

The few seconds their eyes met and held stretched interminably.

"I've made arrangements for you to return on a tour bus that will be leaving in about fifteen minutes." His tone was probably as impersonal as the tour director's.

He helped her on with her coat, his action detached and lacking the usual caring touch that made her spine tingle. They walked in silence. So little time to try to mend the breach between them!

Outside, the snow crunched under their feet. Tourists milled and lined up to board the bus, little puffs of vapor punctuating their chatter.

Laura turned and laid a hand on Geoffrey's arm. "I think we need to talk a little more, Geoffrey. May I wait and go back with you?"

"Afraid not," he said brusquely. "There's some damage to the car, and it will have to be towed. I'll ride back with the driver in the tow truck. You'd better hurry. There won't be another bus until late this afternoon."

"Will you have time later today? I have some things I need to say."

"What more needs to be said? It seems to me that we covered everything rather adequately last night. I'm not much for redundancy."

She winced at the brush-off. "Do you want me to come to work? It looks as if I will be able to be there at the regular time."

"Suit yourself," he said, and looked over her head as if the matter were no concern of his.

"I want to continue," she said as firmly as she could, but her voice quavered in spite of her effort. He shrugged as if he didn't really care.

"There's nothing urgent at the moment, as I already mentioned. However, there is a little correspondence and a few newspaper columns I plan to use sometime in the future, if you like."

The driver honked impatiently. The last person in line had already climbed on the bus. Laura felt the kind of desperation experienced by someone drowning.

"Geoffrey, please. I know that I hurt you terribly last night. I'm truly sorry. I didn't mean to."

The driver admonished her to cease her talk and join the other passengers. Reluctantly she obeyed and the door clamped shut, cutting off Geoffrey's answer if he had one. She sank wearily into a window seat. Had the door also banged shut on any future conversation with him?

The bus climbed a mile or so farther up the mountain to another inn, collected more passengers, then headed back toward Kyoto. A few minutes later it slowed and lumbered around a tow truck that was pulling a black car out of the ditch. Geoffrey, hunched against the cold, stood nearby and gave only a cursory glance at the passing vehicle. His dispassionate gesture hurt her deeply. Was it so easy for him to turn off their love?

An hour later she walked into Geoffrey's condominium to see his housekeeper, Mrs. Fujii, standing in the hall, her mouth working so strangely that Laura wondered if the woman was about to break into tears. On recognizing Laura, she burst into a torrent of Japanese.

"I don't understand," Laura repeated several times, and felt completely helpless and alarmed at the woman's frantic behavior.

At last the woman realized she wasn't communicating and beckoned Laura to follow her upstairs to Geoffrey's office. A devastating scene awaited her. Every drawer had been emptied and dumped on the floor. Every book had been removed from the shelves and hurled into the corners. Laura stared aghast.

"Was anything stolen?" she asked in her slow, careful Japanese.

"I don't think so, but I just arrived and haven't made a thorough search." At least that's what she thought Mrs. Fujii answered.

What could the thieves have wanted? Did Geoffrey store valuable papers or money in his office? Suddenly she thought of his art collection and pointed to the floor above. The woman understood immediately, and the two raced upstairs and down the hall. The room was still locked with no evidence of a break-in. Someone knew Geoffrey kept no papers in there.

Alarm flared again. The file room! Again the two women now hurried to the little room off the library where Geoffrey stored work in progress, research notes and current correspondence. A fireproof safe housed important manuscripts such as novels. Laura closed her eyes at the sight and felt ill. Every file had been emptied, its contents scattered on the floor. The room seemed ankle-deep in Geoffrey's valuable records. Several beer cans added to the litter, and some had spilled their contents over many of the papers. The small fireproof safe was gone. Thank God Geoffrey had already sent his latest novel to the publisher, but what other valuable work might he have stored there?

Mrs. Fujii ran for a carton and started to pile the papers in it.

"No, no!" Laura cried. "First the *junsa*, the police. Don't touch anything. *Denwa*, telephone," she added. Mrs. Fujii nodded and immediately went to the phone on Laura's desk. Laura strained hard to catch the drift of the rapid staccato chatter. Her Japanese was improving, but unless people spoke slowly she still had trouble understanding.

"Suga," 'soon,' the woman said at the conclusion of the conversation. She held up her ten fingers to indicate the number of minutes until the police arrived. Laura went back and surveyed the file room. It would take hours to put everything back in order, not to mention retyping any number of the beer-soaked pages. But she knew she could do it. Her months with

Geoffrey had made her completely familiar with his files and their contents.

In less than the ten minutes, three policemen arrived, businesslike and courteous. The housekeeper showed them the ransacked rooms. Laura explained that Geoffrey had gone to an arts-and-crafts fair at Mount Hei yesterday but she didn't know when he would return. She avoided other details. Geoffrey could fill those in if necessary.

The police went through the house to check for further damage, but to all appearances, it was confined to the two rooms. They worked efficiently, securing fingerprints from beer cans, door handles and files. They took a number of snapshots, and one of the men talked continually into a vest-pocket tape recorder, documenting evidence. As they made ready to leave, Mrs. Fujii asked if she could restore order, and the police gave their assent. She bowed very low, and the men departed.

Now Laura worked quickly. Mrs. Fujii started her usual chores, and Laura took care of the two ransacked rooms. Geoffrey's office went easily enough as she returned books to shelves and organized the usual writer's paraphernalia in a reasonable approximation of its former place. The file room was a different project. Hundreds of pages of typewritten notes, background material for his newspaper columns, had to be resorted according to subject. She spread out the beer-soaked pages to dry and estimated that, after all, there were only a dozen or so that would need retyping.

She stayed at the task through the morning and

into the afternoon, working frantically to complete
and restore the files to their former order. She stopped
for a few minutes' break to enjoy the soup Mrs. Fujii
prepared, then continued. She began to feel tension
increase as she pushed to finish the job before Geoffrey arrived. The break-in was serious, but she didn't
want that problem to override the conversation she
wanted to have with him.

She gathered the now dried and curling pages that
had been soaked with beer and sat down at the typewriter. Some were almost impossible to read, but
she managed to have them all retyped when she
heard Geoffrey's step in the entry hall. She rubbed
the aching muscles in her neck and rose to meet
him.

He stopped abruptly, obviously amazed at finding
her still there, his expression clearly requesting an explanation. Tired lines showed in his face, and dark
circles curved under his eyes. His mood of constraint
still remained as tangible as the afternoon light that
streamed through the windows.

She ached to touch him, to find the elusive words
that would reach him enough to make him turn wel-
coming and loving again. His eyes remained remote,
unchanging.

"You're still working?" he asked finally.

"Yes. I wanted to complete everything, if possible."

"I didn't think there was that much to do." His
cool tone suggested that she must be stalling.

"There is a little more. Shall I return tomorrow?"
He didn't answer right away but allowed the silence

to lengthen until it was charged with negative implications. She walked over to him.

"Geoffrey, give me a straight answer. Do you or do you not want me to remain as your secretary?"

"It's up to you," he said in a monotone. His own opinion seemed apparent. She hated him for leaving it up to her. She wanted him to make the decision. His answer held the fate of their future.

"I wish you'd stop behaving as if we were strangers!" she cried. "I'm a real live person, someone who makes mistakes but someone who loves you!"

"And someone who considers trust a matter of convenience, something to turn on and off like a light switch. What kind of marriage can we build on that tenuous foundation?" he asked, his voice suddenly bitter and charged with emotion.

Tears brimmed, but she ignored them. The conversation had turned unexpectedly treacherous, and she didn't see the point in continuing. She walked past him into the entrance hall, each step uncoordinated as if her brain was sending late messages.

"Oh, yes," she said, pausing at the front door. "In case you're interested, your house was broken into last night." Startled, he began to move toward her in concern.

She brushed him off with a wave of her hand. "Mrs. Fujii will give you the details. I guess the main question here, as far as you and I are concerned, is if you believe our business relationship can still work." *And our personal relationship and our engagement, and even our marriage*, she added silently because she knew his answer would be the same for all four.

She shoved her fists into her pockets to control their trembling as she awaited his answer.

His eyes were bleak. "No, Laura," he said quietly. "I don't think it would work."

CHAPTER TWENTY-THREE

CHRISTMAS MORNING Laura was jolted by fire-crackers exploding beneath her window. A group of revelers staggered down the street bellowing a song off-key, and the musician across the way practiced a piece on the koto at such hysterical speed the rhythm became unintelligible. The sounds hardly seemed evocative of Christmas. Only the temple bell that reverberated in the distance seemed at peace with itself. Scott was right. Japanese celebrated Christmas in the same spirit that Americans observed New Year's. People partied and went to nightclubs and bars. There seemed to be no religious significance.

Kelly had opened his presents the night before and was sleeping late this morning. Laura sat on the floor next to their small tree nursing a cup of coffee. She'd never spent such a lonely Christmas.

The anguish over her break-up with Geoffrey a little over a week ago still continued. She felt empty, dull, as if every ounce of vitality had drained away. A hundred times a day her thoughts took flight and soared up to the mountain inn. It had been a drama in two acts with a tragic ending.

He never truly loved me, she thought now as she

sipped her cold coffee, *or he wouldn't have been so
defensive, so quick to condemn, so unwilling to
listen.* Ending a relationship posed no problem for
him. She wished she could follow suit.

Had he told her the truth? Had she only imagined
Kelly's resemblance to Geoffrey, and was it her
sister, after all, who had deceived her? She wanted to
believe both of them. She wanted to settle her doubts
forever, but no matter how she reasoned, they always
returned to haunt her. Apparently Geoffrey had no
second thoughts. She hadn't heard from him since
the quarrel.

She'd called once to ask about the break-in. Mrs.
Fujii answered, and remembering to slow her Japanese so Laura could understand, she said the police
believed it was caused by friends of the dissident
professor Geoffrey had written about. Apparently
the thieves wanted to remove photographs and other
documentation that could be used against the man.

"I think it's time for you to come back to work,"
Mrs. Fujii said. "Dr. McDermott is one sad man—
crabby, too. I think he needs his secretary."

"Oh?" Laura doubted that. Anyway, he had
several telephones. He could have used any one of
them.

"Yes. He walks around all the time, doesn't tend
to his writing. I tried to cheer him, told him how you
cleaned up his office and file room. You did it fast,
too. He was impressed, let me tell you, but strange
thing, he still didn't look happy. Are you coming
back soon?"

"I don't think so, Mrs. Fujii. I have another posi-

tion now.'' She wished the kind little housekeeper a
Happy New Year and said *sayonara*.

She had found another job at once, working mornings in Ishimoto's bookstore near the language
school, not that she needed the work now. A letter
from her grandmother's lawyer said the long-awaited
annuity would arrive in monthly checks starting the
first of January. Work was a matter of survival.
Keep busy, concentrate on as many tasks as possible.
Maybe if she could exhaust her mind, she would be
able to fall asleep at night.

Mr. Ishimoto, the owner of the book shop, was a
little man who wore thick glasses and a perpetual
smile. He looked a few years younger than God and
seemed almost as wise. Laura adored him immediately. He was infinitely tolerant of the many browsers.
In his own way, that made him a philanthropist.
There were few libraries accessible to the public in
Japan.

There arose one difficulty. Apparently the shop
was a favorite haunt of Geoffrey's. He'd dropped by
a few times to chat with Mr. Ishimoto, who was an
old friend.

Laura didn't work at the counter. Her job involved
filling mail orders and stocking shelves, so thus far
she'd managed to avoid him. Her first day on the job
he'd come in with Marcia Cole, his former secretary
and administrative assistant at Sato. Did she work for
him again? The radiance of her smile indicated some
kind of satisfaction. Perhaps they were right for each
other, after all. Their self-confidence, their sophis-
tication, their good looks seemed eminently in tune.

Irony filled Laura's life in considerable proportion, she mused. The past autumn had brought proposals from two men who could be considered the cream of the crop: Scott, steady and compassionate; Geoffrey, intelligent and exciting. Now Scott would be released from the hospital in a couple of weeks, and an invitation to his and Mariko's wedding, to be held the end of January, lay on her desk. And Geoffrey? Laura looked the other way every time he came into the book shop.

Kelly was up now, so she finished her coffee and fixed his breakfast, which he quickly gulped in order to get back to his model planes. She unconsciously polished counters and stove top until they shone as she lost herself in nostalgia. On holidays, Grandmother Canfield's house had been a gathering place for all their friends. Entertaining had been her forte, a party to decorate the tree, carols sung afterward and the marvelous fragrance of hot mulled wine and home-baked cookies. How different this Christmas could have been. She'd stuffed the lacquer tray she'd bought for Geoffrey far back into the closet.

Suddenly she realized the telephone had rung several times. It was Sachiko.

"If you have no other plans, may I drop by this afternoon?"

"Wonderful. I'd love some company." Yes, she would. It was time she stopped moping around and feeling sorry for herself.

"Thank you," Sachiko said. "Then it's all right if I bring someone along with me?" Her tone was lilting and provocative.

"A mystery guest? How exciting."

Sachiko laughed, a melodious run that spanned an octave. "You know, don't you? Yes, we're getting married. You are our true go-between, so we want to come over and thank you."

What had happened to the sad-faced girl in the tea shop who believed no man would ever marry her? Moreover, what had become of the S.D.O.I., Sachiko's Declaration of Independence?

"So it's love for Sachiko," Laura said. "Sounds like the name of a song. I wish you much happiness."

"*Arigato.* One doesn't shed one's heritage easily, but, Laura-san, I haven't changed my tune as much as you may think. I do go along with my parents now in believing love will flourish if all the ingredients for a good marriage are present. The point is, I made very sure to define a 'good marriage' to my own satisfaction." She giggled. "And of course I had a long list of ingredients."

"'A' plus for Miss Gentle Moon Flower."

"You're surprised, aren't you?"

"After hearing your original S.D.O.I., I wondered."

"Oh, we don't agree perfectly on everything. That would be dull, I think. But when Kenzo wanted to marry me regardless of whether or not I could bear children, I knew I'd found the right man."

"And your parents?"

"I give a little, they give a little. Something new, something old—a good blend for happiness, I believe."

Sachiko invited Laura and Kelly to the Shinto ceremony that would be held at noon on the third of January, then rang off with a promise to arrive early this afternoon.

Later Laura made coffee and sandwiches and arranged a plate of Christmas cookies she and Kelly had decorated. Refreshments ready, she put on the new dress she'd purchased for the holiday season, a blue jersey that exactly matched her eyes and complemented her blond hair. This was the first time she'd worn it. She straightened her posture and gave careful attention to her makeup. Thank goodness for cosmetics, she thought, noting the improvement.

Promptly at two, a knock signaled the arrival of her guests. Sachiko and Kenzo stood holding hands, each bearing a gift.

"Merry Christmas and congratulations!" Laura cried, and beckoned them inside. She served the refreshments as the two shared their plans, excitement surfacing in spite of valiant attempts to behave like proper Japanese and underplay their joy. Sachiko's eyes sparkled. "I think Laura doesn't believe she is our true go-between."

Kenzo broke into a wide smile. "Oh, yes, Tongue-tied-san and Miss Gentle Moon Flower so regard you." Kenzo handed her the presents he and Sachiko had brought and left one under the tree for Kelly. Kenzo's was a leather-bound copy of selected essays and columns by Geoffrey McDermott, Ph.D. Sachiko's package contained a gold chain on which hung a beautiful cultured pearl. Laura clasped it around her neck.

"How thoughtful!" she said, then bent to thumb

through the volume, struggling for control. The book suddenly brought home the extent of her unhappiness. Would the time ever come when Geoffrey would become nothing more than a vague memory rather than this consuming obsession? But this was no time to tell her friends that the relationship had shattered. She was touched by their gesture and said so. Truly, she believed Sachiko had decided wisely and she marveled at the way the young woman's head ruled her heart in the process. But then, Sachiko had the benefit of generations of conditioning.

Kenzo was being sent by his company to the United States the middle of January. The wedding was to be arranged soon so that Sachiko could accompany him. Laura gave them the tea bowls she'd bought at Mount Hei. Kelly came bounding in then, and the conversation centered on him for a while. At last they rose to leave.

At the door they bowed deeply and said goodbye.

"*Sayonara,*" Laura replied. Kenzo stood behind his tiny Sachiko and gave Laura a knowing look over her head. He made a circle with thumb and forefinger.

"Communication," he said, and for once he pronounced it impeccably.

Laura buttoned her sweater and stood on the porch listening to the departing footsteps of her two friends. The city had become paled and tamed under last night's fall of snow. How different now than the recent fiery autumn with its blazing maples and poetic fantasy of moon viewing.

Yes, she'd fallen in love with Kyoto, intrigued at the way it embraced with equal candor an exuberant teenager in jeans and T-shirt or a grandmother in traditional kimono; at its impartial enthusiasm for a Western Christmas or an ancient *matsuri*.

This city had taught her the beauty of understatement, whether in a tea bowl, painting or garden. Its street peddlers' cries and temple bells played a special music that would remain with her always, even that of her persistent if unmusical neighbor, with her ceaseless plunking on her many-stringed koto.

Geoffrey loved this city, too, and in a far more insightful way. Their affection for Kyoto would have enriched their marriage. The thought filled her with poignant longing. Chilled and shivering, she went back inside the house feeling as if she'd been reduced to an anonymous figure.

Except for Sachiko's and Kenzo's visit, the day had seemed interminable. After Kelly went to bed, she curled up on the couch to read the collection of Geoffrey's writing. Too late to receive a certain call? She realized she'd been hoping since early morning. She'd read only a dozen pages when she heard an impatient knock. Her heartbeat quickened. Could it be?

At first she didn't recognize the rumpled-looking man standing on her porch.

"Laura, don't you know me?" he asked, panting as if he'd run up both flights.

"Neil!" He looked so different without a beard, and he'd gained more weight. The dapper Neil had disappeared, and in his place stood a rather seedy-looking man. The change shocked her. Nevertheless, without the beard, she could see the faint physical resemblance to Geoffrey that had bothered her every time she saw him. The shape of the cousins' heads was almost identical, but the chiseled planes of Geoffrey's face couldn't be found in Neil's heavy contours.

He followed her inside, shrugged off his overcoat and settled into a chair. He stroked his chin. "Some gal talked me into shaving it off."

"It's just that you don't look like you anymore."

A pained expression crossed his face. "Good. It's time I changed my personality; the old one didn't have much to offer." He glanced at her spotless kitchen. "Any goodies left? Just got in from Nagoya."

She gave him a tolerant smile. He was always ready to eat. She cut generous slices from the ham she'd baked and made him a couple of sandwiches, brewed fresh coffee and set out the rest of the cookies.

He ate hungrily. "You're just the kind of a girl every man dreams of coming home to," he said between bites.

"Naturally, as long as she feeds him."

He chatted with enthusiasm about an antique bowl he'd just learned was for sale, and he meant to have it. Yes, he certainly sounded like himself, although he didn't look it. Occasionally, she caught a similarity in the timbre of his voice to his cousin's, except Geoffrey's diction was a lot more polished.

"By the way, Neil, why didn't you ever mention that you and Geoffrey were cousins?"

"You mean I've never bragged about being related to a famous author? That's not like me, you know."

"I did think it was odd you didn't say anything."

"I'm sure I told you that first day we met. Remember? What difference does it make?"

"None, I guess. I don't remember that you told me anything about your relationship except you were army buddies."

"Oh, no. I couldn't have said that. I was a P.F.C. Majors never hung around with 'em. Where is he? I stopped by his place just before I came here. No one was around."

Laura took her time refilling his cup. "I wouldn't know. I don't work for him anymore."

He gave her a measuring glance. "You two call it quits? A damn shame."

"I'd rather not discuss it."

"Oh, sure, I understand." He took a bottle of sake out of his overcoat pocket. "Brought you a little Christmas cheer. Not too late for a sample, is it?"

Midnight was too late as far as Laura was concerned, but she didn't want to seem ungrateful. She set out two sake cups, remembering uneasily what Geoffrey had said about Neil's drinking problem. "Shall we warm it?" she asked after she pulled the cork.

He reached for the bottle. "Hell, no, let's not fool around with that." He poured the tiny cups to the brim and consumed his in a single swallow, then poured himself another and drank it in the same fashion. Laura watched uncomfortably. Sake shouldn't be downed like shots of whiskey in a grade-B western movie. One sipped it slowly. When he drank his fourth cup, she grew alarmed. Could he handle it? She still hadn't finished her first drink when he downed still another. He turned the empty cup clockwise as he spoke.

"Actually, I'm in Kyoto to raise some money to buy some priceless items from a bankrupt estate. There's money to be made in the deal, believe me. If I can get the stuff, I have buyers lined up from here to Hokkaido. How about you, Laura? I'll bet you have fifty thousand yen tucked away in your bank account. You can double your money in twenty-four hours if you want to go in with me. What bank gives you that kind of interest?"

"I have no money to invest," she said coolly.

He gauged her sudden change of mood. "Sorry. I didn't mean to push. I get a little overenthusiastic sometimes." Neil had begun to slur his speech, but she was surprised he didn't show more effects from the sake.

"Never mind," he said. "Old Geoff will go for it. Any ideas how I might reach him?"

"Call Marcia Cole at Sato."

"The redhead? Hell, he's probably got her along with him. For business reasons, naturally," he added when he read her expression.

He suddenly yawned and stretched. "Man, I'm beat. Had a big day. I'll just bed down here on your sofa for the night. Don't mind, do you? Do you have a blanket?"

Laura looked down at him in frustration. Yes, she

minded. She minded a lot, and she was appalled at his nerve. What had happened to Neil? He'd always been a fun and entertaining companion. Not in Geoffrey's league, of course, but at least a gentleman.

"If you need taxi money, I'll be glad to lend it to you," Laura said stiffly.

He didn't answer. He was already snoring soundly.

CHAPTER TWENTY-FOUR

IT WAS SACHIKO'S WEDDING DAY, the third noon of the New Year. The large hall in the Miyako Hotel milled with people. At one end the guests gathered for the ceremony around an altar, which simply amounted to a *tokonoma* hung with a scroll bearing the name of a Shinto god.

Banquet tables decorated with arrangements of pink and white camellias filled the rest of the room. Laura sat with a wide-eyed Kelly inhaling the fragrance of pine boughs that festooned the walls. A string quartet performed something by Mozart, the effervescent music lacing the undercurrent of chatter. Laura was so distraught that she was only marginally aware of the activity.

Neil. What was she going to do about that man? He'd disappeared the day after Christmas, then turned up again New Year's Day. The lighthearted charmer had changed to a haunted man who hung around her apartment days and evenings, and went God knew where to spend his nights.

He had an obsequious way of playing on her sympathy and on her natural hospitality. In spite of every means she'd used to discourage him, he'd managed to outwit her.

The situation kept her continually on edge. Neil seemed such a different person that she no longer trusted him. Had he always been like this and she hadn't seen through his good-natured mask, or was it the alcoholism working? He promised to leave as soon as he raised the money he needed. Any day now, he kept saying.

To reach Geoffrey was her only hope, but according to his housekeeper he'd left town the day after Christmas on an assignment to Hokkaido, the northernmost island, something about the Ainus, the Japanese aborigines. She expected him to return momentarily, Mrs. Fujii said.

Laura pried her attention from her worries back to the scene around her and made herself focus on the wedding guests. What went on in their heads? In contrast to their somber dark suits, the men were jovial and greeted friends amid much bowing. It amused Laura to guess social standing according to which person bent down the lowest.

Young women, feminine and graceful in their black ceremonial kimonos, kept their eyes shyly averted, although Laura suspected they missed little of what went on around them. Their sisters in smart Western attire would have been at home in a cosmopolitan gathering anywhere.

Middle-aged ladies seemed to cloak their true thoughts behind pleasant facades, no doubt long practiced. Did they compare their own marriages to the expectations of this modern bride? An elderly woman sat erect, her features aristocratic in her wrinkled face. Not once relaxing her regal mien, she apparently regarded the affair philosophically. And Laura? Could anyone discern the silent weeping for another wedding that might have been?

Was that plum tree in bloom yet at the *ryokan*? She knew she shouldn't think about it but could find no space in her mind large enough to store her anguish.

She envied the ability of the elderly lady to regard life with such serenity. If she were in Laura's place, what would she do about Neil? She shuddered at what the Matsuis were thinking. She'd explained to Seiji one evening when he came to sit with Kelly that the man was Dr. McDermott's cousin, who awaited his return from Hokkaido.

Laura had made her position clear today when Neil arrived back with suitcase in hand.

"I can't let you stay here again," she'd told him quietly. "Go to your cousin's."

"Where do you think I've been the past few days? Geoffrey isn't home yet, and that housekeeper of his got teed off at me for some reason and locked me out."

"Strange. You often stay there, don't you?"

"Yeah, but she happened to catch me looking up something in Geoff's file and got the idea that I was the one who broke into his condo."

"And did you?"

"Why would I do that? I have a standing invitation to stay there." He swayed a little unsteadily, and even at the distance she stood she caught the smell of liquor.

"But you might know something about the break-in?"

He shrugged. "Hell, it could have been a couple of guys I know. Old Geoff was getting pretty nosy about the antique business, collecting a lot of information for a series he planned to do in his columns. Maybe they didn't like that. Hey, aren't you going to let me in?" He gave her an ingratiating smile. "I don't mind sleeping on your sofa. I won't be any trouble. The fact is, I'll only be short of cash for a couple more days, then I'll clear out."

"I'll lend you the money for a room," she said, and was afraid she'd begun to show how frantic she felt.

He looked suddenly penitent. "I'm sorry to be such a bother. I can see that I'm putting you on the spot. But if you could just see your way clear to help me out a little. Are the neighbors giving you a bad time?"

"Please go to a hotel. You may not stay here."

He'd finally left with such a hangdog expression that she couldn't help but feel a little guilty. His rolling gait and morose expression were far removed from the happy occasion where she found herself now.

She realized that the string quartet had stopped. The crowd grew quiet and settled back to watch the ceremony. Sachiko looked fragile and lovely in one of the most beautiful wedding kimonos Laura had ever seen, white brocaded silk piped in floral reds with a short train lined also in red. She carried a fan, *sensu*, in her hand and wore the traditional wide headband. Laura was glad that Sachiko had gone along with her parents in this lovely custom and at the same time was amused at the small ways Sachiko chose to ignore them. She had disdained the lucky day determined for the ceremony by the official go-between and substituted one of her own choosing.

"Shunning the Day of the Monkey or the Day of the Tiger or any other day for that matter is pure nonsense. We determine our own luck," Sachiko had insisted. She reproved the clacking tongues of her aunts who noted the unlucky four years' difference in her and Kenzo's ages. Although she wore the traditional *uchikake*, wedding kimono, she refused to wear the horns of jealousy underneath her headdress. And so it went. In fact, she'd seemed to take delight in plaguing the go-between's pronouncements. He gave in without too much difficulty, Sachiko told her with satisfaction. After all, he took pride in his role in uniting the two prominent Kyoto families, not to mention the prospect of the numerous gifts he could expect.

Now the couple stood in front of the *tokonoma*, and the presiding Shinto priest waved the streamers from his wand to signify that he exorcised any evil influences that might be present. The ceremony was short and included a silent exchange of rings, not customary in a Shinto ceremony. It apparently was an innovation both Sachiko and Kenzo wanted, not only as a symbol of an eternal relationship but as a visible reminder of their vow of fidelity.

They each took the ritual nine sips of sake, and the bride removed the broad floss-silk headband to show that she left her family to join with Kenzo. The ceremony was over.

Sake flowed freely. Waiters passed trays of delicacies so beautifully turned out it seemed almost a crime to eat them. That fact didn't seem to alter Kelly's appetite, and Laura cautioned against his generous samplings.

Everyone moved to the banquet table with Kenzo and Sachiko reigning at the head. Kenzo held his bride's hand and looked at her continually as if still unable to believe he had won her. The two chatted with animation, glancing at each other often, obviously enjoying the festivities. Such outward signs would have disgraced the male image a generation ago.

Waiters served food in small precise servings: raw fish garnished with seaweed and bean curd, mushroom soup, salad of cucumber blossoms and oranges, fish roasted with ginkgo nuts, a noodle dish, rice, crab legs, pickled carrots, melon...the array seemed endless.

As the meal concluded, friends and relatives made toasts and speeches, and the go-between extolled at length the virtues of the distinguished ancestry of both bride and groom. A few guests sang songs from well-known No plays, and others came up with jingles of considerably less noble nature, no doubt influenced by the plentiful sake. Sachiko's pupils from the Suzuki school performed an ensemble selection, and Kelly was a special hit with his recitation of good wishes written by Laura in haiku.

At last the festivities ended, and the hosts left before the guests in good Japanese style. Laura and Kelly made their way from the hotel clutching the elaborately wrapped gifts of fruit presented to each guest by the bride's family.

"May I open mine? We could stop at the park and eat some of it," Kelly said.

"Heavens! How can you force down another bite?"

"Well, then, couldn't we share it with the Matsuis? Do we have to go home right now?"

Laura noted that Kelly no longer mentioned Geoffrey. Although she'd told him that she'd changed jobs and now worked in a bookstore, she hadn't said anything about the breakup. She was certain he sensed what had happened. "It's not always easy for people to have unexpected guests, and it isn't polite to drop in unannounced."

"Neil does. Why does he keep hanging around our place? Can't we go to a movie?"

Laura knew what was bothering him. "You don't want to go home because Neil might be there waiting for us to let him in again?"

Kelly pretended absorption in his fruit basket. "Yeah," he said finally. "He's weird. I don't like him."

They had reached the bus stop. Laura debated. Go home now or find a small inexpensive hotel and wait until Neil left town? There was no one in Kyoto she could turn to at the moment. Scott was still convalescing at the hospital, and Geoffrey was hundreds of miles away on another island. Perhaps he would even prefer her to handle this problem herself. After all, he'd warned her about the man.

"I'm unhappy about Neil, too. I've come to the

end of my patience. Tell me, why don't you like him?''

Kelly knotted his brows in an unaccustomed frown. ''I can't explain exactly. It's like he's always sneaking around. I saw him going through your desk yesterday.''

''Why didn't you tell me?''

''Well, he said you borrowed something from him, and he was looking for it. I thought it was okay.''

Indignation filled her. How to cope? There was something furtive and ugly going on. She felt as if she and Kelly were caught in a tightening net. Well, they were getting out before it was too late.

''And why does he sit around drinking that sake stuff and watching TV all the time? He never lets me see any of my programs.'' Kelly seemed relieved to unload his grievances.

''You're sure he never hurt you?''

''Gee, no. It's more like he wanted to get rid of me. When he first came he promised to take me to a sumo match, but I guess he forgot. Mostly he tells me to get lost. I don't think he likes kids much. I wish Dr. McDermott or Uncle Scott was around. What happened?''

Good question. What happened, indeed, Laura asked herself dismally.

''Listen, Kelly. We're going straight to the Matsuis and ask them to help us.''

''Why don't you tell him we'll sic the police on him? I'll bet they'd throw him out.''

''That's the next step, but the whole situation is so vague.'' She didn't want Kelly to realize how uneasy she'd grown. "We don't know if Neil has broken any laws, and as far as I know, it's not a policeman's duty to throw out unwanted houseguests." Neil hadn't contributed anything except one sack of fruit and the inevitable bottle of sake, which only he consumed. Even more annoying were his untidy habits, which made the little apartment look continually cluttered.

Their bus arrived and they found a seat. Meanwhile, Kelly questioned her continually concerning her plans. Once home, they walked stealthily up the apartment steps so that if Neil waited for them on the porch he wouldn't hear them. Her spirits fell when no one answered at the Matsuis' second-floor apartment.

"They're not home yet," Laura whispered. "They often spend Saturdays visiting relatives in the country. Wait here, and I'll slip upstairs until I can see our landing. If Neil is there, we'll leave and go to a hotel."

She took off her shoes, crept up the next flight and breathed a sigh of relief when there was no sign of the man. She called down to Kelly that the coast was clear, and they entered the house together.

"We'll lock the door, and if he returns we'll pretend we're not home. I won't answer no matter how much he knocks. Tomorrow we'll find somewhere else to stay until he leaves town, I promise."

She braced herself for what might happen. Neil had no compunctions about banging on the door in the middle of the night. He knew the racket would bring her running in order to quiet him. It was humiliating and frustrating.

They drew all the curtains, turned off the lights, lit a candle and spoke in whispers. Kelly seemed to forget his own unhappiness as he got caught up in the scheme and moved around the rooms with excessive quiet, pretending he was a seasoned sleuth. After a while the game wore out, and he went to bed to fall asleep at once. Apparently he had shelved his fears. Laura wished she could do the same.

She called the Matsuis with the intention of alerting them in the event they heard Neil pounding on her door, but there was no answer. She rang Geoffrey's number after rehearsing what to say, hoping her awkwardness wouldn't diminish her present and very real need for help. The Geoffrey she knew would surely respond, but he didn't answer, either. At ten o'clock she bathed and crept into her futon.

Several hours later she woke with a start and sat up to listen. The luminous numbers on the digital clock read two-fifteen. What had wakened her? She heard no dreaded voice calling out her name nor any pounding on the door. Sounds came from the kitchen. That was it. Water running, a drawer sliding shut. She snuggled back into her futon with relief. Kelly. He must have gone in for a drink. Odd, though: Kelly rarely prowled around in the middle of the night. The refrigerator door slammed. She got up and slipped into her robe.

She walked barefoot down the hall and remained in the shadows where she could view the kitchen. Neil stood at the counter making a hefty sandwich from the leftover roast that was supposed to be tomorrow's dinner. The coffeepot perked nearby. He hummed softly under his breath.

"What are you doing here?" Laura asked coldly. Obviously he'd sneaked a key. Was it when he'd rummaged through her desk? He whirled around. His flushed face told her he'd been drinking again. He showed token surprise followed by an affable grin.

"Just a little sandwich. You wouldn't hold out on a poor starving fellow, would you?"

"Take the sandwich and leave, Neil."

"Come on, sweetheart, what happened to all that hospitality?" His voice took on a wheedling overtone that disgusted her.

"I'll ask the questions tonight," she said. "How did you get in?"

He waved a hand in an uncertain gesture. "Oh, that. I borrowed Kelly's key and had one made. It saves a lot of bother."

"That's underhanded. Give me the key," she said firmly. "You can go back to wherever it is you hang out when you're not here, or else go over to your cousin's. I can't allow you to stay here any longer."

He gave her a knowing wink. "Don't tell me the neighbors are beginning to talk?"

"I wouldn't be surprised."

He took his time munching his sandwich and washing it down with gulps of coffee. The silence grew heavy between them. She curled trembling fingers into a fist behind her. What would she do if he wouldn't back down?

He poured a cup of coffee for her and refilled his

own. "Let's talk," he said, and beckoned her to follow him. They sat down on opposite ends of the sofa.

"If you're trying to con me again, forget it," Laura said.

He looked genuinely hurt. "Laura, you don't mean that. Listen, things are finally breaking for me. I've been like a cat on a hot tin roof trying to finance that bankrupt-estate deal. You must be aware of that."

"A neat trick when you spend half your time at my place."

He sighed. "You're making it damn hard for me," he said. For a moment her heart turned over. When he spoke in that quiet tone he sounded exactly like Geoffrey. "Look, I have the feeling you don't trust me anymore. What have I done to offend you? I haven't touched you once, have I?"

At least that was true. "It's just that things don't add up, Neil. A man who's putting together a business deal doesn't sit around drinking and watching TV all day long."

He got up and paced around the room, then slumped down in a chair and put his head in his hands for a few moments. She wished he'd get on with it. All the histrionics were lost on her.

"Okay. I haven't been entirely honest with you, but I was too ashamed to tell you. Things have been going downhill for some time now. The loan I'm trying to negotiate is to save my business. I'm in debt up to my ears, and my creditors are swarming like hornets. Not only that, through no fault of mine, I'm in trouble with the police. That's why I've been hanging around here lying low, hoping they'd forget about me.''

''The police! Why?''

He looked at her warily. '' They seem to think I'm responsible for peddling some of those Thailand fakes.''

''And are you?''

His expression turned sullen. ''Why would a bonafide antique expert get involved with that?'' he muttered as if he asked himself the question. ''So how about it, could you help me out with a couple of thousand dollars? I've only got until Wednesday to come up with some cash, or I'll lose everything.''

Keep cool, Laura cautioned herself. If he admitted hiding from the police, he must be desperate. Neil was a chameleon changing his act whenever necessity called for it.

''Why don't you get a bank loan? Surely your antiques are collateral,'' she asked quietly.

''I've already gone that route. No luck.''

''What about that valuable box of goods that you left here? The way you talked, it must have brought you a pretty profit.''

''Not a single yen. Thailand fakes, the whole caboodle. I bought them from someone I trusted. Come on, Laura, I'll bet you could loan me a couple thousand and never even miss it.'' He laughed bitterly. ''Isn't it worth it to get rid of me?''

''I don't have that much, Neil, but I'll give you every penny I own if you'll get out of my apartment. You've created an impossible situation for Kelly and me. I'll write you a check.''

"You'll cancel it."

"I swear I won't."

His eyes glittered. "Okay. How much?"

"About five hundred and seventy dollars. I'll get my bank book and show you."

"Five hundred and seventy dollars! I don't believe it. You're kidding! That's not even a drop in the bucket." He went over to the counter and poured a water glass full of sake, downed almost half of it and looked at her a long time. "What about your annuity?" His voice took on a sudden hard edge. "What about Granny Canfield and your nifty little inheritance? You see, I know all about that."

"What do you know about my grandmother?" Laura asked in amazement.

"Enough."

"Did you open my mail, or have you been pumping Kelly?"

He grinned, but it looked more like a grimace "Both, if you have to know."

"Then you must realize that my inheritance didn't come in a lump sum. Three hundred a month. I received the first check only a few days ago."

His eyes bulged in anger—or was it frustration? "You're lying!" he cried, then made an obvious effort to control his temper. "Laura, honestly, don't I mean just a little to you?" He put an arm around her shoulders, but she slipped away. Did he actually believe he could win her over by playing on her sympathy? He sickened her. She edged closer to the hall, but he blocked her way, circling like an animal stalking its prey until he stood between her and the escape route.

"My God, Laura, if you only understood my predicament, I know you'd help me." His voice trembled with urgency. "Borrow it. Steal it. I don't give a damn!"

Laura fell back, alarmed at his agitation. "But how? I'm a foreigner here."

"Try Geoffrey. You'll have no trouble getting it out of him, even though I can't."

"I'm not sure if he's home from Hokkaido yet."

He strode over and thrust his face close to hers. "Well, find him. You can locate him if you try hard enough. How would you like old Geoff to know I spent a night here in your apartment? Do you think he'd believe everything was all sweet and innocent?"

Laura was appalled. "You wouldn't!"

"Try me. And what about your relatives? Have them wire it. I need it now, I tell you!" He was working himself into another frenzy. His fists clenched and unclenched, his face flushed a deep red and his mouth grew slack. She hardly recognized the fun-loving Neil she'd known in the pathetic individual who now stood before her. She felt both pity and revulsion.

With studied effort she kept moving away from him as she made her tone easy, conversational. "I don't know how else to tell you, Neil. Somehow you've misjudged my finances."

"There has to be someone you could ask," he cried.

"Please believe me, I no longer have any close relatives."

Anger flared in his face and he grabbed her shoulders, shoving her hard against the wall. "Oh, no? How about that little blond sister of yours? She had plenty to throw around when she was in college."

Laura looked into his bloodshot eyes, and a mountainous wave washed over her. "You're the one!" she cried. "My God, you're the scoundrel who broke Lisa's heart! All this time it was you!" Her knees felt so weak she wondered if she was going to faint.

He hunched his shoulders. "So you finally guessed. I wondered how long it would take you."

Her lips trembled so that she could barely speak. "My sister believed you loved her, believed in that marriage."

"Just a weekend lark. How could she have thought otherwise? We were playing games and she damn well knew it."

"That's not true, and *you* know it!"

"You can't prove a thing."

"Oh, my, what a man of character! And how did you get away with pinning it on Geoffrey?"

"Not too difficult when we were home on leave at the same time. Old Geoff had the misfortune to spend his time in a hospital after an accident. I borrowed his uniform. Amazing what a major's insignia will do for a private." He licked his lips as if relishing the memory.

"Are you aware of the penalty for impersonating an officer?"

"It was worth it and no one was the wiser. Come on, don't look so devastated. Old Geoff always got the breaks. That was one time I had a turn."

"Then you knew who I was from the beginning."

"Not until I found Lisa's picture in your wallet at the fire festival and put two and two together."

"So you stole my purse?"

"Someone handed it to me just like I said. When I looked through it I found the picture. I returned your money, didn't I?"

Every ounce of strength seemed to drain from her body. She supported herself on an adjacent desk, then edged over to a chair and slumped into it. Her throat ached unbearably, and she was afraid she was going to be sick. Her blindness had become a malignancy that consumed truth. *Geoffrey, can you ever forgive me?*

"So how about calling Lisa tomorrow? I'll bet she's married to some affluent professional guy."

"Lisa is dead," Laura said, feeling a numbness take over. "She died ten years ago, mainly of a broken heart when she bore your child." Her hands flew to her mouth. Never should she have revealed that.

"*My* child! My *child*!" he repeated drunkenly and looked incredulous. "Well, I'll be damned. And are you saying that kid you're bringing up is actually mine?"

A gasp and a movement caught their attention. They both turned at once to see Kelly staring at them, his eyes wide and frightened. Dear God, how long had be been standing there?

CHAPTER TWENTY-FIVE

KELLY'S FOOTSTEPS ECHOED down the hall and a door slammed. Laura allowed only a second, then dashed after him. Neil lunged toward her and grabbed her by the arm, pinning it behind her so hard and swiftly she cried out.

"Shut up and listen, you little fool," he snapped, and jerked her around to face him. She writhed and tugged, but Neil only tightened his arm lock. She turned her head away from the sour smell of liquor as he panted over her. His eyes looked like two dark circles, empty of personality or spirit. How could she ever have imagined he resembled Geoffrey?

He held up a key, then dropped it into the pocket of her robe. "For my post-office box. Put the money there by Monday noon," he added with a tight smile, and whipped a gun out from under his jacket. "I know you won't contact the police, because you wouldn't want anything to happen to the kid, would you?" After waving the gun threateningly under her nose he returned it to his belt. "I didn't want to push you this far, honestly, Laura. But you always get things done. It's a great quality. So you go after that money, and I'll get out of your life."

A door slammed and Kelly ran breathlessly into

the room accompanied by Seiji and Mr. Matsui, both wearing *yukatas*, and grim expressions.

Neil made a mocking bow. "Ah, so, we have company."

Kelly rushed over and grabbed Laura's hand. "I ran as fast as I could," he said, looking anxiously into her stricken face. He darted a frightened glance at Neil. What terrible thoughts must be going through the child's head!

"What's the matter here?" Mr. Matsui asked. He appeared small and slight beside Neil's huge bulk. If Neil should go berserk, would the four of them be able to handle him? She didn't know if the Matsuis were skilled in karate or judo, but even so it wouldn't matter much. Neil had a gun.

Suddenly he turned expansive. "Sit down, gentlemen. Have some coffee with us. Sorry you had to get up in the middle of the night for nothing."

The Matsuis didn't move.

Neil shrugged. "Actually, my sister-in-law and I had a little family argument. The lady owes me some money, and I guess I got a little overanxious. Nothing to worry about. Right, Laura?" He patted the place where he hid his gun and dared her to dispute him.

Mr. Matsui looked at Laura as if to seek confirmation. He took in her disheveled hair and obvious anxiety. What must he think? Was it safe to tell him the truth? She didn't think so, not while Neil was in the room. She moved her head barely a fraction to negate Neil's claim. *Stay, please stay with me,* her eyes entreated.

"I think it is too late to collect debts tonight. My son and I will be glad to show you to your car," Mr. Matsui said politely, but his tone was firm and suggested no discussion would follow.

Laura watched Seiji and his father move in, one on each side of Neil. She felt a hysterical impulse to laugh at the Matsuis' understated action.

"Oh, I wouldn't think of troubling you, but thanks, anyway," Neil said affably. "Sorry Kelly bothered you, folks, but kids can get pretty mixed-up when it comes to family problems. Right?" Laura wished Neil would stop saying, "Right." If ever he tarnished a word, that was it.

He rumpled Kelly's hair so hard that the little boy's head bobbed alarmingly. Laura closed her eyes at the pain in Kelly's expression. She knew that the deep hurt came from far more than the rough treatment.

Neil walked out with a lumbering swagger while the four of them watched unmoving and silent. He stopped at the door. "Monday by noon in my post-office box," he reminded her, patting the bulge at his waist as he left.

Laura collapsed into a chair, the ordeal temporarily over. "How can I thank you? You handled the situation perfectly. I was afraid to say anything. He had a gun."

"He's your brother-in-law?" Seiji asked.

"No, and I don't owe him any money, but he's a desperate man."

"I think we must call the police," Mr. Matsui said. Laura shook her head. "I'm afraid. He's threatened us. His cousin is my former employer, Dr. McDermott. I'll try to get in touch with him. He'll know what to do.''

"Lock your door and call Dr. McDermott at once.''

Laura thanked them again, and they went downstairs to their apartment. She turned the key in the lock, then wedged it in place with a nail file. Kelly had gone back into his room. Was there any word at all that would ease the trauma he'd suffered tonight? His room was dark. She turned on a lamp and saw that he lay staring at the ceiling, his face pale, his eyes so bleak that her heart ached for him.

"Kelly?''

He nodded slightly but didn't look at her.

"Is that man really my father?'' The hopeful quiver in his voice pleaded for a negative answer. She knelt beside his futon.

"Yes, I'm afraid so.''

"He's bad, isn't he?''

"Yes, Kelly, he is.''

"Is that why you didn't tell me?''

"I didn't know myself until tonight. I'm as shocked as you are.''

Kelly suddenly pulled the covers over his head. "I don't want him to be my dad!'' Muffled sobs came from under the coverlet.

"He's not a real dad,'' Laura said quietly.

"Oh, yes, he is. He's my real father.'' Kelly's torment was real enough to him. He uncovered his face to check her reaction.

"No, Kelly. But he's your real biological father.''

"Isn't that the same thing? What's the difference?"

Laura groped for words to comfort him, but the night had drained her of energy. Her encounter with Neil had left her exhausted, wrung out. She had nothing left to sustain this child. Her mind stretched back to the years when her own father was alive, how he was always there when she needed him.

She reached over and rested her hand on Kelly's shoulder as he lay now with his back to her. He drew away, but only slightly.

"Kelly?"

"Yes?"

"Believe me, there is a difference. Think about it."

"You're just saying that."

"No, darling, I mean it. Look at it this way. You think of Scott as a very special uncle. You confide in him, you do things for each other. You care about him and he cares about you. You know you're not related, but does that change your feelings for him? He's as close to a wonderful uncle as you'll probably ever know." She leaned over, rested her cheek against his curly head for a moment, then kissed it and turned out the light.

Never had she been so tired. *Locate Geoffrey as soon as possible. Call his housekeeper in the morning.* Lord, how she'd messed up her life! It took all of her remaining energy just to crawl into her futon. Even though she desperately needed to sleep, she went over and over the painful night as if viewing a rerun of some horror movie. But whenever she tried to picture Geoffrey's strong features, she failed. Sleep would not come.

MORNING ARRIVED TOO SOON, sending sunlight like sprays of *mikan* blooms across the *shoji*. Her mind still reeled with Neil's empty promises, the lies, the threats. She felt degraded and gullible. She needed something to make her feel clean again. She took a long hot bath, then went to the kitchen to fix breakfast. Instead, she sat down at the table and laid her head in her arms.

"Do you have a headache?" Kelly asked, his voice full of concern. She hadn't heard him come in. He wore his baseball cap and underneath, his hair was plastered down with so much water that rivulets ran down to his collar. She passed a hand over her eyes as if to do so might clear her thinking. Today must be the Sunday for the scouts' monthly intramural baseball game. After last night, how could he remember?

"Not a headache, darling, just a little weary."

He shifted his weight as if his shoes were too tight and shoved his hands in and out of his pockets. "Well, you don't have to worry about me anymore. I did it."

"Did what?" she asked, alarmed.

"You know, thought about the difference, like you said."

"Oh, and did you sort things out?"

"Yeah, if you mean my real dad and all that stuff."

"You're sure?"

"I get it, honest. Neil is related to me, all right, but you're the real mom and dad to me."

Laura reached for him, and he patted her head awkwardly as he stood in her embrace.

"Hey, Laura, don't forget what you're always telling me. We can handle it, *ganbaro-ne.*"

She nodded, unable to speak, then fixed his breakfast. He'd barely finished when a honk from below announced his ride.

"When you get home from the game, stay with the Matsuis because I may not be home yet. I'm going to try to get in touch with Dr. McDermott. Promise not to come up here. Neil might show up again."

"Don't worry," he said, looking grave and mature, then, after a moment, he took off down the stairway, jet-propelled as usual.

Laura called Geoffrey's number, and this time, to her relief, his housekeeper answered.

"Moshi, moshi?"

"Hai, Dr. McDermott *doko*?"

Once again, the woman forgot to speak slowly for Laura and poured out a stream of almost incomprehensible Japanese. "Miyako" and "Writers' Conference" were among the few words she caught. Geoffrey was going to a conference with Miyako? No. The Miyako Hotel, of course. She dialed and prayed she was right.

The clerk spoke perfect English. Yes, the conference was going on right now. The final session would end in about forty-five minutes. The clerk would be happy to leave a message for Dr. McDermott. Thank God for telephones! But she was still worried. Messages could get lost. Hours could pass before they were delivered.

She made up her mind quickly. She'd head for the hotel. The session ended before noon. If he didn't receive her message by then, how would she be able to find him?

She called a taxi, then phoned Mrs. Matsui about Kelly, and with only token attention to her appearance hurried out to wait for the taxi. Impatiently she paced the street corner watching both directions for her ride. Twenty minutes later it arrived. She could have been halfway there had she taken the bus.

"Miyako, *so; de*—hurry," she said, and realized too late the driver would follow her directions to the letter. She gripped the armrest as the car swerved, honked and weaved in and out of the maze of automobiles, streetcars, buses and motorbikes. *Don't let me be too late,* she prayed, checking her watch every other minute. Despite the cold, her palms were moist with nervousness.

Barely glancing at the handsome entryway of the prestigious Miyako, she hurried into the lobby. At least she was familiar with the layout. She'd come here for Sachiko's wedding. Had it really only been yesterday? It seemed a century.

People thronged the area. She elbowed her way to the desk to ask directions, then hurried to the elevators. All busy. *Wait, hurry up and wait.* Would the doors never open? At last, against all protocol, she pushed her way in front of a group of men in order to secure a place for herself. Then she saw them, Geoffrey and Marcia hurrying out through the lobby toward the entrance.

Laura plowed her way out again, ignoring the disgruntled looks of the other passengers. She edged around a bellhop, his carrier piled high with luggage. A tour group aggressively shoved her aside, making her waste a few more precious seconds. *Damn! Hurry. Run. Call out?* Too much noise. They'd never hear her. *Never mind. Just catch up.* She pushed through the doors, rushed outside and frantically scanned the wide portico.

At the far end, a doorman waved off a taxi with such an extravagant gesture he might have just conducted the final bars of a symphony. The taxi took off down the driveway. The occupants were only too familiar.

"Geoffrey!" Laura cried foolishly as if he could hear her, then realized bystanders had turned to stare. The taxi had already disappeared. She couldn't catch it. Where was he headed? She thought she'd heard the housekeeper mention Miyajima. Was he going to that lovely island with Marcia? Maybe Geoffrey had already received her message and called, she thought in despair. She should have stayed home.

One point seemed clear. No more waiting around for Geoffrey. She would have to act on her own. She and Kelly would take the bullet train, go somewhere, anywhere, hide out until she could safely call the police.

She signaled the doorman for a taxi. The wild ride home didn't faze her. She was preoccupied with everything she had to do. Kelly should have returned by now. She would ask Mrs. Matsui for the name of a small respectable hotel where she and Kelly could stay. *Grab a suitcase. Take off at once.*

The taxi skidded to the curb. She handed the fare to the driver and ran up the flight to the Matsuis'. On the landing she struggled for breath. What had happened to her lungs? She felt light-headed. Panic? How could everything look so normal? The noon sun shone brilliantly, and Mrs. Matsui's smile seemed relaxed and comfortable as she opened the door and beckoned her inside.

"Sit down and have lunch with us. You look as if you need some."

"Thanks. It smells marvelous." Laura inhaled the aroma of good soup. No wonder she felt so dizzy. All she'd had since the wedding was coffee.

Mrs. Matsui looked at her with concern. "Are you all right?"

"Yes, I think so. Last night was a terrible experience, especially for Kelly. Your husband and son were wonderful. I'm so grateful."

"It was Kelly-kun. What a mature child he is."

"Hasn't he come home yet?"

"Oh, yes, I already gave him his lunch. He went to the neighborhood park to play awhile. I reminded him not to go near your apartment."

"Maybe I'm paranoid, but I'd better check," Laura said, and walked to the living-room window that overlooked the playground. From this distance it was difficult to distinguish one child from another.

"He has to be there, but come, we'll go down and see," Mrs. Matsui said, and started down the stairway.

But Laura didn't follow. She didn't need to; she already knew Kelly wasn't there. She ran up the steps, two at a time, to her apartment. The door stood open.

"Kelly!" she screamed. There was no answer. A note was propped on the coffee table. She picked it up with trembling fingers.

Laura, I hate like hell to do this to you, but you're my last resort. Put 2,500,000 yen or ten thousand dollars cash in the post-office box tomorrow as we discussed. If you call the cops, I can promise you that you will never see *my kid* again.

CHAPTER TWENTY-SIX

LAURA STARED AT THE NOTE. The words blurred in and out of focus, and her throat constricted so that she could barely breathe. Ten thousand dollars! He'd said two thousand. There was no possible way for her to come up with either figure. No way at all. Even if she could secure a loan, which was highly unlikely, several days were needed to negotiate it. Surely Neil knew that. He probably figured there was a good chance she could get the money from Geoffrey. Tomorrow was the deadline. Would she be able to locate Geoffrey in time?

Kelly. He must be terrified. Kidnapped by his own father. Surely Neil would not harm him. Still, it took an aberrant set of genes to produce a man like Neil, a man without conscience or feeling. Except for a certain physical resemblance, how totally different he was from Geoffrey. If only Geoffrey had been Kelly's father. Irony never came in small doses, she thought, recalling the months she had fervently hoped there was no such relationship.

Mrs. Matsui ran in then, her face pale with alarm. "He's not there," she cried as Laura dumbly handed the note to her. The older woman read it quickly.

"Oh, no, it's my fault! I should have kept him in my apartment."

"I probably would have done the same. I never expected Neil to do such a thing."

"Call the police!"

Laura pointed to the note. "You see what he threatens. Kyoto is a big city. It might take weeks to find him. First I have to get in touch with Neil's cousin. He'll know what to do."

"Call now."

Laura pressed her hands to her throbbing temples and shook her head. "I don't know where he is but I'm going to sit on the telephone until I find him."

Mrs. Matsui nodded, deep concern in her expression. "Let me know if I can help."

Pinpoints of light whirled before Laura's eyes so that she barely saw Mrs. Matsui leave. She started for the telephone, but it seemed her equilibrium had ceased to function, and she walked uncertainly, hanging on to the furniture until she reached it. She called the Miyako Hotel, then dialed the Sato school and finally Geoffrey's editor. She could tell they thought she was just another tedious female on the trail of this prominent man. As a last resort she called Marcia's apartment. Someone might answer who could give her some information. To her surprise Marcia replied.

"Moshi, moshi?"

"Laura Adams speaking. I have to get in touch with Geoffrey right away. Do you know where he is?"

Marcia's laugh was hearty. "A lot of women would like the answer to that question."

"Please tell me if you know. It's a matter of life and death. My nephew's life!"

"Sorry, wish I could help. I haven't seen him since he dropped me off after the conference. He didn't mention any plans for the rest of the day. Try his house again."

So they hadn't gone to Miyajima together, after all. Even in the midst of her turmoil she felt relieved.

She called Geoffrey's number continually with no results. Where could he be? Would Chizu's folks know, by any chance? They were neighbors. She dialed the number.

Bill Thompson answered. "Miss Adams?... Yes, he's here. You caught us just in time. We're set to take off for a game of golf."

Laura couldn't believe her luck. At last. *Thank God.*

"Laura? Anything wrong?" Geoffrey sounded both guarded and concerned.

"It's Neil. He kidnapped Kelly and wants the ransom by tomorrow."

"My God! That bastard. When did he do it?"

"Today, soon after lunch. He must have nabbed Kelly from the park next door."

"I'll call the police. I just found out that they're after him. Apparently he's been working with a ring that peddled those Thailand replicas. He must have sunk pretty low. Neil has never been the most reliable person, but I never thought he'd do something like this. The police think he's in Tokyo."

"Please don't call the police. Listen!" She read the note.

"Damn! I'm sure he's trying to get enough money

together to leave the country. He tried to borrow cash from me just before I left for Hokkaido. I told him to get lost. If only I'd given it to him!"

"What shall we do?"

"I'll try to find the guy and talk some sense into him."

"Be careful; he has a gun."

"He'd never use it on me. At least, I don't think so."

"But how in the world can you find him?"

"I'm not sure, but I know a few of his hangouts."

She swallowed hard. "He's been hiding in my apartment part of the time."

"Your place!" He sounded stunned.

"He hung around during the days and some evenings and drank a lot. I couldn't get rid of him."

He groaned. "If only you could have told me."

Told him! There was so much she wanted to tell him, but not now.

"It was awful. He's turned into a different person."

"Did he harm you?"

"Not really."

"Stay there. I'll keep in touch."

The hours crept by agonizingly while she prayed over and over that nothing would happen to the man and the boy she loved more than anything in the whole world. She couldn't tell whether Geoffrey was still angry with her. Couldn't he feel her reaching out to him? Didn't he realize how much she needed him, wanted him in her life?

Hours later Geoffrey called to say that he'd

checked with Neil's former partner. The man said he hadn't seen him for months but told him about several small hotels where Neil had been known to stay in the past.

It was well after midnight when the phone rang again.

"He's there, all right," Geoffrey said. "I talked to the clerk. Room 220, second floor at the Oita Hotel. It's above a *pachinko* parlor in a old part of town. He has Kelly with him. The descriptions fit perfectly, even if they've registered under different names. I'm heading over there right now."

"Be careful, Geoffrey."

"Don't worry, I'll have help."

"Suppose Neil leaves in the meantime?"

"He's broke, no car. I don't think he'd chance it. Get some rest. I'll try to deliver Kelly in time for breakfast."

"Let me come with you."

"No way. Trust me." He hung up and she started to pace around the small living room. Get some rest? Geoffrey was out of his mind to think she could rest now. Suppose the clerk dropped the information to Neil that someone was on his trail? Neil was unpredictable. Underneath the affable, happy-go-lucky exterior lurked a deceitful and desperate man. She hadn't seen the real Neil until he had drunk too much to hide it. She could hardly blame Lisa, a far less experienced and younger girl at the time she met him. A cornered man could be treacherous. Neil had already taught her that painful lesson.

It took only a moment to reach a decision. She

must stake out a surveillance on the hotel room until Geoffrey arrived. Geoffrey lived far across town in the suburbs. She could get to the old hotel in ten minutes. She wasn't sure what she'd do if she saw Neil take off with Kelly, but she knew she had to be there. She called a taxi and hurriedly changed to dark wool slacks and sweater, tied a scarf over her head and put on her heavy coat. The taxi arrived almost immediately. At two in the morning, service could be prompt.

She gave the name of the hotel to the driver. He looked at her oddly and seemed to hesitate.

"Bad place for you," he said in Japanese.

"*Hayaku*—be quick!" she said firmly. He sucked in his breath and shook his head, putting the car into gear slowly as if to give her time to change her mind.

Black streets glistened with psychedelic frost from neon lights. Signs flaunted messages in vain to the empty streets. Shafts of shadow and light struck the cab in hypnotic repetition. She looked away from the passing scene and went over the facts Geoffrey had told her. Suddenly her spirits sank. What could she do, a woman alone in the middle of the night? She drew her coat around her and shuddered.

The taxi turned into a narrow street and slowed to a crawl as the driver peered at the shoddy buildings huddled against one another. A block or two later he stopped. Yes, there was a darkened *pachinko* parlor, the Japanese version of the pinball arcade, and above rose a four-story building so narrow that it probably housed not more than two or three rooms on each floor. Its kind could be found in decaying sections of large cities everywhere.

Heart pounding, she paid the fare and stood hesitantly on the poorly lit sidewalk. She was insane to have come here. If the driver hadn't left so promptly, she would have climbed back in the taxi and returned home.

She saw a small all-night café across the street. *Go there first. Have something to eat. Steel your nerves.* Soon she would have to find room 220. Then she would locate a sheltered spot so she could watch until Geoffrey arrived.

Surprisingly, the café was almost full. Who ate meals at this hour of the night? Workers on the way home from a late shift? She sat down at a window table where she had a good view of the seedy hotel's entrance. Two men at the next table played backgammon, drinking beer. A policeman leaned against a counter sipping coffee. She breathed a little easier at the sight of his uniform. He gave her a measuring look, finished his coffee, then apparently reported in on his walkie-talkie and ambled outside, no doubt to resume his beat.

When her order arrived, she hugged the bowl of noodles with her hands to force warmth back into her trembling fingers. Then she ate quickly, keeping an eye on the hotel. A narrow stairway adjacent to the *pachinko* parlor led up to the first floor. Was there a back entrance, she wondered.

Abruptly she stiffened. Chills shot through her, and she held her breath. That voice behind her! It belonged to one of the men playing backgammon.

Neil. She listened to the clink of stones and dice. Conversation was in Japanese, and the men seemed to be arguing over the amount to bet on the game. It was Neil, no question. How much longer would the game last?

She finished the *soba*, swallowing with difficulty, paid the check and hurried across the street and up the stairway to the cubbyhole that served as a lobby. The night clerk dozed, his head on the counter. Soundlessly she slipped past and climbed the creaking stairway to the second level.

The numbers were difficult to read in the dim hall light. Room 220. There it was. The door sagged so unevenly that a crack the width of a pencil showed along the side of the lower half. Faded green paint peeled around the door knob. She knelt and put her ear against the crack. Footsteps behind her! She shrank against the wall and peered over her shoulder. A woman of indeterminate age plodded up to the next floor.

Laura's hands felt clammy inside her gloves, and her heart seemed to shake her with its pounding. She knelt again at the doorway and put her lips to the crack. Was Kelly safe inside, or had Neil locked him in some dingy closet? She had to know.

"Kelly!" she called, and tapped the door lightly. "Kelly!" she called again, and this time heard a muffled sound.

"Laura, is that you?" The child's voice quivered.

Relief made her light-headed. "Yes, darling, everything is going to be all right."

"I thought you'd never find me." He started to cry.

"Are you okay?" Laura asked.

"He tied me to the bed and said he'd shoot me if I screamed."

"Can you move?"

"As far as the bathroom. I can't reach the door."

"Listen, Geoffrey is on his way. I don't have a key, but I'll be hiding on the next landing to see that Neil doesn't take you away."

His sobs grew louder. "Now, Laura. Can't you take me now? This place is awful. Please, I want out of here!"

"Soon, darling. Get back into bed. Pretend you're asleep. Neil mustn't suspect anything. Quickly now, I must go."

The last syllable choked in her throat as iron bands clamped each arm and yanked her to her feet, then closed around her neck.

"Damn it, Laura, what are you doing here?" Neil hissed.

A giant black curtain closed in front of her eyes. Vaguely she heard Kelly scream her name. Unexpectedly, Neil released her and whipped out his gun.

"All right. Let's have it. What's the setup?"

She slumped against the door as air rushed into her lungs. "No setup. I swear I'm alone," she gasped.

"You're lying. You called the police, didn't you?" He waved the gun in her face, hypnotically back and forth like a slow, swinging pendulum.

"I swear, I came alone. Geoffrey should arrive soon. I couldn't stop him. Let me stay with Kelly until Geoffrey comes. He's so frightened. Please, Neil, isn't there a scrap of humanity left in you?"

He unlocked the door and switched on the light. The place was a pigsty, littered with newspapers, beer bottles and *mikan* peels. Kelly sat on the bed, his eyes wide with fear. In seconds Neil untied the rope.

"We're getting out of here. Why in the hell didn't you follow directions?" He herded them outside and down to the lobby. "Call a taxi. Tell the driver to pick us up in front of the Yamaguchi market."

Her mind raced. *Think of something. Stall for time. Anything.* The sleepy clerk watched her uninterestedly. She dared not enlist his help. Neil stood within hearing distance, firmly grasping Kelly's shoulder.

The telephone was pink, which meant it took a ten-yen piece. She fished the coin from her purse and dialed one of the taxi numbers scrawled on a card posted above the telephone. Deliberately she changed the last number and ordered a taxi in a firm voice while at the other end the false number rang repeatedly.

Neil took them out a side door and down a narrow service entrance. Her heart sank. Nothing escaped Neil.

"You didn't think I'd be dumb enough to stand in front of the hotel, did you?" He hurried them through an alley and out by a large corner market, motioning them back into the unlighted entryway. Now they were probably on the street that ran a block south of the hotel. A foul smell of rotting garbage assailed them, and they shivered in the sharp cold and dampness. Kelly clung to her hand, and she tried to give him all the strength she had left to sustain him.

A car sped by, slicing the dark with its headlights, then minutes passed in complete silence. Neil cursed the tardy taxi and ventured out on the deserted street, peering in each direction. Kelly tightened his fingers around hers as if to comfort her. When he grew to manhood he would resemble Geoffrey, not Neil, *if* he had the chance. What would happen when the taxi didn't arrive? Had she made still another foolish mistake? Geoffrey would never find them here.

Two drunks reeled around the corner and burst into a raucous song. They staggered back and forth, then fell on the sidewalk, stretched out a few feet away without interrupting their singing. A scream would bring no help from those two.

A taxi swung around the corner. What fate prompted it to head down the lonely street at this hour? Neil ran to the curb and waved wildly. Brakes squealed as the driver stopped.

Neil ran back and grabbed her and Kelly each by an arm. "Get a move on," he said, and dragged them out of the shadows to the taxi. He opened the door and abruptly backed away.

"My God, Laura, I'll swear you need a keeper!" Geoffrey cried, leaping out the door followed by the night clerk. For a second Neil looked bleakly at Kelly, then made a dash for the dark alley.

The street burst into action. The two drunks, miraculously sobered, rushed after Neil, shouting and pulling guns. Several police rounded the corner to join them. A shot rang in the air. Neil swore, looked wildly in all directions and fired indiscriminately as the police closed in.

Geoffrey pushed Laura and Kelly to the sidewalk and sprawled over them as bullets ricocheted all around them, then silence. A siren sounded in the distance. Geoffrey moaned. One of the policemen ran to help them to their feet, Kelly first. Then Laura rose unsteadily.

But Geoffrey still lay on the sidewalk, a pool of blood beginning to form under his head and shoulder.

CHAPTER TWENTY-SEVEN

LAURA SAT IN THE WAITING ROOM at the hospital. Although it still seemed the middle of the night, every chair was filled. People looked like mannequins, faces frozen, each person dealing with his or her own private fears. The air smelled faintly antiseptic. Once someone walked by with a bouquet of carnations, but the spicy fragrance only added to the funereal mood. Anxiety tore at every nerve.

The chunky nurse at the desk spoke no English, and she talked so rapidly Laura had difficulty understanding her. Apparently the nurse couldn't comprehend Laura's Japanese any better. Laura had asked twice if there was any news yet of Dr. McDermott's condition, but all she could glean was that he still was in surgery. The waiting, oh, Lord, the waiting was killing her!

She had wanted to ride in the ambulance with Geoffrey, but the policemen took her and Kelly to the station. Dazed by the terrible nightmare, she answered questions mechanically, somehow dredging up enough Japanese words so the police understood her, then she gave them Neil's ransom note, which she had in her purse. All through the ordeal she pictured Geoffrey lying on the sidewalk bleeding to death while an eternity passed before the ambulance arrived.

She'd caught a glimpse of Neil, handcuffed, ushered into a car and whisked away. His eyes were dark with defeat and something else. Was it madness? Eventually, two plainclothesmen drove her and Kelly home, and the exhausted boy fell asleep at once at the Matsuis'. She took a taxi to the hospital, and now she waited, the scenes of the past hours turning over in her mind in kaleidoscopic sequence.

Apparently Neil hadn't found it difficult to coax Kelly away from the park and into a taxi yesterday. He'd simply told his son that Laura had been in an accident and wanted them to come and get her. It wasn't until they arrived at the sleazy hotel that Kelly realized he'd been kidnapped.

"What happened then?" Laura had asked him on the way home.

"Nothing much. He said if I'd keep my mouth shut and didn't yell, everything would be okay. If I didn't, he said he'd shoot me. I was pretty scared, but I knew you'd find me."

"You were very brave. I'm proud of you."

"I had funny feelings, though."

"What do you mean?"

"I always thought my dad was a special hero, and all the time he was this creep. But you know something? He didn't feel like my father, and he never said a single thing about it. Isn't that weird?"

"Perhaps he was ashamed."

Kelly looked thoughtful. "Maybe," he said in his

most adult tone. "What I really think is that he never learned how to handle things."

Oh, Kelly, you wise child, you're going to be all right, she thought, and wanted to hug him. She saw a film of moisture cover his eyes, perhaps the final mourning for the man who never existed.

Laura realized she now sat so tensely in the waiting room that her muscles ached. She got up and paced the corridor to ease the stiffness. If only someone spoke English. Her meager Japanese did not include medical jargon.

Dawn broke now, and she stood at the window watching a scatter of snowflakes, a sight she usually regarded with wonder. But today they took on a different meaning. They cluttered the sidewalk like so many little lives trying to survive, streaked the window with tears and turned a little Buddha statue across the street into a barely distinguishable image of a frozen god. On the sidewalks below, a few early risers dug their hands into their pockets, their faces grimacing against the zero invader. She shivered in empathy, found a chair and sat down again.

Don't let Geoffrey die, she prayed over and over. There was still so much she needed to say to him. Her life had been torn apart mainly by lack of communication. Geoffrey had hungered for it all along, begged for it, but for months she'd allowed suspicion and misjudgment to divide them.

"You can forgive if you truly love," one of K.D. Kano's characters said in a recent book. Geoffrey had told her that he loved her. Did his love so quickly die? Apparently humanity existed only in his novels.

Pain and loneliness appeared to be the inevitable outcome of their relationship, but outcomes didn't have to be inevitable if one did something about them.

She took a small note pad from her purse and began to write.

My dearest Geoffrey, I'm sitting in the hospital waiting room praying for your recovery. How can Kelly and I ever tell you how grateful we are for the terrible risk you took?

Then she poured out all the facts of Neil's treachery, including that *he* was Kelly's real father.

It was a tragedy that affected every member of our family. Because of such circumstances, can you understand how my judgment became distorted? I love you, Geoffrey. Can you forgive me?

                                              Laura

She folded the note, wrote Geoffrey's name on the outside and handed it to an orderly.

"Could this be delivered to the patient when he is able to receive it?"

The orderly smiled and nodded, put it on his clipboard and hurried down the corridor.

It was time to brave the desk again. Laura had the feeling she and the nurse intimidated each other the minute they opened their mouths.

"Patient no see visitors," the nurse said, obviously

trying to speak more slowly. "Please go home. Call back later. Maybe he can have visitors after lunch."

Wearily, she found the way out of the hospital and took a bus home. The snow had stopped falling, and already clouds were parting to show a promise of blue skies.

Mrs. Matsui called out to her as she trudged up the steps to her apartment.

"I've just seen Kelly off to school."

"He felt like going?"

"A lively cricket, that one! Come in, I'll give you some breakfast. You look worn-out."

Laura gratefully accepted, and filled in the details of the night's experience as she ate the fragrant miso soup.

"Stay here and rest today. Your apartment will be freezing," Mrs. Matsui said.

"Thanks, but I have to go to work in a few minutes."

"Nonsense. I'll call Mr. Ishimoto and explain."

"Ask if I can switch to the afternoon shift today. He's opening up a new section in his store later this week, and I promised to help stock the shelves today. He's depending on me."

Mrs. Matsui left the room only to return a few moments later.

"All arranged. You don't have to be there until two." She brought out some blankets and indicated the sofa. "I'm going on some errands soon. It will be quiet here. Try to sleep."

Sleep? Never, not with all she had on her mind, but she smiled her appreciation. What would she nave done without this kind neighbor? Exhaustion proved an ally, after all. She snuggled under the blankets and contrary to expectations, she fell asleep at once.

Almost three hours later she awakened. At once she saw the note propped on the end table. "Laura, I called the hospital, and your Dr. McDermott is doing fine." Darling woman! Joy brimmed over and so did the tears. *Call now. No. Save every second for the hospital.* If she hurried, she'd have an hour to visit before she reported for work at two. She raced up to her apartment, bathed, dressed and tied a scarf splashed with plum blossoms around her neck and tried not to think of the significance of the plum tree at the *ryokan.* She noted her high color as she added a touch of lipstick and gave thanks for the restorative powers of a bath and cosmetics. The imminent prospect of seeing Geoffrey had something to do with it, too, she acknowledged.

She took a taxi to the hospital—no time for the bus. She wished she could fly! As the taxi shot through the traffic, its pace matched her soaring spirits. She held imaginary conversations with Geoffrey in which all their misunderstandings were resolved. By the time she reached her destination, she was in a heady state.

At the desk, she flashed a winning smile at the same businesslike nurse, who recognized her right away. Laura couldn't hide her happiness as she asked for Geoffrey's room number.

The nurse was not particularly friendly as she turned to check her files. Laura grew impatient. The nurse barely looked up when she said, "Dr. McDermott gone."

Gone? What did that mean? Laura panicked. "Did he leave any message for me?"

The nurse was obviously annoyed and made it clear she had no more time for Laura by firmly repeating herself. "Dr. McDermott check out this morning. No messages."

"This morning? Is he all right?"

"Only superficial flesh wounds," she said, and turned to the next person awaiting her attention.

Laura ran to a pay telephone at the end of the hall and quickly dialed Geoffrey's number. There was no answer. Where could he be? A hundred places, of course. Wouldn't he try to get in touch with her? Maybe he hadn't received her note. Maybe it was still wandering around the hospital on the orderly's clipboard. She called every five minutes to no avail. An aeon stretched after each try.

Dared she brave the dragon lady one more time? Apparently her shift was over. A young nurse sat in her place.

"*Eigo wakarimasu-ka?* Do you understand English?" Laura asked.

The young woman smiled. "Yes, if you speak slowly."

"I need to get in touch with Dr. McDermott. I understand he left this morning."

"Yes, at nine o'clock. I checked him out myself."

Laura felt her color rise. "Do you know if he planned to go straight home? I mean, his condition warranted that, didn't it?"

The nurse seemed to make a decision whether or not to answer. The hospital no doubt guarded the privacy of its patients.

"He seemed unusually cheerful and fit to me. I believe he said he had a number of things to do because he was leaving on a short vacation. No, he didn't mention where he was going, and neither did the lady who was with him."

Laura stared. *The lady who was with him!* "Thank you," she mumbled, feeling numb. Some minutes later she walked outside to find a taxi. The nurse's words tagged along after her like a pack of unwanted mongrels.

So, he took off on a vacation? Surely not with Marcia. But who else? She thought of the note she had written and squirmed with humiliation. How embarrassing for both of them.

At the book shop she thanked Mr. Ishimoto for changing her schedule for the day and with a heavy heart went up the attractive cantilevered stairway to the new mezzanine. In spite of the turmoil that rendered her almost useless, she made a show of enthusiasm.

"It looks more like a pleasant university reading room than a bookstore," she said.

Mr. Ishimoto grinned and tried not to look too proud. "We must make all our students feel at home. They are tomorrow's best customers."

Before she started shelving books, Mr. Ishimoto asked if she'd be kind enough to water the decorative plants that had been installed earlier in the week. She hauled a sizable watering can from downstairs and began the chore, skirting some scaffolding on which a workman stood as he finished painting the ceiling. A few minutes later he completed his task and started to roll up the drop cloths that were spread on the floor and over some of the book-shelves.

Laura climbed on the scaffolding in order to reach a couple of the hanging plants.

"I'll be through in a minute," she said.

"*Jii iie*—no, no!" the painter cried and gestured frantically. At the same instant, the scaffolding gave way. She dropped the watering can, grabbed for the canvas on the adjacent bookcase and fell to the floor, taking the canvas with her, while scaffolding splayed like Tinker Toys in all directions.

She could hear Mr. Ishimoto's cries of alarm, and heavy footsteps running up the stairway. Hands tugged to free her, but she seemed hopelessly entangled.

"Are you all right?" Mr. Ishimoto called after spieling a torrent of Japanese.

"I think so," Laura said, coughing hard inside her dusty mummylike wrapping.

"Good Lord! What happened here, Sam?" a deep male American voice asked. "Better find something to wipe up that paint before it runs off and ruins your new floor finish."

Laura groaned. Surely that wasn't Geoffrey. Dear God, not now. Not like this!

In frantic Japanese, no doubt accompanied by many gestures, Mr. Ishimoto was explaining the catastrophe.

"You mean someone is under there?" the man asked in a rich baritone. She'd been right. It was Geoffrey. She felt someone tug at the scaffolding that pinned her down.

"Yes, one of our employees," Mr. Ishimoto said. "I do hope she's not hurt." His voice shook with anxiety.

There was a pause. "One of your employees, you say? No, don't tell me. Let me guess. I'll lay a bet it's that new girl you hired just before Christmas. I believe her name was Laura Adams."

At that moment Geoffrey freed her and helped her to her feet. Mr. Ishimoto looked stunned by Geoffrey's accurate guess. Laura, red faced and disheveled, managed a quick glance at Geoffrey. His eyes shone roguishly in spite of an otherwise grave expression.

Laura ran her fingers through her hair, brushed off her dusty clothing and tried to garner a remnant of dignity.

Geoffrey clapped a hand on his friend's shoulder. "Sam, old man," he said confidentially, "I hate to talk like this in front of your new employee, but believe me, it's a matter of survival. Yours. You must fire her. Now. I can assure you she's worse than any poltergeist. With her around, things disappear, fly apart and no telling what all." He gestured grandly to emphasize proof in the mess that surrounded them. "And, take it from me, if there's a bucket of paint anywhere on the premises, I can predict absolutely she will spill it." He leaned closer as if to divulge even more grim details. "Not only that, she talks to plants and makes them grow like nothing you've ever seen in your life. All this greenery you have up here will turn into a jungle. You won't even be able to see the books."

Mr. Ishimoto considered the prospect and shuffled his feet uncomfortably. "So far, Miss Adams has been a very satisfactory employee. I have no real cause to—"

"We're old friends, you and I," Geoffrey interrupted. "And I want to save you a hell of a lot of trouble. Take my advice and let her go this minute. In fact, I'll be glad to remove her myself." Geoffrey took her arm and marched her down the stairs. Mr. Ishimoto followed, openmouthed, and the painter watched in bewilderment.

Laura put her face in her hands. She'd fallen from that scaffold and hit her head. She'd lost her senses. She was hallucinating.

Geoffrey took her hands away from her face and kissed her.

"Don't cry, my darling. It's all right. I love you."

"I love you too, Geoffrey," she said, brushing away her tears.

"Good. So relax, the possibilities are limitless."

Reluctantly they drew apart and realized they'd become the book shop's star attraction. Mr. Ishimoto stared in complete astonishment. The painter carried out the drop cloths shaking his head, and the customers waited in breathless suspense to see what might happen next. Geoffrey gave her a tender smile, took her hand, and they headed out of the shop.

"I can't believe this," Laura said after Geoffrey helped her into his car.

Geoffrey looked happily resigned. "Oh, I can. In fact it's getting repetitious."

A sudden anxiety filled her. "Did you get my letter?"

"Yes, and an earful from the police reporter at the hospital this morning. After your letter, the reporter and Neil's confession, I can't believe my thick skull."

"Oh, I can," she said, mimicking his earlier inflection. "And by the way, was that a lady reporter?"

He shot her an amused look. "Yes, and where were you all morning? I spent half my time trying to reach you."

She groaned. "If I'd only known. Doesn't your wound bother you? Are you certain you're all right?"

"Couldn't be more so. On top of the world, in fact."

He slammed on the brakes to avoid running a red light.

"Would you mind telling me where we're going and why we have to get there in such a hurry?" she asked.

"Well, you don't want to be late for your own wedding, do you? The chaplain is waiting for us."

"Wedding!"

"Of course. I thought you were more observant. Every plum tree in Kyoto is blossoming. The moon is growing fuller by the minute. Not only that, a certain room overlooking the garden is reserved for us at the Mount Hei *ryokan*."

Laura gasped. "You can't be serious!"

"Oh, I moved mountains, but it's all arranged."

Her head whirled. "You've had a busy morning," she said faintly.

"I'm glad you noticed, so sit close to me. A bride

and groom should look the part.'' She leaned her head against his shoulder and put her hand in his, feeling breathless and shy as if she'd met him only once before in another world.

As they left the city and drove through the countryside, an endless Kyoto screen unfolded panel by panel. Cold winter sunlight washed old buildings to furnish gleaming facades, plum blossoms wrote poetry against a red shrine, and on the northern slopes, snow-tipped cedars helped to hold up the sky.

Geoffrey regarded her solemnly. "How do you feel?"

"Not accident-prone, I promise."

He nuzzled the top of her head with his chin. "I'm grateful for large favors. Anything else?"

" 'Bewitched,' I believe, is the word for it."

"Try again. I can think of superior adjectives."

She smiled and reached up to kiss his cheek. "How about 'loving' and 'sexy'?"

He grinned. "Now you're communicating."

"Which is what we should have been doing all along," she said, and meant it sincerely.

His smile faded and he squeezed her hand. "Lord, how I've missed you."

"I'd say your behavior was rather deceiving, then."

"Oh, is that so? Listen, I couldn't sleep at night, and every day I went to Ishimoto's just to get a look at you. Now I know what you went through. My head turned into a one-man debating team: McDermott versus McDermott."

"And I analyzed the word 'loyalty' until it became limp and unrecognizable."

"Worst of all I accused you of not trusting me, but I didn't trust you, either."

"It took you quite a while to figure that out, Geoffrey."

"I know. I'm not as perceptive as you are. All I could think about was the way you took off that day with that little chin of yours in the air. I almost went crazy, especially after I learned how you pushed yourself to clean up that mess."

"I'd hate to admit how easily you could have stopped me."

"False pride, my darling, but I've learned my lesson."

Soon they climbed the winding road that led to the *ryokan*. At the front entrance, the same two little maids Laura remembered stood beaming. They bowed and beckoned her to follow while Geoffrey went on down the hall.

In the room reserved for the bridal couple, they helped her out of her clothing and into the beautiful creamy wedding kimono Geoffrey had asked her to try on months ago in his gallery. Had he always been sure? She reveled in the sensuous feel of the silk as they wrapped the obi around her. With meticulous care, they draped the wide sash in the customary artful bow.

Laura brushed her hair and decided her glowing face required no touch-up cosmetics. She tried a few practice steps, gearing them to the confines of the kimono. The maids chattered their approval and handed her a spray of white camellias, and she walked to the edge of the garden to meet Geoffrey. Her eyes kindled as she joined him. He wore his black ceremonial kimono with grace, comfortable in the ways of this country he loved.

His face lit up in a true caress that told her more clearly than words how beautiful she looked and how much he loved her. She recorded the moment, imprinting it on her mind, a talisman for the rest of her life.

He broke off one of the camellias and tucked it into her hair, then hand in hand they walked through the garden to stand before the flowering plum tree that formed the background for the altar. Nearby she glimpsed a wide-eyed Kelly standing with Mrs. Matsui. Laura flashed a grateful glance at Geoffrey, and her heart swelled as they smiled at the child they would raise as their son.

Laura regarded the plum tree with awe. A month ago it had been barren and covered with snow. Now, under the sapphire sky it sprayed masses of blooms despite remnants of snow glinting in crystal traceries along its branches. A miracle, Laura thought, and felt a joyful stirring inside her. Blossoms in the snow, a symbol of love that survived and bloomed even through a winter of pain.

The chaplain conducted a brief service, and Geoffrey slipped the gold ring on her finger. They kissed gently with the brief tremor that promised greater fulfillment. The moment was hushed. Fragrance of the blossoms eddied around them with only the rush of small bird wings to break the silence. The shining moment enveloped her, drew out the tortured past and granted a blessing for the future.

Good wishes and warm goodbyes followed from Kelly and the few friends who gathered around them. The two doll-like maids bobbed and nodded approval from behind a screen.

Amenities over, Laura and Geoffrey returned to their room. He held out his arms to her, and moving with a slow ease she glided into them. They closed together, assuaging hunger in their little island of serenity.

"Have you forgiven me?" she said.

"I must ask you the same question. It's difficult to see when a huge shadow blocks the light. I should have realized a lot sooner that it was Neil who caused all our problems."

"But in the end he brought us back together."

"And gave me a beautiful son," Geoffrey said gravely.

She stood on tiptoe and laid her cheek against his. "So you won't worry about any more demons?"

"No, my darling. We'll meet none because we conceal none." The scent of blossoms floated in from the garden absorbing the last fragments of remembered pain. His lips touched her forehead, then sought her lips, and for unmeasured time they clung to each other allowing their closeness to nourish and bring them peace.

A little while later he released her "Well, now, Mrs. McDermott, you might as well know right from the start, life with me will be no bed of roses."

She looked startled as she allowed her new name to

sink in. Then she smiled. "Oh, I know that you rant and rave a lot, but I'll try to overlook it."

He tipped up her chin. "And come mud slides, insurrections or tsunamis, I'm resigned to your turning up in the thick of them."

"But together we can handle it. Right, Geoffrey?"

"Right, my darling, we'll handle it. *Ganbaro,* my love, *ganbaro!*"

ABOUT THE AUTHOR

Megan Alexander was born in Washington State, grew up in the Los Angeles area, graduated from U.C.L.A. and now lives in Santa Rosa, a town in northern California's wine and redwood country.

Though Santa Rosa is home to Megan, she has traveled extensively throughout several continents. She particularly enjoyed her three months in Japan and feels her experience there contributed largely to the authentic flavor of *Blossoms in the Snow*.

As well as being an author, Megan is also an accomplished professional pianist and has shared this talent in a number of interesting ways, from performing to supervising and teaching.

Now a full-time writer, Megan has already achieved substantial success. Her first Superromance, *Contract for Marriage*, won the Waldenbooks Award for 1983.

Yours FREE, with a home subscription to SUPERROMANCE ™.

Complete and mail the coupon below today!

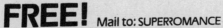

- -

FREE! Mail to: SUPERROMANCE

In the U.S.
2504 West Southern Avenue
Tempe, AZ 85282

In Canada
649 Ontario St.
Stratford, Ontario N5A 6W2

YES, please send me FREE and without any obligation, my **SUPERROMANCE** novel, LOVE BEYOND DESIRE. If you do not hear from me after I have examined my FREE book, please send me the 4 new **SUPERROMANCE** books every month as soon as they come off the press. I understand that I will be billed only $2.50 for each book (total $10.00). There are no shipping and handling or any other hidden charges. There is no minimum number of books that I have to purchase. In fact, I may cancel this arrangement at any time. LOVE BEYOND DESIRE is mine to keep as a FREE gift, even if I do not buy any additional books.

NAME _____ (Please Print)

ADDRESS _____ APT. NO. _____

CITY _____

STATE/PROV. _____ ZIP/POSTAL CODE _____

SIGNATURE (If under 18, parent or guardian must sign.)

134-BPS-KAKS
SUP-SUB-1

This offer is limited to one order per household and not valid to present subscribers. Prices subject to change without notice.
Offer expires July 31, 1984